FATES ENTWINED

ZODIAC WOLVES
BOOK 5

ELIZABETH BRIGGS

FIRE MATED

STELLA & JORDAN

CHAPTER ONE

FATED MATES. Everyone wanted one, right? After all, an entire war had been fought to ensure that every shifter could find their perfect match. The idea that the stars could choose the right partner for us, who would love us and accept us for the rest of our lives, was irresistible. But what happened when the stars chose the wrong person?

Despite the summer heat, a shiver ran down my spine as the setting sun cast an orange glow on the vast meadow before me. The sky looked as though it had been painted with a fiery brush, igniting the world in vibrant shades of gold and crimson, but I barely even noticed. No, my gaze lingered on the way the light glinted off the Leo alpha's golden hair and slid along his tanned, muscular arms. Even across the sprawling field, with his back to me and dozens of other shifters around him, he stood out like a beacon I couldn't ignore.

With a huff, I tore my eyes away and turned toward the

nearby bonfire as it sent sparks into the sky. People said you couldn't fight fate, but staring into the fire, I couldn't help but think there must be a way to tame its flames. There had to be, because I refused to be consumed by this fire that burned within me for the wrong man.

"You okay, Stella?" my brother asked, tearing me out of my thoughts so quickly that I actually jumped.

"Fine." I cleared my throat. "Totally fine."

Kaden gave me a look that made it clear he knew I was full of shit. "You've been tense ever since we got here."

That was the problem with being close to your sibling, you couldn't hide anything from them. But if Kaden found out what was really on my mind he would completely lose his shit, and that was the last thing we needed tonight.

"It's just weird being here," I said, fumbling for an explanation that would appease him. It wasn't a lie either. Just not the whole truth.

His face softened. "I know what you mean. Our pack's first real Convergence."

My shoulders relaxed a little. "I still can't believe it's happening, especially after the last two were such a disaster." At the previous summer solstice, the other Zodiac Wolves had practically chased us off. Then at the winter solstice, we'd spent the entire Convergence fighting the Sun Witches and their allies. It hadn't gone well.

Kaden nodded, his chest puffing out with obvious pride. "Now the Ophiuchus are finally accepted as true members of the Zodiac Wolves. We've proven ourselves, and no one will prevent us from taking part in the Convergence alongside the other packs."

I couldn't help but grin as I gazed out at the meadow before us, taking in the various packs gathered together in a sea of colors and scents, their voices intermingling like a symphony. "Who would've ever thought we'd get here?"

Kaden glanced over at his mate, Ayla, who was taking photos a short distance away, and obvious love shone through his eyes. "We've all come a long way in the last year."

"Mom and Dad would be proud of you," I said, trying to ignore the pang in my chest whenever I thought of them.

He clasped me on the shoulder. "And of you. I'm proud of what we've accomplished together."

"Let's hope the other packs never doubt our place again," I said, crossing my arms. "We've more than earned it."

"They won't," he said, with a touch of a growl in his voice. "We'll make sure of that."

As the bonfire crackled and danced in the fading light, I caught a glimpse of golden hair moving through the crowd toward us. *Jordan.* Raw alpha power emanated from him, a force that drew me in despite my best efforts to resist. My heart raced and my stomach churned with a mixture of dread and something else I refused to acknowledge.

Even though I'd been avoiding Jordan ever since the Leos had arrived yesterday, it seemed like he was always there in the corner of my eye, lurking at the edge of my thoughts. So far I'd managed to stay away, and if I was lucky, I'd make it through the entire Convergence without talking to him. Then we would go home, and I could put him out of my thoughts completely. Out of sight, out of mind.

I made the mistake of glancing his way for a second and my breath hitched as his sky blue eyes caught mine. Something flared in his gaze and he picked up his pace. I quickly looked away, knowing my time was running out. I couldn't face him. Not now.

"I just remembered I need to grab something from my tent," I said, trying to sound casual. "I'll be right back."

"Sure thing," Kaden replied, distracted by another pack member approaching him.

Taking advantage of the moment, I slipped away from the bonfire as quickly as I could. Without looking back, I made my way into the forest that wrapped around the valley where we'd all gathered, knowing the dark trees would shelter me. The cool shadows offered a respite from the heat of the clearing, and I used my Moon Touched gift to cloak myself in invisibility, wanting nothing more than to disappear from the world for a while.

Within the woods, the cool, damp earth beneath my feet grounded me, and the scent of pine and moss filled my lungs. Birds flitted overhead, their joyful chirps filling the air with a harmonious melody that blended seamlessly with the rustling of leaves in the gentle breeze. Still invisible, I stopped and let out a long breath, allowing my shoulders to relax.

To my dismay, Jordan strode confidently into the forest behind me, his movements fluid and graceful, like a predator stalking its prey. Just seeing his cocky smirk made my chest clench. His father had killed my parents, and I'd spent my entire life hating the Leos. I couldn't help but loathe everything about their new alpha too—his cockiness, his arrogance, and the way my pulse raced when I looked at him, like a drumbeat echoing through my veins. I loathed that most of all.

I moved silently but swiftly, darting through the brush to get away from him, but it seemed Jordan was not so easily deterred. I heard his soft footsteps approaching, and the sound of his breath mingling with the rustle of leaves. He was close—too close—and I couldn't help but feel a thrill of excitement at the thought of him seeking me out, even as I tried to convince myself it was the last thing I wanted.

I stilled beside a tree, waiting for him to pass, knowing he couldn't see me, and held my breath as he approached. His shining hair was longer than when we'd last met and a bit unruly as if he'd been dragging his hands through it. He wore a black shirt that did nothing to conceal his broad shoulders or those muscles rippling along his body, along with dark jeans that hugged his hips so well it made it impossible for my eyes not to dip down and wonder what was underneath.

He paused, his gaze sweeping across the forest where I stood. "You know, I'm starting to think you're avoiding me."

Fuck.

"You can't hide from me forever, Stella," he continued, his voice tinged with amusement and something more, something that sent another shiver down my spine. He breathed in sharply, and his eyes closed for a moment. "I can smell you, even if I can't see you."

Damn alphas. Their senses were always so sharp. The air around us crackled with tension, and I knew he wasn't going to let me go this time. I had to face him.

"Leave me alone, Jordan," I snapped, dropping the veil of invisibility.

His entire body focused on me with an intensity that fueled the unwanted fire within me. "I can't do that."

I swallowed hard. "What do you want?"

He took a step toward me. "You feel it, don't you? This...pull between us."

I tried to move back, but the tree was behind me. There was nowhere for me to go. "I don't know what you're talking about."

"You do. I see it in your eyes." His voice was low and husky, and he stepped closer, his broad shoulders blocking out the light, forcing me to acknowledge his presence. "I've felt it from the moment we met. Even before the mating bond with Ayla was broken."

I bit my lip, refusing to look into his eyes, but deep down, I knew he was right. There was an undeniable connection between us, one that had grown stronger since our first meeting. Now that he was no longer falsely mated to another woman, the feeling was overpowering. And yet, I couldn't bring myself to admit it aloud.

"Feelings can be deceiving," I muttered, trying to dart around him.

Jordan reached out and grasped my wrist, stopping me

in my tracks. The warmth of his touch made me gasp, and my gaze jerked up to meet his. The determination I saw on his face sent another shock of heat through me.

"You can deny it all you want, but the second we shift, we'll know it's true," he said.

"Stop," I said, shaking my head as my pulse beat faster. He was too close. I couldn't think like this. "Just shut up."

His fingers tightened around my wrist. "Stella, you're my mate."

Mate. The word I'd tried so hard to ignore hung between us for a few seconds before I managed to jerk my hand away. "No. I can't be your mate."

I shoved past him, needing to break the spell he had over me. On weak knees, I managed to stumble away, though longing filled my chest to the point it became hard to breathe. I pushed it down, focusing on the other emotions I felt around Jordan, like anger and annoyance. That strengthened me, and I picked up speed with each new step.

"Stella, wait!" Jordan called out behind me, and I didn't have to look back to know he was following me. Damn him. Why couldn't he just leave me alone?

I didn't respond, didn't even look back as I stormed out of the forest, stomping the grass beneath my feet with my hurried steps. I emerged near the spot where the Ophiuchus had set up our tents and spotted Ayla in front of the one she shared with Kaden. Her red hair shimmered in the firelight, a striking contrast against the darkening sky, but all I saw were her blue eyes, which looked just like Jordan's.

"Tell your brother to stay away from me," I snapped, not slowing down.

She looked taken aback, her eyebrows darting up with unspoken questions, but she wisely said nothing.

I escaped into my tent, where I knew Jordan wouldn't dare follow. Not with his sister right there, anyway. I roughly closed the flap, shutting out the outside world, and sucked in a breath. I thought I'd feel relief as soon as I stepped inside, but the air in the tent was heavy and oppressive.

I sank down onto my cot, dragging my hands across my face, but Jordan's words continued to haunt me. The worst part was the infuriating knowledge that he was right, and I couldn't deny it any longer. But I wouldn't give in, and wouldn't let my emotions betray me and my pack. I refused to become his mate. Refused to become one of *them*.

No matter the cost, I would not let the Leo pack claim me as their own.

CHAPTER TWO

IN THE DIM light of my tent, I sat with my knees drawn up to my chest, my thoughts a whirlwind of memories and conflicting emotions. Outside I heard raised voices and knew the Convergence was starting. I should have been with the other shifters representing the Ophiuchus, but instead, I was hiding like a coward, all because the Leo alpha would be there too.

The Leo and Ophiuchus packs had once been bitter enemies, but now here we were, reluctant allies bound together by a shared victory over the Sun Witches. The weight of that alliance pressed down on me like a suffocating blanket. I still had a hard time believing my brother could forgive the Leos so easily and accept them as allies after everything they'd done to our pack...and to our family.

I was just a kid when my parents, the former alphas of the Ophiuchus pack, went to the Leos to ask for their help.

The Leo alpha, Dixon, convinced them he would welcome them as guests. Instead, he killed them in cold blood, along with everyone who went with them. We never even got their bodies back to bury them properly.

A year ago, Dixon orchestrated the death of Ayla's family too, when the Leos decimated the Cancer pack at the previous summer Convergence. They later attacked our hidden village, Coronis, with aid from the Sun Witches, all because we'd rescued Ayla. I lost a few good friends that day, and at one point it seemed as though our entire forest would go up in flames, taking our whole village with it. Kaden managed to defeat Dixon in an alpha duel, and Ayla left with Jordan and the Sun Witches to save the rest of our pack.

My hatred of the Leos burned bright every time I thought of them holding my friend captive and how they'd treated her—especially Jordan. The Sun Witches had created a fake mate bond between Jordan and Ayla, and later we learned they'd been telepathically controlling him too. I knew that many of the awful things he'd done were because of their control, but it was still hard for me to separate him from the villain in my mind.

I remembered when we'd first truly met after the winter Convergence, back when our pack couldn't trust a single Leo. Sure, I'd seen Jordan before in passing or during the heat of battle, but this was different. When I laid eyes on him that night something deep within me stirred, an undeniable connection I'd never felt before with anyone else, though I refused to acknowledge it at the time.

As we worked to take down the Sun Witches and free the other Zodiac Wolves, Jordan always seemed to be there, driving me mad with his infuriating presence. He teased and taunted me, a cocky smirk never far from his lips, and it was obvious that the attraction between us was growing more intense by the day, like a forbidden thread that tugged at the deepest parts of my soul. Despite my lingering anger toward the Leos, I found it harder and harder to resist my growing desire for him, especially after I saw Jordan fight a fellow Leo pack member for the role of alpha. The raw power and determination he displayed that day woke something primal within me, and my blood heated at the memory of the way he'd fought with unfailing strength and courage. Not to mention the way his naked body had moved, the sweat and blood gleaming off his muscular skin...

I reached for my water bottle, suddenly parched. I couldn't deny that I wanted Jordan—physically, at least—but that didn't mean I had to act on my desire. Even if everyone else accepted Jordan as an ally or even viewed him as a hero for helping to defeat the Sun Witches, I couldn't separate him from my hatred of the Leos. Over and over they'd tried to take everything from me. My friends. My family. My home. Now they wanted to take my heart too? No fucking way.

A cheer went up outside and reminded me I should be there too, celebrating this occasion with my pack. With a heavy sigh, I dragged myself out of my tent and into the crisp night air. The Convergence meeting was well under-way, led by the Sagittarius alphas beneath the watchful gaze of the stars. By now, Kaden and Ayla's light show must have already finished, and I felt bad that I'd missed it, even though I'd seen them practicing it for weeks.

As I slowly approached the area where hundreds of other shifters were gathered, I heard the Sagittarius alpha speak of moving on after our losses, and I realized I'd also missed the memorial for the shifters we'd lost in the final battle against the Sun Witches. A pang of guilt hit me along with a wave of sadness as I thought of my friend Jack, who'd bravely given his life that night. My eyes burned with tears like they did every time I remembered him, and I silently cursed myself for hiding inside my tent instead of being present for the memorial.

As I joined the crowd, I quickly spotted Ayla and Kaden standing together, holding hands and looking disgustingly in love. The sight tugged at my heart and, for a moment, I wished I could share in that simple happiness. Many others from our pack stood nearby, their faces somber as they gazed toward the center of the gathering, including my friend, Harper, and her twin brother, Dane. Harper gave me a quizzical look as I approached, no doubt wondering where I'd been, while Dane gave me a solemn nod.

I tried to focus on what the Sagittarius alpha was saying, but my gaze landed on Jordan, who stood tall and proud among the throng of wolves. Even with hundreds of other shifters around I picked him out of the crowd easily, and his head jerked toward me as if he sensed my attention. Our eyes met like a clash of fire and ice, and suddenly it became hard for me to breathe. He arched an eyebrow at me, almost as if in invitation, but I shook my head, refusing to give in to the pull that bound us together. A deep frown marred his handsome features, and I forced myself to look away.

Beside him stood the Libra alpha, Ethan, whom I had often flirted with before. He'd even invited me to his bed once, but I'd turned him down. Not because I wasn't attracted to him, but because my best friend Larkin had a crush on him and I couldn't hurt her like that. Life would have been so much easier if he'd been my fated mate though. Ethan was smart, strong, and a great leader, and his calm presence was always a soothing balm. The Libras were close friends with the Ophiuchus pack, and I would have felt at home living among them in Toronto, even as their alpha female. But the stars seemed determined to torment me by binding me to my enemy instead.

I returned Ethan's easy smile and gave him a little wave, but all that did was make Jordan's body tense. As he looked back and forth between me and Ethan, his scowl was like a storm cloud against the starlit sky. Any second now I worried he might actually strike one of us down with a bolt of lightning.

The Sagittarius alpha female suddenly clapped her hands together, drawing my attention. "Now it's time for the moment you have all been waiting for. The mating ritual."

Shit. I should have stayed in my tent.

The Sagittarius alpha female took her mate's hand and smiled at the crowd. "We have a new way of doing the mating ritual this year, now that the Sun Witches no longer control our bonds. Let us give thanks to the Ophiuchus pack, who have never been under the Sun Witches' spells, for guiding us to create a new ritual, one that is true to our nature."

The air was thick with anticipation, and I couldn't help but feel the weight of the gazes landing upon my pack members. We were the newcomers, the outsiders, and the heroes who had freed them, but unlike them, we'd always been able to find our true mates. We'd never needed a mating ritual before, but with so many shifters here it made sense they would want one. From what I'd seen of the Zodiac Wolves, they loved tradition and ceremony.

"Those who are unmated, please remove your clothes, step forward, and shift," the Sagittarius alpha female called out.

All around the gathering, shifters began tossing off their clothes eagerly, including Harper and Dane at my side. A couple of other Ophiuchus joined them, and I knew they were excited to finally be able to find mates outside of our pack. That was one of the reasons we'd fought so hard to join the Zodiac Wolves, after all. Our mating pool had become too small and we worried it would become incestuous if we didn't start reaching beyond our borders. We'd always taken in rogue shifters and even mated with humans and witches before, but what we really needed was to be able to find mates from other packs. That was why my parents had gone to the Leo alpha for help, though we all know how that went. Years later, Kaden had done the impossible and forced the Zodiac Wolves to accept us as one of their own. Only time would tell how that would go, but tonight was a big step. Even if it meant we would lose some of our Ophiuchus shifters to other packs, we would hopefully gain some fresh blood too.

Harper nudged me in the side with her elbow. "Why aren't you getting naked?"

"I'm not looking for anything serious right now." Across the crowd, I spotted Ethan and Jordan removing their clothes too—except as soon as Jordan saw that I wasn't moving to join them, he stopped.

"I hear you," Harper said, as she tore off her bra with zero shame or hesitation and then let down her hair. "I was tempted to skip out too, but curiosity got the better of me. What if my mate is out there in that crowd, waiting for me? I have to know."

I gave her an uneasy smile. "I hope you find what you're looking for."

"Me too. Especially because this place is going to turn into one big orgy in about ten minutes, and I'll be pissed if I'm the only one not getting any." She tilted her head with a grin. "You sure you don't want to join in?"

No. Yes. No. "I'm sure."

She shrugged and shifted into a beautiful brown wolf, while her brother did the same beside her. Together they loped off toward the center of the gathering, along with a few other wolves from our pack. Their fur soon blended in among the shifters from other packs as more and more joined them in the center. This was the reason so many shifters had come to the Convergence, and I knew what happened tonight would shape the destiny of all the packs for years to come. This was the first time these wolves would be able to find their true mates and the excitement in the air was palpable.

Once everyone who wanted to join the ritual was crowded together, the Sagittarius alphas raised their hands to the stars and chanted something that I couldn't quite make out, though I knew it was a prayer asking for true mates to be revealed. The unmated wolves began moving amongst themselves, weaving and circling each other, led by invisible urges and instincts that tugged at their hearts and souls. The first pair matched up quickly, and my heart beat faster as their wolves leaped on one another, then began rolling around in the dirt and nuzzling each other's necks. They darted into the forest just as other wolves joined together, their mating bonds snapping into place as soon as their eyes met. I spotted one of the teachers I worked with get paired up with a dark gray wolf from the Aquarius pack before they raced back toward the tents, presumably to seal the mating bond completely. Longing filled my chest until I felt like it would burst, but I would bet money that none of those wolves were mated to their enemy.

And through it all, I sensed Jordan nearby, his presence a constant hum beneath my skin. I refused to look at him, and when it became too much I turned away, needing to escape from the sea of fur and lust before me. Unfortunately, I nearly ran straight into Ayla and Kaden, whose bodies were entwined under the starlight as they shared a passionate kiss.

"Stella?" Kaden asked as they broke apart. "Is everything okay?"

"You're not shifting tonight?" Ayla added, her voice concerned.

I sighed, wishing I'd escaped sooner. Or better yet, stayed in my tent all night. "No, not this time."

"Why not?" Kaden asked.

I rubbed my arms and tried to keep the emotion out of my voice. "I'm not interested in finding a mate right now. I have enough on my plate as it is."

Kaden raised an eyebrow. "Are you sure?"

Why did everyone keep asking me that? My gaze flicked involuntarily toward the distant figure of Jordan, his golden hair glinting beneath the stars. He stood with his arms crossed, his back stiff, his eyes locked on me with an intensity that could be felt even at a distance. I sucked in a breath and looked away. "I'm sure."

Ayla followed my gaze and then rested a hand on Kaden's arm. "Give her a break. She'll know when the time is right."

"Fine with me," Kaden said. "I don't like the idea of my little sister being rutted by one of the males here anyway."

"I am an adult, you know," I said, rolling my eyes. "I can 'rut' whoever I want."

"Yeah, but I don't want to know about it." He made a disgusted face.

I pictured what would happen if Kaden found out who my mate truly was. Would he set the entire forest ablaze with moon magic? Maybe he'd slam his claws into Jordan's chest? Or would Kaden's head just explode, like something from a cartoon?

Ayla bumped shoulders with her mate and grinned at me. "I think what Kaden is trying to say is that he'd be sad if you found your mate and went to live with another pack so soon."

I swallowed hard at the emotion that swelled in my chest at her words. I couldn't imagine leaving the Ophiuchus pack for any other, but tradition amongst the Zodiac Wolves stated that females always went to join their mates' packs. The one exception was the Virgo pack, which was led by women. In the Ophiuchus pack, we'd never had to worry about such old-fashioned, patriarchal bullshit, since we took in anyone who was mated to one of our members. Now that we were a part of the Zodiac Wolves we'd accepted that our females would leave our pack while new females would join our ranks, thus allowing us to keep our bloodlines strong. Or at least the others had accepted it. I refused to even consider it for myself.

"The Ophiuchus pack is my home, and I have no intention of leaving it," I said.

Kaden nodded, but he still looked concerned. "You can't avoid this forever, Stella. Fate has a way of catching up to us."

Why was everyone suddenly so concerned with me finding a mate? "I know that."

Kaden gave me a pat on the shoulder before he retreated with Ayla to their tent, leaving me alone once more in the throng of shifters. I turned back for one last look at the unmated wolves, their numbers getting smaller as more pairs disappeared into the shadows, and this time I didn't see Jordan anywhere among them. Had he gone off with someone? Not that it mattered to me. Not one bit.

I kicked the dirt as I started back toward my tent. Alone. Just as I wanted.

CHAPTER THREE

I WAS HALFWAY to my tent when my path was blocked by a large, very naked male. At first, all I saw was a broad, tanned chest with rippling muscles and a Capricorn pack mark on his arm, before my eyes traveled up to a handsome face with lots of sharp angles and one very flirtatious grin.

"Hey, gorgeous," the male said, his intentions all too clear in his roaming eyes. "Didn't find your mate tonight? Me neither. But we can still have some fun." He took a step closer. "My tent is right over there. Care to join me?"

"Thanks, but—" I started to reply, but as soon as the words left my mouth, a furious growl tore through the air.

Jordan appeared out of nowhere, his huge hand reaching up to wrap around the other male's throat. The muscles in his arm bulged and his black shirt held on for dear life as he raised the Capricorn into the air by his neck. "Stella is *mine*," he snarled, his voice barely human.

Mine. Jordan's word seemed to ricochet inside of me,

causing a dozen different, conflicting emotions and thoughts to collide, and I could only gape at him with my mouth open.

The Capricorn raised his hands in submission, his eyes wide with fear. "Sorry, alpha! I didn't know!"

Jordan didn't seem to hear him. His fingers turned to claws that threatened to tear the other male's throat out. I couldn't see his face from this angle, but I suspected his eyes were blazing with possessive rage.

"Jordan!" I grabbed his arm and tried to yank him back, but he was too strong. I sank my nails into his skin and tugged harder. "Let him go!"

Jordan's shoulders stiffened at my touch. He threw the other male to the ground, and the Capricorn scurried away like a cowering pup without another glance in my direction. Leaving me alone with the man who'd just claimed me loudly as his own. Good thing no one else was around to hear him, or if they were, they were too busy with their new mates to care.

As Jordan turned to face me, I let go of his arm, though his heat still danced across my palm. "Yours?" I spat, my anger flaring to life. "I am no one's property, least of all yours!"

Jordan huffed. "I don't want you as my property. I want you as my alpha female."

My heart stuttered at his words, but then the thought of being the *Leo* alpha female brought me back to my senses. I clenched my fists at my sides, fighting the urge to reach out and touch him. "For the last time, we are not mates, and I am never, ever going to be your alpha female."

"No?" He cocked his head. "Then shift in front of me and prove there's nothing between us."

I stared defiantly up at him. "I don't have to prove anything to you or anyone else."

Frustration twisted his face. "No, you'd just rather let everyone think you still haven't found your mate. Did you want to go off with that Capricorn? Is that it?"

"No, but I was handling it. And don't you dare threaten any other wolves on my behalf!"

Fire flickered across his eyes as he grabbed my arm. "You think I'm going to let some horny goat put his hands all over what's mine?"

I pushed one hand against his chest. "I. Am. Not. Yours!"

A cocky smirk slid across his lips. "Not yet, but you will be."

My eyes narrowed. "Never."

His firm hand dragged me toward him, and my stupid body obeyed. "What are you going to do, avoid shifting every time I'm nearby? At some point, it will happen. The mate bond will lock into place, and you'll be mine. Why delay the inevitable?" His other arm went around my waist and pulled me against him, his hard chest pressing against my breasts. His voice lowered as he dipped his head. "Just admit you want me as much as I want you."

I put both my hands on his chest to push him away, but instead, they lingered there, like they weren't fully under my control. Desire flared through me at the feel of his body against mine. "I do not want you."

"Liar."

His mouth crashed down on mine and warmth spread through me, like a spark igniting a bonfire. All rational thought fled me as our lips and tongues joined together in an angry, intimate dance. He clutched me to him like he was never letting me go, his fingers digging into my skin, while I clawed at his shirt like a feral animal. This kiss was primal and all-consuming, waking up the wolf inside of me, who howled for more of her mate.

We devoured each other, all those months of pent-up fighting and flirting and eye-fucking finally coming to a culmination. Jordan's hands slid down to my ass and he lifted me up, his mouth never leaving mine. My legs wrapped around him of their own accord, while my fingers slid around his throat, choking him and claiming him all at once. How could I want someone just as much as I hated him?

Then he started walking, and the jolt of movement jerked me back to my senses. I lifted my head and looked around, remembering where we were, and more importantly, *who* we were.

"What are you doing?" I asked, squirming in his grasp.

"Taking you back to my tent," he said, as his strong arms carried me across the field.

Panic and desire warred inside me. "Put me down! I'm not going to your tent!"

With arched eyebrows, he set me down but didn't let me

go. "No? All I can smell is how wet you are for me. It's driving me mad." He brushed his nose against my hair as he breathed in my scent. "At least let me bury my face between your legs so I can taste you."

I gasped at his words and the pulse of heat they caused deep in my core. I hated how much I wanted him to do exactly that and even more, especially after that kiss. But somehow I found enough mental clarity to jerk out of his grip and step back. "Not going to happen."

His eyes flared with lust and rage. "Really? Because a second ago you were ready to fuck me right here in the open."

"That was a mistake." I wiped my lips with the back of my hand, trying to get rid of the intoxicating taste of him. "Stay away from me, Jordan."

He let out a low growl as I spun on my heel and dashed away, leaving him under the mocking stars. The sound of his steps behind me told me he wasn't letting me go so easily. I darted around tents and was so distracted by trying to escape that I ran straight into someone else.

Firm hands caught me and I looked up to see Ethan's handsome face. "You all right, Stella?" he asked, his brows creasing in concern.

I steadied myself and took a step back. "Yeah, fine. Sorry about that."

He gave me a curious look. "In a rush to meet someone? Your mate, maybe?"

"No, I..." I glanced behind me, where Jordan watched us with his arms crossed, possessive animosity radiating from him like waves. I raised my chin and turned back to Ethan. "I don't have a mate."

"I didn't find one tonight either. Maybe next time." Ethan's eyes flickered between me and Jordan. "Are you sure you're all right? Would you like me to walk you back to your tent?"

"I'm fine, really. Just tired. It's been a long day. Thanks though."

I slipped away before Ethan could ask me any more questions or Jordan did something stupid like attack the Libra alpha in a fit of jealous rage. I went invisible and rushed through the camp, trying to escape the chaos in my mind, but there was nowhere that was safe. A sexual frenzy had taken over the Convergence and everyone was under its spell. Tents shook and trembled, while naked bodies writhed on the ground in the shadows of bonfires. The smell of sex was everywhere. And the sounds...don't even get me started on the sounds.

I quickly retreated inside my tent and the flimsy sanctuary it offered, but still felt no relief. A reckless part of me hoped Jordan would find me and was surprised when he didn't, though I knew it was only a temporary reprieve. He was letting me go this time, but soon he would find me again. I had no doubt about that.

I made myself get ready for sleep, but it soon became clear that there would be no rest tonight, not for me or anyone else. Even with a pillow over my head, the sounds of other shifters coupling echoed through the meadow like a chorus of animalistic need. It was as if each moan and growl clawed at my thoughts, digging into the very fibers of my being. Taunting me with what I could have had.

I screamed into my pillow as the memory of Jordan's kiss repeated over and over in my mind. It took everything in my power not to run outside and find his tent to continue what we'd started. The pull between us was undeniable, a force of nature that seemed determined to draw us together despite the obstacles that stood in our way. But how could I allow myself to give in when everything in my past screamed for me to run?

CHAPTER FOUR

THE MORNING SUN pierced through the seams of my tent, forcing my heavy eyelids to flutter open. Memories of the night before flashed through my mind—Jordan's mouth devouring mine, his hands on my skin, my legs wrapped around his hips. My heart raced as I recalled the way he had kissed me and the undeniable passion we'd shared.

I sat up, shaking my head. The kiss meant nothing. Absolutely nothing. I was lonely and he was there. Okay, fine, he was likely my mate, but did that mean I had to accept it? No way. The stars wouldn't choose my fate—I would.

The sounds of the camp stirring greeted me, and I pulled myself together and stepped outside. Shifters from various packs were packing up and saying their goodbyes, ready to head back to their respective territories now that the Convergence was over. The crisp scents of coffee and bacon wafted from several fires, and wolf pups rolled around near the forest edge, eager to play for a bit before their long journeys. A few spots of the meadow were noticeably empty, the tents already removed. The party was over and it was time to go home, at least until the next Convergence at the winter solstice.

I searched for Jordan's tent or any sign of the Leos, but they were gone. Relief washed over me knowing I wouldn't have to face him again anytime soon. Today I would head home with the Ophiuchus pack and forget all about Jordan and the pesky mate bond that kept trying to pull us together. Besides, he'd left without saying goodbye, so he must have realized this thing between us would never work. He needed a nice mate who would be excited about becoming a Leo, and I needed... Well, I wasn't sure exactly. I just knew it wasn't him.

After taking a few minutes to clean up and get dressed, I joined some of the other Ophiuchus for breakfast. I loaded up a paper plate with bacon, eggs, and biscuits, then poured myself some coffee and found a spot next to Harper and Dane at the table. They were already laughing at something one of the other shifters had said, and everyone made space for me as I sat down. The familiarity and ease of being among my pack made me feel right at home immediately. A good reminder of what I would give up if I became the Leo alpha female.

"How did it go last night?" I asked Harper and Dane. "Did you find your mates?"

"No, but we did have some fun," Harper said, grinning suggestively. "You should have joined us."

"Maybe next time," I said, before shoving some eggs in my mouth to avoid saying anything else about my night.

"Marla found her mate," said Carly. She nudged the blond woman beside her, who blushed a little. Like me, they were both teachers back in Coronis.

"An Aquarius!" Marla said, her eyes wide and dreamy. "It all happened so fast. We saw each other and I just knew."

"And then you ran off into the woods and banged for hours," Harper said with a wink, and everyone laughed.

Marla giggled. "Something like that."

"But now you're leaving us," Carly said with a pout. "Who is going to teach your class this year?"

"I don't know." Marla sighed. "I'm going to miss everyone so much."

"Congratulations," I said, my stomach twisting at the thought of her no longer being part of our pack. The three of us had taught the younger pups for years, and it wouldn't be the same without her. "How do you feel about joining the Aquarius?"

"I'm sad to be leaving the Ophiuchus, of course. This will always be my pack." She drew in a breath and looked over to where a couple of Aquarius tents were located. "But this feels right too. I was ready for something new and my mate is perfect. He's everything I could have wanted and I have a feeling I'll fit right in with the Aquarius. But don't worry, I'll come back to visit as much as I can."

I studied her face, wondering how she could be so sure.

She was leaving her home and her pack and everything she had ever known for some man she'd met a few hours ago. Marla had always wanted to be mated though. Maybe she was swept up in the newness of her bond and willing to ignore her fears. Either way, I would miss her.

"Max found a mate too," Carly said, referring to another male in our pack, who did carpentry for the people of Coronis. She leaned forward, her voice lowering. "A male from the Taurus pack."

Harper's eyes widened as she shared a look with Dane. "I wonder how the Taurus feel about that."

The table went quiet as everyone considered it. The other Zodiac packs had never had LGBTQ mate pairs before because the Sun Witches didn't allow them to occur, but in the Ophiuchus pack, we'd always been open to them, at least for as long as I could remember. Our beta, Clayton, was mated to a male who was once in the Sagittarius pack. Even the Sun Witch spells hadn't kept the two of them apart, much like Kaden and Ayla had been drawn together. And how I'd suspected Jordan was my mate even while he was still magically bound to someone else.

"Which pack will they be in?" I asked.

"No one knows yet," Carly said. "The alphas are going to discuss it."

Did that mean we might lose Max too? We weren't very close, but he was a good guy and he'd fixed things around our school before. His presence would be missed if he left us for the Taurus pack, although there was no precedent yet for this sort of thing. It was possible his new mate would join our pack instead.

"Did any of the alphas get mated?" Harper asked.

"No." Carly let out a dramatic sigh and twirled her dark hair. "I was hoping for Ethan myself."

"Everyone was hoping for him," another shifter named Kim said with a laugh.

"Not me," Harper said. "Though I sort of thought he'd end up with Stella."

Dane shook his head and gave me a knowing look. Was it possible he'd seen Jordan kissing me last night? For once, I was glad he never talked.

Every eye at the table turned to me and I cleared my throat and put on a confident smile. "No way. I'm not leaving my pack anytime soon."

While everyone chatted about other shifters who had paired up last night, I got up and threw out the rest of my food, my appetite gone. I was happy for the others who had found their mates, but I didn't want to leave my pack, my home, or my family. But that would be my fate if I allowed this mate bond with Jordan to activate.

On the other hand, I couldn't help but feel a slight bit of jealousy too. Marla seemed so damn confident that the Aquarius pack was where she was meant to be. I longed for that kind of certainty, and I wondered if I would feel it too if I mated with Jordan. No, I couldn't ever imagine calling the Leo pack my home.

But if I was honest with myself, a part of me wished for something more than just being the alpha's little sister.

Before Kaden had mated with Ayla I'd often acted as our pack's unofficial alpha female, taking on many of the leadership roles one would have fulfilled. Now that the Ophiuchus pack had Ayla, they didn't need me as anything more than a kindergarten teacher. When Jordan had said he'd wanted me to be his alpha female, I'd secretly wanted it too. Just not with the Leos.

I headed back to my tent to begin taking it down but spotted Ayla outside of the tent she shared with Kaden. Her red hair gleamed as she bent over her bags, furiously looking for something in them.

"Everything okay?" I asked her.

"Oh, Stella, hi." She straightened up and blew out a long breath. "I can't find my camera anywhere and we need to get going soon, plus I have a meeting with the Taurus alpha in a minute..."

"To talk about Max and his mate?"

"You heard?" She nodded. "There were four other gay or lesbian mate pairs last night among the other packs. No one is sure which packs they should join. Obviously, Max and his mate are welcome to stay with the Ophiuchus pack if they wish, but what about the others? Those packs have never had to deal with this before. It's a good thing because it means people can be with who they love, but it's a big change too. On top of all the other big changes we're already facing."

She seemed so frazzled that I immediately pushed aside my own worries. Ayla was our alpha female now and she'd also become a leader to the other packs, so I knew she wouldn't rest until this was sorted out. Plus, this was a good reminder of why we'd battled so hard for all of these changes. Love was love, and we Ophiuchus would always fight for someone to be with their true mates, even if it made things difficult.

What about your true mate? an annoying part of my brain whispered. I mentally drop-kicked it into oblivion and smiled at Ayla. "Why don't you let each couple choose for themselves?"

"That's a good idea, although I'm not sure the other packs would go for it."

I shrugged. "I always thought it was silly that the females went to the males' packs. What if the males wanted to change packs instead? If it were up to me, everyone should be able to choose where they belong."

Ayla blinked at me. "I've never thought of it that way."

I grinned at her. "Go talk to the other alphas and see what you can do. Meanwhile, I'll find your camera for you."

"Really? Thank you." She pressed a hand to her stomach where my little niece or nephew was growing inside. "I don't know how I lost it in the first place. This preggo brain thing is no joke."

"You have a lot on your mind right now. When did you last have it?"

"Um, let's see, I got up early and took some shots of the sunrise over the camp, and then I went to see this ancient tree with Jordan—oh! I wonder if I left it out there in the forest?" She bit her lip and glanced over at the trees nearby.

I bristled at the mention of the man I was trying not to think about. "Could Jordan have it?"

"I don't think so. We came back together and then the Leos packed up and left. It's a long way back to Arizona and Jordan wanted an early start."

I relaxed again. "I'll find your camera for you. Just tell me how to get to the tree."

"Are you sure?" she asked, just as Kaden called her name from inside the tent. He sounded stressed too.

"Yes, you have enough to deal with. I'll be back in no time."

Her shoulders slumped in relief. "Thanks, Stella."

Ayla gave me some general directions on how to find the tree and I popped into my tent to remove my clothes. With a smooth, practiced shift, my body transformed into my wolf, my senses instantly sharpening as all the scents and sounds intensified. I stretched out my limbs, feeling that sense of freedom that always came with being back in wolf form, and then I took off, weaving through the remaining tents and slipping into the forest.

As I raced through the undergrowth, the wind caressed my black fur, while pine needles cushioned my paws and birds chirped merrily overhead. The sun filtered through the canopy, casting dappled shadows along my path. The sounds of the camp faded away as the scent of damp earth and fresh greenery filled my nostrils, calming my frazzled nerves.

Ayla's directions were good and it didn't take me too long to find the ancient tree. It stood tall and proud, its branches reaching up to the sky like gnarled hands. I couldn't help but be awestruck by its beauty and the sense of timelessness it exuded. As I approached, my fur brushed against the rough bark, and I admired the grooves and ridges that had formed over countless years.

I found Ayla's camera in its bag right at the base of the tree, and I returned to human form to pick it up and put it around my neck. Leaning against the ancient tree, I closed my eyes and took a deep breath. The quiet serenity of the forest wrapped around me like a comforting embrace, providing a much-needed reprieve from the chaos of the Convergence and the turmoil inside me.

I knew I couldn't stay here forever, but for a few precious moments, I tried to forget about everything else and simply exist in this beautiful, peaceful place. It worked at first, but then my thoughts strayed back to Jordan, wondering what the future held for both of us, and whether I'd ever be able to escape the pull of our bond. Was there any point in fighting it?

The sound of rustling leaves and snapping twigs caught my attention, and I pressed my naked back to the tree and glanced around. The disturbance started in one spot in the forest and then spread while getting closer at the same time. I raised my nose and caught the scent of wolves, though none that I immediately recognized.

Reddish fur and gleaming eyes emerged from the brush, surrounding me on all sides. Some of the wolves growled low in their throats, while others bared their teeth, their hackles raised. Every single one looked ready to attack me at any moment. I didn't even need to see their pack marks to know they were Leos.

Panic shot through me as I lived through one of my worst nightmares. Memories flashed of when the Leos attacked my village, their red wolves running through our streets while the Sun Witches burned everything they could. I'd taken the children to safety, while Kaden had killed their alpha—Jordan's father—that day. Were these Leos here for revenge? If they were, they had no idea who they were up against. I was the daughter of alphas, with ancient Moon Witch blood in my veins, and I would go down fighting these Leos with everything I had.

I put Ayla's camera down and let my wolf free again, immediately dropping into a defensive position. There were at least a dozen wolves, and I had no idea which one would make the first move. I had to be ready for anything.

As I bared my teeth at them, the Leos drew closer, circling around me, making sure there was nowhere for me to run. Some of them snapped at me, though none got close enough to actually touch me. Terror flooded my veins, though I refused to cower. Was this how my parents felt before the Leos killed them in cold blood?

Then a familiar scent came to me, the one I'd been unable to stop thinking about since last night. The wolves in front of me parted as a huge red-gold wolf approached from the forest. Sunlight danced off his fur like it was drawn to him, and his blue eyes shone with the fire inside of him. He came for me with the determination of a wolf who had found its prey and was never letting it escape.

A new kind of panic rose up inside me. I started to back away, but there was nowhere for me to go. A soft whine escaped me as I tried to look anywhere but at the alpha approaching me, but it was impossible.

Our eyes met—and the mate bond activated.

CHAPTER FIVE

THE WORLD SLOWED DOWN. Something within me snapped into place as I stared into Jordan's eyes, something I'd always known was there but had never been able to touch before. He was the missing piece of me, the thing I'd been searching for without even realizing it. Through the bond, I knew he felt the same way because we were one being now, not two.

The rest of the forest faded away, and all I knew in that moment was my mate. We both moved toward each other in a rush, colliding in a tangle of fur and claws. We tousled, twisting and rolling through the underbrush, leaves, and dirt scattering around us. Our bodies became entwined in a dance of dominance and submission, but he was too strong and easily pinned me beneath him, our noses almost touching.

Jordan rubbed his face on mine and I couldn't resist the urge to nuzzle against him, reveling in the connection that now bound us together. The scent of him was intoxicating, filling my senses and sending my heart racing. We both shifted back to human form at the same instant, our bodies completely attuned to each other. He kissed along the side of my neck as our naked limbs clung to each other. His hard cock pressed against me and I wanted nothing more than for him to be inside me, making the bond truly complete.

Jordan lifted his head and barked out a command. "Leave us."

Reality crashed back into me as I remembered we were surrounded by a dozen members of his pack, all watching this moment and what we were about to do. A few seconds ago they'd circled me, making me think they were about to attack, and now they were disappearing into the woods at their alpha's command.

Heat flared across my face, and with it came an intense, burning rage. I snarled and pushed Jordan off of me. Hurt and confusion flashed in his eyes as I scrambled up and put as much distance as possible between us.

"What have you done?" I asked, my voice shaking.

The hurt vanished and was replaced by that familiar steely-eyed determination. "What I had to do."

"By getting your pack to attack me?" I could barely breathe as that terror came back to me now. I'd thought I was being ambushed and that I'd have to fight all those wolves for my life. It had brought back so many awful memories of the Leos, reawakening my fear and hatred of them all over again.

"You were never in any danger. I wouldn't let anyone harm you."

"No, you just made me think I was in danger so you could trick me into shifting!" My hands balled into fists at my sides. "You forced the mate bond to activate when you knew I didn't want it!"

Jordan slowly rose to his feet and brushed himself off, drawing my eyes to all that tan, glorious skin on display. Hatred warred with desire inside of me, the mate bond humming between us. Half of me wanted to jump into his arms, and the other half wanted to claw his face off.

"You kissed me last night," he said. "You felt the connection, just like I did. But you were going to leave without a word and go back to your pack like there was nothing between us. I couldn't let that happen. You're my mate, Stella. There's no denying it now."

"You set this whole thing up, didn't you?" Betrayal burned through my veins as I picked up Ayla's camera again. He'd come out here with Ayla this morning. He must have planted her camera here, hoping I would be sent to find it.

"I set up a possible situation and took advantage of it," he said without any trace of guilt.

"And if I didn't come? Would you have found some other way to get me to shift?"

"Yes." His gaze was steady and unapologetic. "I wasn't going to leave without you."

"You knew I didn't want this, but you forced it upon me anyway." I couldn't believe what he'd done, how he'd manipulated me into a situation I'd tried so hard to avoid. I poured every bit of hatred, anger, and betrayal into the bond so he would feel it just as strongly as I did. "You're despicable."

"You're right." He crossed his arms, arrogance radiating from his posture. "I've never claimed to be a saint. You've always known I'm a villain."

"Well, congratulations," I spat. "Your plan worked. We're mates. But this doesn't change anything. I won't abandon my pack for you. I will never be your alpha female. And I would sooner die before becoming a Leo."

He opened and closed his mouth like he was trying to find the right thing to say. Through the bond, I felt a dozen emotions ranging from confusion to regret to desperation, but I was done. I was so fucking done.

I moved right into his space, my eyes locked onto his. "Jordan, I reject you as my mate."

His eyes widened and he stumbled back as though I'd physically punched him in the gut. At my words, the connection between us was severed, vanishing as quickly as it had formed. My soul ached at the loss and something inside of me whimpered at being alone again, but I refused to take back my words.

Jordan straightened up and stared at me. I thought he would be angry, but instead, his eyes shone with a remorse that made my breath quicken. "I suppose I deserve that, after everything I've done."

I had a feeling he didn't just mean today. Tears stung my eyes, but I refused to let them fall. The ache in my chest was nearly unbearable. Every part of me yearned to go to him, to take him into my arms and tell him I needed him, but I couldn't do that. He'd tried to take away my choices, my options, my freedom. I would never look at him as anything but my enemy.

"Yes, you do." I drew in a shaky breath. "I will never forgive you for this."

"Maybe not, but we both know this isn't the end of us." He took a step closer, his voice low. "You may have rejected me, but you can't deny the connection between us, Stella. And deep down, you don't want to."

Anger and hurt clouded my vision, and I couldn't stand to be near him any longer. Without another word, I shifted back into my wolf, grabbed Ayla's camera bag between my teeth, and sprinted away, leaving him standing alone in the forest. This time he didn't chase me.

As I ran, I wondered if I'd ever be able to escape the pull between us. Even with the mate bond severed, the longing for him was a constant ache, a bittersweet reminder of what could have been if only things were different. Maybe if he had given me more time I would have entered the mate bond willingly, once I'd been ready to accept it.

Now we would never know.

CHAPTER SIX

THE OPHIUCHUS PACKED up and left a few hours later, and I made it back to Coronis without another whiff of Jordan's scent. Ayla seemed to sense something was wrong on the drive back, but she had so much on her mind she let me go without an interrogation. Max had decided to return to our pack and brought his new mate, a Taurus named Elliott. The other gay and lesbian mate pairs had also been given the choice of which of their packs to return with, after much heated discussion by the affected alphas. I had a feeling there would be more discussion on the matter soon, followed by a vote of all thirteen alphas. But that wasn't my problem and it never would be, because I'd turned down the chance to become an alpha female.

I ignored the hint of sadness that came with that trail of thought and went straight home, eager to relax with a cup of tea and a good book in my own space. As soon as I arrived at the cottage my shoulders eased and the pressure around my chest didn't seem quite so bad. The small house was pale yellow with a white door and had a garden of herbs on one side and a little stream on the other. Late afternoon sun cast shadows from the large oak tree which I'd used to climb when I was a kid. The golden light danced on the water's surface, casting a warm glow on the surrounding forest. I took a deep breath, inhaling the earthy scent of the trees and the sweet fragrance of the wildflowers that lined the banks.

The quaint little cottage had once been my mother's place, which she'd inherited from her own mother. She'd never lived inside but used it as an art studio and a place to escape from the pressures of being the alpha female. After her death, the house had been abandoned and neither Kaden nor I had been brave enough to venture inside until a few months ago when I'd realized I couldn't spend another day living with my brother and his new mate. Shifter hearing was way too good and those walls were far too thin. Besides, I'd lived with my big brother long enough. It was time for me to get a place of my own.

When I stepped inside, I was greeted with the scents of rosemary, chicken, and potatoes. My roommate Larkin stepped out of the small, dated kitchen and smiled at me. "You're back! I thought you might be hungry, so I'm cooking dinner. How did it go? Tell me everything!"

"It smells delicious." I adjusted my bag on my shoulder. "Give me a minute to put my stuff down and then we'll chat."

I headed to my room, the slightly larger of the two bedrooms in the house, and quickly dropped my bag and stripped out of my travel clothes. Once in my comfy yoga pants and an old ratty T-shirt, I steeled myself for Larkin's interrogation. She was my best friend, but she was also a hopeless romantic, made worse by the fact that she'd never been in a relationship before. Larkin was a Moon Witch who'd been trapped in Lunatera, the realm of the Moon Goddess Selene, for most of her life. Although she was technically in her forties, she appeared to be about fourteen years old. Now that she was living on Earth again she was aging normally once more, and she'd already filled out a little and grown an inch or two taller since I'd first met her. But she still didn't look like an adult yet either.

When I went back out, Larkin already had some tea waiting for me. She sat in her favorite chair, sipping from a mug with a cat in a witch hat on it. "Dinner won't be ready for another half hour, which gives you plenty of time to tell me all about your first real Convergence."

I sank into my usual spot on the sofa and grabbed my tea. "It was good. The Ophiuchus are finally accepted as a real pack. There were a lot of joyous reunions and some surprise matings. It was... intense."

"I bet." Larkin peered at me over her mug. "I'm surprised you're back. I thought for sure you'd be mated with Ethan." She tried to sound casual, but I detected a hint of relief in her voice. She had a huge crush on the Libra alpha, even though he showed no interest in her beyond polite friendship. I couldn't blame him, since Larkin still looked like a kid, after all.

"Nope. Ethan is still unmated, actually."

"Really?" Her eyes lit up with hope for a brief moment before she hid it away. "But what about you? I can't believe none of the males there were your mate."

I hesitated, feeling the weight of my secret pressing down on me. I avoided her eyes and took a long sip of my tea, hoping she'd ask me a question about something else.

Larkin leaned forward, her gaze probing. She could always tell when I was holding something back. "Spit it out, Stella. What aren't you telling me?"

I reluctantly set my mug down. "I didn't shift during the mating ritual."

"What!" Larkin's mouth dropped open in astonishment. "Why not?"

With a deep breath, I confessed, "Because I already knew who my mate was."

"Who?" she asked, her voice barely above a whisper.

I covered my face with my hands. "Jordan."

"Jordan?" Larkin let out a shocked laugh. "Wow. The stars certainly have a wicked sense of humor."

I dropped my hands and glared at her. "This isn't funny."

Her laughter died down as she saw the seriousness in my eyes. "You're right. I'm sorry. What happened?"

"Jordan tricked me into shifting into a wolf, activating the mate bond. I didn't want it. He knew that, and he did it anyway."

Larkin's expression instantly turned sympathetic. "I'm so sorry. That must have been awful."

I clenched my fists, my nails digging into my palms. "I

was furious, and I still am. I rejected him as my mate, and I never want to see him again."

Her eyes widened. "You rejected him?"

"I had to. I can't be with him. Not after what he did." My heart twisted with a mix of bitterness and regret.

"But that means you'll always be alone. You'll never find another mate. You'll never have children."

My heart clenched as she said all the things I'd been trying not to think about. "I know."

She looked like she wanted to say more as she frowned into her mug, but she kept her mouth shut. We both sipped our tea as the weight of my decision settled between us. By rejecting Jordan, I'd doomed both of us to a life without a mate and therefore without children, and a big part of me worried I'd made the wrong decision. Still, I couldn't imagine doing anything else after what he'd done.

Finally, Larkin asked, "What about Kaden and Ayla? Do they know?"

"No, and promise me you won't tell them." I imagined Ayla would try to smooth things over with Jordan, while Kaden would fight to keep us apart. It was better if no one knew.

"I won't, but the truth will come out eventually. Fate has a funny way of making sure we can't escape it." Her expression softened. "You can't avoid Jordan forever. What will you do when you see him again?"

I shook my head, unsure of the answer. The memory of Jordan—his touch, his scent, the warmth of his embrace—haunted me relentlessly, but being his mate filled me with dread. I was trapped between the pull of destiny and the life I wanted, and the way forward seemed more uncertain than ever.

"I don't know. I just can't bear the thought of being his mate and becoming a Leo. I've built my life here, and I don't want to give that up. Especially after he betrayed me. I can't forgive him for that."

"I understand." She reached over and squeezed my hand. "Whatever happens, I'll be here for you."

"Thanks," I murmured, grateful for her unwavering support. I wasn't sure how I was going to get through this, but at least I had a friend who understood what was going on. I knew she was right too. I couldn't escape Jordan forever. At some point, I'd have to face him again, and I had no idea what would happen then.

CHAPTER SEVEN

MONTHS PASSED, and by the time the leaves began to fall, I'd finally gotten to the point where I didn't think about Jordan every single waking hour. I was down to only once or twice a day, and even then it was usually in passing, a fleeting thought that I quickly dismissed. I kept myself busy with fixing up the cottage and teaching the kindergarten class of pups, and I didn't regret my decision at all. Sure, sometimes I woke up in a cold sweat from a nightmare about Jordan, or worse, a sex dream, but I pretended they never happened. Life moved on and so did I, even though it always felt like a part of me was missing. All I could do was learn to live with it.

Did I wonder how Jordan was coping? Sometimes. My ears perked up every time Ayla mentioned him, but she never said much, and I never asked for details. I didn't want to know. What if he was a total mess? What if he'd already moved on? I couldn't decide which was worse.

I walked up the winding dirt road from the cottage to Ayla and Kaden's house, clutching a dish with my famous almond poppy seed bread. Their house, a massive cabin nestled on the edge of the Canadian forest, had once belonged to my parents, and every time I visited a wave of nostalgia washed over me. Though I loved my cottage, my heart swelled at the sight of the place I once called home.

I stepped onto the porch with a bounce in my step and knocked on the door. Ayla and Kaden had been so busy with leading the pack lately that I hadn't seen them in days, and I was looking forward to a cozy dinner together.

The front door creaked open and Ayla emerged, her large belly preceding her. "You're just in time. Dinner's almost ready."

A big smile lit up my face. "You look radiant as always."

"Liar. I look like a whale."

She ushered me inside and the familiar scents of cedar and herbs wafted over me. But as we entered the house, a new scent hit me and my smile fell. I froze in place, my hands tightening around the dish in my hands. It was a miracle I didn't drop it.

Jordan stood by the fireplace, his back to me, but there was no mistaking his broad shoulders and tousled gold hair. When he turned around, his blue eyes met mine, a storm of emotion churning behind them. Anger. Longing. Regret.

"What is he doing here?" I asked, unable to hide the disdain in my voice. I had spent months avoiding any thoughts of him, working tirelessly to push him out of my mind, and now he was standing right in front of me. My heart beat faster at his scent and my eyes devoured the sight of him. His smoldering gaze seemed to bore into me too, igniting a fire that I couldn't extinguish.

"Nice to see you too," Jordan said, his voice dripping with sarcasm.

I whipped around to face Ayla, who had an apologetic look on her face. "You didn't tell me he would be here."

"I'm sorry," she said. "I know there's some tension between you two, but I hoped we could all have a nice dinner together. Besides, there's something we need to discuss with you."

My stomach churned with anxiety. Did Ayla and Kaden know about our mate bond? My gaze slid to Jordan again, who seemed to be as uncomfortable as I was, and for a moment our eyes locked. I saw a flicker of something in their blue depths that made my pulse skip, but then he looked away, his jaw clenching. I got the sense he wanted to race out of this place as fast as I did.

"What's this about?" I asked.

Ayla gave me a pointed look. "We'll talk during dinner. Let's just try to enjoy the evening, all right? Can you do that?"

"Sure," I said, plastering on a fake smile. The last thing I wanted was for my pregnant sister-in-law to have any more stress. I could get through one evening with Jordan. "I brought the almond bread you like."

"You must have read my mind. I've been craving it all day." She took the dish from me and gestured for us to follow her. "Come on. Kaden's been cooking for hours."

Inside the kitchen, Kaden was pulling a large tray of lasagna out of the oven. "It's just about ready. Grab some wine and have a seat."

We sat at the dining table, a palpable tension hanging in the air like a brewing storm. I fought to keep my expression neutral as I took the chair as far as possible from Jordan and poured myself a large glass of wine. As soon as I was done, Jordan grabbed the bottle and did the same. The rest of the evening stretched out before me like an endless chasm, and I had a feeling we were going to need a lot more wine to get through it.

As Ayla and Kaden began serving the food, I couldn't help but wonder what they wanted to discuss. I steadfastly avoided looking at Jordan, but I could feel his eyes on me like a prickle at the back of my neck.

"This tastes amazing," Jordan said after he took his first bite.

Kaden bowed his head slightly. "Thanks. It's our mother's recipe."

The thought of our mother sent a pang through me, especially when I remembered Jordan's pack was the reason she'd been taken from us when I was only a child. It wasn't his fault, of course, but that didn't mean I would ever be able to forget it.

I tried to keep my focus on the delicious meal Kaden had prepared, but even without the mate bond, it was impossible to ignore Jordan's presence across the table. Every time I lifted my gaze to steal a glance at him, my breath caught in my throat. The pull was like an invisible thread yanking my heart toward him. And the way he looked at me... His face held a mixture of longing and frustration, mirroring the turmoil brewing inside me.

"How is it being alpha?" Ayla asked, obviously trying to smother the awkwardness with small talk.

"I'm managing." Jordan's eyes darted to me like he wasn't sure how much to say. "The pack is adjusting to my leadership and my new beta is great. Although last week I fought off another alpha challenge."

I raised my eyebrows, my fork halfway to my mouth. "Another wolf challenged you?"

"Yes, and I'm still here," Jordan drawled. "Disappointed?"

I rolled my eyes and shoved lasagna in my mouth. But seriously, what idiot would fight Jordan? Had they not seen him take out the previous beta the last time he'd been challenged? The memories of him—naked, sweaty, covered in blood, and roaring in triumph—still kept me awake at night in the worst possible way. Jordan was the most vicious fighter I'd ever seen, and that was saying something considering I'd grown up with Kaden.

"Once you have an alpha female, that should end," Kaden said. "No luck at the Convergence?"

Jordan stared at me. The air between us crackled with suppressed emotions, and it became increasingly difficult to breathe. "No."

Kaden waved a hand. "Maybe next time."

Ayla glanced between Jordan and me as if she wanted to say something, but then she hesitated. "How's Griffin?"

Jordan's expression relaxed at the mention of his

younger brother. "Good, although he spends so much time as a wolf I'm worried he's going to be stuck that way."

"That happens a lot when kids first get their wolves," I said. "You should see my kindergarten class. It's a miracle when I can get them to walk on two legs."

"Stella has a lot of experience dealing with this," Kaden said. "Maybe she could help you."

"Helping me is the very last thing Stella wants," Jordan said with a scowl.

I glared at him. "Maybe if you weren't such a—"

Kaden's voice boomed across the table. "Enough."

I slammed down my fork. "Why don't you just tell us what we're doing here already? Enough of this small talk."

Jordan leaned back and crossed his arms. "I told you this was a terrible idea."

Kaden exchanged a glance with Ayla before speaking. "We had a meeting with the alphas earlier today, and Jordan mentioned two young males in his pack went missing recently."

"Missing?" I asked.

Jordan nodded. "They were each gone for forty-eight hours before they stumbled back into town with no memory of where they went or what happened. We think it might be the work of the Sun Witches."

"You think they took them? Why?" I sat up a little straighter at the mention of the Sun Witches. We'd defeated Evanora, their previous leader, and the Sun Witches were now led by Jordan's great-aunt, Brea. But Evanora's daughter, Roxandra, had escaped and still led some Sun Witches who were loyal to her. Up until now, they'd simply vanished, but we knew they'd be back eventually...and when they did, we would be ready.

"No one knows why," Ayla says. "But to have their memories wiped like that..."

"It has to be Roxandra," Jordan growled, his hatred for her evident. "I'm going to find her and stop her, once and for all."

A flash of anger and protectiveness surged through me as well, remembering the pain she had inflicted on him. Not only had she mind controlled him to make him do horrible things as the Leo alpha, but she'd also used that power to sexually assault him. As if that wasn't bad enough, Roxandra had then mind controlled Kaden and nearly destroyed his relationship with Ayla. All I needed was five minutes alone with her and I'd make sure she never mind controlled another person again.

"Have you found anything else connecting this to the Sun Witches?" I asked.

Jordan shook his head. "I've sent out search parties, but we've been unable to find any trail. But I know it was Roxandra. I can feel it."

"We've offered to help Jordan however we can," Ayla said.

Kaden's brow furrowed. "This is the first lead we've had on Roxandra's possible location in all this time. We need to figure out what she's doing with those shifters and make sure she doesn't take any other males."

"What can I do to help?" I asked.

"We need you to go to the Leo pack with Jordan," Ayla said. "You might be able to use your moon magic to recover those shifters' memories or find something the others have missed."

"Me? What about Larkin? She's much more skilled with moon magic than I am."

"Larkin is busy helping the other Moon Witches get settled. Besides, she's still adjusting to life on Earth and doesn't understand pack dynamics like you do. Dealing with the Leo pack could be tricky. I would go myself, but..." She gestured at her very pregnant belly. "It has to be you, Stella."

"You're also the best tracker we have," Kaden said. "We know you have issues with the Leos, which is understandable after what we went through. But you need to put those feelings aside to help these shifters."

"Trust me, I don't like this any more than you do," Jordan said. "But one of the shifters who went missing was my cousin's son. He's only eight. He's back now and seems unharmed, but we need to know what happened to him and make sure it doesn't happen to anyone else."

My heart softened at the hint of fear in his voice. Despite my personal feelings for Jordan, I had a responsibility to help those shifters and stop any more kidnappings. If I got a chance to stop Roxandra at the same time, even better. "I'll do whatever I can. When do we leave?"

"Tomorrow morning," Jordan replied.

"Fine," I said through gritted teeth. As our eyes locked, the air between us seemed to thicken with unspoken desire and tension. Unable to take it any longer, I stood abruptly. "I need some fresh air," I muttered before storming out of the house through the back door.

Once outside on the deck overlooking the forest, I inhaled the cool night air, feeling as though I could finally breathe again. My mind raced, wondering how I would survive this mission without either strangling Jordan or kissing him. It would be tricky, but I couldn't say no. Not when kids were going missing and I might be able to stop it.

The back door closed behind me, and I heard footsteps on the deck. Jordan's scent filled my nose as he moved to stand beside me. I studiously ignored him, staring into the dark forest.

"This isn't how I wanted our reunion to go either, you know." His voice was rough with some emotion I couldn't identify.

I scoffed, still not looking at him. "I didn't want a reunion at all. I was perfectly happy pretending you didn't exist."

"And how's that working out for you? We both knew we'd have to face each other again sooner or later."

"Did you ask them to get me to help you?" I finally turned toward him. "Is this your twisted way of forcing me to be with you?"

He scowled, hurt and anger flickering in his eyes. "No, this wasn't my idea. I wanted Ayla or Larkin to help me. If it were up to me, you'd stay here, where it's safe."

"Why should I believe you?" I shot back. "You tricked me into activating the mate bond, even though you knew I didn't want it."

"I know, and I'm sorry for that. I thought if you experienced our bond, you might understand..." He shook his head and his expression hardened. "Forget it. What's done is done, and all I care about now is protecting my pack and stopping Roxandra."

The sexual tension between us was palpable, like a live wire sparking and crackling in the air, and I fought the urge to move closer to him. "I'll find her, have no doubt about that. But don't expect me to fall into your arms just because we're stuck working together."

He glared back at me, his anger mirroring my own. "Don't worry, I won't be holding my breath. As soon as this is done, you can return here and go back to forgetting I exist."

He turned his back on me, his shoulders rigid as he stormed back into the house. I waited a few minutes before following him, already dreading what tomorrow would bring.

CHAPTER EIGHT

MORNING CAME WAY TOO SOON, especially after a night with little sleep. Outside my bedroom window, the sun crept above the horizon, painting the sky in shades of pink and orange while I stuffed everything I needed into a duffel bag. I'd packed enough clothes for a few days, but it was impossible to know how long I'd be with the Leos. It was Saturday, and with any luck, I'd be back before school started again on Monday. Otherwise, they would have to find someone to cover my class for me.

After a quick shower, I stood in front of the mirror, my heart racing as I took in my reflection. Long, dark brown hair framed my face, and my blue eyes looked back at me with uncertainty. On my bare arm, my Ophiuchus pack mark stood out, reminding me of my place in the world. I tried to imagine a Leo mark there instead and shuddered.

When I emerged from my room, Larkin was waiting in the kitchen with a sympathetic smile and the faint scent of lavender I'd come to associate with her. She handed me a travel mug full of coffee. "Thought you might need this."

"Thanks. You're my hero." I grabbed a granola bar to shove in my mouth when I got a chance. I didn't think I'd be able to stomach anything heavier. The thought of going to the Leo pack had my guts twisted in knots.

"You don't have to do this if you don't want to."

"Are you offering to go instead?"

"No..." She poured herself a cup of coffee. "I have to go to Lunatera and meet with some of the Moon Witches who want to move to Earth. But even if I could go, we both know you're a better choice."

She had a point. Even though the Ophiuchus treated Larkin like a member of our pack, other shifters tended to be suspicious or even fearful of her. It didn't matter that she and the other Moon Witches were our allies and had helped free the Zodiac Wolves, to them she would always be an outsider. She wasn't a shifter and never would be one, and even worse, she was a witch. After everything the Sun Witches had done, many shifters wanted nothing to do with magic of any kind.

"It'll be fine," I said, trying to sound confident. "I'll deal with this issue and be back before you know it."

"And Jordan?" she asked, looking skeptical.

"He won't be a problem."

She gave me a sly grin. "Are you sure? Because we both know enemies to lovers is the hottest trope."

I snorted. "Only in romance novels."

"Oh, that reminds me. I just finished this book and I

know you'll love it. Take it with you so you have an excuse to bury your nose in a book and ignore Jordan." She picked up a hardcover and handed it to me. It had a discreet cover with a dagger and a crown covered in frost.

"*Of Swords and Snow?*" I asked, opening up the flap to read the inside.

"It's about a fae princess of the summer court whose family was killed by an evil king from the winter court. She sneaks into his castle to seduce the crown prince and take her revenge on the entire family, but then she discovers they're fated mates." Larkin spoke quickly, her eyes flashing with excitement like they always did when she talked about a good book. "It's the perfect enemies to lovers book and the spice is..." She made the chef's kiss gesture.

"It sounds good. Thanks." I shoved the book into my bag. Larkin and I had bonded from the start over our love of books, especially romance novels. She'd once told me they were the only thing that got her through her long years living in Lunatera. Even now she read a couple books every week, as if she wanted to cram as much romance into her life as possible since she couldn't experience it herself.

"You'll love it. The only problem is that the second one isn't out for two more months, and I'm not sure how I'm going to endure the wait. I need you to read it and suffer with me."

"That's what friends are for. Shared suffering." I glanced at the clock with a sense of dread. "Speaking of suffering, I should go."

"Promise me you'll be careful," she said, wrapping her slender arms around me in a tight embrace.

I hugged her tightly. "I promise."

"Don't forget all the spells I taught you. And if anything happens with Jordan..." She hesitated. "Just trust your heart. It will know what to do."

"I'll try."

"If you do have hot hate sex..." She let out a dramatic, wistful sigh. "Enjoy it for me, okay?"

I huffed. "That's not going to happen."

"Sure it won't."

I hefted the bag over my shoulder and headed out, taking a deep breath as I started on the path to Kaden and Ayla's house. The morning had that crisp chill in the air that signaled autumn was fully upon us, and I soaked in the beauty of the leaves changing colors all around me. I'd never lived anywhere except in this forest and knew my way through it like the back of my hand. Now I would be heading to the Leo pack lands, which were about as opposite to Coronis as you could get. Did they even have seasons in Arizona, or was it just hot and sunny all the time?

When I arrived at the house, Ayla was already waiting outside, head tilted up as if listening to something only she could hear, with a small smile on her face. She seemed so content and sure of her place in the world, the complete opposite of when she'd first arrived here all those months ago. Back then she'd been nervous and awkward, with a sharp tongue to hide how vulnerable she really felt. All of that was gone now, replaced with a powerful, serene alpha female who knew exactly who she was and where she belonged. I envied her for that.

She flashed that smile at me. "All ready to go?"

"Where's Jordan?"

"He should be here any minute." She paused, studying me. "He's not so bad, you know, if you give him a chance."

"You have to say that because he's your brother."

"Maybe, but he was also there for me when no one else was, and he's trying to change. He's already grown so much and—"

Whatever she was about to say was cut off when the front door opened and Jordan emerged from the house.

"Sorry I'm late." He strode toward us with a confident smile, his hair framing his face in soft golden waves, his blue eyes unapologetic. The tight-fitting black shirt he wore did little to hide the broad expanse of his chest and lean waist.

"Needed more time to make yourself pretty?" I asked.

He fixed me with that cocky grin I so loathed. "No, I always look this good."

I rolled my eyes. "You're here now, so let's just get going."

"No need to sound so enthusiastic." He turned toward Ayla. "We better go before Stella changes her mind."

"I'm on it." She took both our hands in hers. "Here we go. One, two, three..."

Jordan's body stiffened as the world around us went dark for a moment, before reforming again as an entirely new place I'd never seen before. I'd teleported with Ayla a few times before and had never been bothered by it, but Jordan yanked his hand away and bent over as though he was trying not to retch.

"Sorry, I tried to give you some more warning this time," Ayla said, patting his back.

"Can't handle a little moon magic?" I asked with a smirk.

"He's always hated my teleporting," Ayla replied. "Too much Sun Witch blood maybe."

"I'm fine," Jordan said, straightening up and casting us both a hard look. "Thanks for the ride, Ayla."

"Anytime." She gave Jordan a hug, then turned to give me one too. "Take care of yourselves, and call me if you need me."

We said our goodbyes and Ayla vanished, leaving me in the middle of the Leo town with Jordan. Basically, my worst nightmare come to life.

The weather was warmer here, the morning sun beating down on my skin with an intensity I hadn't felt back in Canada. Numerous buildings and homes with clay roofs stood in front of me, all in shades of beige, like they wanted to blend into the desert surrounding us. Palm trees blew in the wind, while succulents and long grasses grew along the sidewalks and in front of houses, along with some red and white flowers I didn't recognize. In the distance, I spotted towering mountain ranges and a vast sky dotted by a handful of clouds.

There was no forest. No creek. No familiar scents at all. It was the complete opposite of Coronis in every way.

"Welcome to Daybreak, Arizona," Jordan said. "What do you think?"

"Too much sun," I said, shading my eyes.

"Not for a Leo."

I scowled and followed him down the street. Ayla had left us in a suburban area and Jordan led us to a large two-story house at the end of a cul-de-sac. Like the other nearby homes, there was no grass in the front, just a rugged mix of rocks, succulents, palm trees, and other desert plants I didn't recognize.

"Please tell me you're taking me to a nice bed and break-fast," I said.

"Sorry to disappoint you, but you'll be staying with me." He unlocked the front door and opened it wide. "But I do have a nice bed and I can make some mean pancakes."

"I don't want anything to do with your bed. Or your pancakes."

He smirked as we stepped inside. "You'll change your mind once you try them."

We stood in an entryway that led to a big open-concept area with a living room, dining room, and kitchen, all illuminated by bright sunlight through the huge windows and skylights. Beautiful wood floors stretched across the space, but there were no rugs on them and no pictures or art on the walls. Other than a few pieces of furniture, along with a massive TV, the place looked pretty bare. On the far side, huge sliding glass doors led out to a pool surrounded by palm trees and lounge chairs, like something from a resort hotel. There was even an outdoor bar and kitchen area.

I spent a few seconds admiring the place before turning back to Jordan. "Let's get one thing straight. I won't be trying your bed or your pancakes. I'm only going to be here for a few days, and when this is over, I'll go back to my pack. Nothing will change between us. Got it?"

"Oh, I'm well aware you want nothing to do with me." His smirk vanished and his jaw clenched. "Come on. I'll show you to your room."

He led me up the stairs, his shoulders stiff, and something like regret or guilt flickered through me, making me nearly apologize for my harsh words. But they were the truth, and there was no sense in letting him think something else might happen here. Even if I couldn't help but stare at his very nice ass in those dark jeans as I followed him up the stairs. I mean, who wouldn't stare? It was right there in my face.

"My room is here," he said, gesturing at a closed door. "This one is yours." He opened the room next to his and I went inside. Like downstairs, it was pretty bare, except for a bed and a side table with a clock and a lamp on it, which was all I really needed anyway.

I set my bag on the bed. "Thanks."

"I'll let you get settled in. Once you're ready, we can figure out a plan."

I opened my mouth to say something to ease the uncomfortable ache in my chest, which only grew when I saw his tormented eyes. But nothing came out, and he shut the door a moment later.

This was going to be harder than I'd thought.

CHAPTER NINE

AFTER A QUICK DISCUSSION, Jordan and I decided I should speak with both males who'd gone missing to see if I could uncover any new clues as to what happened. Even though we could have walked, Jordan insisted we take his large black SUV, which looked like it had just been polished.

"Would you rather we take the convertible?" he'd asked, gesturing at the red sports car in his garage.

"Of course not," I'd scoffed, even though I secretly wondered what it would be like to cruise around in it.

It was a short drive to the first house, and we were let inside without hesitation. Jordan introduced the woman at the door as Gwen, his cousin, before introducing me. "This is Stella. She's from the Ophiuchus pack, and she's helping me investigate the disappearances."

I smiled and shook Gwen's hand when she offered it.

She was a bit older than us, probably in her forties or so, and seemed very kind, if a bit frazzled.

"Nice to meet you," she said, as she led us further inside. Everything in the house looked fairly clean and modern, but there were kid's toys everywhere. "How can I help you?"

"We're wondering if we can talk to Russell," Jordan said.

"Of course." She called out his name, and then I heard the sound of feet on the stairs. Two children rushed into the room—the boy who must be eight-year-old Russell, and a younger girl who was clearly his sister. Gwen held out her arm and the two of them came over to her. "Russell, Jordan and his friend are going to talk to you for a few minutes, okay?"

Russell looked over at us with a frown but said, "Okay."

Gwen took the girl into the other room, and we all sat down in the living room. Russell had hair the color of straw, a face full of freckles, and bounced on the couch like he had a hard time sitting still.

I looked over at Jordan and said in a low voice, "Let me handle this." I wasn't sure if Jordan was good around kids or not, but I knew I'd be able to handle whatever Russell threw at us. Being a kindergarten teacher had prepared me for anything.

Jordan shrugged. "That's why you're here."

I hadn't expected him to let me take over so easily, but I didn't question it. I settled into the chair near Russell and smiled. "Hi, Russell. My name is Stella."

"Hi." Russell picked up a pencil and started scribbling on the page in front of him. Various art supplies were scattered around the table and on the floor, along with half-finished drawings in a variety of colors.

"What are you drawing?" I knew from experience that it wouldn't be best to just start questioning him right away. Kids tended to clam up when a stranger started interrogating them.

"A wolf." He turned the sketchbook toward me. A blob that vaguely looked like a dog or a horse stared back.

"Very nice," I said. "I like the way you did the fur."

"I also like drawing people, but I'm not very good at it."

"I bet if you practice, you'll get better. People are really hard to draw."

Russell started drawing another shape next to his first wolf. "Or maybe I'll just keep drawing wolves."

"That's fine, too."

"Do you draw?" Russell asked after a few minutes.

"Yes, I teach kindergarten back where I live, so I draw with my students a lot." I paused. "Have you ever tried drawing what happened to you when you went missing?"

Russell threw the pencil down. "I already told everyone that I don't remember anything."

"That's okay. I'm here to help you with that. You see...I have magic." I wiggled my fingers in front of his face.

Russell looked at my hands for a few moments, and then up to me. He seemed curious, which was a good sign. "Real magic?"

"Yes." I lowered my voice like I was sharing a secret. "Don't tell anyone, but I'm part witch."

"No way."

"Why don't you tell me what you do remember, and I'll see if I can use my magic to fill in the blanks."

Russell stared at me and I thought he might bolt, but then he sighed and said, "I was out with Stephanie—that's my sister—playing out by the Nose. I don't remember what happened after that until I was walking back into town sometime later."

"What's the Nose?" I asked.

"It's a big hill outside of town that's shaped like a nose," Jordan said.

I nodded and turned back to Russell. "Do you remember anything about the time in between, even if it's just a few flashes or memories?"

Russell shook his head.

"I'm going to try to do a little bit of magic on you now if that's okay."

Russell nodded and sat up straighter. "Is it going to look cool?"

"Maybe," I said a few words in ancient Greek and pushed the magic toward him, trying to draw out those missing memories. But when I pushed I felt something like a block in his mind, something that felt like heat and bright light. Sun magic. I pulled back immediately.

Russell gave me a skeptical look. "There weren't any sparks or anything. Are you sure it worked?"

"I'm not sure. I'd like to try one more time." I didn't want to push any harder than I already was because it might hurt him. With his mind still so young and developing, there was no telling what a spell like this could do if I pushed too hard.

Especially with sun magic, which I knew very little about. Ayla would be better equipped to handle Sun Witch magic, but even then, she wasn't an expert in it. But maybe if I tried a slightly different spell...

Russell's brow furrowed. "Maybe if I concentrate, too."

"That's a good idea."

I said a few new words in ancient Greek, adding a little bit of glowing light to my hands, which I held near Russell's head. His eyes widened as I kept chanting, this time trying to slip around the block in his mind, and this time I got a few flashes of images. Somewhere dark and cool. A rocky ceiling. A cave, maybe?

I tried to dig deeper, but the images slipped away from me like water. The sun magic was firmly blocking everything else, and I didn't think I could remove it without hurting Russell.

I ended the spell and the glow around my hands faded. "Thank you, Russell."

He sat up a little straighter. "That was so cool. Did it work that time?"

"Yes, a little bit."

"Probably because I was concentrating," he said with that certainty that only a kid can possess.

"No doubt," Jordan said, giving the kid's shoulder a squeeze. "You did great."

We left the house a few minutes later, and as soon as we got into the car, Jordan asked, "What did you find out?"

"There was a block in his mind, hiding his memories, and I'm pretty sure it was sun magic."

Jordan swore under his breath. "I knew it."

"I couldn't remove it without hurting him, but I did get a tiny glimpse from his memories. It looked like he was being held somewhere dark, cold, and rocky, like maybe in a cave."

"Not much to go on." He gripped the steering wheel hard, though he didn't start the car. "We asked Stephanie what happened too, but she didn't see anything. She turned around and he was gone. Like he just vanished. I suspected then it was the Sun Witches." His fingers tightened until his knuckles were white. "Now we know for sure."

"How long was Russell missing for?"

"Two days."

My heart ached for his poor family. "That must have been terrifying for everyone."

Jordan ran a hand over his face. "Tell me about it."

I buckled my seat belt. "Let's talk to the other male who went missing."

Jordan drove us to a local coffee shop, where he said the other male worked. I'd expected another kid, not the nineteen-year-old guy behind the counter who fixed us a latte while also explaining that he remembered nothing. According to him, he'd been smoking weed a few miles outside the town to avoid getting in trouble with his parents, and he didn't remember anything after that until he was walking back into town a few days later.

I felt comfortable pushing a little bit harder with his mind since he was an adult, but I still couldn't remove the block or get around it. I did manage to see a few flashes of memories that were very similar to what I'd seen in Russell's mind. Somewhere dark, possibly in a cave. But nothing more.

Once that was done, Jordan drove us out of town to check out the two locations where the males went missing so I could see them for myself. As I stared out of the window, I watched the buildings and houses fade away while the road stretched out ahead, disappearing into the distance as it wound its way through the desert landscape. The midday sun cast a warm, golden glow over the rugged terrain, which wasn't as barren or desolate as I'd originally thought it would be.

I rolled down the window, letting the warm, dry air wash over me, carrying with it the faint scent of plants I didn't recognize. To our left, towering mesas rose up from the desert floor, their sheer cliffs bathed in the warm light of the sun. To our right, the desert stretched out endlessly, dotted with the occasional cactus or scrubby bush. The colors seemed to shift and change with each passing mile, from the rich reds and oranges of the rocky outcrops to the soft, sandy hues of the land. It was a vast canvas of earthy hues and striking contrasts, and I couldn't help but admire its beauty.

It was very different from where I'd previously lived, but I had to grudgingly admit that it wasn't all that bad.

"Thank you again for helping us," Jordan said. "I know you don't want to be here, but I really appreciate it."

"I'm glad I can help." I studied his face while he drove, noting the lines of worry on his forehead and the tension in his jaw. These kidnappings had obviously been weighing heavily on him as an alpha. "Don't worry. We're going to get to the bottom of this."

"I just can't believe this is happening right under my nose and there's nothing I can do to stop it. When I find Roxandra..." His voice trailed off in a growl.

"I know," I said, ignoring the urge to reach out and physically comfort him. "We won't let her get away with this."

Jordan nodded, and then he waved as we passed a few Leos on patrol. The air changed a few seconds later, a tingle inside me that told me I'd passed through magic.

"What was that?" I asked.

"Sun magic wards. Brea put them there to protect my pack from Roxandra, should she ever return."

"Somehow I don't think it's a coincidence that both males were taken outside of those wards." I tilted my head. "But couldn't Roxandra just remove them?"

"She could, but my mother would feel it and raise the alarm." He glanced at me. "She's part Sun Witch too."

"So I've heard."

Jordan pointed as we approached a large hill which did look like a nose if I squinted. "We're here."

We spent the rest of the day investigating the two locations where the males had gone missing. I used all of my tracking skills and even some moon magic to try and uncover some new clues but found nothing except a few lingering traces of sun magic. Not enough to prove they'd actually been there or uncover what they'd done or where they'd gone. Larkin might have been able to find something more, but all Jordan had was me.

I could tell he was getting frustrated by our lack of progress too, even though he didn't take it out on me. I didn't blame him either. We'd spent the entire day searching, and in the end, I had what? A few glimpses of somewhere dark, and nothing more. Nothing we could actually use to find Roxandra or stop her from taking any more males. Which meant I wasn't going home anytime soon.

CHAPTER TEN

DOING ALL that magic had given me a massive headache, and Jordan seemed to sense I wasn't in the mood to chat during our trip back to Daybreak. To my surprise, he didn't drive us to his house but kept going to a different part of town I hadn't been to yet.

"Where are we going?" I asked.

"We're going to get something to eat. You look like you need it."

I started to argue but then sighed. "Fine."

"I know dinner with me is probably the last thing you want, but my beta's wife owns this amazing Mexican restaurant. You'll love it."

"That does sound good. I could use a margarita or five."

Jordan grinned. "I'm sure we can make that happen."

He took us to downtown Daybreak, which was larger than Coronis and a lot more colorful, with adobe buildings and a southwestern style that fit the Arizona desert perfectly. We drove past a couple of cute restaurants with outside seating and string lights, a bookstore, a bakery, and some clothing stores. On the other side of the street, I saw a small grocery store that looked locally owned, and there was a nice park with a playground and a few good patches of grass.

We parked in front of a restaurant called Paco's with a bright green and red awning, and Jordan pulled the door open for me. A delicious aroma hit my nose as we stepped inside the cool, dark space, where a woman with curly dark hair and a warm smile greeted us.

"Jordan!" she said, kissing his cheek. "Who is this lovely lady you've brought tonight?"

"This is Stella, of the Ophiuchus pack," he said.

"I'm Ana," she said, giving me an unexpected hug. "It is so nice to meet you. Jordan has never brought a woman here before, you know."

"Oh, um..." I fumbled, unsure how to respond.

"Come sit down. I have the best table ready for you." She led us to a red booth with a window that overlooked the park, where we could watch people jogging along the trail or kids playing on the playground as the sun set behind them.

Ana handed us the menus, took our drink orders, and left us to decide what we wanted to eat. I tried to focus on the menu, but I kept looking out at the town instead.

"This town is different than I expected," I eventually said.

"You mean, we're not as horrible as you thought we'd be?" Jordan said as he closed his menu.

"Something like that." I considered my words carefully. "The last time I was around your pack was when they were in hiding with the Scorpios and you had to fight to become alpha. Back then there was a heavy scent of fear and anger around the Leos, but I don't sense any of that now. Everyone has been very kind, and for the most part, people seem happy too."

"I've put a lot of effort in the last few months to make changes in my pack. My father and his beta ruled the Leos with an iron fist, and then we were under the control of the Sun Witches, but now we're free." His eyes shone with determination as he spoke. "I want us to be a different pack than we were before. A better one, embracing the best qualities of Leo instead of the worst. A pack that people respect instead of fear."

"That's surprisingly mature of you," I said.

"I am occasionally capable of that, believe it or not." He glanced at the park outside. "One thing I've focused on is giving everyone a sense of stability while making sure the town is secure and my people feel safe. But these recent kidnappings threaten to destroy all that."

Damn him, he was making me feel sympathetic again. And despite my better judgment, I wanted to help him. "Tomorrow we'll keep looking for clues. Do you know of any nearby caves that might match the one I saw?"

"Possibly. I'll get us a map of all the local caves so we can start narrowing them down."

When Ana came back with our margaritas and asked us what we wanted to order, I flipped through my menu again but felt completely overwhelmed by all the choices. "What do you recommend?" I asked Jordan. "I don't get much authentic Mexican food where I live, and I have no idea what to order."

He grinned at me. "In that case, you should get the combo number three. Beef taco, cheese enchilada, and chile relleno. That way you get a taste of all the best things here."

"Okay, I'll have that." I raised my eyebrows. "I shouldn't trust you, but I will. Just this once."

Jordan laughed and it sent a rush of warmth through me. He ordered his food while I took a sip of my margarita to hide how flustered it made me.

We discussed a few more ideas for finding Roxandra, and before I knew it, the food had arrived. By then I was ravenous, thanks to using so much magic today. I took a bite of everything on my plate, letting the rich flavors melt into my mouth, and groaned. "I hate to admit it, but you were right. This is delicious."

Jordan put a hand over his heart. "Wow, I think that's the nicest thing you've ever said to me."

I couldn't help but grin. "Don't get used to it."

"I wouldn't dare, but I do want a recording of you saying I was right. Can you say it again into my phone?"

"No way. And don't bother telling anyone what I said because no one will believe it."

"True." He leaned forward, flashing me some of that trademark Jordan smolder. "I'll just have to get you to say it again somehow."

I pointed at him with my fork. "That is not going to happen."

He sat back with a cocky smirk. "Challenge accepted."

I rolled my eyes and went back to eating, certain I would never utter those words again.

"Tell me about yourself," Jordan said after a few minutes. "I know you're a kindergarten teacher, and Kaden says you're the best tracker in his pack, but I'd like to know more."

I took another sip of my margarita. "This isn't a date, Jordan."

"I know that." He looked like he wanted to say more, but then shook his head and looked away. "Never mind."

That vulnerability that I sometimes glimpsed in his eyes was back, and it made my chest ache. "What do you want to know?"

"Everything," he said, meeting my gaze with an intensity that took my breath away.

Luckily Ana saved me in that moment by asking if we wanted dessert, and Jordan ordered us some churros.

"Ayla mentioned that you like to read," he said. "She says you have a book club with Larkin where you all read romance novels. Is that your favorite genre?"

I threw my napkin on the table, ready to throw down with him next. "Go ahead. Make fun of me for liking them."

He held up his hands. "Whoa, I'm not making fun of you. I think you should read whatever you want. I just want to know what you like about them."

"They're the perfect escape, and they always have a happy ending so they're comforting to read. After the last few years, I really needed that." I tilted my head and smirked at him. "And everyone knows the men in romance novels are so much better than men in real life."

"Ouch. I guess I'll need to read some of your favorite books so I can take notes."

My breath caught at that, and I had to quickly come up with a snarky comment so he wouldn't see how much his comment affected me. "You, read a book?"

"Why does that surprise you?" He played with the straw of his margarita, almost like he was nervous. "I like to read too, actually."

My eyebrows shot up at that, but before I could come up with an answer, Ana brought us a plate of warm churros. I'd never had a churro before, and I moaned as the first one melted into my mouth. "Oh no. I'm going to want to eat like twenty of these. I can't believe you'd do this to me."

"Stella's weakness is churros," Jordan said, mock writing it down. "Good to know."

"Don't change the subject. What do you like to read? Don't tell me you're secretly into romance novels, too."

"Mostly I read mysteries and thrillers. Sometimes a bit of sci-fi too."

"Really?" I asked, unable to hide my surprise. I'd never expected Jordan, of all people, to be a reader.

He shrugged. "I read a lot of stuff. I like graphic novels too."

I grinned. "Of course a Leo would like superheroes."

"Who doesn't?" he asked, but then his face turned serious. "I used to read them with my brother, Griffin. He had a hard time reading as a kid, and our dad... Let's just say he didn't like it when we showed any kind of weakness. I wanted to protect Griffin from his anger, so I got some graphic novels from the library for us to read together. It worked, and then it became one of our favorite things to do together. When our parents were fighting and throwing things at each other, we'd hide in our room under the covers with a flashlight and read about Batman or Daredevil. Like you said, it was an escape."

I stared at Jordan with my mouth open, unable to look away, my heart beating faster with every new tidbit he revealed. I'd known the previous Leo alpha was evil, but I'd never realized he was so awful to his own family. Or that Jordan had done everything he could to protect his little brother from it. With every word, Jordan revealed new hidden depths to himself and made it even harder for me to hate him. And the fact that Jordan felt comfortable enough to open up to me about something so personal, even after I'd done nothing but tease him and act sarcastic, made me feel like the biggest asshole ever.

"That's..." I stumbled over my words, unsure how to reply. "Thank you for sharing that."

"Sure," Jordan said, rubbing the back of his neck and avoiding my gaze. "Well, are you done? Unless you want more churros, of course. I could ask Ana to get us a container of them."

"Oh no. I've already eaten so many. Please don't tempt me with more."

"That might be difficult." His cocky smirk was back. "I'm nothing if not tempting."

I threw an ice cube at him and he laughed, then paid the bill without letting me look at it. Ana gave me another hug and made me promise to return, and then we headed outside. It had cooled off a lot now that the sun was down, and I rubbed my arms as we walked to the car, looking up at the clear sky above.

"Chilly?" Jordan asked. "I wish I had a jacket so I could not give it to you."

He actually made me snort with that one. "You just can't help being a jerk sometimes, can you?"

"It's all part of my charm," he said with a grin, as he opened the car door for me.

"Is what what you call it when you drive someone to murderous thoughts?"

"Aha, so you admit you have been thinking about me."

"Only the best places to hide your body."

He slid into the driver's seat. "We both know that's not what you want to do with my body."

My cheeks flushed, and I was glad the car was dark so he wouldn't see. "Don't get any ideas. I plan to curl up in bed with a book as soon as we get back, before going to sleep early."

"One of your romance novels?" Jordan asked as he started the car. "Think of me during the steamy parts."

"You wish," I said. "Remember what I said about men in books being better?"

But later that night, when I cracked open the book

Larkin had given me, I had a hard time getting lost in the pages. Especially when the hero appeared, and all his lines sounded in my head like Jordan's confident drawl.

"He just had to be cocky and blond too," I muttered as I flipped the book closed. Every time the heroine noticed the hero's chiseled muscles and sharp jawline, all I could picture was the man in the room next to mine. I tossed the book on the side table and turned off the light, cursing the Leo alpha in my head. I wouldn't catch feelings for him, I *wouldn't*. But even as my eyes drifted closed, I knew I was already losing that battle.

CHAPTER ELEVEN

WHEN I WENT DOWNSTAIRS the next morning, there was no sign of Jordan anywhere, except for a large stack of pancakes on the kitchen island, along with a note.

Here are your pancakes, as promised. Sorry I'm not there to share them with you. I'll be back soon. —J

I scowled and set the note down, then considered the pancakes and maple syrup in front of me. I'd told Jordan I wouldn't eat his pancakes, but it was hard to resist them when they were right in front of me, taunting me like that. He'd done this on purpose, knowing I wouldn't be able to resist. I couldn't let him win.

But just a little taste wouldn't hurt, right? I tore a bit of pancake off and popped it in my mouth. They were probably terrible anyway.

They weren't.

My eyes fluttered shut, and I was glad Jordan wasn't around to see my reaction. I hated to admit it, but his pancakes were delicious, which made me even more annoyed because now I had to eat them.

Cursing Jordan in my head, I poured syrup on the pancakes and sat down at the counter to eat them. It had been a while since I'd had homemade pancakes, and before I knew it, they were all gone. *Damn you, Jordan.*

I cleaned my plate and silverware, and put the syrup back in the cabinet, like maybe if I erased the scene of the crime then it never actually happened.

I went back upstairs to shower and get dressed, then unpacked one of the Moon Witch spell books Larkin had given me. I took it back downstairs to read while I waited for Jordan to return. I could text him to ask how long he would be, but I didn't want to make it seem like I was anxiously waiting for him to come back.

For the next hour, I lounged on the couch and scanned the pages of the spell book, looking for anything that might help us. When I heard Jordan's car pulling into the garage, I shut the book with a sigh, frustrated that I hadn't found anything useful.

"Good morning." His eyes fell on the note beside the very absent pancakes and he smirked. "I see you had breakfast."

"I don't know what you're talking about."

"Sure you don't." He set his keys down on a side table. "Sorry I left without telling you this morning. You were sleeping and I didn't want to wake you. My mother called me and was really upset because Griffin hadn't come home for a few days. I was worried he might have been taken by

Roxandra, but after some searching, I found him at a friend's house."

"I'm glad he was okay."

He pinched the bridge of his nose, his forehead creased with worry. "Me too, although I was pissed at him for making us worry so much when he knows what's going on with the kidnappings. So now he's not speaking to me again and I've made everything worse, as usual."

My voice softened. "He's your brother and you just want him to be safe. He'll get over it soon."

"Maybe." He didn't sound convinced. "Griffin's been struggling a lot these last few months. I just wish I knew how to get through to him."

"He's a teenager," I said with a shrug. "You were probably like that too."

"Yes and no." He sat on a chair across from me. "I was a little shit, no doubt about that. But if I'd done anything like what Griffin did today, my dad would have beaten the shit out of me. And sometimes that's exactly what I wanted." He stretched out his long legs as he stared off into space. "I spent most of my teenage years making sure his focus was directed on me and not my brother. My dad said I was protecting Griffin too much, that he'd grow up soft, but I didn't care. I took every punishment meant for him and I'd do it again. But now..." He spread his hands. "Once I became alpha things changed between us, and I never see him anymore."

My heart ached for Jordan and his brother and everything they'd been through. "I've worked with some teens before. I can try to talk to him if you'd like."

Jordan looked at me, surprised. "Thank you. That would be great."

"No problem." I shifted in my seat, suddenly uncomfortable. What was I thinking, offering even more help to the Leo alpha? But I couldn't just do nothing either. Not when he needed me.

Jordan cleared his throat after an awkward pause. "I was able to get my beta Cannon to make me a map of all the caves in our area. He's the one who has explored most of them." He pulled a few folded pieces of paper out of his back pocket and smoothed them out on the table in front of me. "We can start searching them today if you're open to that."

"I'm ready to go anytime."

As we both stood up, Jordan asked, "Should I ask some of the other Leos to come with us? I'm sure we could spare a couple of people to help us search."

"No, I'd rather do this without any distractions." In truth, I was a bit worried about being around the Leos. Everyone had been nice so far, but I keenly remembered the Leos surrounding me in the forest, circling me until Jordan arrived to activate the mate bond. I still didn't trust them. "Let me put this book upstairs and get my shoes on, and then I'll be ready to go."

Jordan nodded and leaned against the counter. He crossed his arms over his chest, looking over at the space where the pancakes had been, and smiled.

I never should have eaten those pancakes.

THE FIRST CAVE WAS A BUST.

Like the one in my vision, it was dark and damp, but this one had stalactites hanging down from the ceiling, and the one in my vision didn't. I glanced up at them and hoped for the hundredth time that one wasn't going to fall down and crush me.

"Sense anything?" Jordan asked from a little farther in the cave. He shined his flashlight back at me, and I lifted my hand against the glare.

"No. You?"

"Nope. I caught the scent of some other members of my pack, but not the males who went missing."

"I can't detect any magic, and this doesn't look like the one in my vision either."

Jordan nodded. "Let's head out and move on to the second cave."

Together we returned to the mouth of the cave. As soon as we were outside, I took a deep breath of fresh air and let my shoulders relax.

"Not a fan of caves, eh?" Jordan asked.

"I can handle it," I replied, my tone a little harsher than I'd intended.

Jordan held his hands up, and I started to apologize as we walked away back to the truck. Before I could get a full sentence out, Jordan's phone buzzed in his pocket.

"It's Cannon, my beta." He frowned as he looked down

at the screen and answered the call. "You're on speaker. What's up?"

"I have bad news," Cannon said, his voice gruff. "Another male went missing outside of town."

"Fuck," Jordan said. "Who was it?"

"Miles Crenshaw."

Jordan looked up at me. "One of the younger males who was on patrol outside the wards yesterday." He spoke back into the phone. "Who was he paired up with?"

"Dustin Haller," Cannon said. "He won't stop talking about how Miles went behind a tree to pee, and then he was just gone."

"What's the location?"

"I'll send it to your phone now."

"We'll be right there."

Jordan jumped into the car and started it without another word, and I hurried to keep up with him. As the tires peeled off, he stared at the road, his eyes blazing with fury and fear. I could only imagine how he must be feeling, knowing people in his pack were being taken right under his nose, especially when he'd tried so hard to make them feel safe and secure.

I reached out and took his hand. "We're going to find him. I promise."

Jordan blinked at me like he was confused. Then he squeezed my hand once before letting it go.

He didn't say a single word during the entire trip, which was short because he drove like a Sun Witch was chasing us.

When we arrived at the place where Miles had

vanished, I spotted a young man sitting in the dirt with his head in his hands. An older man with a shaved head and a dark beard stood near a tree, and he waved at us when we stopped.

As soon as we got out of the car, the younger guy raised his head from his hands. "I'm so sorry," Dustin said. "It's my fault. I took my eye off of Miles for a second, and he disappeared."

Jordan patted him on the shoulder. "It's not your fault. You did the right thing by calling us right away."

"Thanks for coming so quickly," the man with the beard said to us. He held out a large hand to me. "I'm Cannon."

"Stella. Nice to meet you."

"I already scouted the area," he told us. "Miles's scent is here, but then it just vanishes. There's no way to follow it."

"Any trace of the Sun Witches?" Jordan asked.

Cannon spread his hands. "Not that I can tell, but I'm not an expert on that."

"Let me try." I muttered a few words in ancient Greek and gestured around us in every direction. Over by a nearby tree, presumably the one Miles went to pee behind, red sparkles appeared in the air, hovering in place. "There."

Jordan walked over and inhaled sharply. His shoulders stiffened and he let out a low growl. "Roxandra."

"Are you sure?" I asked. The scent was so faint I couldn't detect it, not in my human form anyway, but Jordan's senses were sharper than mine.

"Trust me," Jordan said with a scowl. "I'd recognize her scent anywhere."

I nodded. "Can you follow it?"

He tore off his clothes without hesitation and I tried very hard not to stare at his naked body, but damn. All those muscles. That ass. *Seriously, Stella, this is not the time.*

He shifted into a huge red wolf that looked golden under the light of the midday sun and raised his black nose into the air. He padded around the tree and then out into the dirt a few feet away, but after a few minutes, he returned and shifted back. "Her scent is here, and that's it. Like she popped into existence, grabbed him, and vanished again."

"She might have taken him to Solundra," I said, biting my lip. If that was the case, there was no way we'd be able to find her. "But maybe she returned to Earth in another spot. I might be able to cast a spell that will track her down."

Jordan dragged his shirt back over his head. "Do it."

I focused on the shimmering red traces of her magic that still hung in the air and cast my own magic out at it while uttering a few words in ancient Greek. Normally I liked to track things with my ears, nose, and eyes, but that wouldn't work in this situation. My own silvery magic wrapped around the red sparkles and then took off like a shooting star, heading north. I could still sense it though, like an invisible beacon leading me forward through the desert and then underground.

"I know where they are." I kicked off my shoes and started to remove the rest of my clothes. "Follow me. It'll be easier in wolf form."

Jordan told Cannon to wait here with Dustin, then tore off his shirt again. We shifted together, my black wolf about half the size of his red one. A pang went through me as I remembered the last time we'd been wolves together, but I pushed it aside and took off at a run. Jordan followed me without hesitation, and we headed for some rocks in the distance, barely visible against the sun-bleached desert. If my magic was correct, Roxandra should be in a cave there...and we were ready to face her.

CHAPTER TWELVE

AS WE VENTURED into the cave, the walls seemed to close in around me, their jagged edges reaching out like gnarled fingers to ensnare me in their grasp. This cave was a lot smaller than the last one we'd been in and the air was cool and musty, filled with the earthy scent of damp rock and ancient minerals. I crept through the darkness with Jordan beside me, and even though I'd made us invisible, we were both careful to make sure our footsteps were silent. Every instinct urged me to turn around and flee, but my magic had led me here, and there was no turning back now. Especially once Jordan inhaled sharply and let out a low growl. I didn't need to be able to speak with him to know what he meant. Roxandra was here.

The cave opened up into a larger chamber, and I paused to take in the scene before me. Faint light spilled in from the top of the cavern, which stretched out before leading off into hidden alcoves waiting to be explored. Roxandra stood in the center with a young man with dark hair, who appeared to be unconscious on the ground at her feet. She was dressed in a red hooded robe and she appeared to be casting some sort of spell over Miles that caused a faint glow to surround him. I caught a glimpse of her cruel but beautiful face, marred only by the slash of claw marks across one eye, a scar that Ayla had given her.

My plan was for us to sneak up on her and take her out since we were invisible, but Jordan had other ideas. He charged her without warning, moving far enough away from me that he became visible again. Roxandra sensed him before he got to her and threw her arm out, sending out a wave of magic that sent him flying back.

"Hello, Jordan," Roxandra said with a triumphant smile. "It sure took you long enough to find me. I was starting to think I'd have to tear through your pathetic little wards and come visit you at home soon just to get your attention."

Jordan growled and shook off her magic, creeping toward her again like he was prepared to attack at any moment. I whined low in my throat, trying to warn him to stay back, but he didn't even look at me. Once he was only a few few from Roxandra he shifted back to human form. "Let my pack member go."

"Oh, Jordan. I have missed you. So much passion." Roxandra reached out as if she wanted to touch him, but Jordan batted her hand away with a snarl. "How about I offer to give this male back and leave the Leo pack alone for good?"

"In return for what? I know you wouldn't do that out of the kindness of the heart you don't fucking have."

"In return for you." Her eyes gleamed with hunger as she looked his naked body up and down like she wanted to take a bite. Jealousy and rage surged inside me, and I had to hold myself back from lunging for her. *Mine*, my wolf growled inside me. It must not have gotten the memo that he was no longer my mate. But I sure as hell wasn't letting Roxandra have him either.

Jordan tensed, and I thought it was because of what Roxandra said, but then I caught movement out of the corner of my eye. I quickly whipped my head around to see some movement in the shadows. Dark shapes formed into unnaturally beautiful men with sharp fangs who moved with a lethal grace toward Roxandra. At the sight of the vampires, some primal instinct inside me snarled and snapped, desperate to bite their heads off.

Shit, I realized, with a burst of fear. *It's a trap.*

"As you can see, I've brought some friends, and they're very hungry," Roxandra said. "It would be a shame if they had to visit your little town next."

"I have a better idea," Jordan said, his hands turning to claws. "How about I kill you all, and make sure you never hurt my pack again."

He swiped toward Roxandra, who darted out of the way just in time, but two vampires came up behind him. I didn't have time to shift back and warn Jordan, and I needed to protect him while his back was vulnerable. It was a gut reaction, one I didn't even have time to think about because

Jordan's life was in danger. All I knew was that I had to defend him.

I lunged toward the vampires, snarling and snapping my teeth as my invisibility dropped. I tried to keep them back away from Jordan, but one of them darted around me. I set my teeth in his shoulder and ripped his arm off. The vampire shrieked, and chaos erupted all around us. Together, Jordan and I fought the vampires, but they were so fast it was impossible to keep them all off at once. I dodged a particularly nasty blow and tore off a vampire's head, then spit his blood out on the cave floor.

With a flash of light, something painfully hot burned into my side. I let out a sharp whine as I staggered back, while Roxandra prepared another blast of sun magic. I rolled out of the way just in time, but that only sent another wave of pain through me. I shifted back to human form, clutching my burned side, and sent one of the vampires careening into the wall of the cave with a blast of moonlight. He landed on a stalagmite and was impaled, and I turned back to fight off another one, but the burning pain became too strong and my legs gave out under me. I collapsed on the stone floor, while the vampires circled around me like sharks closing in on their prey.

"No!" Jordan yelled. A wave of fire burst out of him, roaring through the cave like an unleashed dragon. Every vampire it came into contact with burst into flames immediately. The fire avoided me completely, while Roxandra used her own magic to protect herself from the blast.

It was over in an instant. The vampires fell to ashes, and

Jordan stepped back, looking down at his hands like he couldn't believe what he'd just done. I couldn't believe it either. Jordan had just used sun magic. How was it possible?

Roxandra clapped her hands together and laughed. "I knew you were the one! The first male with sun magic in decades. If I'd known all it took to unlock your magic was to threaten this female shifter, I would have done it much earlier." She conjured another blazing fireball in her hand. "Can you do it again? Or do you need to hear her scream first?"

Jordan moved to stand right over me, baring his teeth at Roxandra. "Get away from my mate."

The word *mate* echoed around the empty cavern, final and damning. Roxandra's face went from smug to shocked in an instant. Her mouth opened and closed a few times before she said, "No...she can't be."

She seemed to be momentarily stunned by this news, and that distraction was exactly what I needed. Using the last of my strength, I formed a shard of razor-sharp moonlight in my hand, then hurled it at her. It hit her shoulder, landing deep inside, and she screamed. A moment later, she disappeared in a puff of smoke.

I slumped back down onto the ground, my body trembling. Was I going into shock? Probably.

Jordan immediately dropped to my side. He inspected my injuries, then lifted my head with his hands and looked into my eyes. "You're going to be okay. I'm going to get you out of here."

"Careful, you're acting like you care," I said, as my eyes fluttered shut.

"Is it that obvious?" His strong arms wrapped around me, and a second later he lifted me up, clutching me to his chest. "Just stay with me, Stella."

"Okay," I muttered, my head spinning as he carried me out of the cave.

The last thing I remembered thinking was that being in Jordan's arms wasn't quite as awful as I thought it would be.

CHAPTER THIRTEEN

I OPENED my eyes to an unfamiliar ceiling. It took a few seconds too long, but I remembered I was with the Leo pack and in the guest bedroom in Jordan's house. My body ached a bit, like I'd just been healed, and I vividly recalled the battle against Roxandra...right up until I'd passed out in Jordan's arms.

"Nice of you to finally join us," Jordan said. He sat on a chair beside my bed, his legs stretched out like he'd been there a while.

I sat up slowly to make sure I wasn't still hurt. I was in my pajamas, and I wondered if Jordan had put them on me since I'd been naked when I passed out.

"What happened?" I asked. "Is Miles okay?"

"He's fine and he's back home. Like the others, there were no lasting effects except the memory loss. The vampires that attacked us are all dead, and Roxandra is gone."

I let out a sigh. "I wish we'd caught her, but I'm glad we all made it out."

"Barely," Jordan said, his brow furrowing. "You were pretty banged up when I brought you back here. I even asked my mom to come heal you with her sun magic."

I pictured the huge burst of fire circling the cave before it engulfed the vampires and burnt them to a crisp. "You used sun magic in the cave, didn't you?"

"It seems that way. I've never had magic before, but seeing you injured and in danger..." He sucked in a breath. "I guess it awoke this power in me."

I didn't want to think about the fact that it was seeing me injured that had awakened the power in him. "How is that possible?"

"I guess it means that the curse that Helios, the Sun God, put on the Sun Witches has been broken with the death of Evanora. Males born with Sun Witch blood can now use magic. Or at least, I can." He leaned back in his chair and looked out the window, where sunset was falling. "I'm going to have to tell my mother and Brea about what happened. They'll be thrilled."

"They're not the only ones. Roxandra set up a trap for you. She already wanted you, and now that she saw you use fire magic, she'll be even more relentless. She'll never leave us alone until she's dead."

Jordan looked back at me, his jaw set. "I don't plan to let her escape next time."

"Me neither."

"What I still need to figure out," Jordan continued after a moment. "Is why she was taking the other Leo males."

"You're right. She could have taken anyone to lure you in or made it more obvious that she just wanted you to come find her. There were never any notes or any signs that it was her. She was hiding what she was doing by blocking their memories."

Jordan scowled. "Whatever it is, it can't be anything good."

I pushed the covers off of my lap and swung my legs over the side of the bed. I winced as I tried to stand. I was still pretty sore, even though most of the damage was already healed. In a few hours, I'd be as good as new.

Jordan stood quickly and put a hand on my elbow. "Careful, let me help you."

I let him take a lot of my weight as he wrapped his hands around my elbows and hoisted me up. He was a lot closer than I'd expected, and he didn't let go of my arm. My breath caught in my chest as I looked up at him. I didn't move away, and for a few moments, we breathed the same air.

He slid his hand along my arm, heat trailing in the wake of his hand, and cupped my shoulder. I held perfectly still, not wanting to move for fear that I'd lean into it. I should have pulled away, but I didn't.

His eyes skipped between mine, before dipping down to settle on my lips. I licked them subconsciously and then caught what I was doing. I didn't want him to get the wrong idea like I was trying to flirt, so I cleared my throat. "Thank you for saving me."

"Thank you for helping me save Miles," Jordan said.

I swayed forward, just a bit, caught in the magnetic pull of his gaze. I should have stepped back, I really should have. Was he going to kiss me? Would I let him?

Then he opened his mouth and ruined it all. "Stella...I want you to be my mate."

I jerked back, reeling. "What?"

"Hear me out," Jordan said, tightening his hand around my shoulder. "If you were a Leo, you would be immune to fire. Roxandra couldn't hurt you like that ever again."

I shook my head and stepped back. "I can't do that."

Jordan looked like he might argue a bit more, but then he sighed. "Sorry. I know you don't want me. But when I saw her hurt you like that..." He ran a hand through his hair. "I just want you to be safe."

He looked so wounded and it killed me. "It's not that I don't want you. But I can't be your mate. I'm sorry."

"I understand. But will you stay a little longer to help protect the town?" Jordan asked. "In case Roxandra attacks again, I mean."

"I'll stay. I plan to see this through and make sure she is stopped for good. I just need to let the teachers at my school know that I might not be back for a while."

"Thanks. If you hadn't been there today..." He shook his head. "I can't even imagine what might have happened."

I took his hand and gave it a squeeze. "We're going to stop her. I promise."

"I know we are." Jordan's shoulders loosened a bit and he flashed a dim smile. "I'm going to make dinner, and you can come down whenever you're ready. It shouldn't take more than an hour."

"Thank you." I didn't breathe until the door closed behind him.

I headed into the bathroom, determined to ignore everything about what had just happened. I stripped out of my clothes and stepped into the shower, letting the hot water wash away the grime of the cave.

I thought about what had happened, the deep fear I'd felt when I saw Jordan so close to Roxandra. It wasn't that I didn't think he could hold his own. I knew he could, but Roxandra was dangerous. Her creepy smile that said she owned him made me want to rip her to shreds with my claws and teeth. I tried to convince myself that it was just because I didn't like the idea of her controlling any wolf again, but I knew I was just lying to myself.

I frowned and scrubbed my hair with shampoo. I tipped my head back and let the water wash away the dirty suds and waited for the anger to fade. It didn't.

Roxandra had tried to steal *my* man.

Except Jordan wasn't really my man. Was he? I picked up the conditioner, shaking it a bit more viciously than I needed to. I slathered it into the ends of my hair and worked it up as I tried to come to terms with how I felt about Jordan.

I'd rejected him, which should have made it easier to let go of this strange anger, but it didn't. I still felt possessive of him. The thought of anyone else touching him made my hackles rise, and my inner wolf growled that he was mine. Was that from the mating bond? No, I'd surely felt it break.

So why was I feeling this way now? And why did the thought of him uncovering his own magic to protect me make me feel so...good?

I sighed as I turned off the water and stepped out to dry off and get dressed. Nothing made sense anymore. All the conviction I'd had about how awful he was had vanished. This was all uncharted territory, and no one had bothered to give me a way to navigate it.

I pushed the thoughts away. There really wasn't anything I could do about them. I'd told him no, and I wasn't going to change my mind.

I went downstairs, lifting my nose as I got closer to the kitchen. The smell of something savory made me realize how ravenous I was. As I reached the kitchen, I took a moment to watch Jordan tasting something in a big pot.

"What are you cooking?" I asked.

"Just some of my famous chili," Jordan said, flashing me a smile. "I hope you're ready for some heat."

I raised an eyebrow at him. "Bring it on. I could use a little spice in my life."

Fuck, why did I say that? What was wrong with me?

Jordan huffed out a laugh. "Are you not getting enough spice from your romance novels?"

I ducked my head as I remembered my book last night, and how easily the hero had been superimposed with the picture of Jordan and his ridiculously perfect face and body. "Romance novels and toys can only do so much," I said because I couldn't seem to help myself. "Sometimes I need something more."

Jordan dropped the spoon into the pot and set the lid on top. He rounded the counter of the island, crowding in close to my space. I stepped back, but there was only a wall behind my back. I leaned against it. My breath came fast as I tilted my head back to look at Jordan.

"I can help you with your spice problem," he said, with a wicked gleam in his eye.

It triggered something low in my gut. I sucked in a breath as pleasure flooded me. I wanted to lean in and push further, but—we were flirting, weren't we?

I carefully slid around Jordan and leaned against the counter. "Thanks, but I have it under control."

Jordan grinned and went back to the pot of chili. "Fine, but if you change your mind, it's an open offer."

What was I thinking? Telling him no, I didn't want him as my mate, and then immediately turning around and flirting? I wanted to shake some sense into myself, but Jordan seemed to make it all disappear just by flashing me one of his cocky smiles.

"Dinner will be ready in a few minutes. Why don't you go sit down? I'll bring you a bowl since you're probably still a little sore."

"Thank you." I sat at the dining table, which he'd already set. Damn him, why was he being so thoughtful?

"Here you go," he said, as he brought two bowls over. "My famous chili. With a little extra spice, just for you."

"It better be pretty damn spicy for how much you're warning me," I said as I spooned some into my mouth. Intense flavors burst over my tongue and I momentarily lost my train of thought. Jordan watched me chew and swallow. It was good, probably the best chili I'd ever had, but I wasn't about to give him that satisfaction.

"So?" he asked.

"It's all right," I lied.

Jordan leaned back, grinning. "Liar. You love it."

"I do not," I said. "It's passable at best."

Jordan made a noncommittal noise.

I glared at him. "Fine, it's probably the best chili I've ever had. Are you happy now?"

"Aha! I knew it!" He pumped his fist. "But is it spicy enough? Or do you need a little more...help?"

"It's the perfect amount of spice, thank you."

"Good." He paused and watched me eat. "How is the book you're reading? What's it about?"

I was surprised he was asking, but he genuinely seemed to want to know. "It's a fae romance with two enemy royals. I haven't gotten very far into it though. Too much on my mind."

Jordan nodded. "I haven't had much time to read lately either. Or play video games. Or do anything fun. Being alpha is a lot of work."

"I bet." I glanced over at the giant TV on the other side of the room. "What kind of games do you like to play?"

"Everything. Adventure, puzzles, fighting, roleplaying... I used to play a bunch of games with my brother, but we haven't done that in a while. I know he wanted to play the new Star Wars game that just came out, but I've barely even seen him. And when I do, we just fight."

"Oh, I've been wanting to play that too! If he doesn't come around, maybe we can play together."

"Really?" Jordan asked. "You play video games."

"Sometimes, yeah. I used to play a lot with Kaden too. It's a fun way to unwind after a long day."

"Definitely."

We talked some more about games we used to play, laughing at how silly some of the old ones were and how much we loved them anyway. Before I knew it, I'd had a second bowl of chili and found myself really enjoying my evening.

And I realized I was starting to not hate Jordan. Not at all.

In fact... I kind of liked him.

The thought was terrifying.

CHAPTER FOURTEEN

THE NEXT DAY, Jordan took me to the fanciest house in town, a massive, gated mansion with a lush lawn that must have cost a fortune to maintain. As he clicked a little fob on his car's visor to open the gate, I peered into the yard, where a large fountain of a lion sprayed as we passed it. The house itself was done in the same southwestern style as the rest of the town, but on a much larger scale, with huge pillars and several balconies along the second floor. I bet it looked gorgeous at night.

"Wow," I said as we pulled into the circular driveway. "You weren't kidding when you said your mom's place was big."

"It was my dad's," he said as he parked and turned the car off. We'd taken the red convertible today, and it was as much fun as I'd expected. "Only the best for the alpha. It passed to my mom when he died. Now it's just her and Griffin. She offered it to me, but I want nothing to do with it."

I hesitated to get out of the car, drumming my fingers on my thigh. I wasn't excited about this at all, but there was no avoiding this conversation.

"You're nervous," Jordan said.

I tucked my hand under my thigh. "No."

"You are," Jordan said. "You think I haven't picked up some of your tells by now?"

"Fine, I'm nervous. Your mom was married to the man who killed my parents. For all I know, she was involved in that too, maybe even helped him."

"It's possible. My mother is a formidable woman. But she also had a difficult relationship with my dad. She was forced by the Sun Witches to marry him, but they were not true mates." He smiled, but there wasn't any amusement in it. He mostly looked sad. "Hence why my real father was actually the Cancer alpha. Griffin's too."

"Right," I said, remembering when Ayla had told me about it. "Let's just get this over with." Staying in the car would send a very clear signal, and I didn't want to appear weak in front of Jordan's mom. Especially after she'd healed me yesterday.

We walked up the huge steps together, and I reached out to touch a pillar. I couldn't begin to imagine just how much this place had cost. Jordan pulled his keys out of his pocket and inserted one into the lock, letting us in with a shout to let his mom know we were there. Inside, the floors were all pale marble, and my shoes made a strange noise that echoed around the huge interior. Jordan didn't seem ill at ease, but then he'd grown up in this house.

I braced myself as I heard footsteps coming from down one of the halls tucked away from the main entrance. A tall blonde woman appeared, wearing a cream-colored dress that showed off her impressive physique, even at her age.

"There you are." She came over and kissed Jordan's cheek, placing her hands on his shoulders and studying him. "You look well, even after your fight yesterday."

"I'm fine," Jordan said. "I wasn't the one who got hurt."

She turned to me, studying me like she was checking over my injuries, but said nothing.

"Hi, I'm Stella," I said, trying to ease the awkward tension in the air. "Thank you for healing me yesterday."

"You're welcome." She spoke with a cool, almost haughty vibe. "You may call me Debra."

"Have you seen Griffin?" Jordan asked.

Debra's hands twitched like she wanted to cross her arms, but she kept them at her sides. "No. He's run off again." Underneath her frosty exterior, I could tell that she was frustrated.

"I'll talk to him."

"Tell me, son," she said, turning back to look at me. "Why did you bring the Ophiuchus-Moon Witch here?"

Jordan hesitated, glancing at me, and I worried he might mention the mate bond. Debra was already treating me with a bit of hostility. Did she know I was Jordan's mate and had rejected him?

"I brought Stella to help us with the kidnappings," Jordan said. "She's the best tracker in the Ophiuchus pack, and her moon magic helped us yesterday when Miles went missing. I wouldn't have been able to find the trail, but she did, and we were able to discover Roxandra was behind all of the disappearances."

Debra raised her eyebrows. "Oh?"

"I don't know what Roxandra wants with the Leo males, but she definitely wants Jordan," I said before Jordan could gloss over that part. He seemed like the type of son who wouldn't want to worry his mother, but I thought it was important that she knew. "She's not going to stop after what happened."

"And what was that?" She scowled at Jordan. "You didn't mention any of this yesterday when I came over."

"I was too busy worrying about Stella then," he muttered. "But yesterday... I used sun magic to fight Roxandra and her vampires."

"Really?" Debra asked. "That's incredible. This is a great thing for the Sun Witches because it means the curse has broken. But it puts you in even more danger."

Jordan squared his shoulders. "I can look after myself."

"I know you can, but you still need to be careful. You should go to Solundra and begin training with Brea." Jordan opened his mouth to protest, but Debra lifted a hand. To my surprise, Jordan listened. "You'd be safe there, too. Roxandra couldn't get to you there, under Brea's protection."

Jordan shook his head. "I can't leave my people, I'm their alpha. My place is here, with them."

Debra sighed. "I'd argue with you, but I'm used to dealing with stubborn alphas. It's like arguing with a brick wall."

"I'll train with Brea after we've dealt with Roxandra."

"Fine." Debra frowned. "But I'm worried that if you have magic, Griffin might as well. He'll be at risk from Roxandra too, maybe even more so because he doesn't understand how dangerous she is."

Jordan nodded. "I promise I won't let any harm come to him."

The thought of Roxandra grabbing Jordan's younger brother, to use him as bait, or worse...I shuddered. "I can put some moon magic wards up around the town. They'll help protect everyone from Roxandra, or at least alert us if she tries to enter."

I saw the surprise flash across Debra's face before she hid it. She must have made a hell of an alpha female back in the day. "That's a good idea," she said. "Thank you."

"I don't want any more harm to come to any of the people here. We've all suffered enough at the hands of Evanora and Roxandra." That, at least, we could all agree on, I figured.

Jordan's phone buzzed in his pocket. He fished it out, frowned down at the screen, and then looked up at us. "Sorry, I have to take this."

I watched him walk down the hall Debra had appeared from as he answered the phone. When I turned back to look at Debra, she was studying me again. The full weight of her gaze on me made me squirm now that there was no Jordan to distract her. I held my ground and didn't fidget, but it was hard not to.

Finally, Debra said, "You look a lot like your mother."

Anger sparked immediately and I stiffened, clenching my hands into fists. I didn't want to give Debra the satisfaction of knowing how deep her words cut me, but she must have seen some of it on my face.

"You have every right to be mad," Debra said. "If I were in your position, I'd want to rip my head off too." She sighed and looked away, her pale eyes drifting over the white, polished interior of her house. "You don't have any reason to believe me, but I am sorry about what happened to your parents."

I wanted to tell her where she could shove her apology, but I didn't dare open my mouth. I wasn't sure what would come out if I did.

"I won't ask for your forgiveness," Debra continued. "I didn't kill them, but I didn't stop my husband either. I didn't stop him from doing a lot of things back then. But I should have."

There was a starkness to her words, an honesty that I hadn't expected would bring me any peace. But I found my hands unclenching at her admission.

I forced the words out. "I heard the former alpha was hard to disobey. I doubt you had much choice."

"No, but I should have tried harder. He did so many things and I looked the other way because I didn't want to deal with his wrath or the Sun Witches who forced me to mate with him." She shook her head once, brusquely like she could physically shake remembering him away. "But my son will be a better alpha than he ever was. He is everything I ever wanted him to be."

"He is," I said softly. I'd seen it myself over the last few days. The Jordan I'd seen as my enemy wasn't anything like the Jordan I knew now.

"He needs a strong woman to keep him in line though. Someone who isn't afraid to argue with him and challenge his ideas. Are you that woman?"

I sucked in a breath. "You know he's my mate then?"

"Of course I do. I'm part Sun Witch. We wrote the book on studying and manipulating the mate bonds, after all. And I know what it's like when there's a true bond too. The Cancer alpha was my real mate, but we weren't allowed to be together." She sighed and brushed some of her long, blonde hair back out of her face. "I never would have imagined the stars would put Jordan with an Ophiuchus and a Moon Witch, but the Sun Witches did a lot of damage trying to change fate. I'm not going to be the one to say what's right and what's wrong."

"Well, you don't have to worry. Jordan isn't my mate. Not anymore."

She gave me a coy smile. "No?"

Before I could argue some more, Jordan returned from down the hall. "That was Cannon," he said, shoving his phone back into his pocket. "People are getting nervous about the kidnappings, and I need to do some damage control."

"I can start working on the wards while you do that," I said. "We can get more done today apart rather than working together."

Debra reached out and put her hand on Jordan's shoulder. "Be careful."

"I will," Jordan said and gave her a quick hug. "I won't go outside the wards today, and I'll make sure Griffin is safe too."

"Thank you."

We said our goodbyes, and then Debra floated back the way she'd come, silent as a ghost. I watched her go with a frown. She'd given me a lot to think about.

"Are you okay?" Jordan asked as we walked toward his car. "You're very quiet. I'm sorry, I didn't mean to leave you alone with my mother."

"I'm fine," I said, which wasn't quite a lie. I didn't know how to feel. I'd built my parent's killer up in my head to be this monstrous, rage-filled man. Debra wasn't him, but she'd been married to him and she hadn't stopped him. But maybe she hadn't been able to stop him either. Maybe she was just as much a victim of Evanora's Sun Witches and the former Leo alpha as Jordan had been.

"If she was rude or anything—"

"It was fine. I'm touched that you care, but I promise, I'm okay."

"Good." He paused in front of the convertible, then handed me his keys. "You should take my car. It's not too far for me to walk."

"Are you sure?"

"Yes, it'll be faster for you to do the wards that way. Plus it will make me feel better, knowing you can drive away if Roxandra shows up again."

"Thank you," I said, palming the keys with some hesitation. It felt weird to be saying goodbye, even if it was just temporary. How had this change happened so quickly between us?

Suddenly Jordan pulled me into a crushing hug, wrapping his arms around me completely. I stiffened at first, raising my hands to shove him away, but I couldn't. He was so warm and muscular and he smelled good, like a mix of sunshine and sage. I closed my eyes and leaned into him, letting my hands rest on his shoulders.

"Be safe." His voice was a little gruffer than usual, and something in my heart twinged.

"You too." I pulled away and headed to the driver's side. I had to admit, I was pretty excited to drive Jordan's sports car, especially on such a beautiful day. The top was already down, and I couldn't wait to feel that warm desert air in my hair as I sped away.

When I got inside, Jordan whistled. "You look good in it."

I winked at him. "Damn right, I do."

He laughed and the sound sent a rush of heat through me. I drove off before the flirting continued, although I found myself wishing Jordan was by my side.

But I'd worry about that later. Right now I had work to do.

CHAPTER FIFTEEN

I SHIELDED my eyes as I stepped across the Sun Witch wards and started walking along the perimeter. The hot, dry desert air was so different from what I was used to, and I took a sip from the water bottle Jordan had made sure I brought. I was surprised how hot it was out under the sun even though it was fall. I was used to cool breezes and the changing leaves, but this felt like summer back in Coronis. I had a brief pang of homesickness as I thought about home. I missed the deep cover of the leaves in the forest and I missed my pack. I missed working with the children and seeing Kaden, Ayla, and Larkin every day. But to my surprise, I didn't hate this place either.

I paused along the perimeter and looked out at the vast Arizona desert. I still was shocked by how beautiful it was, in its own way. Everything was so open, with warm colors and cool rock formations. Someday I'd like to explore it more as a wolf, to breathe in the desert's scents and chase the trails of lizards and other animals I'd never encounter back home. With Jordan, maybe. The thought wasn't as unwelcome as it would have been just a few days ago.

I continued walking outside the perimeter of the town, eyes fixed on a rock formation with a couple of scraggly trees in the distance. That would be a good landmark to start at and mark my progress with. It should only take me a few hours to do the wards, and then I would go back to Jordan's place and relax by the pool as my reward. Maybe I'd even get a chance to read my book.

As I got closer to the rock formation, I noticed that there was a reddish-gold wolf standing there that looked like a smaller version of Jordan. He didn't run away, but simply watched me as I approached.

I waved and set my water bottle down on one of the rocks. "Hey. Are you Griffin?"

The wolf took a few steps back and then shifted back into his human form. He moved to stand behind a boulder, which covered him from the waist down while frowning at me. "How'd you know?"

I shrugged. "Your wolf looks a lot like Jordan's wolf."

He eyed me for a few heartbeats before speaking again. "Are you that Ophiuchus who is staying with Jordan?"

"I am."

Griffin nodded and then looked away again, messing with a loose set of pebbles that sat on top of one of the bigger boulders. I remembered telling Jordan that I would talk to Griffin sometime, to try and see what was up with him. I sat on a large boulder and took another sip of water.

"It's quiet out here," I said. "A nice place to get away for a while."

"I guess."

"Jordan says he never sees you anymore. He says you're always out here as a wolf."

Griffin snorted and flicked one of the pebbles onto the ground. It skittered across the sandy basin and then landed close to the trunk of one of the trees. "Yeah, like he cares."

I raised my eyebrows. From just the few surly words Griffin had said, I was pretty sure I knew what was up. "Of course he cares. He misses you."

"No, he doesn't," Griffin said, flinging another rock into the trees. "He's so busy being alpha that he doesn't have time for me anymore."

"I know what you mean. My older brother is the alpha of the Ophiuchus pack. I know it can get pretty lonely sometimes, but being alpha is a lot of work. He has a lot of stuff to figure out, especially after the Sun Witches left the Leo pack in chaos." Griffin glanced at me, and I offered him a tentative smile. "But Jordan still cares about you a lot. He talks about you all the time."

Griffin shifted uncomfortably. "Whatever."

"He does," I insisted, leaning forward. Griffin had his head cocked toward me, and I knew he was hanging onto every word I said. "He told me all about how you guys used to read graphic novels and play video games together."

Griffin shrugged. "We're not kids anymore. I grew out of that stuff, and he did too. We have other things to do."

"What, like hang around the rocks just outside of the

village?" I asked, keeping my tone light and teasing. Griffin didn't smile. "Just because you're not kids anymore doesn't mean you can't still do those things together."

"I guess," Griffin said, but he didn't sound very convinced.

"He got that new game you wanted." Jordan had shown it to me last night, over our empty bowls of chili. It was still in its packaging. He'd said he wanted to save it for Griffin, so they could play it for the first time together.

Finally, Griffin looked up at me, eyes wide with surprise. "He did? He didn't tell me that."

Gotcha, I thought smugly as I leaned forward. "Yeah, he's been waiting to play it with you. But if you're not around, I might have to get in there with him. And that would be really bad."

Griffin frowned. "Why?"

I grinned. "Because I'd totally kick his ass."

Griffin wrinkled his nose at me. He looked startlingly like a younger version of Jordan. "You're a gamer?"

"Yep. My brother and I used to play too, until alpha stuff got to be too much for him too. Trust me when I say that I know what you're going through a little too well."

"Huh," Griffin said.

"I miss it a lot, actually," I said. "Maybe the three of us could play it sometime? I saw Jordan had an extra controller."

"Maybe," Griffin said with a shrug. He didn't look as angry now, and I knew he'd think about it for a bit. I bet he'd come around.

"It'll be good to remind Jordan that he has a life outside of being an alpha," I said. "Sometimes it's important to unwind with your family."

Griffin threw another rock. It rebounded off the trunk of the closest tree, chipping some bark off. "Fine. But I want something in return."

"What's that?"

"I heard Jordan talking to some of the other pack members. He said you were the best tracker in the Ophiuchus pack, and that you taught others. Including Ayla."

Had Jordan been bragging about me? "That's true."

"Can you teach me?"

Something warm burst in my chest as I smiled at him. "I'd like that a lot. It's a good skill to have."

He cocked his head at me. "Does that mean you're sticking around for a while?"

"For a while, yeah."

"Cool," Griffin said with typical teenage nonchalance, but I saw a hint of excitement in his blue eyes.

I smothered another smile and picked my water bottle up. "Be careful out here, okay?"

"Yeah, yeah. See you around." He shifted back into his wolf and loped away before I could say anything else.

I shook my head as I watched him leave, smiling to myself. Teenagers. Then I took a bigger drink of water and began summoning moon magic to create the wards. It was time-consuming and energy-sucking, and a faint headache started behind my eyes as I worked my way around the village. The sun magic and moon magic worked better together than I expected, my wards weaving together with the previous ones to offer added protection against anyone who might do harm to the pack.

By the time I made it back to the rock formations and placed the last ward, I was sweating, parched, and bone-tired. The sun was high in the sky and my stomach rumbled as I considered the walk back to where I'd parked Jordan's car. *I should have brought something to eat.*

"You look a little tired," Jordan said.

I jumped and glanced over toward him. He grinned at me and lifted two plastic bags. My nostrils flared as I caught the scent of food, and my stomach rumbled again, louder.

"You have perfect timing," I said. "I was just thinking that I needed lunch."

"I thought you'd probably be hungry after working so hard all morning, so I brought sandwiches. I wasn't sure what kind you liked, so I got a couple different ones, plus some pasta salad. You can take your pick."

I was touched he'd gone to so much effort. "Thank you."

"Would you like to have a picnic out here before we go back?" he asked, gesturing toward the scraggly trees, which offered a tiny bit of shade.

"I'd like that."

Jordan handed me one of the bags as we moved under the tree Griffin had been throwing rocks at. From his back-pack, he pulled out a blanket for us to sit on. I dug around in the bags, checking out each sandwich, but they all sounded good and I wanted to try a bunch of them. In the end, Jordan and I split each sandwich so I could sample every one. We sat in companionable silence for a few minutes, eating our food. Jordan's knee brushed against mine, and I didn't move away.

"I spoke to Griffin," I said, once my stomach was feeling a lot better and my headache had vanished. "I think he's feeling a bit...ignored. He misses you."

"Really?" Jordan asked, furrowing his brow. "I guess we haven't hung out much lately. Being alpha has taken up a lot of my time."

"He didn't know you had the new game he wanted, but I think he'd like to play it with you. He also asked me to teach him tracking."

"Oh yeah?" He arched an eyebrow.

"It might be good for him. Give him a way to redirect all that energy he has."

Jordan let out a breath. "Thank you. For talking to him. It means a lot."

"He and I have a lot in common," I said. "I also have a brother who is an alpha. I know what it's like."

"Yeah, you do." Jordan looked out at the view of the desert as we ate, his eyes thoughtful.

I took another bite of my turkey sandwich. "This is delicious. Thank you again for bringing it."

"You deserve it. I felt the moon magic as soon as I crossed the wards. Oh, that reminds me, there's something I want to show you." He reached for his backpack and pulled out a dark brown leather-bound book with a radiant sun embossed on the front. "My mom gave me a book of Sun

Witch spells. I tried to take a look at it, but it's overwhelming."

I leaned over, tracing the old, carved leather cover with my fingers. "Let me guess, it's all in ancient Greek?" He nodded and pulled a face. "It can take a long time to learn, and then the spells themselves can be really tricky."

Jordan let out a frustrated breath. "There's no way I have time to learn all that right now." He tossed the book on the blanket. "Can't you just teach me? You know all about magic."

"I know a bit about moon magic, most of it from Larkin, but I don't know anything about sun magic. You could ask Ayla. She's gotten pretty good at it."

"I don't want to ask Ayla," Jordan said, holding my gaze. "I only want you."

I swallowed, my throat suddenly dry even though I'd just drank a bunch of water. The double meaning in his words wasn't lost on me. I reached past him and picked the book up. "I'll take a look at it," I said, ignoring the heat of Jordan's gaze and how those words made me feel.

"Thanks." He balled up the last of the sandwich wrappers and began cleaning up.

I thumbed through the book, scanning the pages. Ancient Greek wasn't too hard for me anymore, thanks to all the tutoring from Larkin over the last few months, but I still had to slow down and try to figure out some of the terminology that was foreign to me. "A lot of it is similar to moon magic, in theory anyway. I think I could get you started on the basics at least."

Jordan stood up and brushed off his jeans. "That would be great. I want to be ready in case Roxandra or any vampires come back, but I want to make sure I don't accidentally set anyone on fire either."

"We'd probably better get away from the trees," I said, heading toward the big, open space that surrounded most of the Leo village. "We don't want you to light them on fire and burn them all down."

Jordan snorted but followed me a good distance away from anything that might be flammable. "Now what?"

"Try to empty your mind of everything, then repeat after me." I recited the phrase I'd seen in the book, listed as one of the beginner spells.

Jordan repeated it, tripping over the unfamiliar pronunciation. I said it again, and Jordan repeated it, more confident this time.

"Good," I said. "Now concentrate on keeping your mind calm and blank while you say it."

Jordan tried, but nothing happened. He did it over and over, while the sun beat down on us, and sweat formed on our foreheads.

Eventually, Jordan kicked a rock in frustration. "This is pointless. I'm never going to learn this shit."

A short distance away, a scraggly tumbleweed caught on fire, bursting into an inferno in the time it took me to blink. I yelped and shot some cooling moon magic at it before it blew toward the trees.

Jordan's jaw dropped. "Did I do that?"

"It sure as hell wasn't me," I muttered.

"Oops." He grinned and rubbed the back of his neck. "Now if only I knew how I did it."

"Hmm. Maybe sun magic is fueled by passion, whereas moon magic needs a clear, calm mind."

He flashed me one of his cocky smiles. "If it's passion you want, I've got plenty to spare."

I shoved at him playfully with my shoulder. "Prove it. Show me you can do it again."

"What do I get as a reward?" he asked.

"What do you want?"

"A kiss."

"You'll have to really impress me to get that."

"I do love a challenge." He rubbed his hands together and repeated the words. Nothing happened.

I decided to try a slightly different technique. "Forget the words. You don't even really need them for magic—they just help you focus. Instead, think about something that makes you really angry and hold your hand out in front of you. Direct your anger toward that."

"Anger is easy. All I have to do is think about Roxandra." Jordan held his hand out, a vein throbbing in his forehead as he concentrated. A moment later, a small flame appeared in his palm. I sucked in a breath, but I didn't want to break his concentration as the fire grew.

"I did it!" The flame immediately extinguished, but he was beaming, and his smile was as warm as the sun across my skin.

"You did it!" I clapped my hands together. "You're a fast learner."

"I have a good teacher," he said and grabbed me around the waist. I shrieked, but I didn't try to get away as Jordan spun me around once and then pulled me closer. "Now how about that kiss?"

I kissed him on the cheek with a smirk, and he groaned and let me go, but he was still grinning. Something passed between us, and I wanted to kiss him for real. But it was too much, too fast. I was still trying to sort through everything I felt about him.

"We should probably start heading back," I said. "But we can do this again."

"And by 'this' you mean...?"

"The training." I smacked him on the shoulder. *Stupid, insufferable alpha,* I thought and turned away before he could see my grin. Or how close I was to actually kissing him.

CHAPTER SIXTEEN

SINCE I'D BEEN able to complete the wards in one day, I was able to spend the next few days wandering around town, getting to know the people while watching out for any attacks or kidnappings. True to my word, I also kept training Jordan, even though watching him improve at fire magic so quickly made it hard for me to keep my distance. He was earnest about learning, underneath all the banter and flirting, and he always looked so happy when he figured something out. Frankly, I was getting tired of pushing him away.

I made sure to check the wards every day, but so far there was no sign that anyone had tried to get past them. Roxandra hadn't returned to claim Jordan yet, but I knew it was only a matter of time. I tried not to stress about it, but it was hard to not let it get to me.

To try and take my mind off of everything, I stopped by the bookstore I'd seen the first night I'd walked downtown with Jordan. *Paws And Prose* was a cute little shop with new and used books and a charming display in the front with some fall-themed books. I smiled as I glimpsed the twitching tail of a brown tabby cat sunning itself underneath a display of historical fiction.

Some bells chimed on the door as I pushed it open, and a woman behind the counter glanced up over the thin-wired glasses perched on her nose. She looked to be about my age, with brown skin and black hair pulled up into a knot on the top of her forehead. "Welcome in," she said and immediately turned her gaze back to her book. "Let me know if I can help you find anything."

"Thanks," I said with a smile. I knew the feeling all too well of getting caught up in a good book.

I closed the door behind me and looked around. There were several free-standing shelves of nonfiction in the front and floor-to-ceiling fiction shelves along the outer walls. I made a beeline to the romance section and spent a few minutes looking around, then grabbed a book I thought Larkin might like. Maybe we could choose this one for our next book club pick.

As I headed back to the counter to buy it, I studied the young woman in front of me. Something about her seemed off somehow, and I realized it was the glasses. Shifters didn't need them. Why was she wearing them?

"Oh, this is a good one," she said, as she rang up the book. "You're the Ophiuchus staying with Jordan, aren't you?"

"Yeah, I'm Stella."

"Nice to meet you. I'm Moumi."

"Are you the owner of this store?"

"I am," she said, grinning. "I opened it about six months ago. It's always been my dream to own a bookstore, and thanks to our new alpha, now I do."

I tilted my head. "Thanks to Jordan?"

She put the book in a small plastic bag for me with the shop's logo of a wolf with glasses reading a book. "Up until Jordan became alpha, I wasn't allowed to be a true Leo, because I'm half-human."

"Oh," I said, feeling like an idiot. That explained the glasses. I remembered Ayla had grown up in the Cancer pack but never was really one of them either. I still had a hard time believing the packs could be so cruel—the Ophiuchus accepted everyone.

"As soon as Jordan became alpha, that was one of the first things he changed." She proudly flashed the Leo symbol on her arm. "He also loaned me the money to open this place."

"That's..." I found myself at a loss of words. "That was really nice of him to do all that."

She nodded. "He's the best thing that's ever happened to our pack."

"It sounds like it." I tried to change the subject with the first thing I could come up with. "Did you go to the Convergence?"

"No, I skipped it." She pushed her glasses back on her nose. "I just became a Leo and got my store open. I don't want to find a mate right now and have to give all that up when I'm forced to join his pack."

I sighed. "I know exactly what you mean. It's something I wish the alphas would change."

"You could work to change it..." A slow smile spread across her face. "If you became our alpha female."

I didn't know what to say to that, so I glanced at the book she'd turned face down on the counter and did a double take. "Oh, you're reading *Of Swords and Snow.*"

Moumi perked up. "Do you know it?"

"I just started it a few days ago. I'm really liking it so far."

"The love interest is so hot, isn't he?"

I hummed in agreement and tried to not blush again as I remembered that I kept seeing him as Jordan in my mind.

"I heard the sequel is supposed to be even spicier than this one," she continued. "I could put in an order for you if you'd like. It's coming out in a couple of weeks, and I could have it here on release date."

I wanted to say yes, but I didn't know when I'd be going back to the Ophiuchus pack. "I'd better wait," I said, shaking my head. "But thank you."

"I understand completely, but you should know that most of the pack members are hoping that you'll stay. Including me."

I blinked a few times. "Really? Why?"

Moumi shrugged. "Everyone knows you're Jordan's mate and that you rejected him, but the fact that you're here now gives us hope. Personally, I think you'd be good for Jordan and the rest of the Leos."

"Does everyone think that?"

"Most do, but some don't. You know no one can ever agree on anything in a pack."

"I know all about that," I said with a snort, thinking about all the times Kaden had come back to the house grumbling about how the Ophiuchus pack fought like toddlers. I'd had to help him settle some disputes in the past and knew how stubborn some people could be about even the smallest things.

"I don't know if I'm ready to make a decision about that yet," I finally said. "I'm still trying to figure out my path. I had my whole life back at the Ophiuchus pack, but coming here has opened my eyes to a lot of things. Not that you need to hear about that. Sorry."

Moumi put her hand over mine. "It's okay. I know the Leos haven't always been kind to you or your people, but there are many of us who want to change the future of our pack." She pulled her hand back and adjusted her glasses again. "Whatever you decide, I'd love to grab some coffee and chat about books sometime. You can never have too many book friends."

"I'd like that too," I said with a genuine smile.

After saying my goodbyes to Moumi and exchanging numbers so we could set up a coffee date, I headed back to the house, feeling better than I had in days. Was Moumi right? If I stayed here, would I be accepted? And could I really make a difference in the future of the Zodiac Wolves as an alpha female?

Jordan was in the kitchen when I got there, cooking

again. He looked up and smiled as I kicked off my shoes and padded over to the kitchen.

"What are you making?" I asked.

"Something for dinner," he said. "It's a surprise."

"Oh, a surprise?" I asked. "I don't really like those."

"I promise you'll like this one," he said. "Did you like the bookstore?"

"I loved it," I said and held up my new book. "Moumi was so nice. I didn't know you had a bookstore with such a good selection out here either."

"Moumi's the one to thank for that," Jordan said. "She knows a lot more about books than I do. I gave her some pointers on the graphic novels section, but everything else she picked out. People donate their books as well."

"It's perfect," I said, smiling. "Do you need help with anything?"

"No, you just relax," Jordan said. "Go read your book by the pool, if you'd like."

I hesitated for a moment. I didn't want to leave him in the kitchen alone like this. I hopped up onto the counter next to where he had some vegetables set out to put into the frying pan and watched him move around the kitchen for a few minutes.

"Thank you for sticking around," Jordan said after a few minutes. He dipped his finger into a sauce and lifted it to his mouth, then put some more salt in.

"In the kitchen?" I asked.

"Well, yes," Jordan said. "But I meant in general. I know it's difficult for you."

"It's not as hard as I thought it would be, honestly," I said. "I had a lot of bad feelings about the Leos, and while I can't say some of them weren't justified, I've also seen the other side of your pack over the past week."

"I know my pack has done some bad things in the past, and so have I while I was under the control of the Sun Witches, but I'm not my father," Jordan said, glancing at me.

"I know that now."

"I want my pack to be better," Jordan said. "I want to epitomize the best traits of the Leos going forward. We've gotten a bad rap as being arrogant, aggressive, and domineering, but we're so much more than that. I want to show the rest of the Zodiac Wolves that we can be trusted."

"I think you're doing a great job so far," I said.

Jordan set down the spoon he was using to stir the sauce and came over to me. He picked my hand up, lacing our fingers together. "I'm doing the best that I can, but I need your help."

I looked down at our joined hands, hesitating. "My help?"

"Yes."

"I'm not sure if I'm the right person for that."

"You are." He squeezed my hand. "Stella, I'm sorry for what happened at the Convergence. How the Leos cornered you and forced you into shifting to activate the mate bond. I regret it, and I wish I'd done it differently."

"I know," I whispered. "But it still happened."

"If I could take it back and redo it all, I would." His brow furrowed. "At least let me try to explain why I did it."

"I'm listening."

"After what Roxandra did to me..." Jordan swallowed and looked away. "I've had a hard time getting over it."

Anger flashed through me, as it did anytime I remembered what Jordan had endured at the hands of Roxandra, and how she'd forced him to have sex with her through mind control. But I kept quiet, getting the sense that Jordan didn't want to be interrupted before he could get the next words out.

"At the Convergence, I worried you only wanted me for my body, like Roxandra did," he finally said.

"No, Jordan," I said, feeling sick to my stomach at the thought. "That's not it at all."

"You kissed me. You clearly wanted to have sex. But you didn't want *me*." He dragged a hand through his hair. "What was I supposed to think? I was so scared that if I let you leave without activating the mate bond, we'd never be together. But now I know you only wanted me *because* of the mate bond, and somehow that's even worse."

I stayed quiet, even though I wanted to protest. A week ago, I'd have said he was right and all we'd had was the mate bond. But that wasn't true, and I was starting to suspect it had never been true.

He squeezed my hand again and let me go, taking a step back. "I'm glad you rejected me. I deserved it after what I did. And now that the mate bond is gone, I know what I feel for you is real."

"Jordan," I breathed. Out of everything he could have said, I hadn't expected that. My throat tightened. "It wasn't like that. I didn't want you because I was scared of what being your mate meant. It meant I would become a Leo, and at the time I couldn't imagine anything worse."

"And now?"

I wrapped my hand around the back of his head and pulled him close. "Now I think you should shut up and kiss me already."

Surprise flickered across his face, but then he didn't hesitate at all before taking my face in his hands and slanting his lips across mine. I slid myself toward the edge of the counter so I could press my body against his. He made a surprised grunt, and smoothed his hands down my shoulders, along my breasts, and to my hips. I deepened the kiss and arched my body against his, while Jordan growled against my lips.

He was right. What I was feeling wasn't because of the mate bond. It was just us, and it was time to figure out what exactly that meant.

CHAPTER SEVENTEEN

THE KISS DEEPENED as Jordan let his hands roam across my body. Everywhere he touched felt like warm licks of fire against my skin, and it made me want him even more.

Jordan broke away, breathing hard. "Let me turn the stove off."

"Hurry up," I said, holding onto his shirt a second longer as he moved away. I already missed the heat of his body against mine.

The moment he had the stove turned off, he came back and kissed me again, harder this time. I reached for the hem of his shirt and slid my hands underneath. His body was so strong, and I'd be lying if I said I hadn't thought about what it would feel like under my hands. I'd gotten a bit of a taste at the Convergence, but now I could take my time and truly explore him.

I broke away from his lips and pushed him back just enough to pull the fabric over his head. He took off my shirt in return and made an appreciative noise as I unhooked my bra and tossed it to the kitchen floor.

"You're so gorgeous," he said. "Do you know how long I've been thinking about this?"

"Since the Convergence?"

"No. Since the moment I met you."

I didn't answer him but pulled him close, needing his lips on mine again. I was already breathless, and his words only added to the desire burning through my veins.

He kissed his way down my neck and across my collarbone, while his hands explored my breasts. His mouth replaced one of his hands and his tongue swirled around my nipple. A jolt of pleasure shot through me and I grabbed his shoulders, digging my fingers into his muscles.

His hands continued down to my hips, then he pulled me off the counter and worked to remove my jeans and everything else I had on. When I stood before him completely naked, his eyes swept up my body and one of those cocky smiles spread across his face. He looked like he was seeing a priceless piece of art, one he'd just purchased for himself, and it made my skin tingle.

He lifted me up by the waist and set me back down on the counter. I gasped, surprised by his strength, and by the cold granite against my ass. But all thoughts flew from my head when Jordan's big hands gripped my thighs and began spreading them wide.

I let out a shuddering breath as he pushed my legs apart. He licked his lips and kept eye contact with me as he kissed the sensitive skin along my inner thighs. I braced my hands on the counter, anticipating what would come next. He kissed up and down both my legs, never letting his lips travel too high. I let out a whimper, needing him to touch me where I wanted.

"Please," I whispered.

Jordan leaned in, his mouth just an inch from my center. His hot breath caressed me, and my whole body shuddered, then went boneless as he licked a long, searing stripe up my pussy.

"You taste good," he said. "Just like I imagined."

"Fuck, Jordan," I said, breathless. He hummed and latched his lips around my clit, swirling his tongue around it. I arched my back and dug my fingers into his thick, golden hair. He growled a little as I tugged on the strands, his hands moving to grip my ass and drag me even closer to his face.

Then he plunged his tongue into me, fucking me with it. He gripped my hips tightly, keeping me in place, and I moaned, loud and long. I couldn't help but grind against his face, chasing the pleasure.

Jordan brought a hand up and used his thumb to rub my clit as he continued to fuck me with his tongue. It sent a bolt of heat straight through me, and I tugged against his hair even harder.

"Jordan...I'm so close," I panted.

Jordan hummed, the vibration adding to the pleasure pooling low in my stomach. My whole body started to shake. I was right on the edge, and I needed him to push me over.

He replaced his tongue with two of his fingers and curled them upward. He stroked his fingers along the soft spot inside me, and at the same time, circled his tongue around my clit.

I came with a scream, yelling his name, and gripping Jordan's hair so tight it had to be painful. He kept up his attention to my clit, drawing out my orgasm. Wave after wave of pleasure coursed through me, and it seemed to last forever.

When it was finally over, I was trembling and could barely catch my breath, but I still craved more. I grabbed Jordan by the back of his neck and dragged him up for a kiss. His lips were soft, and he tasted like me. I wrapped my legs around his waist and pulled him closer, wondering how I would ever get enough of him. Through his jeans, the hard length of his cock pressed against me, and I rubbed myself along it. I wanted him inside me, fucking me hard and fast. Why had we waited so long to do this? I couldn't remember anymore.

"You sounded so good yelling my name," Jordan growled. "I want to hear you scream it again."

"Make me," I said, cupping him through his jeans. He was big and hard and I wanted to feel him inside of me even more now.

The doorbell rang, and we both froze. A second later, someone knocked on the door.

I looked up at Jordan, my eyes wide. "Who's that?"

"I have no idea," Jordan said with a scowl. "I wasn't expecting anyone."

He handed me my clothes and I slid off the counter,

pulling my pants up quickly as my legs continued to shake with aftershocks of pleasure. Shit, where was my bra?

The knock came again, more insistent this time.

No time for the bra. I struggled into my shirt, shoving a hand through my hair after I caught sight of how wild Jordan looked. I only hoped whoever was on the other side of the door wouldn't judge us for looking like this, or be able to tell what we'd been doing. Then again, there was no hiding the smell of sex from a shifter.

Jordan pulled the door open, still shirtless, and Kaden and Ayla stood on the other side. Out of all the people who could have stood outside, they were the absolute last people I wanted to see me like this. Especially my brother. Shit.

Ayla put her hand over her mouth and her eyes went wide. She hid it quickly enough, but I caught her stifling an almost involuntary laugh as she looked us both over.

Kaden's gaze lingered on Jordan's disheveled hair and then went to my skewed clothes. He raised his eyebrows, and I could have sworn the air around us plummeted ten degrees. "What the hell is going on here?" he asked, blunt and straight to the point as usual. "Are you two together?"

"Kaden," Ayla said, putting a hand on his shoulder. "We don't know what's going on—"

"We've been texting both of you, and neither of you was answering. So we decided to come by to see if you were okay," Kaden said, cutting Ayla off. "I thought you were in danger, not... Whatever the hell this is."

"We're fine," I said. "We've just both been...busy."

"Yeah, I can see you've been real 'busy,'" Kaden said with a scowl.

I pressed a hand to my forehead. How was this my life? "Why don't you come inside and sit down?"

"Good idea," Ayla said as she came inside, dragging Kaden in after her.

"Can I get you anything?" Jordan asked them. He didn't look as uncomfortable or awkward as I expected him to be.

"Yeah, you can put on a damn shirt," Kaden said.

"Like you're one to talk," Ayla said, rolling her eyes before turning back to Jordan. "Some water would be great, thank you."

Jordan left to get the water from the kitchen while I led Kaden and Ayla to the living room area. The tension was off the charts, and I awkwardly cleared my throat as I heard the tap running and the sound of glasses being filled. I was pretty sure my face was beet red, and I couldn't look at Kaden at all.

"I can't believe the two of you are..." Kaden trailed off and made another vague gesture as he sat on the sofa with Ayla.

"I'm an adult," I said. "I can be with whoever I want."

"Yeah, but...him?" Kaden asked. "Out of everyone, you had to choose him?"

I didn't, I wanted to say, but I bit my tongue again. The less Kaden knew about how complicated our situation was, the better. And it wasn't really true, not anymore. I'd chosen Jordan today, without any mate bond forcing us together.

"Try not to sound so horrified," Jordan said, as he

returned with glasses of water for Kaden and Ayla. He'd put his shirt on as well.

Ayla took her glass from Jordan with a wry grin. "I knew it. You're mates, aren't you?"

Kaden, who had just taken a sip of his water, choked. "I'm sorry, what?"

I supposed there was no way to hide it. We might as well air out all the dirty laundry now and get it over with. "We were," I said, as he took another sip of water. "Until I rejected him."

Kaden choked again, and this time, he set the water down on the coffee table, hard. When I glanced up, he was glaring at me. "You *rejected* him? What the fuck?"

I threw up my hands. "Do you want me to be Jordan's mate or not?"

"Well, no. But you can't just reject him!"

I crossed my arms. "Too late."

With a smile, Ayla gestured to where Jordan stood behind me instead of sitting in the other chair. "It doesn't look like it worked very well."

"It's complicated," Jordan said. "We're still trying to figure things out."

Kaden growled deep in his throat, and then he was up, moving across the room so fast it was a blur. Before I could even react, he grabbed Jordan and slammed him into the wall.

"Kaden!" I yelled, one second away from prying him off of Jordan, but Ayla held me back.

Kaden had his forearm on Jordan's throat, his face

twisted in rage, but the Leo alpha just looked back at him like he was bored. "My, my, isn't this familiar," Jordan said dryly. "I thought your days of pinning me against walls was over."

"I'll tear you apart if you hurt my sister," Kaden snarled and pressed his arm a little harder against Jordan's throat.

Ayla and I shared a look. *Damn overprotective alphas.* I wanted to snap at him that I could take care of myself, but Kaden had always been extra protective of me, ever since our parents had died.

"I would never do anything to hurt Stella," Jordan choked out. He glanced over at me. "I love her."

CHAPTER EIGHTEEN

EVERYONE FROZE as those three little words rang out through the air.

Kaden recovered first. "Oh... Shit."

He let Jordan go and stepped back, while I opened and closed my mouth a few times, trying to figure out what I was feeling. My heart raced so fast I worried it might jump out of my chest and run out the front door. Jordan...loved me?

Kaden looked back and forth between Jordan and me for a minute, rubbing his jaw like he wasn't sure what to do now. "Sorry," he eventually said.

Ayla grabbed his arm and yanked him back to the sofa. "If the alphas are done posturing, maybe we can sit down and have a real conversation now."

"I was just making dinner," Jordan said. "You're welcome to share it with us."

"That would be great," Ayla said.

While Jordan disappeared into the kitchen once more, I

got everyone to move to the dining table and then I set out forks and knives. My head was still spinning from what Jordan had said. I wasn't sure how to respond. Did he expect me to say it back? I wasn't sure I could. Not yet.

When Jordan said the food was ready, we all headed into the kitchen to load up our plates with spaghetti. He raised his eyebrows at me as he handed me a plate and our fingers brushed. I gave him a smile so he knew I wasn't upset with him. He visibly relaxed as he passed plates around, and soon we were all digging in.

"I had no idea that you cooked," Kaden said to Jordan.

"I didn't before, not really." He met my eyes. "But it's more fun when you have someone to cook for. I asked my mom to send me all her recipes. This is one that she used to always make. Hopefully, it turned out okay."

"It's really good," Ayla said with a smile for her brother.

"So what brought you guys here today?" Jordan asked. "Not that we mind you stopping by, but it'd be nice to have some advance warning next time..."

Ayla gave us a sheepish grin. "Sorry about that. I got worried when you guys weren't answering my texts so I grabbed Kaden and teleported us over. Blame the pregnancy hormones. They're making me a bit nutty."

"No kidding..." Kaden muttered, and she smacked him on the arm. "Mostly we want to know what's going on with the missing males and the Sun Witches."

Jordan and I launched into a long tale, trying to cover everything that had happened since I'd arrived. So much had changed over the past few days, and it was a lot to fit into one conversation. When we mentioned Roxandra and the vampires, Kaden's hand tightened on his fork and his eyes narrowed.

"It's concerning that she still has so many allies among the vampires," he said.

"I know," I said. "I guess they still believe she'll help them break the Sun Curse."

"Or they're just using her blood to help them walk in the daylight," Jordan said.

"The two of you fought them off by yourselves?" Ayla asked.

"We did," I said, meeting Jordan's eyes. "Thanks to Jordan's new sun magic."

"What?" Ayla asked with a laugh. "You used magic?"

"I did, and not just that one time," Jordan said, sitting up like a proud lion. "Stella's been training me, and I'm starting to be able to control it."

"That's amazing!" Ayla said while Kaden looked less pleased. "I'll have to loan you the Sun Witch tome I have. Once you're ready, of course. Oh, this is so exciting. Do you think Griffin has magic too?"

"We're not sure yet," Jordan said.

"The Sun Witches must be thrilled to know that the curse is broken," Ayla said.

"But it means Roxandra will be even more relentless in pursuing Jordan," I said.

"Do you need us to stay and help?" Kaden asked.

"I appreciate the offer, but we're fine," Jordan said.

Kaden nodded. "If you change your mind, let us know.

We can send some warriors to help patrol. Although we've had our own disappearance too."

"What do you mean?" I asked, suddenly worried.

"An older Moon Witch named Maricar has gone missing from Coronis," Kaden said. "We're not sure if she went exploring and got lost, or if someone took her, but we can't find her. We've sent some people to see if they can pick up her trail, but so far we've found nothing."

"Oh no," I said, a bit of panic rising up in my chest at the thought of a Moon Witch wandering around alone. They'd all been living in Lunatera so long that they didn't understand the modern world, and sometimes they got confused easily. "I hope she comes back soon, and that she's okay. Larkin must be so upset."

"She is," Ayla said with a sigh. "But we'll keep looking for her."

They continued to update me on other things happening in Coronis, and while I missed everyone a lot, I found myself not as homesick as I expected. My village kept going without me there, and it was clear I was needed more here right now.

As Ayla talked, I watched as Jordan popped a cherry in his mouth, stem and all. He held my gaze, looking smug, and I wondered what he was doing now. When he opened his mouth, the cherry was gone and the stem was tied into a knot.

"Show off," I mouthed to him. I knew all too well how good he was with his tongue. I squeezed my legs together, heat pooling between them again.

When I looked up, Kaden was looking at me, eyebrows raised. "Unbelievable," he muttered and shook his head. Jordan looked at him, the perfect picture of innocence like he didn't know what Kaden was talking about.

"On that note, I think it's time we got going," Ayla said, rising to her feet. "We just wanted to check on you, but it seems like you're doing fine. Better than fine, even."

"Thanks for dinner," Kaden said grudgingly as he followed Ayla to the door. "Stella, do you want to stay here, or come back with us to Coronis?"

"I'm going to stay here," I said. There was still work to do with the Leo pack, and the thought of leaving Jordan didn't sit right in my chest either.

Kaden's eyebrows shot up on his forehead, while Ayla looked pleased and Jordan looked surprised. "If that's what you want," Kaden finally said. I could tell it would take him a while to get used to the idea of me being with Jordan, but he was trying.

"I'll walk you both out," I said. Jordan said goodbye, giving Ayla a quick hug, and then I walked Ayla and Kaden outside.

Ayla pulled me into a hug. "I'm happy for both of you," she whispered, squeezing me tight.

When she stepped back, Kaden stood with his hands in his pockets. He grunted and avoided looking at me in the eye. "Be careful."

I hugged him. "I will. You both stay safe too, okay?"

"We will," Ayla said. She gave us a wave, and then she and Kaden vanished as she teleported them away.

When I returned inside, Jordan was cleaning up in the kitchen. I moved to help him, but he caught my wrist in his hand, spinning me to face him.

"What does this mean?" he asked. "That you're staying."

I remembered the way he'd said he loved me without any hesitation and swallowed. "It means I'm willing to see where this thing between us goes."

He grinned and arched an eyebrow. "And where would you like it to go right now?"

"I have an idea." I ran my hand down his shirt and paused, right above the waistband of his jeans. I wasn't ready to go all the way, not when it might bring the mate bond back. But I could do something else. "I have to find some way to thank you for what you did earlier, after all."

"You don't need to thank me," he said. "But I'm not going to stop you either."

I dragged him out to the plush rug in the living room and removed his shirt, slower this time. Then Jordan let out a breath as I dropped to my knees in front of him, keeping eye contact as I slid my hands across his stomach.

"Fuck, Stella," he said, his voice a little strained. "You look so good. I never imagined I'd have you on your knees like this."

I unbuttoned his jeans and tugged them down, then his boxer briefs went with them. When his cock sprung free, I ran my hand over it. It was big and hard, and I felt a thrill shoot through me, knowing he was turned on because of me.

Jordan groaned and threw his head back, eyes closing. I stroked him slowly, teasingly. His hands clenched and unclenched at his sides, and I could tell he was trying to be patient.

"Is this okay?" I asked.

"Don't stop," he said, his voice rough and full of need. "Please."

"Since you asked so nicely," I teased, before licking him from base to tip. He moaned, and his body jerked at the sensation.

I took him into my mouth and slid down his length, swirling my tongue around him. He wrapped his fingers in my hair and pulled slightly. I let him guide me deeper until the head of his cock hit the back of my throat.

He was panting, and his fingers were still entwined in my hair. I looked up, meeting his eyes. There was so much raw desire there, it made me feel powerful. I sucked on him and he thrust into my mouth. I gagged a little but quickly adjusted to the sensation.

"Good girl," Jordan said. "Look how good you are at taking my cock. Like it was made for you. Fuck, maybe it was."

He started moving his hips, and I relaxed my jaw, letting him use me however he wanted. His movements grew more erratic and he groaned, his cock twitching against my tongue. I never thought I'd be able to render Jordan speechless. Who knew all I needed to do was take his cock into my mouth this whole time?

It was heady to see the Leo alpha, undone like this. I felt like the most powerful woman in the world on my knees with Jordan's hands in my hair and cradling my neck.

"Stella," he gasped out, losing his rhythm. I liked the way my name sounded like that, strained and on the cusp of orgasm. His hands tightened in my hair suddenly, and he moved to pull out. I shook my head and took him deeper, as deep as I could. I wanted to taste him when he came.

Jordan cursed and exploded down my throat. I closed my eyes and savored the feeling of him on my tongue. I swallowed every last drop.

I let his length slide out of my mouth and took in a few deep breaths of air. He pulled me up into his arms and into a deep kiss. His hand tangled in my hair, and his tongue slid against mine.

He pulled back and rested his forehead against mine. "Damn, Stella," Jordan said, still sounding breathless. "Thank you for staying."

"I'm glad I did," I whispered.

CHAPTER NINETEEN

I WAS JUST STEPPING out of the elementary school when Jordan's red convertible drove up. The sun glinted off his tanned, muscular skin, his golden hair blew in the breeze, and my heart felt like it might burst at the sight of him.

"Hey there." He climbed out of the car and moved to open the door for me. Who knew Jordan was such a gentleman?

"Hey yourself." I lifted up on my tiptoes to kiss him. He slid his arm around me and pulled me even closer. I let my hands roam down his chest, unwilling to part yet.

Over the last few days, we'd done everything except have sex. We'd explored each other's bodies, learning every dip and curve of skin, but we hadn't taken that final step yet. Sex was what sealed the mating bond, and I wasn't sure what would happen if we went that far. Would the bond return, or would it remain broken forever? A part of me was scared to find out. What if we'd permanently ruined something that might have been great, if only things had been different?

"How was it today?" Jordan asked. He'd sent me over early this morning to talk to the elementary school teachers, since they were struggling with the kids turning into wolves all the time. They'd never had to deal with this issue before when everyone's wolves were locked away until they were adults, and now they weren't sure how to handle it. In the Ophiuchus pack we'd never had our wolves locked away, so I had a lot of experience dealing with kids who couldn't control their shifting yet or just preferred being on four legs, and I'd jumped at the chance to help.

"It was good," I said with a big smile. I loved working with the kids today and the other teachers too. I missed my students back home, but I could see how easily I could help here too, and how much I was needed. Everyone was also incredibly nice to me, showing me a completely different side of the Leo pack than I'd expected. "They asked me to come back again when I can."

He grinned back at me. "Of course they did. You're amazing. The middle school and high school have already asked me if you can come visit them too."

"I'd be happy to help them too, if I can. Although I think I'm best with little kids."

"You're way too modest. My mom says Griffin is doing so much better this week."

That was another project I'd been working on. Every afternoon, after Griffin finished school, we went out into the desert and worked on his tracking skills. The boy was a natural and picked up on things quickly, and he was also showing me all sorts of interesting plants and animals I'd never encountered back in Canada. Yesterday we'd followed the very stinky trail of something he called a "skunk pig"—an animal called a javelina, which was like a weird cross between a rodent and a pig. Then we'd headed home and finally played that video game with Jordan, who kicked both of our butts. We were already planning another night for a rematch.

Even though I still missed my home in Coronis, I was slowly carving out a place for myself here without even realizing it. I checked the wards every day and looked for signs of Roxandra, but she remained elusive, but at least no more males were taken. Moumi and I met up regularly for coffee and book chat, and Jordan and I often went to Paco's to hang out with Ana and Cannon and drink way too many margaritas. I even went with Jordan to a few of the Leo pack meetings, listening on the sidelines as he calmly dealt with whatever issues his people were having. And every day, Jordan and I grew closer and closer, and I delayed my return to the Ophiuchus pack a little longer.

But I was still hesitant to become the Leo alpha female. No matter how happy I was here among them, it didn't change the fact that this was the pack that had killed my parents, and been the bitter enemies of the Ophiuchus for a long time. But then again, was this really the same pack? The alpha that had orchestrated and carried out the brutal murder of my parents was long gone. I'd gotten some sharp looks from some of the older pack members, and when I'd asked Jordan about it, he'd said that some of them still followed his father's ways. But they were in the minority, and most of the pack was eager to put that in the past. They wanted to grow and change as a pack, and this was where Jordan and I could really make a difference.

I didn't realize I was staring out of the windshield—or that we were already halfway home—until Jordan put his hand on my knee.

"What's on your mind?" he asked. "You look like you're pretty deep in thought."

"Oh, um." I didn't want to tell him that I was still unsure of becoming his alpha female. "I was just wondering why Roxandra hasn't done anything yet."

"I've been thinking about that too." Jordan squeezed my knee. "I think she's staying away because she's scared of you."

"She should be scared," I muttered, imagining all the things I wanted to do to Roxandra if I ever got her alone.

Jordan grinned. "I love how fierce you are."

Oh, there it was again. The L word. He hadn't said it since that night with Kaden and Ayla and I'd chosen to pretend it had never happened...but now it was back. Did he really love me? How could he be so sure?

"Where are we going?" I asked, as I realized we were heading out toward the desert instead of to his house.

"I'm taking you to one of my favorite places. It's a new moon tonight, and the view of the stars is going to be incredible."

I raised my eyebrows, wondering where exactly we were heading but willing to go along with it. "Did you bring food?"

He chuffed. "Do you even need to ask? Of course I did. I brought wine too."

"Sounds romantic."

He glanced over at me. "I hope so."

Butterflies fluttered in my stomach as we drove, while the sun moved lower and lower in the sky. We didn't speak again for the rest of the drive, which took about twenty minutes.

When Jordan finally parked, he pulled two backpacks out of the trunk. "Take off your clothes and put them in the black one. We're going on foot from here."

I nodded, eager to see where he was taking me. We both removed our clothes and put them away, then shifted at the same time. My black wolf brushed up against the side of his red wolf, telling him I was ready. We each picked up a backpack in our mouths, and then we took off.

Jordan had parked us next to a very large red rock formation, and he led me up a steep path toward the top. On foot it would have been a challenge, but as a wolf we were able to climb it easily and quickly. We reached the top just as the sun met the horizon and painted the never ending sky in a rainbow of colors that took my breath away. The rock formation jutted out at the top, forming a smooth ledge that reached up toward the sky, and that's where Jordan took me. From this spot, we could see the entire valley below, and I marveled at everything I saw there. Not some dry, desolate desert, but a land filled with life, color, and beauty. I'd come here thinking there would be nothing to love, and instead I'd discovered a place I continuously wanted to explore.

Jordan raised his head and let out a long, crooning howl, and I lifted my nose and joined him a second later. It was an ode to the beauty of the land and the sky, a goodbye to day and a hello to night, and a celebration of being alive, together, in this moment.

When our song ended, we both shifted back and stood together holding hands, letting the cool breeze dance across our skin while the sky darkened around us and the stars began to slowly appear.

"Thank you for bringing me here," I said. "It's so beautiful."

Jordan nodded. "This is where I used to come when I needed to escape my father. When I was angry at everyone and everything, when it was all too much and I didn't know how I could take another second of it, coming here always calmed me down."

I squeezed his hand. "I can see why."

Jordan turned to face me. "I've never brought anyone else here before. Only you."

My breath caught in my throat. "I'm honored."

He took both of my hands in his before speaking again. "Stella, there's so much I want to say that I don't even know where to start. I'm sorry for forcing the mate bond. I'm sorry for everything the Leo pack has done to you. I'm sorry for—"

"Stop. You don't need to apologize anymore." I stepped closer and kissed him. "I forgive you for everything, and I'm sorry for rejecting you and for everything I did too. The past is done. Let's focus on moving forward."

"I'd like that, as long as we're doing it together." His fingers tightened around mine. "Stella, I want you to stay."

"I am staying."

"Not just until the end of this thing with the Sun Witches, but always." He swallowed hard. "I know you don't feel like you belong here, but I can't imagine my life without you in it anymore. You make me a better man, and a better alpha. My pack needs you. I need you. And more than that... I love you. Not because of the mate bond, but because you're clever and kind, strong and loyal, brave and funny. You're never afraid to keep me in line. You go out of your way to help others. You charge into danger to protect people you don't even know. You're generous with your time and your love. You're an Ophiuchus at heart, but a Leo in your soul. You belong here, with us. With me. As my mate and my alpha female."

My heart felt like it had expanded to fill this entire, endless sky. "Jordan—"

"You don't need to say anything." He let go of my hands. "I'm not going to pressure you or force you to make a decision tonight. I just wanted you to know how I feel so—"

"Jordan!"

He blinked. "Yeah?"

"Shut up."

I lunged to close the distance between us and threw my arms around his neck. Jordan hardly got a chance to let out a startled noise before I sealed our lips together, standing on my toes to reach him. He kissed me back and let his hands slide around my waist, while I melted against him. He was strong and he was safe.

He was *mine*.

I broke away from our kiss and stared into his eyes. "I'm not going anywhere."

His hands tightened on my naked skin. "Good."

The next words were so big and heavy that they clung to my tongue, but I finally got them out.

"I love you too...and I want you as my mate."

The second I said them, something jolted between us, knocking the breath out of me. Jordan's eyes widened and I felt his surprise and excitement, but most of all, his love.

The mate bond.

CHAPTER TWENTY

JORDAN LET OUT A DELIGHTED LAUGH, and I felt his awe and amazement before he swept me up in his arms. "The mate bond," he said between quick kisses to my lips. "I didn't know if it would come back."

"Me neither." To my relief, it was not only back, but even stronger than before. A connection formed between us that was so deep and powerful it sent shivers down my spine, and every nerve in my body tingled with the intensity of it.

Desire flared between us both as the kissing grew more intense and the mate bond demanded to be sealed. Jordan broke apart and I nearly howled in disappointment, until he opened one of the backpacks and pulled out a blanket, then set it down on the ground for us. An instant later, he swept me off my feet and into his arms. I shrieked and grabbed his neck as he carried me bridal style toward the blanket. He laid me out under the stars, which twinkled their approval above us, and then lowered himself over me. All that hard naked skin, and that body that concealed the big heart inside my mate. I wanted it. No, I *needed* it.

I was done denying myself, and done pretending like I didn't want this. I'd held off because I wasn't sure if I was ready, but I'd never been more sure of anything in this moment.

I was ready to truly be Jordan's mate.

I wrapped my arms around his neck and pulled him into a deeper kiss, while his cock nudged between my legs. Jordan let out a low growl as I opened for him, positioning him so the head of his cock could rub against my pussy and my clit. He slid back and forth, sending flickers of heat through me.

"I don't think I can go slow," he said, nuzzling my neck. "I've wanted this for too long."

"We have time for slow later. I'm not going anywhere." I nipped at his ear. "Claim me hard and fast."

"Fuck," he growled, and thrust inside me.

I moaned as Jordan filled me completely, stretching me open with pleasure that almost bordered on pain. When he started moving, it somehow got even better. He drove into me, hard and fast, the way I'd asked. The sound of our flesh slapping together filled the air and I gripped his shoulders, trying to anchor myself. It felt like every inch of my body was on fire, and each of his thrusts fanned the flames higher.

"So good," I managed to get out, between his fervent thrusts. I couldn't believe how perfect we fit together. How right this felt. I never wanted it to end.

"We're just getting started," Jordan said with a grin. "I'm going to make you forget your own name."

"So cocky." I thrust my hips up at him. "Prove it then."

He grabbed one of my legs and hooked it over his arm, opening me wider. His cock drove even deeper, and a hoarse cry ripped from my throat. My entire body shook, and my toes curled into the cool dirt. Jordan reached down, his hand sliding between us, and started rubbing circles around my clit. My hips bucked up against him, and I couldn't keep quiet anymore.

"Jordan," I cried out, clawing at his shoulders.

"That's it." He grunted as he bottomed out inside me. "Let the whole damn world know who your mate is."

Jordan set a quick, ruthless pace that had me on the verge of an orgasm almost instantly. His fingers kept moving on my clit, and his cock stroked me just right inside. He'd spent the last few days learning what I liked, and he knew exactly how to get me to come—multiple times.

I screamed his name as the pleasure built up inside me, and then I grabbed his shoulders and pulled him down toward me just as it exploded. If Jordan wanted everyone to know he was my mate, then I would make sure no one would miss it.

With a growl, I sunk my fangs into the soft spot between his neck and shoulder, marking him as mine just as the orgasm swept through me. He let out a hoarse groan as he thrust harder, and the taste of his blood and sweat in my mouth only made my pleasure grow. I wrapped my legs around him, nails digging into his back, as the orgasm went on for what felt like forever.

When some sense had returned to me, I licked the spot on his neck where I'd bitten him. "Now everyone will know you're mine."

"Fierce," Jordan said, touching his neck with a dark smile. "I like it. But now it's my turn."

He pulled out of me, and with rough hands he turned me over onto my hands and knees. With no warning he wrapped one hand around my neck, while the other gripped my hips, and then his cock slammed into me from behind, pleasure exploding through me. It was too much and not enough. I was still sensitive from the last orgasm, and his rough handling had me teetering on the edge already.

He leaned over and nipped at my ear, before whispering, "You're mine, and I'm not letting you escape this time."

He slammed into me and his fingers dug into the flesh at my hips, no doubt leaving marks. The hand around my throat was gentle but firm, and the way he pounded into me was rough and exactly what I wanted. We both let our animal sides take over, our inner wolves demanding us to move harder and faster, and I felt his claws emerge and dip into my skin.

He pulled me back hard against his cock, which hit me in a spot that had me trembling right on the edge of another orgasm. I shouted his name to the sky and any stars who might be listening, and then that hand on my throat pulled me back to him. With a final growl, he sank his teeth into my neck, marking me as his mate. Pain and pleasure burst through me at the same time, while his cock swelled inside me and we came together. It was the most intense thing I'd ever experienced, with his cock buried deep in my pussy, his teeth biting my neck, and his claws digging into my skin.

My whole body shook as the mate bond solidified between us. The connection was so intense I could almost see through Jordan's eyes, feel every breeze across his skin, and smell every scent that hit his nose. He was a part of me, and I was a part of him, and that would never change.

We collapsed onto the blanket together and Jordan held me in his arms while we stared at each other.

"I'm never letting you go again," he said, tracing his finger across my cheek.

"If you try, I'll bite you," I warned.

"You can bite me anytime you want."

I rolled him onto his back and climbed on top of him, nuzzling the spot where I bit him. "Oh, yeah? You'd like that, wouldn't you?"

He rolled his hips, his cock already hard again. "Very much."

"Then I'll do it again and again, so you're always reminded that I'm your mate."

He took my face in his hands, meeting my eyes. "Stella, I'll never forget. I will always be yours."

And with those words, the last piece of my resistance fell away and I kissed him hard, showing him I was completely his too. Then I sank down onto his perfect cock and rode him while the stars watched. They'd brought us together, after all, and it felt only right that we did this with the Milky Way shining down on us. I tilted my head up to the endless sky and gave a silent prayer of thanks as Jordan and I brought each other to heaven once more.

CHAPTER TWENTY-ONE

WE SOMEHOW MADE it back home later that night, and spent the next day having lots of sex—now that the mate bond was in place, we were insatiable—and hatching a plan to lure out Roxandra. If Jordan was correct, and my presence was the problem, then I had an idea for how to get her attention.

The next morning, we woke early and headed out of town together in Jordan's truck. The sun was just starting to come up as we drove past the town's wards, and the rock formations glowed red in the distance. Anticipation made my heart beat faster, but I was ready to get this over with. Jordan and the rest of the Leos would never be safe until we dealt with Roxandra.

Jordan parked in a clearing near a tiny stream, and together we hiked up to the top of a small mesa that overlooked it. The cave where we'd battled Roxandra before was nearby, but I hoped we wouldn't have to go back in there.

Jordan stretched out his arms and headed for the center of the mesa. "This seems like a good spot to practice. Lots of sunlight. Maybe it will help."

I moved to stand across from him, holding Debra's Sun Witch spell book. "Good idea. Let's try the basic spell to summon fire in your hand."

"That one again?" He rolled his eyes dramatically. "You know I already mastered that."

"Did you?" I crossed my arms. "Show me."

We spent a few minutes running through the things Jordan already knew how to do. He was getting better every time we practiced, and I felt a small glow of pride in my chest as I watched him hold the flame, switch it from hand to hand, and then snuff it out and restart it.

"See?" He flashed me an arrogant look. "Easy."

I snorted. "Fine. You've got the basics down. But now we're going to focus on making the fire bigger while keeping it in control. That's a lot harder. Especially for someone like you."

His eyes narrowed. "What's that supposed to mean?"

"Nothing," I muttered. "Just don't lose your temper and we'll be fine."

He scowled at me and summoned another flame. As he glared at me, the flame grew bigger and bigger, and then suddenly it exploded in a burst that sent us both flying back.

"You idiot," I snapped, as I got to my feet and brushed myself off. "You have to keep your emotions under control."

"I had them under control," he growled as he stood up.

"Obviously not!"

He waved his arms around. "It's hard to keep them in control when I can feel you judging me over there!"

"I'm not judging, I'm trying to teach you. Now do it again, but try to keep your shit together this time."

He snarled and summoned another flame and shot it at me, missing by a mile. I jumped and let out a screech.

"What the fuck, Jordan!"

"Sorry, I must have lost control," he sneered.

I threw up my hands. "I can't teach you like this. You act like a toddler who throws a fit the second something goes wrong. I've taught kindergarteners with more patience than you!"

Jordan got right up in my face, his eyes bright with anger. "Maybe the problem isn't me, it's you. Maybe you're just a bad teacher."

I poked my finger at his chest. "Or maybe you're a terrible student."

"Maybe you just don't want me to get better at sun magic because then I'll be more powerful than you."

"Maybe you need to get your ego in check!" We were both yelling at each other now, and I could only hope Roxandra was taking notice, because my heart couldn't take much more of this.

"This was a mistake," he said, stepping back. "All of it."

"What do you mean?" I asked.

"I don't want you as my teacher, and I don't want you."

My jaw dropped. "Jordan—"

He took a step back, his face stony. "Go back to the Ophiuchus. We don't need you anymore."

"No..."

He pointed back toward the town. "Go. Just...go."

I let out a sob that wasn't entirely fake and turned away from him, then shifted into my wolf form, not even bothering to remove my clothes first. I shook away the torn shreds, kicked off my shoes, and ran down the path as fast as I could.

I ran until Jordan was out of sight, and then ducked behind some agave to catch my breath. That fight had taken a lot out of me, even though it was all part of our plan. I hoped Jordan knew I didn't mean any of those things I'd said. We'd had to make the fight look convincing, so Roxandra would truly believe I was gone. Assuming she'd been listening, of course.

I turned invisible and then headed back to the mesa, retracing my steps. I made sure to move silently as I drew near and kept my ears perked, listening for anything out of the ordinary. That's when I heard her voice.

"Oh, Jordan," she practically purred. "It's about time you got rid of that moon wolf."

"Roxandra! How long have you been here?" Jordan asked, as I climbed faster.

"Long enough to see that she had no business trying to teach you sun magic. But I'm here now. I can teach you everything you need to know."

I reached the top of the mesa, still invisible, but kept my distance. I didn't want her to sense my moon magic yet.

Jordan sat on a large rock, gazing at Roxandra, who was

in her red hooded robes and had her back to me. "You can teach me things that Stella can't?"

"You know I can." She ran a hand along his shoulder. "And we can finally be together."

Jordan paused, as if he was considering. "Things with you were so much easier."

My heart clenched, knowing how hard this must be for him, but he delivered the line flawlessly. *Good job,* I thought to Jordan, even thought I knew he couldn't hear me. *Playing on her feelings for you.*

"I know." Her hand moved to cup his cheek and she gazed at him with hunger. "It can be like that again. The two of us."

"The two of us," Jordan said with a suggestive grin.

She leaned forward like she was about to kiss him. "You're the key to everything I need. I want your body, your blood, and your baby."

Jordan's face flickered with distaste, just for a moment, but he smoothed it away so fast that I hoped Roxandra didn't notice. Meanwhile, my wolf screamed at me to destroy this bitch who wanted my man.

"What do you want my blood for?" Jordan asked, as he rose to his feet.

"All in good time," Roxandra said, squeezing his arm. "You're too pretty to worry about things like that. Come back with me, and you'll know everything soon."

"First tell me why you were taking the males in my pack. It couldn't just be to get my attention."

She sighed. "I was testing their blood to see if they had

any sun magic, but their blood wasn't strong enough. Not for what I need. But yours...yours is perfect."

Jordan grabbed Roxandra's arm and dragged her to the center of the mesa, his face twisting with anger. "That's all I needed to know. Now I'll make sure you never hurt anyone again."

That was my cue. I muttered words in ancient Greek and moon magic lit up along the ground in a circle, forming a cage around Roxandra. I'd laid the trap last night, under the stars and the tiny sliver of a moon, when my magic would be stronger.

Surprise flashed across Roxandra's face, but then she laughed. "You didn't think this would hold me, did you?"

Fire exploded out of her, burning through my cage and setting her free in an instant. Fuck, she was so strong. I was a pretty good Moon Witch, but I would never be at Roxandra's level. Only Larkin and Ayla would be able to fight her as equals. But I wasn't alone.

Jordan's claws were out and he slashed at Roxandra, but she managed to dodge away, faster than should have been possible. I gathered more moon magic and shot shards of it at her, which she batted away easily. Then there was a huge flash of light, as if the sun was suddenly in our eyes, and I had to look away. When I did, Roxandra was standing beside Jordan, who was clutching his arm. He reached for her but his reaction was painfully slow, and she easily moved back. A second later, Jordan crumpled to the ground in a heap.

"No!" I yelled and gathered more magic, but it was too late.

Roxandra reached down to take Jordan's arm, and then the two of them vanished in a puff of smoke.

I quickly latched onto the mate bond between us, trying to figure out where she was taking him, but my sense of him fizzled out immediately. I reached into the empty space, yelling Jordan's name, but there was nothing.

I slumped to my knees and stared at the spot where Jordan had just been. Where could she have taken him that the mate bond wouldn't be able to follow?

No, I thought. *Anything but there.* But it was the only thing that made sense. Roxandra must have taken Jordan to the one place she knew I couldn't follow.

Solundra.

CHAPTER TWENTY-TWO

PANIC SET in not long after I realized where Roxandra had taken Jordan. I had no idea how to save him in Solundra, or what I was supposed to do next. I stared at the space where he'd disappeared, replaying those last few moments. It had all happened so fast, and it was all my fault. My plan had failed, my magic wasn't strong enough, and now Jordan was gone.

I remembered the way Roxandra had smiled at him, like he was a slab of meat. She wanted his blood for something, and whatever it was, it couldn't be good. My stomach twisted at the thought of her trying to use his body to make a baby, but no—that was not going to happen. I was going to get him back.

There was one person in Daybreak who might know how to get to Solundra. I raced back to Jordan's truck, threw on the extra clothes that I'd packed, and then drove at reckless speeds toward town, to the one house I least wanted to visit.

The gate opened for me as soon as I pulled up, and I parked right next to the fountain and jumped out, racing toward the mansion's front door.

Debra opened it before I could knock, her expression worried. "What's wrong?"

"Roxandra. She took Jordan to Solundra."

Fear flashed in her eyes, but then her face became steel again. "Come inside."

"Mom?" A familiar voice asked, as Debra swept me into the house. Griffin raced down the stairs and spotted me. "What are you doing here? Where's Jordan?"

"Jordan's been taken," I said. "I need to get to Solundra."

"How do you know he's there?" Debra asked.

"Roxandra vanished with him, and I..." I hesitated, but this news would come out soon enough. "I can't feel him through the mate bond anymore."

Debra's eyebrows shot up. "So you've become mates then?" She nodded, not even waiting for the answer. "Good. That will help once we get to Solundra."

"We?" I asked.

"Obviously I'm coming with you." She gave me a stern look. "Your moon magic won't work in Solundra. You'll need all the help you can get."

"I'm coming too," Griffin said, standing up straighter.

Debra shot him a sharp look. "Absolutely not."

He gave her a look that reminded me of Jordan when he

was upset. "You can't keep acting like I'm a kid! I can help too."

"It's too dangerous for you there," Debra said. "I won't let Roxandra take you too."

Griffin let out a frustrated noise and stormed out of the room. I supposed that was his way of backing down. I didn't have time to worry about him though.

Debra pinched the bridge of her nose and then shook it off. "I can open a bridge to Solundra, but we'll need to bring some warriors who can fight vampires and witches. You need to rally them quickly."

My mind immediately went to my family and friends, but I couldn't ask them for help. Larkin's magic wouldn't work in Solundra, and Ayla was about to have a baby—I couldn't ask her to go. I wouldn't risk my brother's life either. No, I had to do this alone. "I don't have anyone who can come."

"Nonsense. You're the Leo alpha female now. You have an entire pack of warriors at your service."

Me? Rally the Leos? It was one thing to be Jordan's mate in private, but being the alpha female of the Leo pack and expecting them to follow me was a whole other matter. I wasn't sure I could do it, or that any of them would even listen to me. But what other choice did I have?

For Jordan, I would try.

I stood up straighter, summoning the courage that the Leos were known for. "Okay. Let me see what I can do."

Debra's lips curved into a small smile, and for the first time I actually saw a hint of pride in her eyes.

I SHADED my eyes against the sun and turned to look at the assembled Leo warriors. I was surprised by how many people had volunteered when I'd asked them to come. Most of them I didn't know by name, but after I'd called Cannon and explained to him what was going on, he'd jumped into action and summoned all the warriors he could get on short notice. Now we stood at the edge of the town, still inside of the wards, while Debra prepared to open the portal.

Griffin stood to the side, hands shoved in his pockets. I could tell that he was still put out by not being able to join us, so I caught his eye and motioned for him to come over. He looked reluctant, but shuffled over.

I dropped my voice low as he came close. "I know you want to come with us, but I need someone here who can protect everyone while we're in Solundra. While we're gone, you're the acting alpha."

Griffin's eyes widened. "Me? Are you sure?"

I patted him on the shoulder. "I know you can handle it, and it will make me feel better knowing the pack is safe while I'm gone."

Griffin straightened. "I'll do my best."

I nodded, and gave his shoulder one last pat before I walked over to Debra, who was watching Griffin.

"Thank you," she said. "I was worried he'd try to sneak inside the portal with us."

"No problem," I said. "We're ready when you are."

"Then let's begin. I'll need a few minutes to open the

portal." She turned away and raised her hands, muttering something in ancient Greek while light gathered in her hands.

I turned back toward the gathered warriors, seeing some faces I recognized and many I didn't. "Thank you all for coming so quickly. We're going into Solundra, the realm of Helios, to track down Roxandra and rescue Jordan. We don't know what we will face there, but I know whatever we find, the Leos will be ready for it. Leos are creatures of the sun, immune to fire, and nothing can stop us from finding our alpha."

The Leos roared and howled in response, their faces ranging from eager to angry to determined. But not one of them was scared, at least on the outside. The Leos were truly a mighty pack.

The portal burst into life with a flash of light, which settled into a shimmering golden vortex in front of Debra. She nodded to me, signaling it was ready, and I turned to Cannon.

The beta stepped forward first. "For the alpha!" he cried, before striding through the portal.

Once the other warriors saw him go in, they quickly followed, going through the shimmering portal one by one until only Debra and I remained. I took a deep breath and looked around, taking in the town and the people watching one more time, before stepping through.

There was a brief pinch at the base of my spine and the feeling of falling, and then I was on the other side. The first thing I noticed was how sunny and warm it was, like a perfect summer day with just enough shade from nearby trees and a slight breeze in my hair. The sun looked huge in the sky, and a little too close for my liking, but I supposed that was to be expected in the realm of the sun god.

We stood in a grassy area with olive trees and flowers, very different from the desert town we'd just left behind. Lush green hills rose in the distance, and on top of them was a huge Greek structure with gleaming white columns and a giant statue of what I assumed was Helios in front. Dozens of smaller structures dotted the hill around the structure, along with some roads that led up to it.

Debra appeared through the portal, which then closed behind her. She followed my gaze. "That's Helopolis, where the Sun Witches live. My aunt Brea should be there now, along with the Sun Witches she's convinced to join her side. The rest follow Roxandra."

"Should we go there?" I asked.

"No, we don't have time. Roxandra won't be hiding there, and it will take too long to find Brea and try to get help. We're on our own."

"But then where do we go?"

"You tell us," Debra said.

Right. I closed my eyes and breathed in the warm air, opening up my connection with Jordan while saying a small prayer to Helios—my first one ever. Jordan was a true child of the sun as both a Leo and a Sun Witch, and I had to believe the god would want us to rescue him.

The mate bond flared to life in an instant, so strong it made me wonder if the god had heard my prayers. I felt

Jordan's life force, alive but weakened, and it tugged on me, urging me to move forward.

"I know how to find him," I said.

Debra raised her eyebrows. "You can feel the mate bond? Lead the way then."

I gestured toward the warriors and raised my voice. "I know where Jordan is. Follow me."

The other warriors moved forward without hesitation, following my lead, and a little thrill shot through me. I led us north, away from the hills where the Sun Witches lived, toward a denser forest. The trees were completely different from the kinds I was used to near my home, these ones suited for a much warmer climate. As we entered the forest, I was surprised by how beautiful it was. I'd expected Solundra to be a desert like Arizona, but this was the opposite. Lush, thick greenery carpeted the ground with brightly colored flowers poking out of the earth and bright green trees hanging over us. Small streams and brooks bubbled and flowed throughout the landscape with crystal clear water. They were small enough that we could step or jump over them easily, and when I dipped my hand into one of them, it was pleasantly cool. I took a sip, and felt immediately refreshed. The perfect way to cool off on a hot summer's day.

"It's not what I expected at all," I said to Debra, who was watching me.

"You expected a lifeless desert, didn't you?"

"Yeah," I said. "How did you—"

"I know what you think of the Sun Witch's magic,"

Debra said, lifting her chin. "You've watched it destroy and burn, but there's more to it than that. True sun magic is about life and growth, not just fire and destruction. Before Evanora twisted and corrupted us, the Sun Witches were healers and gardeners, not just warriors. That's what the new Sun Witches are trying to get back to now, under Brea's leadership."

"I didn't know that," I said. "But I'd like to learn more about it."

Debra sniffed, but I thought she looked pleased at my answer. "Later. Right now we need to find my son."

Jordan. The reminder of why we were here sent a pang through my chest, and I started walking faster. There would be time to wonder about Solundra and sun magic later.

With each step, I felt us growing closer, and it took everything I had not to break into a run and go crashing through the trees until I found him. When one of our scouts returned an hour later and mentioned a small structure up ahead surrounded by vampires, I knew that's where Jordan had to be. I sensed him nearby, though he was still weakened by whatever Roxandra had done to him.

I'm coming, I told him through the mate bond, hoping he would feel it. *Stay strong.*

"The structure is made of solid brick and only has one entrance, along with multiple large windows that could be breached," the scout said. "I counted at least five vampires in the surrounding area, but there could be more."

"Good work," Cannon said.

"He's in there," I said, my skin tingling with anticipation. "I can feel it."

"How do you want to proceed?" Cannon asked.

"Have one group take out all the vampires surrounding the structure. Make it noisy so it draws out any more in the area or inside the structure. With that attack as a distraction, Debra and I will sneak inside and rescue Jordan."

Cannon nodded. "I'll send two wolves with you as backup."

"Good, but tell them to leave Roxandra to me."

"Understood."

He gave a signal to the rest of the warriors behind us, and everyone began shedding their clothes, including Cannon and Debra. Within seconds, there were a dozen red wolves quietly fanning out through the woods toward the vampires, whose scents were easily detected by our sensitive noses. I took off my own clothes as well and tried to use my gift to make everyone invisible, but of course it didn't work. No moon magic in Solundra.

Debra's red wolf moved alongside me, along with two others I didn't know, and we crept through the forest together, making no sound at all. We stopped behind some thick ferns at the edge of the clearing, where I spotted the brick cabin where Jordan had to be held. There were tall windows on either side of the door that shone with light, but I would need to get closer to see what was inside.

Suddenly the other Leos throughout the forest let out their trademark roar, which made enemies either panic or flee in terror, before the sounds of fighting broke out. As snarls and growls filled the air, I sent out another prayer to Helios to watch over his favorite pack.

Two Sun Witches in orange robes burst out of the front door, scanning the forest.

Charge, I told the other Leos by my side, and they split up and attacked without question. The witches threw fireballs at them, but the flames washed right over them. Leos were immune to fire, after all. Before the two witches could cast another spell my two wolves were on them, tearing out their throats without mercy, while Debra and I were rushing into the house to find Roxandra—and Jordan.

CHAPTER TWENTY-THREE

THE CABIN SEEMED to consist of one large room, and I spotted Roxandra immediately as I dashed inside. She stood over a small cauldron, which I didn't know witches actually used, and was stirring some kind of bubbling potion in it. On the other side of her were two small beds, with Jordan in one, and an older woman who looked vaguely familiar in the other—both of them unconscious and bleeding from large gashes in their arms. The woman wore an old-fashioned cloth dress with moons on the hem, and Kaden and Ayla's words drifted to the front of my mind. They'd been worried about a missing Moon Witch—Maricar—and hoped she hadn't gotten lost in the woods. Now I realized she'd been kidnapped by Roxandra and had been in Solundra this whole time. But why?

As Debra and I raced into the room, Roxandra spun toward us, clutching a golden chalice in one hand that glowed slightly. Blood sloshed out of it and dripped on the floor, and the scent of my mate's blood made me see red. She'd hurt him, and now she was going to pay.

I lunged straight for Roxandra, knocking the chalice out of her hands with my teeth. It fell to the floor and the golden light dimmed as blood spilled everywhere.

"Hello, little moon wolf," she said, and kicked me. I tried to dodge, but she was so damn fast. Her kick caught me square in the chest and I went sprawling. How was she so strong? I got up and snarled at Roxandra, preparing to launch myself at her again.

She raised her hands and shot fire at me so quickly there was no way for me to dodge. I flinched and closed my eyes as the flames hit me...and did nothing.

"What—" Roxandra started, before hitting me with more fire. I stalked toward her with a wolfish grin on my face as the flames rolled off my back. Fire couldn't hurt me anymore.

I was a Leo now.

That had been Jordan's idea, and this time, I'd agreed. He'd secretly made me a member of his pack, making me the true alpha female, even if no one knew about it yet. And the look on Roxandra's face made it all worth it.

I snapped at Roxandra while she was still caught off guard by my sudden immunity to her fire magic, and managed to catch her arm with my teeth. She screamed and flashed bright white light in my eyes, which made me flinch back. I let her go and she darted away, still impossibly fast.

"You can't beat me," she said. "Even if you're immune to

fire now, I've been using vampire blood to make myself stronger and faster."

Behind her, I spotted Debra back in human form, using sun magic to heal Jordan. All I had to do was keep Roxandra distracted a little longer so Debra could get him out of here.

I growled low in my throat, my ears twitching, and bared my teeth in a challenge. Roxandra grabbed a silver dagger off the table and raised it as I approached.

"Jordan is mine," Roxandra snarled as she lunged for me with the knife, but I easily dodged out of the way. "And he was mine long before you got him in your bed."

If looks could kill, I would have turned her into a big pile of ashes. I snapped at her leg, catching just a bit of her calf and a big chunk of fabric. Her red robe ripped from ankle to knee, and exposed her bleeding calf underneath. Her knife scraped along my back, but I twisted before it did any real damage, and then slammed her against the wall with my side.

She fell to the floor, and I pinned her with one paw on her throat and the other on her chest. Roxandra beat weakly at my paws as I cut off her air. On the other side of the room, Jordan drew in a deep, sharp breath that I could hear even over the din of the fighting. He sat up and Debra hugged him.

"Are you okay?" she asked.

"I'm fine," Jordan said. He looked a little pale and his hair was disheveled, but overall he did seem to be okay. The wound on his arm was already mostly healed. He looked over at the Moon Witch. "But she needs your help."

Debra let go of her son and moved over to Maricar to begin healing her. Jordan stood, and caught sight of me standing over Roxandra. I felt a mixture of relief, pride, and love surge through the mate bond as he looked at me, followed by anger and hatred as he focused on Roxandra.

"Get off me, you mangy beast," Roxandra yelled, then squirmed out from under me using her stolen vampire speed and strength, but Jordan was there, and he punched her in face. She went down hard, but got back up again impossibly fast, touching the spot on her cheek where he'd hit her.

"Careful how you talk to my mate," Jordan said.

"Jordan," she pleaded. "We're meant to be together, ruling both the Zodiac Wolves and the Sun Witches. You said you wanted that too."

Jordan's fists clenched at his side. "That wasn't me. You had me under your control. Nothing we had together was real. I didn't want it then, and I definitely don't want it now."

"But you're the future of the Sun Witches. We need you. I need you!"

"I might be the future, but you're not. And I won't let you hurt anyone else." He grabbed Roxandra by the throat, while she threw useless fireballs at him and tore at his chest. But no matter how strong her stolen vampire blood had made her, Jordan was still stronger. "I want my eyes to be the last thing you see."

With a fierce roar, he grew claws and reached into her chest, ripping her heart out in one quick, violent motion. He crushed it between his claws while Roxandra blinked at him while the life suddenly left her body. He dropped her sagging form to the floor, where blood spurted out of the gaping hole in her chest.

Jordan flung her heart away from him with a snarl. He was breathing hard, like he'd been fighting her for a long time. I rubbed against his side, and he put his hand on top of my head.

"I knew you'd come for me," he said, stroking the spot between my ears.

I shifted back and threw my arms around him. "Always. I love you."

He held me close. "I love you too."

Debra finished healing Maricar and then rushed over to check on her son again. The Moon Witch sat at the edge of the bed with her head in her hands. While Debra hugged Jordan, I glanced around the room, taking in the cauldron, the chalice, and the spilled blood.

"What was going on here?" I asked Jordan. "Why did she take you and the Moon Witch?"

Jordan bent down and picked up the chalice. "She was doing a spell to remove the Sun Curse from the vampires in order to gain their total loyalty. She needed the blood of a male Sun Witch and a female Moon Witch to complete it. She'd had the Moon Witch for a while, but she couldn't find any males with strong enough Sun Witch blood. Except for me."

I bent down and picked up the chalice, studying it. The Sun Curse prevented vampires from going in the sunlight. The wolves had once had a similar curse on us, the Moon Curse, which caused us to lose control of our wolves and our minds during a full moon. It had been removed long ago by the Moon Witches, but the Sun Witches had never removed the curse from the vampires. Instead they gave the vampires their blood, allowing them to temporarily walk in the sun, in return for their loyalty. That was how they kept manipulating and controlling them—just like they'd controlled the Zodiac Wolves for years.

The remaining vampires surrendered once they realized Roxandra was dead, and Cannon and the other Leos rounded them up and brought them to us in the cabin. A small, unexpected swell of pride went through me at the sight of my wolves returning alive and triumphant.

"We surrender," a male vampire said, dipping his head in a sign of submission. "But please, finish the spell, I'm begging you. We will be loyal to whoever breaks the curse."

"Why should we trust you?" Jordan asked.

The vampire got down on his knees slowly. "A vampire's word is unbreakable, and I can speak for all of us when I swear we will serve the Leo pack if you finish the spell and break the curse."

Jordan and I shared a wary look. Could we trust them? But then I thought of Killian, the vampire who worked with the Moon Witches, who was currently living in Coronis. He couldn't go out during the daylight either, and he proved that not all vampires were evil. Maybe they just needed a chance to change and do better, like the Leo pack once did.

"We don't want your servitude," I said, and Jordan

nodded beside me. "We don't want to control you like the Sun Witches did."

The vampire looked up at me, eyes wide and a little bit hesitant. "What is it that you want then?"

"A truce between vampires and shifters. No more fighting, no more attacks. We don't need to be allies, but we will not be enemies anymore either. I know it might be hard with our history, but we're only enemies because the witches made us that way. It's time we all broke free of them and charted a new path, one of peace this time." I took Jordan's hand and smiled at him. "You'd be surprised what you can do when you try to turn over a fresh leaf."

The vampire inclined his head and stood back up, then gave us a low bow. "We agree. If you break the curse, we will call a truce, and there will be peace between vampires and shifters."

"Are you sure about this?" Cannon asked us.

"I know what it's like being controlled by the Sun Witches," Jordan said. "As long as the Sun Curse exists, the vampires can never truly be free."

I grinned at him. "We freed the Zodiac Wolves. Why not the vampires too?"

He raised my hand to his lips and kissed it. "This is why I love you."

"How do we do the spell?" I asked.

"Roxandra's spell book is open to the page," Jordan said, gesturing toward an ancient-looking tome on a nearby table. "I don't think I'm good enough to do the spell yet though."

"I'll do it," Debra said.

"Then all we need is blood." Jordan took the chalice from me and grabbed Roxandra's dagger off the floor, then sliced into his arm again. He collected the blood in the chalice, and then handed the knife to me.

I was about to hand it to Maricar, who looked like she might pass out again at any moment, when I realized Jordan had given it to me for a reason. Up until the last few months, I'd never considered myself a Moon Witch, just a wolf with a few extra powers, but all that had changed. I'd gotten comfortable at casting real magic, even during combat, and I'd even helped Jordan learn sun magic.

I cut myself and took the chalice to collect the blood. Once there was enough, Debra took it from me and began chanting words in ancient Greek. The chalice began to glow while she swirled it in a clockwise motion, mixing the blood together. Then she poured the blood into the cauldron and continued chanting, waving her hands over the glowing potion brewing inside.

Everyone stood and watched in silence as she went through the spell, the glow getting brighter and brighter until it looked like it was sunlight itself trapped in the cauldron. When it became too bright to even look at, Debra dipped the chalice into it, and then offered it to the vampire who had spoken earlier.

"Thank you," he said, looking around at all of us while the chalice glowed in his hand. "It means a lot that you would trust us with this. We won't let you down."

I squeezed Jordan's hand as the vampire tilted the chalice up and drank the contents. The light flowed into him, illuminating him from the inside out. It looked like someone had taken the world's strongest flashlight to his throat, and then his chest. I could see the outlines of his ribcage as it slid down his throat and settled in his stomach. Then, the magic spread out, lighting him up so brightly that I had to lift my hand to my face and squint my eyes. The other vampires in the room started glowing as well, and they all lifted their arms like they were going to take flight.

I was surprised to find tears in my eyes as I watched. Every vampire in Solundra was suffused with the light, and somehow I knew that every vampire back on Earth was too. The centuries-old curse truly was breaking, and the vampires would finally be free to come out of the shadows.

All at once, the light disappeared, as if someone had blown out a candle.

"Thank you," the vampire said, staring at the chalice in awe. "It worked. I can feel the difference."

A wave of agreement went through the rest of the vampires as they nodded their heads and made affirmative noises. I breathed a sigh of relief and smiled at them. "Congratulations. How does it feel to have the curse broken?"

"Like being reborn." The vampire came up to me and extended his hand. "My name is Ferdinand of House Desmodus. It is a pleasure to be at peace with you."

I hesitated, waiting to feel that instinctual urge to kill any and all vampires...but it was gone. The Sun Curse must have been responsible for that too. Yet another way they manipulated us.

I looked to Jordan, waiting for him to step forward and

take the lead, but he gestured for me to respond. His faith in me gave my strength, and I smiled and gripped the vampire's hand. "I'm Stella, alpha female of the Leo pack, and this is my mate, Jordan."

Damn, it felt good to say that out loud.

Jordan grinned at me, and then reached out to shake Ferdinand's hand next. "We look forward to working with you on this truce."

Things happened quickly after that. I took Roxandra's spell book, figuring it was safest with us, while the Leos gathered the wounded and Debra prepared a portal outside that would take us back to Daybreak. Once the house was empty, Jordan set the interior on fire and held me close as we watched Roxandra's body burn.

"It's finally over." He closed his eyes as a tremor ran through him. "I'm free."

CHAPTER TWENTY-FOUR

"THANK you all for coming tonight to honor my lovely alpha female, Stella," Jordan said into the mic while he gazed out at the crowd gathered before him. "I'm so honored she chose to be my mate, and that she's agreed to help me lead the Leo pack. Since coming here a month ago, Stella has helped me stop the threat to our people and negotiated a truce with the vampires, while also working with our teachers and kids to make our community even stronger." He took my hand and gave me a bright smile. "With Stella by my side, I know we will make this pack the best it can be —a shining example to all of the other Zodiac Wolves, showing we can change and grow into something bigger and better no matter what happened in our past." He brought my hand to his lips and kissed it, then handed me the mic.

"When I first found out Jordan was my mate, I was scared and hesitant. The Leo pack had taken a lot from me and I didn't think I would ever be able to get over that. But coming here and meeting all of you really opened my eyes and made me realize that was the Leo pack of the past, not the present. Jordan is not his father. He is not the previous alpha. He is so much better. I couldn't be happier to be his mate and be your alpha female." I raised my champagne glass. "To the Leos!"

Dozens of other glasses raised in the air while people shouted out, "To the Leos!" We all toasted and drank, and then I passed the mic off to Ana, who was hosting this party at the park outside her restaurant.

"Thank you Jordan and Stella. I know I for one can't wait to see what's next for our pack. But now it's time to party!"

The crowd cheered and then the band started playing music. Some people paired off to dance, while others went to get some of Ana's amazing food, and a few came up to congratulate us on our mating. In the Ophiuchus pack we had a tradition of having a big celebration when the alpha found his mate, and I'd asked Jordan if we could do something similar for the Leos. He'd jumped at the idea, eager to show me off to everyone. Maybe a little too eager, if I was honest, but I couldn't complain.

The last few weeks had passed in a blur. After negotiating the truce with the vampires, I returned to my cottage in Coronis and packed all my things to officially move into Jordan's house and take my place as the Leo pack's alpha female. I'd also started working at the local elementary school as a consultant and sometimes substitute teacher, which I loved. It let me work with kids again, while also giving me plenty of time to help Jordan manage the pack. Of course, the best part was waking up beside Jordan every morning and coming home to him at night.

Once some of the pack members finished congratulating us, Ayla and Kaden walked over. Or rather, Kaden walked, with his hand protectively on Ayla's back, while she waddled over. She was seven months pregnant and glowing with happiness.

"Congratulations, you two," Ayla said. "We're just so happy for you both."

I pulled Ayla into a hug. "Thank you. You look good."

"You do too," Ayla said, grinning at me. "The Arizona sun is doing wonderful things to your skin. You look killer with a tan."

"And how's my little niece or nephew?" I asked.

Ayla rubbed her large bump. "Hiccuping again. I swear, it never stops!"

"Thanks for coming tonight," Jordan said, giving Ayla a hug. Then he reached out and offered Kaden a hand. After a moment's hesitation, my brother shook it.

"You two aren't going to go after each other again, are you?" I asked, shooting Kaden a glare.

"Not tonight," Kaden said with a wry grin. "Believe it or not, I think being here is good for you, and even better for the Leo pack. We miss you back in Coronis though."

"I miss you guys too," I said. "But I'm happy here."

"Good." Kaden looked to Jordan, his eyes turning icy. "But if you ever hurt my sister, I *will* come after you."

Jordan rolled his eyes. "There's the Kaden we know and love."

"If Jordan hurts me, I'm perfectly capable of kicking his ass myself," I said.

"I suppose," Kaden grumbled.

"We're going to get some food," Ayla said, grabbing Kaden's arm. "I heard the burritos are amazing and this baby is starving. We'll catch up more later."

After they wandered off toward the food tables, we were surrounded by more Leos wanting to talk to us and congratulate us, and when there was a short lull, Wesley approached. Jordan squeezed my hand as his half-brother, the Cancer pack alpha, approached and everyone around us went quiet.

"You came," Jordan said, a little surprised.

"Of course I did." Wesley gave Jordan one of those manly back-patting hugs, which Jordan returned. All around us, I heard people whispering and saw many faces looking on. The Cancer and Leo packs had been at war for as long as anyone could remember, but now their alphas were brothers. Everyone wanted to see how this would play out. Wesley gave me a quick hug next. "I had to come and give you my congratulations in person."

"I think this is the first time in decades that a Cancer alpha has come to visit the Leos," Jordan said. "In case you're wondering why everyone is staring."

Wesley laughed. "It is strange to be here, but a good kind of strange."

Jordan grinned. "Our fathers are probably rolling in their graves at this very moment, which just makes it even better."

"No kidding. But we're family now, so hopefully we'll be visiting each other a lot from now on."

"We would love that," I said.

Wesley looked back and forth between us, shaking his head. "I still can't believe you two ended up together."

"Watch out," Jordan said. "You'll be next if you aren't careful."

"I'm not sure that's in the cards." His smile faltered and his gaze looked past us, at someone in the crowd.

I turned and spotted Mira, Ayla's best friend, clutching a baby in one arm while carrying a plate of food in the other. Her hair was pulled back from her pretty face, and she wore a cute sundress. Was there some history there, between the two of them? I really liked Mira, who'd remained strong over the last few months despite losing her mate and having a baby at the same time. And Wesley seemed like the kind of guy who would step up to the plate to be a dad. Maybe the two of them had a chance.

"If you want something, you have to go after it." Jordan said with a knowing grin. "That's what I did, and look where it got me."

I scoffed and punched Jordan lightly in the shoulder. "Yeah, but maybe don't go after it the same way Jordan did. That backfired terribly."

Jordan grunted. "We got there in the end. That's all that matters."

"Whatever Jordan did, I'll aim to do the opposite," Wesley said with a laugh.

After Wesley left, we received another unusual visitor— the vampire Killian. He was unbelievably beautiful, and it was hard not to stare at him as he approached. But unlike every other time I'd met him, I no longer felt the instinctual response to tear his throat out. It was gone now that the Sun Curse was broken.

"It's good to see you again," I said to Killian. "Thanks for coming."

"It is truly my honor," he said, dropping into a formal bow. "I offer you my sincerest congratulations on your mating, and my deepest thanks for breaking the Sun Curse and negotiating a truce with the vampires."

"We're happy we could help bring peace to our people," I said.

Jordan nodded. "If anyone knows what it's like to be controlled and manipulated by the Sun Witches, it's me. I didn't want your people to suffer that way any longer."

"The two of you have started a new era. One of peace. I've been in contact with the other vampire Houses and they've all agreed to uphold the truce. Some of the Houses might even wish to be your allies someday. Either way, we are all in your debt."

"We would be happy to forge new alliances," I said, and was rather proud of myself for sounding so diplomatic. I was seriously killing this alpha female job.

After Killian left, I could tell we were about to be swarmed by more people but I needed a break. I grabbed

Jordan's hand and dragged him toward the food tables. "Come on. I need some tacos."

We got in line and piled up our plates with food, then went to find our table. Debra and Griffin were already seated there, eating their own food, along with Brea. My footsteps slowed as we approached. I'd seen the Sun Witch before from a distance, and up close she was even more intimidating, but when Jordan introduced us, she smiled.

"It's nice to meet you in person," Brea said, shaking my hand. "Thank you for taking care of Roxandra for us."

"It was our pleasure," I said with a slightly feral grin.

"Now that she's been dealt with, we can start your training," she said to Jordan.

"I've already learned a lot," he replied. "Stella's been helping me."

I shrugged. "I've done the best I can, but he really needs a Sun Witch to help him with the more advanced spells."

"Yes, it's impressive how much you've been able to teach him," Brea said.

"What about Griffin?" Jordan asked. "Can you train him too?"

Brea glanced over at Griffin, who perked up at the sound of his name. "You've been exhibiting signs of magic as well, haven't you?"

"Um," he started, glancing at me like he was asking permission. I nodded. "I've set things on fire a few times by accident."

It was true. Just the other day, Griffin had gotten frustrated during one of our tracking sessions, and he'd lit a bush on fire. He might not have control over his sun magic yet, but he was turning into a fine tracker. He listened well and had a keen nose, and he only had to learn things once to integrate them. I had no doubt he'd be a master at tracking soon.

He'd been hanging out a lot at Jordan's house lately too, and we spent many nights together all playing video games. The fact that he wasn't running off by himself all the time made Debra much happier too.

While the others continued chatting, I excused myself to get up and get a margarita. I waved at Madison and Mira, who were chatting together at another table, and planned to speak to them later.

"Stella!" Larkin launched herself into my arms and hugged me tight. "I'm going to miss you so much. You have to promise to visit me back in Coronis sometime."

I hugged her back. "Of course I will. I still have to visit my grump of a brother and make sure he isn't scaring everyone off with his scowling and growling. And Ayla will be having her baby soon, and they'll probably need help with that. Afterward, I can just come to see you, and we can catch up on the books we're reading. Or you know, you could come visit me here anytime."

She blinked back tears. "I knew this was going to happen when you left, but I am really happy for you. I told you that enemies to lovers was the hottest trope, after all."

"Yes, you were right. That reminds me. There's someone here you absolutely have to meet. You're going to love her."

I searched for Moumi in the crowd. She was talking to a

few of the other younger Leo members, and when I called her name, she quickly said goodbye and walked over.

"Hey, Moumi, this is Larkin, my Moon Witch friend who loves romance novels as much as we do."

Moumi's eyes lit up. "Nice to meet you, Larkin," she said and extended her hand. "I own the bookstore here in Daybreak."

"Woah," Larkin said. "That's so cool. Owning a cozy little bookstore is the ultimate reader fantasy. I would love to see it sometime."

"You can come by anytime." Moumi turned to smile at me. "That reminds me, I got the sequel to *Of Swords And Snow* in today, so you can pick it up next time you come by."

"Oh my goddess, I'm dying to read that one," Larkin said, her voice rising to a squeak. "I loved the first one."

"Me too!" Moumi said.

I could tell the two of them were going to be fast friends, so I got my margarita and left them to chat about the other books they'd been reading lately. Many Leos stopped me to introduce themselves and congratulate me on my way back to my table, and everyone was overwhelmingly kind and accepting. I couldn't believe how quickly they'd accepted me and made me one of their own. Despite all my initial hesitations and prejudices, I'd come to realize that, once given a chance, Leos truly did have the biggest hearts.

"There you are," Jordan said, wrapping an arm around my waist as I approached. "Care to dance?"

"Sure, after I drink this margarita."

Jordan suddenly stiffened beside me, and I turned to see

Ethan approaching. He looked as handsome as ever tonight, but he'd never made my pulse race like Jordan did.

"Hello, Ethan," Jordan said in a tone that was anything but friendly.

Ethan only smiled, as if Jordan's attitude just amused him. "I'm so very happy for you both," he said, embracing me in a warm hug. I could practically feel the air heating up as Jordan imagined setting Ethan on fire.

"Thank you," I said.

Ethan offered his hand to Jordan, who reluctantly shook it. "Good to see you, Jordan."

We exchanged a few more awkward pleasantries, and then Jordan's displeasure turned into a full-on glare as Ethan walked away.

I nudged him in the side. "Stop it. There was never anything between us."

Jordan let out a low growl. "Maybe, but I know he wanted more with you."

"He did, but it was never going to work out between us. Besides, ever since I met you, you were the only one I wanted. No matter how much I tried to deny it."

Jordan dropped the glare and flashed me a cocky grin. "And who could blame you?"

I rolled my eyes. "I take back everything I just said."

"Too late." He dragged me close and kissed me. "You're my mate now and everyone knows it."

I let out a dramatic sigh. "I guess you really can't fight fate."

He gripped me around the waist and dragged me close. "No, but why would you want to?"

Before I could answer, he pulled me in for a kiss, and several people around us let out a cheer. I laughed against his lips as he suddenly lowered me into a dip, showing off for the crowd. And for the first time in months, instead of rejecting my fate, I embraced it with open arms.

WATER FATED

MIRA & WESLEY

CHAPTER ONE

BEING a single mom was a lot like being a really exhausted superhero.

Case in point: I was dragging my large suitcase across the frozen ground with one hand while pushing Adriana in her stroller in the other hand, while simultaneously juggling her diaper bag on my arm plus a gigantic bag of presents for Ayla and her baby. How? I had no idea. This kind of coordination had never been possible before I became a widow and a mother, but now I was a freaking expert at doing ten things at once—and doing everything on my own.

"Thank you so much for coming to get us," I said to Larkin, who stood waiting for me in the ice-covered front yard. She was bundled up in a big poofy jacket that only made her look even more like a kid. Sometimes it was hard to forget she wasn't really one.

"It's no problem at all." She gave me a big smile, which

highlighted the cute freckles on her nose. "I'm happy to help since Ayla is too pregnant to teleport anyone these days. Here, let me take that." She reached for my suitcase.

"Thanks. I had no idea that all Moon Witches could teleport."

"We can teleport to Lunatera and that's it, thanks to this tattoo." She raised her hand and showed me a moon tattoo on her finger that matched the one I'd seen on Ayla before. "But we can open portals to Lunatera for other people too, and from there, we can open another portal back to anywhere on Earth that we've been before. It's like teleporting but not as fast, and a bit more work."

"We really appreciate it." I checked on Adriana, but she was happily bundled up in her stroller and babbling away.

"Are you all set?" Larkin asked.

I glanced back at the house where I'd been living ever since I'd joined the Pisces pack here in Alaska. It was cute and cozy, but it was Aiden's parents' home, and I still felt like a guest there. I had a bedroom I'd once shared with Aiden, and that was it. Now all it did was remind me that he was gone. I was eager to get away from it—and my in-laws—for a few days.

I turned back to Larkin and plastered on a smile. "Yes, we're ready."

She raised her hand and said a few words I didn't understand, opening a shimmering silver portal in front of us. "Go on in."

I took a deep breath and pushed the stroller through,

then let it out once we were on the other side, standing on a beautiful beach with a large full moon hanging low over us. I'd never been to Lunatera before, even though I had a tiny bit of Moon Witch blood in my veins. I could summon some moonlight to lighten up a dark room, but that was about it. There had never been any reason for me to visit before, nor any time, but now I found myself wishing I could see more of it. Someday maybe, when Adriana was older.

Larkin stepped through, dragging my suitcase, and the portal closed behind her.

I listened to the tranquil lap of waves while a light breeze tickled my hair. The weather here was warmer than it had been back in Alaska. "It's so beautiful."

"It is."

Larkin allowed me a few moments to soak it all in before she opened the next portal. I adjusted the bags on my arms and pushed Adriana through it, feeling a little tingle on my skin as the magic touched me, and then I was standing outside of Ayla and Kaden's large house on the edge of a forest. A few snowflakes hit my face, but the ground wasn't covered yet, which made me think it had just started snowing.

"Kaden said it was going to snow today," Larkin said after she came through the portal and closed it behind her. "I didn't think it would be until later though."

The front door opened and a very pregnant Ayla beamed at us. "You're here!"

I maneuvered the stroller up the stairs and then gave

Ayla a big hug. "I wouldn't miss it! You were such a huge help to me after I had Adriana, and I want to be there for you too."

"Come inside, both of you," Ayla said, stepping back. "I've got the fire going, and I'll make us some hot chocolate."

"No, no, I'll do it," I said, after setting down my things. I got Adriana out of her stroller and set her down on the floor. "You need to rest, and I still remember where everything is. This is why I'm here after all."

"Fine, but only because moving is a struggle at the moment," Ayla said, before sinking into a comfortable armchair with a groan.

While Larkin took my bags up to my room, I set about making hot chocolate for the three of us. I'd stayed with Ayla and Kaden after I had Adriana when the grief of losing Aiden combined with the post-pregnancy hormone crash and the difficulties of being a new mom all got to be too much for me. I would forever be in their debt for helping me out during that time, and now it was my turn to help them. Ayla was supposed to have her baby any day now, and she had no parents to help her out. Sure, she had Celeste, the Moon Witch High Priestess, but they didn't have that kind of relationship. As Ayla's oldest and closest friend, it was my duty and honor to help her with whatever I could during this time. Plus I was just really freaking excited that she was going to be a mom too.

When the hot chocolate was ready, the three of us sat down by the fireplace, while Adriana crawled across the floor and played with some of the toys I'd brought.

"Mm, this is exactly what I needed," Larkin said, as she took a sip of her hot chocolate.

"Me too. Thanks, Mira." Ayla smiled at me over her mug. "We haven't really had a chance to just sit and catch up for a while. How are things in the Pisces pack?"

I tried to keep the smile pinned on my face, but any warmth I'd felt before evaporated just like that. I'd hoped that I could avoid talking about this, but both Larkin and Ayla waited expectantly for me to answer.

"Fine," I said and took a sip of my hot chocolate to avoid having to say anything else.

"Wow," Ayla said. "Tell your face that."

"Really. It's fine, I'm just tired, keeping up with Adriana and everything."

"We've been friends for years. Do you really think I don't know when you're lying? Come on, what's going on Mira?"

"Is something wrong with the Pisces pack?" Larkin asked.

"No, nothing like that." I closed my eyes for a moment before beginning. "The Pisces pack has been nothing but kind and welcoming to me. Their town in Alaska is so beautiful sometimes I can't believe it's real. But everything there reminds me of Aiden. I only moved there because I was mated to him, and now that he's gone..." My voice wavered and I had to stop a moment to compose myself. "I'm just a bit lonely, that's all."

Larkin made a sympathetic noise. "You must miss him terribly."

"I'm not sure if my heart will ever heal from the pain of losing my mate." My chest hurt just saying the words out loud, but I looked down at Adriana, who'd crawled over to me and was offering one of her toys. She smiled, all gums and chubby cheeks, and the ache eased a tiny bit. "The only thing that makes it bearable is knowing he lives on in Adriana."

Ayla sipped her hot chocolate as I spoke, her eyebrows drawn down in a frown. "Is there anyone in the pack you're close to? Anyone you can talk to?"

I shook my head. "No, I haven't been able to connect with anyone. My in-laws are nice, and I'm grateful to them for everything, but they really only care about their grand-daughter." I felt awful admitting that out loud. They'd done their best to make me feel included, but it was always clear that Adriana came first for them. "They can be a little controlling, too. They're always telling me how Adriana should be raised. And there's no escape since I'm a guest in their home."

"I'm sorry," Ayla said. "I had no idea it was so hard for you."

"Don't be sorry. I know they mean well, and they're grieving too. Aiden was their only child and his loss was very hard on them. Adriana is all they have left too." The mood in the room had darkened, and I straightened up, waving the words away. "But enough of that. I'm just relieved to get away for a while and visit my friends. I'm sure all I need is a little vacation and I'll be as good as new. How about you both? How have things been going?"

Ayla put her mug down on the coffee table, groaning as she leaned forward, and then let out a contented sigh as she settled back onto her chair. "Not much is new. We're just waiting for the baby to arrive. I'm getting pretty impatient, but my due date isn't for another few days." She rubbed her hands along her sides and pulled a face. "I can hardly move at this point, and it makes it hard to get up and pee. Which I have to do constantly."

I chuckled softly while picking Adriana up off the floor and setting her on my lap. "I remember those days. But it'll all be worth it once the baby is here."

"I can't wait," Ayla said with a sigh. "I just wish he or she would hurry up already."

"How about you, Larkin?" I asked.

"I've been really busy," she said, as she stretched her legs out toward the fire. "I'm trying to find a place for the Moon Witches to settle now that many have agreed to return to Earth. At the moment they're staying here with the Ophiuchus pack, but it's so crowded. We need our own town that we can settle into."

"Maybe you should talk to Ethan about it," Ayla said with a little gleam in her eye. Everyone knew Larkin had a crush on the Libra alpha. "He might have some good ideas since he works in real estate."

Larkin stared very hard at the mug in her hands as a blush rose up her cheeks. "Maybe I'll ask him sometime. But one of the biggest problems we have is that the witches have been living in Lunatera so long, none of them have any money."

"Oh, that does make it trickier," I said.

"Not only that," Larkin said, eyes blazing as she sat up straighter. She must have been saving this up for someone who would listen to her. "They have no credit, no IDs, no addresses, and no history on Earth to use in the human world. A lot of them are really struggling to adapt to modern times too. They'd been in Lunatera for decades or even centuries, and there are so many new technological advances and things that they can't easily pick up on. I'm afraid they're going to struggle and want to give up on returning to Earth at all."

"I'd love to help in any way I can," I said. "Not just while I'm here, but when I go back home too. I can do some research on places to live, or answer their questions about how to use a tablet, or whatever else you need."

"Thank you so much," Larkin said. "I'd love that."

I opened my mouth to tell her that it was no trouble, but before I could, Ayla stiffened, putting a hand to her stomach. Her brows knitted and she sucked in a sharp breath.

"What's wrong?" I asked. "Are you having a contraction?"

"No," Ayla said, but it came out strained.

I set Adriana down on the floor by her toys again. "You are."

"Okay, you're right. It might just be a fake one though. I've had some before and thought that it was the baby coming, but it turned out to be a false alarm. I've been having these since this morning, and they're just getting worse, but I wasn't sure if it was real this time."

"That one didn't look fake." I got up from my seat to put my hands on Ayla's shoulders. "I think you're in labor, and we need to get you to the midwife."

"We should wait a bit," Ayla said. "I don't want to bother her again if it's just another false alarm."

I frowned, rubbing her shoulders. She looked so uncomfortable and I wanted to argue, but I knew how stubborn Ayla could be when she wanted. Just as I opened my mouth to ask her to reconsider, she stiffened again, eyes going wide with pain.

"Maybe you're right. I think they're getting worse. Can you hand me my phone? I'll text Kaden to let him know."

I looked around for a few seconds, trying to find Ayla's phone. It was over on the kitchen island, and I swooped down to grab it and hand it to her. She sent off a text just as another contraction hit her. They were definitely getting closer together now.

We rushed around getting everything Ayla would need to take with her, while she groaned from her spot by the fire, and then Kaden burst into the room. "I'm here! Is it time?"

"It's time," I said, shoving Ayla's overnight bag in his hand, while Larkin took hold of Ayla's hand and helped her to her feet.

"Larkin, would you go to Lunatera and tell Celeste that it's time, please?" Ayla asked as she and Kaden headed for the front door.

"I'm on it!" Larkin replied. She gave Ayla a quick hug, wished her luck, and then vanished, leaving behind only a few silver sparkles that quickly dissipated.

Ayla slipped her shoes on and then glanced back at me. "Oh, and Mira? Could you please call Stella and Jordan to let them know I'm in labor? Wesley too?"

I hesitated. I had Wesley's number saved in my phone, of course. I thought about reaching out sometimes, just to hear a familiar voice, but I never quite managed to do it. But this wasn't about me. It was about Ayla. "I'll call them right now and let them know."

"Thank you." She bit her lip, hesitating at the door.

I hurried up to Ayla and hugged her tight. "Everything is going to be fine. You're so strong, and your baby is too."

Ayla nodded and smiled, but it didn't quite reach her eyes. I knew she was worried about the pregnancy and about the baby, but she had a lot of good people looking out for her. And everything I'd said was true—Ayla was the strongest person I knew.

"Good luck." I kissed her cheek before ushering them out the door. "I'll take care of everything here."

Kaden helped Ayla out of the door, and I closed it behind them. I sighed, turning around to look at the empty house. Adriana made a questioning noise, crawling toward me, and I leaned down to pick her up.

"Don't worry about Ayla. She's going to be just fine, and then you'll have a new friend." I ran my hand over her dark hair and she looked up at me, her brown eyes wide like she understood what I was saying. "Would you like that? A friend?"

Adriana babbled in response with what I assumed was a

yes, but who knew with babies? She could be asking me for a snack, for all I knew. I put her in the high chair in the kitchen, which was already set up in preparation for the new baby, and got out some of the baby puffs I'd brought with me. That would keep her happy while I made my phone calls.

I pulled my phone out of my pocket and typed in Wesley's name. *Might as well get the hardest one done first,* I thought and pressed the call button.

Please go to voicemail, I thought as the phone rang once, twice, and then again. But of course, Wesley picked up.

"Mira?" He asked, instead of saying hello. "Are you okay?"

"Oh, I'm fine," I said, blushing. Why was I blushing? All he'd done was ask if I was okay. "I'm calling about Ayla. She's in labor, and we wanted to let you know. Kaden just took her to the midwife."

"Thanks for letting me know. I'll be there as soon as I can."

"Okay. Good. Um, I guess I'll see you soon then. Safe travels."

"See you soon," he said and hung up.

I sat down on the couch, still flushed. I hadn't expected him to drop everything and come right away, but I should have because it was exactly the kind of thing Wesley would do. I also should have realized that coming here would mean seeing Wesley again too, but I'd been trying to avoid any thoughts of him over the last few months. Now there was hardly any time to prepare myself to see him again. But it was fine. We were both here for Ayla and the baby, and that was it. Nothing was going to happen, because nothing ever happened with Wesley. Which was exactly what I wanted. Right?

Right.

CHAPTER TWO

I TURNED the light off in the guest bedroom and pulled the covers back on the bed, ready to crash. Ayla had arrived safely at the midwife and this time she definitely was in labor. Kaden had relayed that the midwife said it could take all night or even longer, so there was no use staying up and waiting.

I thought about staying up anyway, but I was exhausted. I'd spent the afternoon cleaning up the house so everything would be all ready when they got home and then gave Adriana her dinner and a bath. She'd been a little fussy when I put her down in her travel cot for the night, not used to being anywhere but our home in the Pisces pack, but finally she was asleep and I was ready to crash too. Kaden assured me that he would call if anything changed, and I had my volume turned up so it would wake me up.

Just as I sat down on the mattress, a knock sounded from

the front door. I paused. Who would be stopping by this late?

I crept past Adriana's cot and headed downstairs to look through the window right beside the door. Wesley stood on the porch, gazing out at the forest. My heart leaped and then sank into my stomach. I swallowed hard and unlocked the door.

Wesley turned, his blue eyes tired and his clothes rumpled, but looking handsome as always. His brown hair had a slightly windswept look to it, and his skin shone with a healthy tan from being outside by the sea so much. My breath caught at the sight of him in front of me, my knees suddenly weak. I gripped the side of the doorframe for support.

"Hey," I said, and hoped it didn't sound as nervous as I felt. "I didn't think you'd be here so fast."

Wesley didn't respond right away, his eyes slowly sliding over my face, down to my neck, and then all the way to my feet. It had been months since I'd seen him last, but here he was, standing in front of me. My heart picked up its pace, pounding in my chest, and I hoped he couldn't hear it.

As his eyes landed back on mine, there was a sharp tug in my chest. It was so strong, I had to plant my feet to stop myself from stepping forward. I looked away, but the over-whelming desire to go to him remained.

Wesley cleared his throat. "I hopped on the first plane I could."

"Ayla's still in labor, but you can come inside if you'd like." Wait, why did I say that? Being alone with Wesley was the last thing I wanted. But what else was I supposed to do—slam the door in his face? This was his sister's house, after all.

"Thanks." He carried a large duffel bag on his shoulder, which he set carefully on the floor, before taking his heavy jacket off and hanging it up. I tried not to watch him, but my gaze kept going back to him no matter how hard I tried to focus on anything else. He wore a charcoal sweater that clung to his chest, along with jeans that fit him perfectly, and it was really hard not to stare at him. I'd had a crush on Wesley my entire life, as long as I could remember, from back when he was my best friend's older brother. But now he was a man, and the alpha of his pack, and he radiated power and masculinity in a way that made my mouth water.

Stop it, I told myself. *You are a widow and a mom and Wesley is off limits!*

"Do you want some water?" I asked awkwardly as we stood by the front door and avoided looking at each other.

"No, I'm good, thanks." He put his hands in his jeans pockets and cleared his throat again. "How is Ayla doing?"

"She's fine. The baby is just taking its sweet time. I just checked in with Kaden a few hours ago and he said it could be a while."

"I'm glad she has so many friends and family here to look after her. Including you."

"And now you," I said, feeling the flush returning to my cheeks.

Wesley grinned. "And now me. Speaking of babies, how is Adriana doing?"

"Good," I said, my stupid heart softening at Wesley's question. I didn't expect him to think of me or Adriana at a time like this, but that was Wesley. Always worrying about everyone. That was why he made a good alpha. "She's asleep right now. Are you sure you don't want anything? Maybe some tea?"

Wesley shrugged. "Some tea would be nice, I suppose. Thank you."

We stepped into the kitchen and I immediately headed for the kettle. I was grateful for something to keep my hands busy, but as I filled it from the tap and set it on the stove, the silence became more deafening.

Wesley's eyes followed me, and I became very aware that I was wearing only a thin black nightgown with nothing on underneath it. No wonder he'd been staring at me. I wanted to hug my hands to my body and hide myself, but that would just draw attention to my lack of proper clothing. I glanced down and saw my nipples, which were extra large due to breastfeeding, on full display through the thin fabric. How embarrassing.

I kept my eyes down, away from Wesley, and hoped he couldn't see me blushing. I felt like a kid again with a hopeless crush on my best friend's older brother, following him around and waiting for him to notice me. I hadn't felt like that for a long time, not since I'd been mated to Aiden. But now those feelings were back and stronger than ever before.

Finally, the silence became too much to bear and I had to say something. "How are you doing?"

"I'm fine," Wesley said, leaning against the doorframe

with his arms crossed. "I've spent the last few months moving the Cancer pack off the island and back to our village now that the threat from the Sun Witches is over."

A twinge of bittersweet happiness went through me. I was glad my old pack members were able to return to their home, but I missed it too. "That's great news," I said and hoped he couldn't hear the sadness in my tone. I turned away and busied myself with pulling mugs and tea bags out of the cupboard. "I bet it was hard to be in hiding for so long."

"It was," Wesley said. "You know, you're always welcome to come back anytime."

I wrapped my hand around the handle of one of the mugs and squeezed a bit to ground myself. "I'm not a Cancer anymore. My parents are dead. I have nothing there."

"You have me," Wesley said, his voice low and much closer than before. I hadn't even heard him cross the room, but when I turned around he was right behind me.

"Wesley—" I started but stopped as he took my hand and unwrapped my fingers from the mug. He threaded his fingers through mine and leaned against the counter.

"I feel this undeniable pull toward you." His bright blue eyes stared into mine, and I worried I might drown in them if I didn't look away. "Do you feel it too?"

I nodded before I could even think about lying, my heart pounding in my chest as I breathed in his scent. Salt and sea and shore pine. It was as familiar and comforting as I remembered. He smelled like *home*.

"I'm pretty sure we both know what that means," Wesley said.

The hope in his voice made my heart twinge, but I finally managed to look away. "I can't do this. I already had a mate."

Wesley's hand tightened around mine. "What happened to your mate was a tragedy, but it doesn't mean that you have to spend the rest of your life alone. Aiden was in the past, but I could be your future if you'll let me."

I pulled my hand away and went back to making our tea. "I had a teenage crush on you, but that's it. I'm an adult now, with responsibilities. I have a kid to look after." I sniffed and began pouring the water into the mugs. "Why would you want a single mom anyway? You're handsome, smart, and a powerful alpha. You could have anyone."

He moved up behind me again, setting his hands on my hips. His breath tickled my ears as he leaned in close. "The only one I want is you."

I set the kettle down and spun around, shocked by his words. "What?"

Wesley's hands stayed on my hips like they belonged there. "I don't care that you had a mate before, or that you have a kid. I want you, and everything that comes with that." He dipped his head, his lips so close to mine. "You belong with the Cancer pack. Your daughter too."

I sucked in a breath at his words. A desperate, hungry part of me wanted to give in. But it wasn't that easy. "Adriana is a Pisces. She can't—"

Wesley lifted his hand and touched my lips, silencing me. "It's okay if you aren't ready."

He stroked his thumb against my jaw and I shivered. It felt so good, and it had been so long since anyone had touched me like this. I swayed in closer to him, that pull between us growing stronger and stronger. I wanted to kiss him, to touch him back. I braced my other hand on the counter, trying to stop myself from reaching for him. I knew if I gave in, there'd be no turning back.

"I'll wait for you," Wesley said. "As long as you need."

I lifted my head toward him, waiting for him to kiss me and undo me completely, but he didn't close that final distance between us. Instead, he took my hand and pressed his lips to the back of it, which was somehow even worse, especially when I saw the look on his face. Like it pained him to hold back, but he had no other choice. He would never cross that line, not until I said it was okay, because that was the kind of man that Wesley was.

He let me go, leaving me reeling. I leaned back hard against the counter, watching as he took a few steps back. *I should say something,* I thought, but my mouth and my brain both seemed to have stopped functioning properly.

"It's late," he said. "I'd better get going."

I followed him out of the kitchen like a lost puppy, abandoning our tea. He slid his arms into his jacket and wouldn't meet my eyes as he leaned over to grab his duffel bag.

"Where are you going?" I asked. "Aren't you staying here with us?"

Wesley smiled sadly and shook his head. "I don't think that would be a good idea."

He opened the front door and paused, like he wanted to say something else, or maybe was waiting for me to tell him to stay. It would be easy. I could make up an excuse like I didn't like the idea of staying here alone. But then what? There was no future for us. The idea alone was too wild for me to even consider. And tomorrow, when his mind was clear, he'd realize that too.

"Good night, Wesley," I said.

He dipped his head in response, and then he was gone. I closed the door and leaned against it, listening to the sound of a car starting and then driving away. It felt like a part of my heart went with him.

Maybe I should go after him. I eyed the keys to Ayla's car hanging on the hook by the door. It would be easy enough to chase him down and tell him to come back.

Upstairs, Adriana let out a shrill, loud cry. I sighed and shook my head. What was I thinking? That I'd run out into the night and chase down someone who wasn't even my mate and beg him to stay here with me? I couldn't leave her, and it would be silly to pretend that I was the old Mira, who could do things like that. I was a mom now and Adriana would always come first. Getting involved with Wesley would only complicate things, especially since he was the Cancer alpha. Adriana was a Pisces, and so I had to be one too.

I sighed and headed upstairs to settle Adriana and give her some milk. She kept crying until I picked her up and settled her in my arms. She made an expression that reminded me so much of Aiden that my throat tightened with emotion. I'd already lost a mate once. It didn't matter that the mate bond between us had been created by the Sun Witches, it felt real to us at the time. Losing him had been like losing part of my soul, and I wasn't sure I could ever get close to anyone again after going through that. Not even Wesley.

Adriana was asleep again, and I pressed a kiss to her tiny nose. "We're going to be fine together, just you and me. Isn't that right, my sweet girl?"

She didn't answer, of course. I looked out the window at the snow still falling and hoped that it was true.

CHAPTER THREE

IN THE MORNING I received a bunch of texts letting me know the baby had arrived and everyone was doing well. Adriana and I spent the day inside since the snow had fallen all night, leaving huge, dense drifts of it all around the village. Eventually, Ayla told me she was ready for visitors, so after lunch, I packed Adriana up in our borrowed car and drove to the midwife's house. I couldn't wait to meet the new baby and check in on Ayla too.

I knocked on the door, holding Adriana in one arm and my diaper bag in the other, and was surprised when Stella opened it.

"Mira! You're here, come in!" She hugged me gingerly, careful not to crush Adriana between us, and ushered me into the midwife's house. We stepped into a welcoming living room, where Jordan was standing by the fireplace. As I entered, he gave me a little wave, and I gave him one in return. I was still surprised about Stella being mated to

Jordan. I never would have expected the two of them to be mates, but there was no denying that they seemed to be happy now.

Stella smiled down at Adriana. "Isn't she just the cutest thing? Can I hold her?"

"Please," I said.

Stella took her gently, bouncing her a little, and Adriana giggled. "She's gotten so big! And she looks just like Aiden."

"Yes, she does. How are things going in the Leo pack?"

Stella held Adriana closer to her so she could focus on me. "Everything is going well, much to my surprise."

"Stella's selling herself short," Jordan said, smiling at Stella. "She's really settled in as my alpha female and is also working at the local elementary school."

"That's great," I said, feeling both happy and envious, all at once. They both seemed so...content. Even when I'd been mated, I'd never felt that way. Maybe because my mate bond had been a lie. Would a real one feel different?

"Hey everyone." Kaden stepped into the hallway, carrying a small bundle in his arms close to his chest. As he drew closer, I saw brilliant blue eyes and fuzzy white hair. "I'd like to introduce you all to my son, Jack."

"Oh, Kaden." Stella's eyes immediately filled with tears and she wiped at them, no doubt thinking of her good friend, Jack. Like Aiden, he'd given his life in the final battle against the Sun Witches. "That's the perfect name."

"Hello, little nephew," Jordan said, peering down at the baby.

"He's beautiful," I said, smiling at Kaden. "I'm so happy for you."

He nodded. "Ayla was asking for you. Feel free to go back and see her."

"Go," Stella said, hefting Adriana up on her hip. "I don't mind holding her while you two chat."

"Thank you." It was nice to have some help with Adriana, even if only for a few minutes.

I stepped past Kaden and knocked on the door he'd come out of. A tired, familiar voice said, "Come in," and I pushed the door open.

The midwife smiled at me while pressing a cool washcloth to Ayla's face. My beautiful friend was tired and sweaty, but she looked radiant.

"I'll give you a few minutes, but call me if you need anything," the midwife said, before leaving the room.

"How are you doing?" I asked as the door closed behind me.

"I'm tired and sore but I've never been happier in my life," Ayla said with an exhausted smile.

"You did such a good job." I kissed Ayla's forehead. "Now you just need to rest and heal. Let us do everything else."

"Sounds good to me."

I adjusted her pillows and blankets, fussing over her. "Do you have a lot more visitors coming?"

"Just Larkin and Celeste, but they should be here soon."

"What about Wesley?" I asked. "I'm surprised he's not here too."

Ayla sat up a little in bed and took a sip of water. "Oh, you just missed him. He came by really early this morning when I was still in labor. He just went back to the cabin to get some rest."

"Oh... Good."

Ayla pinned me with one of her knowing looks. "Were you hoping to see him here?"

"No!" My response was a bit too vehement and I coughed. "I mean, um, we saw each other last night."

She perked up at that. "Oh really."

I held up a hand. "Nothing happened."

"Not yet..."

"Not ever."

Ayla took my hand. "Why not? It's obvious the two of you are mates. I think you should give it a chance."

"It's not that easy," I said, giving her hand a squeeze before pulling away. "Even if I wanted to be with Wesley, I can't be a Cancer again. Not when Adriana is a Pisces."

"I understand. The moment I saw Jack, I knew I'd do anything to keep him safe. But you deserve to be happy, and Adriana wants that too." Her voice lowered. "So would Aiden."

I blinked away the sudden sting of tears. I'd spent so much time thinking about what was best for Adriana and ignoring what was best for me. But maybe having a mother who wasn't miserable *was* what was best for my daughter.

"The stars are bringing the two of you together for a reason," Ayla continued. "And the more you fight it, the more miserable you'll both be."

"You're right," I said, sniffling and swiping at my eyes. "I'll go talk to Wesley. I can't promise anything more, but we can at least talk."

"That's all I can ask for. He's staying in a cabin just outside of the village. Kaden can give you directions." She shooed me away. "Now get out of here, and don't come back until you've worked things out with my brother."

I laughed and stood up. "All right, all right, I'm going, but I'll be back in a bit. I promise."

"Don't worry about me." She settled back against her pillows. "In fact, take all the time you need. You know everyone will be fussing over Jack and me for the next few days."

"Good. You're always so busy helping everyone else. You deserve to be fussed over for a bit." I leaned over and gave her a hug. "I'll see you soon."

Hopefully, Ayla would be able to get a little bit of rest before the next visitors came. I closed Ayla's door and headed back toward the living room, where Stella was holding baby Jack, while Adriana crawled on the floor toward Jordan, who held out a small, squishy ball to her. Kaden was standing to the side speaking with his beta, Clayton, who had clearly just come from outside. His hair was dusted with snow, along with his coat and boots. Neither of them were smiling.

"The storm has gotten worse," Clayton said in a low voice. "It's moving in fast, and in a few hours we're all going to be snowed in."

"We need to make sure everyone gets to their homes and has supplies," Kaden said. "I can—"

"No." Clayton put a hand on Kaden's arm and shook his head. "You get your family home. I'll handle everything else."

Kaden clapped Clayton on the back. "Thank you. I know the town will be in good hands with you."

I chewed my lip, worried. Ayla had said that Wesley was staying in a cabin just outside of the village. Would he be out there by himself in the snow?

After Clayton left, I approached Kaden. "Can you give me directions to where Wesley is staying? I need to talk to him."

"Sure." He gave me quick directions to a spot just outside the village, and then added, "The road's a bit bumpy because we don't use that cabin very often. It's one of our older cabins and not very big or very warm. Usually Killian lives there, but he's visiting some other vampires at the moment."

"Why is Wesley staying there?" I asked, panic rising in my chest at the thought of Wesley out there alone during the storm.

"It's the only place we had available," Kaden said. "With the Moon Witches staying here, we're packed full."

"Couldn't he stay at your place?"

Kaden hesitated. "He could, but he asked to stay somewhere else."

Great. Wesley was out in the middle of nowhere in a freezing cold cabin all alone because of me. Did he even have supplies there? What if he got snowed in for days? "He probably doesn't know about the storm coming, does he?"

"I doubt it," he said. "He left before we knew how bad it was going to get."

Ayla called for Kaden, who rushed into the room to check on her like the most overprotective alpha ever. I fumbled for my phone in my pocket and dialed Wesley's number. His phone rang several times and then went to voicemail.

"He's not answering," I said to Stella and Jordan, who were watching me intently. "I need to find him and make him come back to Kaden's house before it's too late. It's my fault he's out there in the first place."

"We can watch Adriana while you go," Stella said.

"Are you sure?" I asked. "You really don't have to."

"It's no trouble at all." Stella glanced over at Jordan, who nodded. "Besides, it's good practice for us. You see... I'm pregnant. Surprise!"

"Congratulations!" I said, giving her a quick hug. "You'll make great parents I'm sure."

"Thank you," said Jordan. "We weren't expecting it to happen so quickly."

I picked up Adriana and gave her a kiss. "Mommy has to go out for a few minutes, but Auntie Stella and Uncle Jordan are going to watch you, okay? I promise I'll be back soon." I handed her to Stella again but hesitated. "Everything you need is in her diaper bag. Are you sure you'll be okay?"

"We'll be fine, I promise." Stella bounced Adriana on her hip like a natural. She'd been a kindergarten teacher before, so she was used to dealing with kids, and Adriana already seemed to love her.

"Go," Jordan said. "We'll call you if we have any trouble."

"Thank you," I said, relieved that I wouldn't have to take Adriana out into this storm. "I'll be back as soon as I can."

I gripped my coat tighter and ventured out into the storm, intent on fixing what I'd messed up last night.

CHAPTER FOUR

AS I DROVE out of town the snow really started coming down, faster than anyone expected, and once I turned where Kaden had instructed, there wasn't even a road or a set of tire tracks to follow. My borrowed car wasn't suited for this much snow, but I wasn't sure anything short of an off-road vehicle would be able to handle it either.

I slowed down, trying to pull my car through the heavier snow, but soon it was impossible to make it through. I stopped and turned my car off, staring out at the forest in front of me. There wasn't time to go back and try to find a better car to reach Wesley. I'd have to do something on my own, without my car. The thought of abandoning it gave me anxiety, but I didn't have a choice if I wanted to reach Wesley in time to bring him back to town before the storm got even worse.

I stripped out of my clothes quickly and left the keys in

the visor above the driver's side. Then I hopped out of the car, slammed the door shut, and shifted before the cold hit me too hard. My brown wolf exploded out of me and I was instantly warmer, thanks to my fur coat, but I didn't want to be out here when the storm truly hit.

I continued on toward where I thought the cabin might be, my paws sinking into the thick snow. The whole world around me was white, and I squinted my eyes and flattened my ears, but it was hard to see very far. My nose twitched, but I didn't smell anything useful. The cabin had to be nearby though, so I kept going, letting my instincts guide me.

As the wind howled around me, turning the snow into something closer to a blizzard, I wondered if I'd made a huge mistake. What was I thinking, leaving Adriana to come out here alone? I debated heading back to the car, but at this point, I wasn't sure I'd be able to find it. I spun around but saw nothing except snow-covered trees on either side of me. Where was this damn cabin?

I let out a howl, desperate and frustrated. I didn't expect anyone to answer, but to my surprise, over the sound of the wind, I heard an answering howl. One my soul instantly recognized. Wesley!

I bolted toward the sound, energy renewed. If I could just pick up on Wesley's scent, I'd be able to find him. He was close, I could feel it. I ran through the snow as fast as my four legs would take me, no longer feeling the cold. All that mattered was reaching him.

I howled again, and he answered, long and low, but a lot

closer now. I lifted my nose to the air, trying to catch his scent. There, just on the edge of the wind, a trace of salt and sea. I turned my head, trying to pinpoint it, and spotted a dark shape appearing in the distance.

Wesley's gray wolf bounded toward me, huge and majestic. Relief made my legs go weak, and I let out a soft whine as he approached, my tail wagging. He put his head against mine and nuzzled me, huffing out a pleased breath. His fur was warm and mostly dry. I leaned into him and rubbed my chin against his flank, so happy to see him that I was nearly vibrating from it.

I'd come here to talk to Wesley, but after desperately trying to find him in a snowstorm, everything seemed clear. He was my mate, and there was no way I was going to let him slip out of my fingers again. At that moment, I didn't care about pack politics or the fact that I was a widow and a single mom, all I knew was that Wesley was my true mate and I was done denying it.

I pulled back and looked him in the eyes, triggering the mate bond. The connection snapped into place immediately and felt so natural as if it had always been there and we'd finally realized it. The gaping hole in my soul, the part that was destroyed when Aiden died, was filled again with something new and wonderful, making me complete once more. I would always love Aiden and would miss him for the rest of my life, but there was room in my heart for Wesley too, I realized. I didn't have to be alone anymore.

Wesley licked my face and then nudged me forward. He jerked his head back the way he'd come from, and I dipped my head in assent, signaling I would follow. Together we ran off into the woods, and the snow-covered forest was beautiful now that I was no longer worried about finding Wesley anymore. We chased each other through the trees, dodging fallen branches and running just out of reach of each other. It had been a long time since I'd had fun like this, just running through the snow without a care in the world. My heart swelled with joy, the new mate bond thrumming strong between us.

The cabin appeared out of nowhere, a welcoming sight with bright windows and smoke coming out of the chimney. I let out a breath of relief, my ears drooping. No matter how much fun it was to chase Wesley through the snow, I was still cold down to my bones and ready to get inside.

Wesley shoved the door open in his wolf form and jerked his head for me to go in before him, and I quickly leaped over the entryway. Immediately, the warmth hit me like a wall, and I whimpered in relief. Wesley pulled the door shut with his teeth and shook his fur out before shifting back. I quickly followed suit, shivers returning the moment I was standing on two feet.

We stood, facing each other, completely naked. Wesley's eyes trailed down my body slowly, while I devoured the sight of him too. He had the body of a swimmer, with long, lean muscles and broad shoulders, and his cock was already hard and beautiful. For me.

"What were you doing out there in this storm?" Wesley asked.

"I came to find you. I was worried about you being out here all alone."

"Did you mean to activate the mate bond?" There was so much in his gaze, so much that was unsaid. He wanted this, wanted *me*, but he was holding himself back in case it had been an accident.

"I did. I've wanted you my entire life and I'm done trying to fight it." I cleared my throat. "That is, if you want me too."

Wesley closed the distance between us in response, pulling me into his arms and crushing our bodies together. His head lowered and his lips claimed mine in a kiss that had me melting against him. I was enveloped in the warmth and safety of his embrace, his scent surrounding me, his taste consuming me. Kissing Wesley was like nothing I'd felt before. Even with Aiden, it had never been this intense, and desire washed over me like an ocean wave, becoming all-consuming. Everything else faded from my mind as Wesley picked me up and wrapped my legs around his hips, his hard cock rubbing against me.

"Feel that? That's how much I want you. Not just now, but always." He pressed hot kisses along the side of my neck, making me moan. "But once I'm inside you, you're mine. I'm never letting you go. Do you understand?"

"Yes. I want that." I squeezed my legs tighter around him. "Make me yours."

With a low growl, he spun us around and carried us to a couch, then set me down on it. The fireplace crackled with heat a few feet away as he spread my legs and kneeled between them.

"You're so fucking beautiful," Wesley whispered. He took one of my hands, lifting it to his lips. He kissed each finger and pressed my palm against his cheek and nuzzled it like he was still his wolf. He was hot, practically burning up and I leaned into that heat. I wanted more and pulled him back to my lips, needing to taste him too.

He pressed me back against the couch with a firm hand and then began a long, thorough exploration of my body. I had no idea how he could hold himself back so long, with the mate bond burning inside us, begging to be sealed. All I could think of was his cock inside me, and I knew it had to be torture for him too, but Wesley was all about restraint. He took his time, dragging his tongue across my neck, my shoulders, and my breasts, until I was crying out, begging him for more. But he didn't listen, just kept moving down to my belly and my hips, kissing all my stretch marks like they were beauty marks. By the time his mouth moved to my thighs, and then between them, I was so turned on I was whimpering. When his tongue finally flicked my clit, I nearly came right then.

"Wesley!" I cried. "I need you inside me."

"I want to taste you first." His fingers traced my pussy, feeling how wet I was. "I've been dreaming of this moment for so long."

He lowered his mouth and licked me again, sliding his tongue between my folds and then up to flick my clit. The pleasure was almost overwhelming, but I couldn't stop him, didn't want to stop him. Every nerve ending in my body was alight, and my toes curled as his tongue circled my clit.

When he sucked it, I was lost. The pleasure overwhelmed me and I was shaking as I came against his mouth.

"You taste even better than I imagined," he said as he moved back up, bracing himself on his forearms and brushing his lips against mine. "Are you ready for more, my mate?"

"Yes, please." I wrapped my arms around his neck, drawing him closer. "I don't know how much longer I can wait."

He yanked me down on top of him, so I was straddling him. "Then take what's yours."

I reached between us, taking his cock in my hand. It was so hard and silky smooth, and I couldn't resist running my thumb over the tip.

Wesley's hand was tight on my hips, his fingers digging in. "Be sure, because once we do this, we can't undo it."

"I'm sure." I leaned down and pressed a kiss to his lips, then adjusted my hips so his cock slid inside me with one swift motion. It was like coming home. The mate bond snapped into place, and everything became clear. Wesley was mine, and I was his, and the rest of the world faded away. It was just us and our wolves. We didn't need anything else.

He groaned and his head fell back, but he never took his eyes off me. I started to move, slowly at first, savoring the feeling of him filling me so completely. He let me take control, setting the pace, and finding the position that made us both feel good.

It felt so fucking good, finally having him inside me. I'd

fantasized about this back when I was younger and unmated, but this was better than all of those fantasies put together. Pleasure flared hot in the pit of my stomach, and I rode him faster, wanting more friction.

As our pleasure built, his grip tightened, and soon he was helping me move, holding me down against him and thrusting up. We moved together in a rhythm as old as time itself, our bodies joined in a primal dance.

As I rode him, I felt our connection growing inside us. Wesley was the alpha and I was his female, and together we made each other stronger. Wesley must have felt it too, because his eyes were wide, staring at me with awe.

"Can you feel it?" Wesley asked as he ground my hips down on his cock. "The mate bond strengthening?"

"I feel it." The pleasure built until it was almost too much to bear, but I couldn't look away. It was the most beautiful thing I'd ever seen. "I've never felt anything like it before."

He groaned at that, and I leaned down and grabbed onto his shoulders, needing something to hold onto, to ground me in this moment as the pleasure threatened to drag me away. He wrapped his arms around me as our animal nature took over, and his teeth clamped down on my neck. He kept thrusting up as he marked me as his mate, and a mix of pain and pleasure sent me over the edge. I let out a long howl as my pussy clenched around his cock, and his movements grew wild and rough in response. I sank my teeth into his shoulder in return, and then we were both coming, shuddering and gasping as the pleasure consumed us.

Together we collapsed onto the rug in front of the fireplace, with his cock still buried inside of me. My breath and heartbeat slowed, and I snuggled closer to him, putting my head on his chest.

"My mate," he said.

"Always," I answered.

CHAPTER FIVE

WESLEY STROKED a hand through my hair and pressed a kiss to my forehead. The crackle of the fire and the howling wind outside were the only sounds for a few minutes as we caught our breath.

"Are you warmed up now?" he asked.

I nuzzled against him. "Yes, much better."

He let out a soft laugh. "I can't believe you came to find me in the middle of a snowstorm."

"I was worried about you, out here all alone by yourself with no supplies. My plan was to bring you back to Kaden's place, but you see how well that went."

"I couldn't believe it when I heard you howl. I thought I must be imagining things at first, but then I caught your scent." He tightened his arms around me. "But I'm glad you're here."

"Me too." I sat up and glanced around. I'd hardly looked around the cabin when I first came in since all I had eyes for was Wesley, but it wasn't as bad as Kaden had made it out to be. Sure, it was outdated, but it wasn't like it had holes in the roof or anything. Wesley would have been fine here on his own. But if I hadn't come looking for him, this may have never happened.

Through the windows, I could see that night had fallen, and I realized how late it had gotten. Panic shot through me at the realization that I'd left Adriana with other people all this time, and that the storm must be getting worse with each passing second.

"Oh shit," I said, scrambling to my feet. "Can I use your phone?"

Wesley frowned but got up and passed me his phone without asking why. I dialed Stella, but after a few moments of dead air, the call dropped. I pulled it away from my ear to check that it wasn't dead and saw the words *no service* flashing in the top corner.

"Of course," I muttered.

Fine. We'd have to try to get back on foot, as wolves. It would be miserable, but we could do it.

But when I opened the front door, a huge pile of snow fell through and landed on my feet, followed by freezing wind that instantly stole away any warmth I had left. The blizzard was raging, and I could barely see three feet in front of the door.

"Mira," Wesley said, coming up behind me. "There's no way we're getting out in that. We're snowed in."

"We have to try." I closed the door again and leaned against it. "They'll be worried sick about us, and I need to make sure Adriana is okay. Surely if we take it slow, we can make it back to the car."

"And then what?" Wesley pulled me away from the pile of snow beside the door. "It's not safe outside right now. Our best bet is to stay here overnight, and in the morning when the sun is out we'll be able to dig our way out and make it back to town."

"But what about Adriana?" I asked, panic rising in my stomach. "I've never spent a night away from her before, and I told Stella and Jordan I would be back."

"She's fine," Wesley wrapped an arm around me and led me back toward the fire. "I know you're worried, but Adriana is surrounded by people who will take good care of her. You'll see her tomorrow, and in the meantime, we should try to relax and enjoy our new mate bond."

I sighed. He was right, as much as I didn't want to admit it. There really wasn't anything we could do, but it didn't change the fact that I felt like the worst mother ever for leaving Adriana behind. I trusted Stella and Jordan with my life, but they had no idea how Adriana's bedtime ritual went, or what foods she liked for dinner, and did they even know how to change a diaper? I felt guilty about abandoning my baby with them for such a long time and worried Adriana would be upset that I was gone so long. I wasn't sure if I'd be able to relax until I laid eyes on her again. That was the nature of being a mom.

"I left my clothes in my car," I said, a weak, last protest. "What am I going to wear?"

"You can wear one of my shirts." He grinned and slid a

hand down to cup my ass. "Or I could find other ways to keep you warm..."

I laughed a little, my cheeks flushing. "Haven't you had enough of me for one night?"

Wesley nipped my shoulder playfully. "Now that I've had a taste of you, I'll never have enough."

"Later," I said, swatting at his chest. "Do you want to give me a tour of the place?"

"The only place you need to know about is the bedroom," Wesley said. "But fine. There's a bathroom down the hall, and a small kitchen over there."

The kitchen was more of a nook in the wall opposite the living room, but there was a sink, a fridge, an old stove and oven, and a microwave. It would do for the night. I stepped inside and opened the pantry, finding some bread, crackers, and more food than I anticipated.

"This is better than I expected," I said, moving to the fridge to check out its contents. "I thought I'd come out here and find you trying to start a fire with wet wood and snow coming in through the holes in the roof."

Wesley leaned against the counter. "Were you thinking we'd have to huddle for warmth?"

"The thought may have crossed my mind."

"We still can."

He picked me up and threw me over his shoulder like I weighed nothing. I shrieked, grabbing onto his shoulders as he carried me down the hall past the bathroom. He opened the door to the bedroom and spun me around once. I shrieked again, giggling as he moved over to the bed and set me down.

"I'm going to make love to you all night," he said, crawling on top of me. "All morning too, if you'll let me."

"We'll see," I said, dragging my fingers through his hair while spreading my legs for him. "I bet I'll tire you out before morning."

"Oh, you're on," Wesley said and grabbed my hips.

I smiled, my heart so full with the new mate bond and the pure joy at having someone to be close to again. And then Wesley made sure I didn't worry about anything for the rest of the night.

I WOKE up to watery sunlight and my head pillowed on Wesley's chest. The bed was more comfortable than I thought it would be, and warmer too. I made a soft, contented noise as Wesley's scent filled my nose. Memories of last night played in my head on repeat, and I sighed again as I remembered how attentive Wesley had been, giving me everything I wanted and more.

"Good morning," Wesley said, tightening his hand around my waist.

"Good morning." I stretched my feet out, basking in the silence, the warmth, and the feeling of having Wesley so close to me. This was the perfect way to wake up, and I wished that I could have it every morning. Not that Wesley was my mate, maybe I could.

Wesley began kissing my neck, but the desire that swept through me was overpowered by hunger.

"Go get me a shirt," I said, shoving at his shoulder. "We'll have time for more of that after breakfast. I'm starving."

"Fine, but after we eat some food, I'm eating you next." Wesley nipped me on the shoulder with his teeth before pulling away. He returned with a gray T-shirt and handed it to me.

I crawled out of bed and slipped it over my head. It was big, falling to my thighs with the neck threatening to slide off of one shoulder, but it smelled like him. I lifted it to my nose and inhaled his scent. This was better than my clothes, I decided.

"I like the way that looks on you," he said with a low growl, his eyes going feral.

"You can take it off me later." I walked past him into the kitchen. "I saw some eggs and bacon in the fridge. I can make that, while you make some coffee and toast. Does that sound good?"

"Delicious."

From the kitchen window, I could see nothing but snow in the sunlight and hoped we'd be able to get out of there once some of it melted away. I worried about Adriana and hoped she'd had a good night with Stella and Jordan, but I'd also accepted that there was nothing I could do to get back to her right now. I'd tried calling again two more times, but there was still no signal here. *She's fine,* I told myself over and over, while I pulled out the eggs and bacon from the fridge.

Wesley made the coffee, and we worked in silence for a few minutes, brushing elbows and giving each other smiles as we moved around each other in the small space. Once the coffee percolated and the eggs and bacon sizzled in the skillet, I leaned against the fridge door and smiled at Wesley.

He raised his eyebrows. "What?"

"I still can't believe you're my mate. I keep waiting to wake up and find out it's all been a dream or something. I had a crush on you when I was younger, for as long as I can remember."

"I know," Wesley said, sounding amused. "You used to follow me around and stared at me like I'd hung the stars. It wasn't hard to figure out."

"How embarrassing. I'm surprised you put up with it."

Wesley shrugged. "I never disliked having you around, even though half the time you looked at the floor more than you looked at me."

I snorted. "You never saw me as anything except your little sister's friend."

"That was true when we were younger, but things changed."

"After I was mated to Aiden, I assumed that all my feelings for you were nothing. Just a teenage crush that I'd grow out of." I turned away to pull plates and mugs out of the cabinets, just to give my hands something to do.

"But then?"

I rinsed out the mugs before answering him. "But then I

figured out that the mate bonds were fake." I swallowed and braced my hands on the sink. I wasn't sure if I could look at Wesley for this next part. "Every time you were around, my feelings for you resurfaced and I felt like I was being torn in two. I tried to deny it because I loved Aiden too, and we were going to have a baby together..." My throat closed up and I couldn't continue.

Wesley moved up behind me and rubbed my back. "It's okay."

I swallowed and tried to get the words out. "I felt so guilty for having feelings for both of you, especially because Aiden was so good to me. He was so kind, so patient, and stood up for me when it mattered. I never wanted to hurt him. Even if our bond was fake, it felt real. But at the same time, deep down I knew I should have been with you all along."

Wesley wrapped his arms around me and buried his face in my hair. "I'm glad you were mated to him."

I turned to look at him, surprised. "Really?"

"Aiden was a good man, and the Pisces pack kept you safe. If you hadn't been mated to him, you might have been killed during the Cancer pack massacre." A shudder ran through him. "I barely survived, and I lost my parents that night. For months, I thought I'd lost my sister too. The one comfort I had during that time was knowing you made it out alive."

Tears flooded my eyes at the memory of my first Convergence. I'd said goodbye to my parents when I'd joined the Pisces pack, not realizing it would be for the last time. Like so many others in the Cancer pack, they'd been murdered by the Leos and their allies that night. I wasn't a warrior, and I had no doubt I would have died alongside them without the protection of the Pisces pack.

"Not only that," Wesley said, wiping away a tear running down my cheek. "But Aiden gave you Adriana."

I blinked back my tears. "You're right. I wouldn't change that for the world. I'm glad I had my time with him. I'll always miss him, but I know he'd want me to be happy."

"And I will do everything in my power to make you and Adriana happy." Wesley grabbed my hand and squeezed it. "Mira, come back to the Cancer pack with me and be my alpha female."

I wanted to say yes, more than anything, but it wasn't only me I had to think about. "But what about Adriana? She's a Pisces."

Wesley poured coffee for both of us. "You both belong with me in the Cancer pack. The stars have decided you're my mate, and that means Adriana is my family too."

I loved Wesley even more for saying that, but I was still worried. "I'm not sure the Pisces will see it that way."

"They'll just have to get over it," he said with a low growl, his eyes flashing with power, reminding me he was an alpha, and what an alpha wanted, he got.

I put my arms around him and kissed him, ignoring the bacon burning behind me. "Thank you."

Wesley pulled back and looked at me with a confused expression. "For what?"

"For being you," I said. "Now let's eat before the food gets cold."

Wesley laughed and shook his head as he plated up the food. I watched him, imagining many future mornings like this, except with Adriana in the kitchen too.

Maybe he's right, I thought as I took my plate. *Maybe we really can be a family.*

CHAPTER SIX

I SIGHED with relief as my borrowed car came into view, piled high with snow, but the shape was unmistakable. It had taken us most of the morning and early afternoon to dig ourselves out of the cabin and make our way back down to the road, but we'd finally managed it. Now Wesley and I bounded toward the car, trudging through melting snow that was nearly as tall as I was in my wolf form.

Once we reached the car we shifted back, and I pulled my frigid clothes out and quickly dressed. Wesley had his own clothes in a backpack that he'd been carrying in his mouth, and he put them on while I tried to start the car. It didn't want to start at first, but after a few tries and some coaxing words, it finally was running.

We waited for the car to heat up, our hands rubbing together in the meantime to keep warm. I found my phone, but there was no service here either apparently. I sighed and shoved it in my pockets. *I'll be there soon, baby girl.*

"What's the weather like back home?" I asked Wesley.

He grinned at me. "I like that you called it 'home.' It's been cold and rainy, but no snow yet."

"That sounds about right." I closed my eyes for a moment, remembering Delphinus, the Cancer pack village, which was on the coast a bit north of Vancouver. I couldn't believe I would be going back there again. I hadn't officially given Wesley my answer yet, but it seemed inevitable. I was his mate. How could I return to the Pisces pack when half my soul would be with the Cancer pack?

Once the car was ready, I carefully made a U-turn, testing the car's ability to handle this amount of snow. The car drove fine, but I made sure to go slowly the whole time. After we made it back to the main road, everything cleared off a bit and it seemed like someone had been by to plow it recently.

"Can you check if we have service yet?" I asked.

Wesley nodded. "I'll text to make sure everything is okay."

I waited anxiously, driving slowly to make sure we didn't slide on the snow or the places where it had melted. Wesley texted a few people, and then his phone chimed.

"That's Stella. She says everything is fine, and Adriana was no trouble at all," he said and grinned up at me. "See?"

I let out a long breath, as some of the stress left my body in a rush. "Thanks for checking in with them. Tell them we'll be there soon."

It wasn't long before I pulled into Kaden's driveway, and together Wesley and I walked up to the house. The driveway hadn't been plowed yet, and all the cars were still covered with snow. The steps had been swept though, and I kicked snow off my boots as I went up, not wanting to track it onto the porch. I knocked, and Ayla opened the door, looking tired but healthy.

"Oh, you're back!" She hugged Wesley tightly, and then me. "I'm so glad you're both okay. We couldn't get ahold of you, but I figured you'd made it and just didn't have service."

"You're right," I said. "Sorry I couldn't call."

"We were fine," Wesley said, wrapping an arm around my shoulders. "Better than fine."

Ayla grinned. "I'm happy you two worked everything out."

"We did," I said. "You were right, as usual."

"Finally someone admits it," she said with a laugh. "Come inside and relax. You must be exhausted."

Everyone was gathered in the living room, chatting and sitting around the fire, which was roaring and huge to keep everyone warm. Kaden was holding Jack, whose fuzzy shock of white hair stood out against the grey blanket he'd been swaddled in, and Ayla sat back down next to Jordan and leaned in to ask him something I couldn't quite hear over the buzz of everyone else talking.

Larkin and Stella, who were sitting on the floor, looked up in tandem as I walked around the couch. "Oh, your mom's here," Stella said, pointing. Adriana followed the movement, her eyes bright and her cheeks rosy. "I told you she'd be here soon, didn't I?"

Adriana giggled and clapped her hands together. The

last bit of worry I'd been holding onto unraveled. I rushed over and picked her up off the floor. Adriana cooed and pressed her little hands against my cheeks. I kissed her forehead, then her cheeks, and then her hands. "Oh, I'm so glad to see you, my sweet girl," I said, hugging her close.

"Hi there," Wesley said, waving to Adriana. "We haven't officially met. I'm Wesley."

Adriana smiled at him and waved back, cooing softly. I moved in close, and Adriana leaned forward and rubbed her hands along his stubble. Wesley laughed softly and Adriana giggled as well.

"Oh, she likes you," I said.

"I like her too." He took her hand and squeezed it gently. "I hope we can become good friends."

"I'm so happy you're both okay," Ayla said again. "And that you figured everything out."

Wesley wrapped one arm around me and Adriana. "I'm pleased my mate found me out in the snow."

I blushed and shoved at his arm good-naturedly. "He's the one who found me. I would have been walking around all night looking for his cabin if he hadn't returned my howl."

"Sounds like fate brought you together," Stella said with a knowing gleam in her eye. "Congratulations."

Larkin, Jordan, and Kaden echoed her thoughts, and I relaxed a little more. It was nice to have their acceptance, even if they weren't really the people I was worried about. Having people on our side would make it easier to deal with whatever fallout waited back at the Pisces pack.

"It's funny," Larkin said. "I always thought this kind of stuff only happened in romance novels."

"What stuff?" I asked.

Stella snorted. "Sex."

I covered Adriana's ears and pretended to be outraged. "Hush, there's children present."

"Not what I meant, but yes," Larkin said with a laugh. "The whole snowed-in-a-cabin trope. Who knew it was so effective?"

Wesley laughed and pulled me over to one of the couches, where we sat Adriana down so she could clamber over both of us. As we settled in and everyone fell back into the discussions they'd been having before our arrival, I leaned back into Wesley's arms. This was the most content I'd felt in ages, and as I looked over at Wesley, wearing an easy smile, I realized that he felt the same way.

"GOODBYE," I said, closing the door behind Larkin. She waved as she ran down the steps and into the road. I shook my head as I watched her go. "I wish she would have let me give her a ride."

I knew she'd be fine. She was tougher than she looked, but I still felt protective over her, just like I felt protective over Stella and Ayla. Maybe it was a mom thing. Once you had a baby, suddenly you wanted to look after everyone you cared about. Or maybe it was a Cancer thing. My mother had been like that too, always taking care of everyone and anything, from lost kids to stray dogs to elderly neighbors. I missed her so much.

Stella and Jordan had left about an hour before, saying they needed to catch up on some sleep. I'd felt bad, knowing it was Adriana who had kept them up, but Stella assured me that it was more than okay and that it was good practice since she'd be dealing with late nights and early mornings soon enough.

Ayla and Kaden had headed upstairs a few minutes before Larkin left to settle Jack down to sleep, and Wesley was back in the living room with Adriana.

I headed back in to sit down on the couch and watch them for a few minutes. Wesley was seated on the floor, lifting one of Adriana's toy cars and making whooshing noises to make it fly. Adriana giggled and reached for it, and Wesley immediately let her have it.

"You're so good with her," I said. "She already loves you."

Wesley turned to look at me and smiled. "I'm glad. I wanted to get a good score from the toughest judge in the house."

I nudged at him with my foot, grinning. Wesley grabbed it and pulled me forward. I went, laughing, and ended up on the floor with him and Adriana. She climbed onto my lap, and Wesley resumed playing with her toy car, swinging it through the air.

I grabbed for it, pretending to miss it, and Adriana watched, engrossed as we play-fought for the toy. Eventually, she grabbed it from us and started running it along Wesley's leg. He held very still, looking down at her.

My heart ached from being so full as I watched the two of them interact. I could already feel in my soul that I'd made the right choice. Wesley would love her like his own child, that much was clear already. I felt confident that Aiden would want this too. He really always had wanted to make me happy, and after his death, I was sure he'd give his blessing for me to move on. Especially if it was also the best thing for Adriana.

Uneasiness returned just as fast though as I thought about the impending phone conversation I'd have to have with Aiden's parents. They wouldn't let Adriana go without a fight, and they'd probably try to tell me that I was making a selfish decision. I was scared of what that conversation would bring, but I tried to push it out of my mind.

Adriana rubbed her eyes a few moments later, knocking me out of my ruminations. "Oh, she's getting tired," I said, and Wesley dropped the toy. "I should put her to bed before she gets cranky from being up too late."

I picked her up and started heading up the stairs, bouncing Adriana and humming to her as I climbed the stairs. To my surprise, as I opened my door, Wesley followed me.

"What is it?" I asked.

Wesley motioned toward her crib. "I want to learn how to do it all, so I can help you out. I know I won't be of much help for a bit, but I'm a fast learner."

I frowned and shifted Adriana over to one hip. "Are you

sure you're ready for this whole dad thing? It's a lot, and it's not all fun, and it was thrust upon you suddenly. I don't expect you to pick it all up right away."

Wesley took Adriana from my arms and gave her a kiss on the cheek. "You're wrong. I've been preparing to be a dad for months, ever since I saw you at the Convergence and knew you were my mate. I was just waiting for you to come around to the idea."

I was momentarily breathless. "You were so sure I'd say yes?"

Wesley grinned. "I knew I'd win you over eventually with my stunning good looks and impeccable charm."

"Well, it worked."

Wesley wrapped his free arm around me, pulling us into a group hug. "Mira, I want this. I want you, and Adriana, and everything that comes with you both. I'm prepared for the not-so-good days, as well as the good ones, and I want us to be a real family."

My heart swelled, and I leaned in to kiss him. "You're perfect." I pulled back, but I left a hand on his chest. "I'm ready to give you my answer now."

"Your answer?" His eyes widened.

I drew in a breath. "We're coming with you. We'll join the Cancer pack. I don't care what the Pisces pack says."

He touched my cheek in wonder. "My mate. My alpha female." And then he touched Adriana's cheek. "And my daughter. I'm so happy you'll be coming home with me soon."

"Me too." I stepped aside and pulled out Adriana's pajamas. "We really should put Adriana to bed though, so we can have some alone time."

"What a good incentive to learn quickly," he said with a grin.

CHAPTER SEVEN

I OPENED my car window and breathed in deeply before letting out a sigh. We were back in the Cancer pack village, and it felt exactly like coming home. The cool air was tinged with the briny scent of the ocean, and I tilted my head back, letting the sea breeze wash over me, along with the distant sound of waves lapping against the shore and the docks.

We'd stayed with Ayla and Kaden for a week, helping them adjust to parenthood, and I'd called my in-laws during that time and explained everything to them. They hadn't been happy at all, unwilling to even entertain the idea of me leaving the Pisces pack to join the Cancer pack. They'd told me to come back immediately and argued that I couldn't take Adriana away from them or from their pack. It had escalated to yelling, and I'd hung up on them after several failed attempts to get them to calm down. I wasn't sure what would happen with them next, but I couldn't worry about that now. It didn't matter if I never went back to the Pisces pack to collect my things. I had everything I needed right here.

Wesley smiled over at me as he slowed down, driving through familiar streets. I glanced over my shoulder, but Adriana was still asleep in the back. She'd traveled incredibly well the whole way, first on the airplane and then in Wesley's car. I couldn't wait for her to wake up and see her new home.

I hadn't been back here for over a year, since we'd all left for the Convergence. I'd gone straight to the Pisces pack, and there hadn't been a chance to come back for the rest of my things after the Leos slaughtered much of the Cancer pack that night. After that, it wasn't safe to come back here, and then once it was, I'd had a baby to look after.

As we drove through the main part of town, I noted that some of the shops I remembered were closed, and there was a distinct lack of the usual activity. No children running in the streets, and very few pack members loitering around outside the stores.

"It seems different," I said, turning to look at Wesley. "Quieter."

"We're still trying to get back to living in the village after being in hiding for so long, and our numbers are fewer these days. Entire families were wiped out, or only left behind orphans who were too young to go to the Convergence." His voice went a bit quieter, and he clenched the steering wheel. "Barely anyone made it out alive that day."

"I know." I reached over and put my hand on his knee. "I

can't imagine how hard it must have been for you, becoming alpha so suddenly after so much loss."

"It wasn't easy, and a part of me will never forgive the packs that were involved, or the Sun Witches for what they did. So much of our pack was wiped out that night. But we're crabs. We're tough, and like water, we adapt and change. That's what I've focused on this last year."

"You're an incredible alpha."

He ducked his head. "I don't know about that, but I've done the best I can for our people. I'm glad you'll be by my side as my alpha female going forward though."

He turned down a familiar street, and my throat clogged up as I realized where we were going. I looked down at my hands, trying to get ahold of my emotions, but I'd hardly had any time to process my parents' deaths when there was so much going on with the Leo pack and then the Sun Witches.

Wesley stopped, and I forced myself to look up. The house stood, familiar as ever with its blue paint and white awnings, but I could tell even from the outside that it was empty. Tears welled up, and I was helpless to stop them as I remembered my parents caring for me and making sure that I had a good childhood. Good and bad memories alike returned to me. My mother making pancakes for me and Ayla. My father reading a book to me before bed. My mother arguing with my father while I listened from my room. My father coming home, injured after he'd challenged the alpha and lost. They both wanted our pack to be better. To return to the ideals that the Cancer pack once held. But they'd failed, and the alpha had punished our entire family in return.

Now that I was going to become alpha female, maybe I could finish what they'd started.

"This is your house now," Wesley said. "You're the only surviving member of your family."

"I miss them so much." I shook my head, sniffling as tears continued running down my cheeks. There were so many good memories there, but all I could remember now was that my parents were dead and that this house would always be empty and echoing. There wouldn't be anyone calling my name from downstairs, or giving me a hug after a long day. "I'm not sure if I can face it. Not yet."

Wesley reached over and took my hand. He laced our fingers together and squeezed. "It's okay," he said, voice warm. "It'll be here for whenever you're ready. You can decide when that is."

"Can I see where we'll be living?" I asked, wiping the tears away. There would be time to grieve later. Right now, I wanted to settle in and make sure Adriana felt comfortable here.

Wesley nodded and put the car into reverse. He drove back the way we'd come and then turned toward the ocean. We drove up the road that led to the alpha's residence, a huge two-story house that perched at the very top of a cliff and overlooked the ocean.

"I always loved this house," I said as we drove up. "It's so gorgeous, and the ocean views... Incredible."

"It's yours now." He still hadn't let go of my hand and he squeezed it again.

I opened my mouth, but before I could even think of what to say, I noticed a group of people standing in the driveway. I recognized almost all of them. My teachers, distant cousins, and people I went to school with. I was so relieved to see them alive, but what were they doing here?

"What's going on?" I asked.

"Everyone wants to meet their new alpha female," Wesley said. "They were so excited to hear you were coming home."

He put the car into park and looked over at me expectantly. I felt frozen with nerves, looking at all the people outside. It hadn't truly hit me yet, that being Wesley's mate included being alpha female and a leader to all of these people. I'd thought about it in vague terms, but seeing all these people I knew made me realize that things would change. They would look to me for advice and help now. Was I ready for all that responsibility?

"What's wrong?" Wesley asked.

"I don't know if I can get out," I said. "I never planned to be alpha female. I never wanted it. I just wanted a quiet life near the water with my handsome mate and my family."

"You can still have all of that. You have the handsome mate, after all."

I swallowed hard. I was too nervous to laugh, but I appreciated his attempt at lightening the situation.

"Mira, you're exactly what the Cancer pack needs right now. We're all just trying to heal after what happened."

I nodded slowly. "I'll try."

"That's really all we can do," Wesley said. "It's all I'm doing, too."

"Well, you're doing a really good job of it. You were born to do it, after all."

"And I think you'll do a good job, too." Wesley turned off the car. "I'm going to get out but take your time getting Adriana. There's no rush."

I nodded and watched as he exited the car. A few of the people turned with him, walking up to him to talk. I watched them for a few moments, noticing how Wesley turned to answer everyone with a smile. He really *was* a good alpha.

Most of the people continued looking at me, and I sighed, unclicking my seat belt and getting out. Adriana blinked dark sleepy eyes at me as I unbuckled her from her car seat, and I carefully picked her up. She yawned and instantly turned her head toward the sound of the waves, drawn to them just as I was.

A few of the people came forward to greet me. "Mira," someone said. "Welcome home." A few others echoed it, and when I finally chanced a glance up, they were all smiling. Something in me eased. I'd been afraid that when they saw my daughter, they might change their tune a little, but no one seemed to be upset about her presence.

"Mira, your daughter is so beautiful. What's her name?" someone else asked, an old teacher of mine.

"Adriana," I said, pressing my hand to her head and cupping her neck.

"Hello, Adriana," Julie, one of my cousins, said. "We're so happy you're here."

My heart softened at the genuine welcome. They let me pass, and I made my way up to where Wesley waited at the foot of the steps. My smile became more genuine, and I nodded hello to all of the people I knew and thanked them.

Once I made it up to the porch, Wesley put his arm around me and looked out at the gathered group of people. "Thank you so much for coming. I'm so honored that you'd take time out of your day to greet my new mate, but it's been a long journey, and we all need to rest. There will be time to catch up later, and I'll answer any questions you have then. I know I've been away for a few days, and there are some matters I need to attend to, but we can discuss them in the next day or two."

A murmur went through the crowd, and a few people nodded. The group slowly dispersed, with many calling goodbye as they left. I raised my hand and waved to them, and then Wesley led me up the steps.

He unlocked the door and motioned for me to go inside in front of him. The house mostly looked like I remembered, but emptier, like Wesley had been getting rid of things. Jackie had decorated it in a very modern style, with gray, white, and black furniture. Beautiful, but a bit cold. I could already imagine ways I could keep the best pieces but spruce things up with some new art, decorative pillows, and accent pieces.

When he noticed me looking around he shrugged. "I figured I didn't need all of my parent's stuff. A lot of it wasn't really my taste, but I haven't had a chance to make it mine yet."

"I understand that. We've all been a bit busy this last year."

Wesley blew out an amused breath. "I was hoping you could help me make it a home. Feel free to change or buy anything you want for it.

"Really?" I asked.

"I meant it when I said this would be your place as well. I want us to make it a home together. A perfect place for all three of us."

Adriana shifted in my arms and made a disgruntled little noise. I shushed her and ran my hand down her back, but it didn't do any good. She started crying, and I realized it had been hours since she'd eaten.

"I bet she's hungry," I said. "I'd better get her something to eat."

"I'll get it, in just a minute. Can I show you something first?"

"Sure." I followed him as he went upstairs, shushing and soothing Adriana as best as I could.

Wesley stopped in front of a door that I remembered well. Whenever I'd come to visit Ayla, I could see him coming in and out of his room, which he usually kept shut. *Stay out of my room,* he had said more than once, when he was a sulky teenager.

"Wasn't this your bedroom?" I asked.

"It was."

Wesley grinned at me and swung the door open. I

peered inside, and gasped at the sight of a crib, some toys, a bookshelf with a few picture books, and a huge mobile hanging from the ceiling. The walls were painted a beautiful sea green, with hand-painted mermaids and other sea creatures all over. Front and center was a very detailed, beautiful crab to represent the Cancer pack, but swimming beside it was a large fish, representing the Pisces pack.

"This is so beautiful," I said. "How did you do this?"

Wesley shook his head. "I didn't. Everyone in the Cancer pack came together to get the room ready for your arrival."

"I can't believe it." I turned Adriana around so she could see the room. She paused in her fussing, enamored by the bright colors and sea creatures. "This is going to be your new room. Isn't it perfect?"

Wesley kissed Adriana's forehead, and then mine. I closed my eyes, leaned into him, and hugged Adriana close. Now I truly felt like I was home, more than I ever had in the Pisces pack, and it was all because Wesley and the rest of the pack made sure I felt like we were welcome here.

CHAPTER EIGHT

THE SOUNDS of hundreds of shifters outside of my tent were almost overwhelming, their voices overlapping and feet crunching through the snow, while a few wolves howled in the distance. Today was the winter solstice, and we were all getting ready for the Convergence, hosted by the Capricorn pack this time. I stood up from my folding chair and pulled the flap of my tent open to peer outside as a particularly loud shout caught my attention.

My breath misted in the air in front of me as I looked out at all the shifters milling about. A few of the other Cancer pack members were setting up their tents, or walking between bonfires to chat with each other. I still could hardly believe that I was here with the Cancer pack again, instead of with the Pisces pack. Not only that, but I was here as the Cancer pack's alpha female. I rubbed my hand over my chest. Even though I couldn't actually feel the pack mark over my heart I knew it was there, though I kept expecting to wake up and find it had all been a pleasant dream.

Movement caught my attention, and I turned toward it with a smile, feeling my mate approaching. Wesley waved and held Adriana's head close to him as he picked up his pace to a light jog to reach me faster. She babbled and giggled at being jostled around in the carrier, and I just shook my head with a smile as they approached.

"Hey," I said, and couldn't stop grinning at the sight of Adriana in her baby carrier on Wesley's chest. She had a cute little hat on, and despite the cold air, she looked happy to be outside, especially with Wesley.

"Hey, yourself," Wesley said as he stopped in front of the tent, and then leaned over to kiss me.

"How was everyone?" I asked. He'd left about half an hour before to say hello to the other alphas and to make sure everything was running smoothly, while I stayed behind to finish unpacking Adriana's things and get us settled in for the night.

"Stella and Jordan just arrived with the Leos. But Ayla and Kaden aren't here. I saw their beta, Clayton, and his partner here representing the Ophiuchus pack."

"That makes sense. It's too soon for Ayla or Kaden to travel so far with a newborn."

Wesley hummed in agreement and bounced Adriana a bit as she fussed. "I haven't had a chance to speak with Ethan or Madison yet, they were both busy."

"There will be time, I'm sure, once everyone is settled in. It's hectic out there, isn't it?"

Wesley sighed. "Tell me about it. I can hardly hear myself think."

I was about to ask about the Pisces pack when two figures I recognized all too well were walking quickly toward our tent. My heart immediately sank into my stomach. "Don't look now," I said through teeth gritted in a fake smile, "but Adriana's grandparents are headed this way."

Wesley ignored me completely and looked over at them. I kept my smile in place as they approached. If looks could kill, Aiden's parents would have incinerated me on the spot. None of us had spoken since that awful phone call two weeks ago. I had planned to visit them after the holidays to get my sparse belongings and try to work things out with them in person. I'd hoped that we'd be able to come to an agreement that would benefit both of us—and most importantly, Adriana. Meeting them on my own terms would have made me feel a lot more comfortable, but it looked like we were doing this right now, whether I was ready or not.

"Hi," I said as they looked between me and Wesley. "Ruth, Kevin, this is Wesley, my mate. Wesley, this is Ruth and Kevin, Aiden's parents."

For a moment neither of them said anything, and my anxiety skyrocketed. I hoped that we could keep things civil between us now, but from the tension in the air, it looked like that might be out of the question.

"I'm glad you're here," I said, keeping my voice polite. "I've been wanting to talk to you."

"We have nothing to talk about," Ruth said. "You've

kidnapped a member of the Pisces pack and we want her back."

"Kidnapped?" I asked, startled. "She's my daughter!"

"We're not looking for a fight," Kevin added. "We just came here to get Adriana and take her home."

I growled low in my throat. "No."

"It wasn't a question," Ruth said, crossing her arms. "It's a demand. Adriana needs to be back in the Pisces pack, where she belongs."

Wesley stepped forward, teeth bared as he wrapped his arms around Adriana. "No one is taking my daughter," he said. "She belongs in the Cancer pack, with her mother, my alpha female."

Ruth shook her head. "Adriana isn't your family. I don't know what Mira has been telling you, but she is *Aiden's* child. She deserves to be back with her pack. Adriana is all we have left of him."

"She is also my daughter," I said. "And I'm part of the Cancer pack now."

"Adriana is a Pisces and she must be raised with her pack." Kevin glared at Wesley, not backing down.

"Then I'll make her a Cancer," Wesley said.

Ruth took a step back and put a hand to her chest. "You can't do that! It's not right."

"Adriana will always be a Pisces." Kevin stepped closer to Wesley, his finger just a few inches away from his chest. It was either very brave or very stupid of him to get so close to an alpha like this.

Wesley growled, low in his throat, and Adriana fussed

between them. My hands itched to take Adriana away, but I trusted that Wesley would keep her safe, even in a conflict like this. I wanted to tell him it wouldn't escalate to a fight, but I didn't know. I'd never seen Aiden's parents this angry before. They'd been quiet in their grief after his death, and they'd never yelled at me until the phone call. I knew they were upset, but we'd all had more than enough fighting in the past couple of years. I didn't want to see packs at each other's throats again in my life if I could help it.

"Please." I put my hands out to the sides, physically separating Wesley and Kevin. "Let's talk about this, and we can try to come to a peaceful resolution."

"There's nothing to talk about," Ruth snapped. "You stole our granddaughter from us and won't let her come home."

"Surely we can figure something out," I pleaded, looking between everyone. "It doesn't have to be like this. I know we all want what's best for Adriana."

"No," Kevin said. "I think we're beyond talking. We tried to come over here and give you a chance, but your *mate* —" he spat the word like it was a curse— "said he would turn our granddaughter into a Cancer. That's not how things should be done, and I don't think the other alphas would be very happy to hear about what's been said here."

"That's right," Ruth said, baring her teeth. "We're going to take this to the alpha council and see what they have to say about it."

"You can't take my daughter away from me," I said, tears clogging my throat as I fought to get the words out.

"We're not monsters," Ruth said as if affronted by the idea. "If you want to be with Adriana, you can come back to the Pisces pack too. You're always welcome to live with us."

"Wait—" I started, but Kevin cut me off by raising a hand.

"No," Kevin said, shaking his head. "You've made your choice, and we've made ours. You'll be hearing from the alphas soon."

He turned and started walking back the way he'd come. Ruth looked at Adriana for one long moment with sadness in her eyes and then followed her mate.

I turned to Wesley, on the verge of tears and shaking. I couldn't suppress the shivers as they wracked my body. "I don't see a way out of this. The Pisces alpha will take their side. The other alphas might too. What if I have to leave and go back to the Pisces pack?"

Wesley wrapped his arms around me, completely engulfing me. "Everything is going to be fine. I'm not going to let anyone take you away."

I wrapped my arms around Wesley and Adriana, squeezing my eyes shut tight. He sounded so sure, but I wasn't. As far as I knew, there had never been a situation like this before, but now with the fake mate bonds broken and real ones emerging, everything was changing. "How can you be sure?"

"I lost my family once, and I'm never losing them again," Wesley said. "I promise."

"I'm scared," I whispered. "I already lost my mate once."

"That's not going to happen again."

I wanted so badly to believe him, but I wasn't sure that I could. I knew in my heart that I'd have to do what was best for Adriana, even if that meant leaving happiness behind. I wasn't going to let her grow up without her mom.

Wesley squeezed me tighter, but gentle enough that Adriana was still safe between us. He was so good with Adriana and he wanted to be her dad so badly, but it might not be possible now. And didn't Adriana deserve to grow up with a dad too? Maybe not her real one, but one who would love her, guide her, and protect her just as much as Aiden would?

But if the alphas decided Adriana had to return to the Pisces, I already knew I would have no choice but to follow.

Would I be forced to give up the mate I'd just found for the sake of my daughter?

CHAPTER NINE

I LOOKED around the large tent, nerves turning my stomach and setting me on edge. A few of the other alphas had already gathered, sitting in a circle of fold-up chairs, but some had yet to arrive.

Wesley held his hand out to me, and his face looked more calm than I expected. I took his hand and squeezed, hard.

"We're going to be fine," Wesley said to me under his breath. I wanted to believe him, but I just didn't see how this could end in a way that would satisfy everyone.

I wanted to squeeze Adriana tightly to me, to breathe in her familiar smell and look into her eyes, but we'd left her back with Stella for this. She'd told me that even though she wouldn't make it to the meeting, Jordan would be speaking up on my behalf. I caught his eye and gave him a weak smile, and he nodded in response. It comforted me to see that at least one of the alphas would be on our side, but I didn't know if it would be enough.

I wished Ayla was here. She'd been my rock throughout my whole life, and now she was my sister too. I knew she would fight for us no matter what. But she was at home with her new baby, as she should be. We had to fight this battle on our own.

A few more alphas stepped into the tent, and pretty soon, all thirteen packs were present and accounted for. Wesley pulled me forward and we joined the circle of alphas.

I eyed the new Pisces alpha, Fisher, as I took my seat next to Wesley. He had Aiden's nose and chin, but his hair was lighter and he had a perpetual frown on his face. He avoided my gaze, and I couldn't help but feel a bit of petty hatred toward him. Fisher was Aiden's cousin, and if he had stepped up when his father, Amos, had died at the hands of the vampires, Aiden might still be here. It was only because Fisher was too much of a wimp to stand up to the Sun Witches that Aiden had become alpha and fought at the last battle, losing his life to make sure all the Zodiac Wolves were free. Now that the danger had passed, Fisher had finally taken over as alpha. I had a feeling he wouldn't hold it long though. He would be challenged, and he would lose, and the Pisces pack would be better for it.

"Now that we're all here, let's get started," Ethan said, standing and stepping forward into the circle of chairs so he could look at all of the alphas. There was a murmur of agreement, and Ethan clasped his hands together in front of him.

He looked cool and put together as always. "The Pisces pack has a grievance with the Cancer pack that they would like addressed."

Fisher nodded at Ethan, but he still refused to meet my gaze. Coward.

Ethan continued, looking around at the other alphas. "For those of you who don't know, Adriana is nine months old and the daughter of Aiden, the former alpha of the Pisces pack. Her mother, Mira, has now been mated to the Cancer pack alpha." He motioned toward me, and the weight of a dozen eyes fell on me. "Mira and Adriana have gone to live with the Cancer pack, but the Pisces pack wants Adriana back. Since it was the Pisces pack who brought this grievance to us, we'll let Fischer speak first."

Fisher stood up and put his shoulders back, finally looking like the Pisces pack alpha he was. He looked around the circle of gathered alphas before speaking. "Adriana was born a Pisces and is part of the alpha family's bloodline. She is all that my family has left of Aiden, and Ruth and Kevin are beside themselves with grief over not only losing their son, but their granddaughter as well." He turned to look at me, his brow knitted in sadness. "We've always treated Mira well. We took her in and we see her as a member of our pack and our family. But now she has betrayed us by running off to the Cancer pack and taking Adriana with her. She didn't give us any warning, or any chance to stop her."

A murmur ran through the assembled pack alphas, and a few of the gazes turned a little less friendly from where they fell onto me. I wanted to protest his words, but it wasn't my turn to speak yet, so I tried to keep my head up and my back straight.

"Even if Mira chooses to go back to the Cancer pack, as is her right since her mate is part of the Cancer pack, she *doesn't* have the right to take Adriana away from her pack." He paused and looked around again. "I'm sure you all understand how important it is that Adriana be raised in the Pisces pack. She is a Pisces, and the daughter of an alpha, and she should be among her people, her pack."

"What is it you're asking for?" Ethan asked.

"Ruth and Kevin, the grandparents of Adriana, want full custody of Adriana. I hope the other alphas will agree that this is the best course of action, for both Adriana and the Cancer and Pisces packs."

"Thank you," Ethan said. I tried to read his face, to see if he was more sympathetic toward Fisher and the Pisces pack now, but he had an incredible poker face. It was part of what had made him such a good leader for the packs to lean on for support and guidance during the months leading up to the final battle. Fisher sat back down, and Ethan paused a moment before continuing. "The Cancer pack can now speak."

Wesley stood up, and I could almost taste the tension pouring off of him in waves. His earlier easygoing attitude was gone, after hearing the Pisces alpha speak.

"It's true. Mira and I discovered we were mates recently when we both visited my sister in the Ophiuchus pack. She is my alpha female and belongs with the Cancer pack. Surely none of you can argue against a true mate bond. But you can't really expect to take a child away from her own mother either, can you?"

A few of the other alphas murmured and shifted in response, and I knew deep in my heart that I had to be the one to plead my case with the alphas, and hopefully appeal to Fisher's better nature, if he had one. I had to fight for my family. I had run from too many fights in my life, but I wouldn't run from this one.

I reached up and put my hand on Wesley's arm before he could continue. He must have seen my thoughts reflected in my eyes, because he immediately nodded, and covered my hand with his own. He sat back down, and I braced myself as I stood up and looked around the circle. No one was outwardly hostile, not even Fisher. He looked uneasy like he didn't want to be making these decisions at all. I swallowed and hoped that this meant I still had a chance to plead my case.

"I'm extremely grateful to the Pisces pack for everything they've done for me. Especially after my family was killed, they were good to take me in and give me a home. I truly loved Aiden and always will mourn his loss. It was never my intention to take Adriana away from the Pisces pack, but I am mated to Wesley." I drew in a breath, standing even taller. "I'm now the alpha female and I belong with the Cancer pack. Adriana is still a Pisces and Aiden's child. She always will be, and no one will ever take that away." I clenched my fists. It shouldn't have gotten to the point where Wesley threatened to make Adriana a Cancer, but he'd been angry in the moment. "But Adriana is also my child, and I will not let my child be taken away from me."

I turned to look at the other alphas, trying to gauge their reactions. There still wasn't any outright sympathy, but everyone seemed a little wary to jump to conclusions.

"I know that Ruth and Kevin are doing this out of grief. I understand because I feel that grief, too. I lost my mate and the father of my child, just like they lost their son. I have no intention of keeping Adriana away from the Pisces pack or from her grandparents. I would like to visit them as much as possible, and Ruth and Kevin are also welcome to come to the Cancer pack as well." Thinking of Aiden's death made me clench my fists as I added, "Isn't that what we fought the Sun Witches for? A chance for us to be united again—not packs fighting against each other, but living in harmony, sharing resources, working together. Adriana doesn't need to be a Pisces or a Cancer. She can be both."

With those words, I sat back down, and Wesley put his hand on my thigh and gave me a proud smile. I had no idea if what I said would get through to the other alphas, but I'd made my case as best as I could.

Ethan stood up again. "Thank you, Fisher and Mira, for showing us both sides of this issue. This is a matter we all needed to talk about, that goes beyond the Cancer and Pisces pack, and beyond this current conflict. Many of us have been discussing how families have been torn apart and recreated among the different packs because of the severing of the fake mate bonds and the emergence of new ones."

I raised my eyebrows. It made sense, I supposed. Lots of

people were under the fake mate bonds, and lots of them had decided to break them. Some of them had probably even lost their mates during the last battle, like I had.

"We need to decide how to handle this before we start fighting again," Ethan said.

"Surely you don't plan to take a child away from her mother," Jordan said.

Madison, the Virgo alpha, cleared her throat. "That's not going to happen."

"That isn't the solution," the Aries alpha said, frowning. "But it isn't right for a Pisces child to be raised away from her pack either. What separates her from being a Cancer then?"

The Sagittarius alpha rolled his eyes. "You're thinking too black and white, as usual."

The Aries alpha visibly bristled, and the tensions rose. A few other alphas started muttering, and to my right, Wesley tensed. I grabbed onto his hand as the arguing grew louder, and panic started rising inside of me. This was exactly what I didn't want to happen. I was so sick of fighting, of having these conflicts, and of nothing ever being truly solved.

"Perhaps the Zodiac Wolves need to stop worrying so much about pack divisions," Clayton said, rising to his feet as he spoke for the Ophiuchus pack. "Mira's right. This is what our people fought and died for."

"I agree," Wesley said. "It's time for the packs to stop being so isolationist, and start being one united nation. Wasn't that the whole point of breaking free of the Sun Witches? To prove that we weren't the angry, rabid animals they thought we were? We need to encourage our people to travel between the packs. We need to start building alliances instead of starting wars." Wesley looked over at Fisher. "The Cancer and Pisces packs used to be great allies, and I hope that can be true again now."

"I agree," Ethan said. "If you think about it, very few people these days truly belong to one pack. They may have grown up in one but found their mate in another. Some have even moved to a third pack. But the thing that unites us is that we are all Zodiac Wolves."

The Scorpio alpha piped up. "This is all good and wonderful, but the distance between the packs is a big problem. We can't all teleport around like the Sun or Moon Witches. We're so spread out, and I don't see a way to resolve these problems until we can find a viable solution."

I sat up straight as I remembered Larkin talking about the problems the Moon Witches were having with obtaining money. "I think I have an idea," I said. "But I'll need to talk to Larkin first."

CHAPTER TEN

THE OCEAN BREEZE whipped through my dark hair, drawing it back from my face as I turned to stare out at the sea. I smiled and closed my eyes briefly, soaking in the feeling of being back by the waters where I'd grown up. If I got to spend every day down here, I wasn't sure if it would ever be enough.

The warmth in the air promised that spring was here, and today was beautiful and sunny, especially out on the beach. The breeze was still a bit chilly, but it definitely wasn't cold enough to be off-putting to the Cancer pack, or the Pisces for that matter.

An excited shriek caught my attention. Adriana toddled unsteadily toward me on the beach, wearing a pink onesie with a big number one on it. I scooped her up and pressed a kiss to the top of her head.

"Happy birthday," I said. "Are you excited for your party to start?"

She cooed happily and clapped her hands. I hugged her before setting her back down. She immediately tried to stand up, but fell back down and then picked up a handful of sand. She let it sift through her fingers, entranced.

Just as I straightened up, Ayla appeared with Kaden and Jack, who was now three months old. His hair was still white and fluffy, but he'd grown a lot during the last three months. My heart grew, seeing my nephew so healthy and happy, along with his parents.

Wesley walked over to greet them, shaking Kaden's hand and giving Ayla a hug before all of them came over to see me. Ayla and Kaden looked content and happy, if a little tired.

I embraced Ayla. "I'm so happy to see you all. Thank you for coming."

"I'm glad we could make it," she said. "Are you ready for this?"

I nodded. It wasn't all fun and games today, even though it would seem that way to Adriana, oblivious as she crawled and walked around in the sand. Today would be the ultimate test to see if my big proposal would work, and all the packs were waiting to see how it went.

"It's going to work," Wesley said. "Don't worry."

I smiled at his surety and leaned into his side for a moment. "I know."

We all turned as a swirling, bright portal appeared out of nowhere, growing bigger and bigger until it was about six feet tall and six feet wide. Larkin stepped through first, hands held up and her brow knitted in concentration. My excitement spiked at seeing her, but I refrained from rushing forward, just in case it broke her concentration.

Stella and Jordan were the next ones through, and Larkin opened her eyes and smiled as she let go of the magic. Slowly, the portal closed, and she dusted her hands off before following Jordan and Stella over to where we all stood. Stella was shining with that pregnancy glow, and I saw the first hints of a baby bump on her. We all exchanged hellos, hugs, and handshakes, and then I turned to Larkin.

"Is everything going according to plan?" I asked.

Larkin looked down along the beach, shielding her eyes from the sun. "Yes. They'll be here any moment."

"Perfect. Thanks so much for organizing this with me."

"No, thank you for coming up with the idea. If this works, it will help the Moon Witches so much."

"It will help everyone," I said with a smile.

I'd talked to Larkin about the solution to everyone's problems as soon as I could after the meeting at the Convergence. The Moon Witches would offer teleportation services—for a fee, naturally—to all of the Zodiac Wolves, allowing shifters to travel between packs any time they wanted. This gave the Moon Witches a legitimate way to earn money and independence, which they could use to start their own village. It also allowed the Zodiac Wolves who were torn between packs to feel less separate from each other. As part of that, each pack was making sure they had accommodations for visitors too.

Including the Cancer pack. I'd decided to make my old family home into a bed and breakfast for traveling shifters, witches, and even vampires if the time ever came that we'd need to house them. I was looking forward to using my childhood house for the benefit of our pack, and to have it full of people again. I knew my parents would want that too.

There was another shimmer in the air, and then another, as more portals opened along the beach. Moon Witches I didn't recognize stepped through first before ushering their guests through. Ethan came from the one closest and then shook the Moon Witch's hand. Madison came from another, and then Ruth and Kevin came from the third. They looked up and down the beach until they spotted Adriana, and ran over.

"Little fish," Ruth said, picking Adriana up and spinning her around. Kevin took her next and hugged her close.

"Welcome," I said, smiling warmly at Ruth and Kevin. It was good to have them here, despite the slight awkwardness that still lingered in the air between us. I was glad we'd been able to come to this peaceful resolution, and hopefully, after some time there would be nothing but warmth between us.

The other alphas had all agreed that Adriana should stay with us in the Cancer pack, as long as she also spent time with members of the Pisces pack too. Ruth and Kevin, once they calmed down, agreed to their terms, especially once I told everyone my plan to involve the Moon Witches. In the end, we all wanted what best for Adriana.

Ruth took Adriana back, who giggled and reached up to play with her hair. "Thank you so much for inviting us."

"We're excited to stay for a while and spend some time

with our granddaughter," Kevin added, putting his arm around Ruth's shoulder.

"I'm glad you were able to make it," I said. "How was the travel?"

"I kept expecting it to be bumpy or something," Kevin said. "But we just stepped through, and now we're here."

"Good. Are you okay with watching Adriana while I say hello to the other guests?"

Ruth and Kevin nodded, seemingly entranced by Adriana, who also looked delighted to see her grandparents again. A huge wave of relief passed through me at the sight of them together. I'd never wanted to take Adriana away from her Pisces family, and I was so happy she would grow up knowing them too.

Around us, more people were arriving, both from the Cancer pack and from the portals. Some people set presents for Adriana on the table we'd set up earlier, while others grabbed drinks and food from the buffet. They'd already started mingling, with shifters from all different packs talking to the Cancers who had joined us for Adriana's party. I moved between the groups, thanking everyone for coming and checking in with how they were doing.

After saying hello to everyone, I circled back around to see Adriana playing in the sand, with Ruth, Kevin, and Wesley beside her. Wesley handed her a little shovel and showed her how to dig a hole. He'd settled so easily into his role as Adriana's dad like he was meant to do this all along. I couldn't ask for a better partner.

I just wished being alpha female came as naturally to

me. I had never been interested in pack politics and had always tuned Wesley out when he talked about it before when we'd both been younger. Now I simply focused on the parts that I felt comfortable with, and Wesley kept assuring me that I was doing a good job. I cared a lot about helping others, and lots of people in the pack needed help after what we'd all been through at the hands of the Sun Witches. I'd been able to help people get homes and jobs and also made sure that no one was alone or hungry.

The Cancer pack had lost its way before, under the previous alpha, but I knew that Wesley was capable of turning it around. And even if I still wasn't sure about being alpha female, I would stand beside him and help however I could. We would rebuild our pack and make it even stronger than it was before—I was sure about that.

Wesley handed Adriana off to Ruth, who took her out to the water. I watched them as Ruth held her upright and let the cold water flow over her bare feet. Adriana shrieked and giggled, and everyone around her laughed at her sheer joy.

Wesley came over to me and wrapped his arms around me. I leaned into his kiss, letting my body melt against his. I still couldn't get over how well we fit together, and how perfect this was. I looked out at Adriana, still laughing and kicking her feet while Ruth held her up to let her splash the water.

"I think this might be the happiest day of my life," Wesley murmured to me. "What are you thinking about?"

"I was just thinking that this is the first time I've ever felt really content. It's like this is where I'm supposed to be. I belong here, with my family in the Cancer pack, and as the alpha female."

"I agree," Wesley said. "You're taking to it like a fish to water. Or should I say crab?"

I rolled my eyes at his joke but then hugged him tight. "I'm sorry you had to wait for so long."

"I didn't know it before, but things were meant to happen this way. I always felt like I was waiting for something, and now I realize this is what I've been waiting for. This exactly." He smiled at me and pressed a kiss to my forehead. "You not only brought together our family, but this is mending a rift between the Cancer and Pisces packs. I couldn't have done that myself."

"I'm sure you could have," I said. "You're good at keeping the peace."

"Maybe, but you made it happen faster than I could have. And you're working with Larkin and the others to bring the entire Zodiac Wolves packs together, and that's not something just anyone could do."

I looked down, blushing. "Thank you."

"I know that Aiden would be very proud of you."

My eyes clouded with tears. That wound still hurt, and I knew it would likely hurt for the rest of my life, even if being with Wesley made it easier. I'd loved Aiden, and I was glad that Wesley was willing to talk about him and honor his memory. "I hope so."

Wesley turned away as someone called his name. I hung back, looking out at the water for a bit longer. Maybe Wesley was right. Maybe I was helping bring all the packs together, to be better than they'd ever been before. I hoped I could have that much of an impact as alpha female.

A fish with rainbow scales leaped out of the water, closer to shore than I'd ever seen before. It hovered in the air, the sun glinting off its fins, and I swore that our eyes connected for the briefest moment before it dove back into the sea. I blinked as I watched the ripples fade, and then smiled.

Thank you, I thought to Aiden. It felt like he'd given me his blessing, and that was all I needed.

I turned away from the water and went back to join my family, eager to celebrate this new beginning.

AIR KISSED

LARKIN & ETHAN

CHAPTER ONE

I FIDDLED with the hem of my shirt as I rode the elevator up to Ethan's office. I could see how pale I was in the reflection of the shiny metal doors, my freckles more pronounced than ever, and I tried to paste a confident smile onto my face. It didn't work, and I quickly dropped it in favor of smoothing my light blond hair. I'd recently cut it short in an effort to make myself look older, but I was starting to think it had the opposite effect, making me look like a pixie. Not that Ethan would even notice, I thought with a sigh.

A few months ago, I'd started working with the Libra alpha to find a good place for the Moon Witches to live. I'd initially reached out to him on Ayla's recommendation since he worked in real estate here in Toronto and owned many properties and hotels. We'd traded emails back and forth over the last few months to narrow down the options, and there was one in particular that looked perfect. Today I was here to discuss it with Ethan so I could decide if I wanted to look at it in person.

As the elevator neared the penthouse, nervous butterflies fluttered around my stomach, while my heart beat at dangerous speeds. I was starting to second-guess that cup of coffee I'd had before coming here. I wished I could say it was the property I was excited and nervous about, but that would be a lie.

Though I would never confess it out loud, I'd loved Ethan from the moment I'd set eyes on him, right after I returned to Earth with Ayla. Since then, I'd spent every moment either pining for him or trying to get over him. Every time there was a Convergence I feared he would get his mate, but he was still single. Even so, I would never have a chance with him. He only saw me as a friend.

And who could blame him? I was stuck inside of a teenage body after living most of my life in Lunatera, where time didn't flow like it did here on Earth. I was in my early forties, but on the outside, I didn't look a day over fifteen. No decent guy would even consider me romantically, and Ethan was the best guy I knew. Nothing would ever happen between us while I looked like this, but it didn't stop my crush on him from growing into something unmanageable.

The elevator dinged and the doors opened onto the top floor, where Ethan's office was. I sucked in a bracing breath before stepping out into the nice lobby, which was smooth and sleek with large windows overlooking Toronto. The front desk was empty, and I hesitated in front of it.

Ethan came walking down the hallway with an easy

smile on his face and the whole world seemed to stop. His dark hair framed his face in ways that made his sharp cheekbones and strong jawline look good enough to lick. He wore a dark gray suit that was tailored to perfection, fitting his body so well that it made me want to weep. His white shirt was unbuttoned at his neck, showing off a bit of tan skin with the slightest hint of black ink teasing what was underneath.

And his eyes? I could lose myself in them forever. They were cool gray, like the moon itself, and the moment I looked into them I fell madly in love all over again—and had my heart broken because I knew he could never be mine.

Goddess, I was such a fool to come here in person.

"I thought I heard the elevator," he said, completely oblivious to the total meltdown I was having at the sight of him. "Sorry, my assistant took the day off for her son's birthday. Come in my office and we'll get started."

He motioned for me to follow him, and I jerked myself out of my starstruck haze. "Hi," I said. *Hi?* Couldn't I think of anything better to say? No, because I didn't trust my mouth right now. I wanted to smack myself in the forehead like that emoji with the hand over its face. Yep, that was me, one big giant facepalm when Ethan was around.

"It's nice to see you, Larkin," he said, and my stomach swooped, my knees nearly giving out on me.

I clutched the doorframe leading into his office to try to get a hold of myself. *Keep it together,* I told myself over and over. Ethan walked over to his desk, which was huge and made of cherry wood, and then took off his jacket. I stood, frozen in place, as he set it on his chair, and then rolled up his shirt sleeves, revealing the tattoos inked all along his arms.

He noticed me standing like a scared rabbit and his smile dropped. "Are you all right?"

I scurried across the room toward his desk, my cheeks going red. "Yes, sorry. I, um, forgot to eat this morning."

"Ah." In a few strides, he was across the room, bending before a mini fridge. He grabbed a bottle of water, then busied himself with some things while I sat down in a very comfortable chair in front of his desk. A few moments later, he set a plate in front of me with a beautiful arrangement of crackers, some fancy-looking cheese, peppered salami, and red grapes. "Here we are. I'm sorry it's not much. Would you like me to order you something instead?"

"No, this is perfect. Thank you." His thoughtfulness only made my chest ache with longing. Why did he have to be so damn nice?

Ethan sat behind his desk while I took a cracker and spread some cheese on it just to have something to do with my hands. He clicked a few things on his computer. "You're interested in the former hunting and fishing resort on Halcyon Lake, right?"

I nodded, forcing myself to focus on the reason I was here. Ethan and I had researched a lot of different places, including private islands, ghost towns, RV parks, and many more. In the end, the former resort at Halcyon Lake seemed to be the best bet in terms of location and amenities. It was about a four-hour drive from Toronto and seemed like the perfect mix of secluded and private, yet it wasn't so remote that getting supplies would be a problem. Since it was a former resort, there was already a main lodge we could use as a town hall, plus twelve cabins already built that could act as housing for the Moon Witches. With sixty acres of land, there was tons of potential to add more housing over time, along with stores and restaurants and anything else we needed. Water, electricity, and sewage were already taken care of, and there were nearby cellphone towers, which meant that even though it was a little off the beaten path, it wouldn't be like living in Lunatera and completely cut off from the world. To top it all off, our land would be surrounded by protected wilderness, so there would never be any threat of others building close to us.

"It looks perfect on paper." I popped a grape in my mouth. He'd gotten me all this delicious food, and it seemed silly to waste it.

"It does." Ethan shot me another blinding smile. Part of me wanted to ask him to tone it down, but then I'd have to get into *why* I needed him to not smile at me like that, and that was too embarrassing to even think about. "I think we should visit it together and see how much work it needs."

"I'd like that," I said before I could think better of it. "You know more about this sort of thing than I do. I'd be lost if I went there by myself."

"That's why I'm here." He glanced at something on his computer screen. "We should probably talk about costs before we get too much further though. The resort is listed at three and a half million, which includes all the land and water rights, plus all the buildings, boats, and all the equipment."

I sat up straighter, my heart beating like a humming-bird. I'd never seen that much money in my life, and I could hardly conceptualize it. The other Moon Witches weren't any richer, either. "I don't know how we will afford that."

"That's where the Libra pack comes in. We will give the Moon Witches a loan that you can slowly pay off over time."

"By the Libra pack, you mean you, right?" I asked.

"Of course."

I laughed a little, my head spinning. "You're just going to buy us a three-and-a-half million-dollar resort?"

Ethan shrugged. "That's what I do."

"Even so, it will take us an eternity to pay you back. Especially with interest on top." Like me, the other Moon Witches had been stuck in Lunatera for decades or even centuries. I'd convinced some of them to return to Earth with me, and thanks to Mira's smart thinking, they'd been able to earn money by teleporting shifters to different packs. It was a slow process, but we were all beginning to get bank accounts, credit cards, and driver's licenses—all the things we needed to exist in the modern world. "We're not exactly rolling in cash at the moment."

"I did have an idea about that." He paused, checking to see if I was interested before continuing. "If you want to turn this into a real town that will grow and sustain many genera-tions, you'll need to think beyond housing a few Moon Witches."

I paused in the middle of making a cracker-cheese-salami sandwich. "What do you mean?"

Ethan drummed his fingers on the desk. "If you got other people to live in your town, they could help pay off the debt too."

"Are you talking about inviting humans to live there? Because I can already tell you the answer will be no."

"Not humans, no. But there are other supernatural beings who might be interested in living in your town. For example, some shifters are not fitting neatly into one pack or another, especially after the changes with the mate bonds. They might want to live there, outside of the packs, either temporarily or forever."

My initial reaction was to reject his idea, but then I considered his words and saw his point. Many of the Moon Witches were, quite frankly, little old ladies who had no idea how to survive in the modern world. Sometimes it felt like half my time was spent showing them how to use microwaves or thermostats. And computers or smartphones? Forget it. Most of them wouldn't even touch them. There would be great advantages to having other people living in the town who could help keep it running while paying off the loan too.

"I see your point," I said. "I'll talk to the Moon Witches about this, but I doubt they'll like it."

"That's all you can really do," he said. "We can try to think of other ways for your people to earn money as well, but I think this way is the best. Not just for the loan, but for your people's long-term survival."

I nodded. It was something that had been on my mind too. There were some couples among the Moon Witches who were excited about being able to start a family now that they'd returned to Earth, but their numbers were small. If we wanted our people to last more than another generation or two, we needed to breed with outsiders. We couldn't do it alone.

"I'll try to persuade them," I said.

"Good." He furrowed his brow as he looked at his computer. "I can set up a visit to Halcyon Lake in two days. Does that work for you?"

"Yes, that's perfect."

"Great. We'll leave from here early in the morning. Pack a bag so we can spend the night if needed."

My throat went dry at the thought. It sounded like a lot of time alone with Ethan out in the wilderness. I wanted it and I dreaded it all at once. I forced myself to smile. "I'm so excited to see it in person."

"You're going to love it." Ethan stood up and leaned against his desk, and I tried not to stare at his long profile. "Is there anything else you want to talk about?"

Yes, I want to confess my undying love for you. "No, I think that's it."

"Then let me walk you out," Ethan said, ever the gentleman.

We walked to the elevator in a comfortable silence, and then I turned to him. "Thank you so much. Really, I would be so lost without your help."

"I know it's been really hard for you and the rest of the

Moon Witches, and after all the help you gave the Zodiac Wolves against the Sun Witches, it's the least I can do."

"But still," I said. "You've gone above and beyond. I really can't thank you enough."

"Anything for you," he said, and my stomach swooped. I knew he didn't mean anything by it, but the phrase still took my breath away.

Some wild impulse grabbed me then and I threw myself at him, giving him a quick hug. It was like something had taken control of my body, turning me into a much more confident version of myself. When his arms wrapped around me in response, I found myself lifting up on my tiptoes to brush a kiss against his cheek. But Ethan turned his head at that exact moment and my lips accidentally brushed his mouth instead.

Something short-circuited in my brain. *His mouth! Was touching! Mine!*

The moment was ruined when he stepped back so fast that I nearly stumbled. I caught myself and realized what had happened, my cheeks flaring with heat. I'd *kissed* him, and it hadn't even been on purpose.

"I'm so sorry," Ethan said, holding up his hands, looking panicked. "I didn't mean for that to happen. It was an accident. I would never..." He trailed off, and the panic started looking a little closer to horror.

Never? My stomach sank, and I was so embarrassed I wanted to melt right into the floor below me. There was nothing but panic and horror in his eyes at the realization that he'd kissed me.

"It's okay," I said, though my voice sounded a little hysterical. I pressed the elevator down button approximately three hundred times. "It was my fault."

Ethan looked like he wanted to say something more, but the elevator doors opened at that moment, saving me from any more embarrassment. I stepped inside and slapped my hand on the button for the first floor. "Uh, well, goodbye," I said, as I met his eyes briefly. It was the least eloquent thing I could have said, but it was better than screaming, which is what I really wanted to do.

The second the elevator doors shut, I slumped against the wall, breathing like I was about to have a panic attack. When the doors opened, I stumbled into the main lobby and outside, barely noticing anything around me. At some point, I teleported away, though I barely remembered doing it. I just needed to get out of there.

I found myself stepping into the house I had lived in for decades in Lunatera. It was the only place that really felt like home, even though I had complicated feelings about it. It had been both my prison and my sanctuary for years, but now I rarely came back here. I looked around the familiar surroundings—my favorite couch, all the romance novels I'd bought over the years, everything I hadn't taken with me to the Ophiuchus pack lands when I'd moved there—but just felt sick to my stomach. I'd secretly harbored my crush on Ethan for years, and even though it was dumb, I'd always hoped that maybe someday he could think of me as something more than a friend. But from the look on his face after our kiss, I knew that was impossible.

I sank to the ground and covered my face with my hands. "This is the worst day ever," I groaned.

Not only was that my first kiss with Ethan, but it was also my first kiss *ever*. I'd thought about what my first kiss would be like so many times. I'd read about magical first kisses and how the entire world felt right when you kissed someone you loved. It hadn't been like that at all for me. Either the romance novels were lying, or I was the problem. I couldn't decide which was worse.

Somehow I had to go and talk about Ethan's plan with the other Moon Witches, but I wasn't sure if I'd ever be able to move from this spot again. I wished that the ground would open up and suck me into it, but of course that didn't happen. I didn't have that kind of luck.

I thumped my head back against the door and wondered how the hell I was supposed to ever face Ethan again.

CHAPTER TWO

WELL, *that went about as badly as expected.*

I sighed as I transported to Earth, eager to leave Lunatera behind after my meeting with the Moon Witches. They hadn't liked the idea of sharing their town, naturally. I'd hoped that they would at least be open to considering it, but the moment I'd brought it up, everyone had protested. Unfortunately, no one had an alternative solution either. We'd gone back and forth for almost an hour before I'd bowed out and told them that they had to think about it or come up with a better option.

I'd known they would hate the idea of sharing their town, but I'd underestimated just how much. I'd hoped that a few of them would at least be open to talking about it, realizing this would be the key to us saving our people, but they'd refused to even listen.

I returned to Coronis near the cottage I used to share with Stella before she'd moved to live with Jordan and the

Leos. Now the only other inhabitant was a cat named Luna, who'd been given to me by Elsa and Kena, two Moon Witches I'd known my entire life. They'd been together for centuries and had dozens of cats instead of children, and once they came to Earth they naturally brought their babies too. A few months later, their cats all started having kittens, and suddenly the people of Coronis never had a mouse problem again. Luna was one of the first born, a little gray tabby who acted like my trusted familiar some days, and like a houseguest who barely tolerated my presence the rest of the time.

Today she was happy to see me, which was a relief. She darted out from my bedroom and meowed loudly, stepping between my legs and rubbing her head against my calves.

"I hope you had a better day than me." I leaned down and scratched behind her ears. She butted her head against my hand and I smiled for the first time in hours. She was cute, and I was glad I had her, especially now that Stella was gone.

"You're probably hungry, huh?" I asked before going to the pantry and getting Luna's food out. She waited patiently while I filled her bowl, and then happily ate while I peered out of one of the windows, feeling restless. Usually, coming home to Luna after a long day and letting her curl up in my lap was enough to lift my spirits, but today was an exception. I couldn't stop replaying the accidental kiss and the mortifying moments that had followed it over and over in my head.

Tonight was a full moon, and I felt its call deep in my

bones, summoning me to come outside and bathe in its light. I ached to share the experience of the full moon with someone, anyone. But Stella, Mira, and Ayla were all mated, and either pregnant or dealing with their kids. I could try to find Harper, but I knew how the wolves got on the full moons. I didn't know what—or who—she was doing tonight and I definitely didn't want to get in the middle of any of that. At least it was May, which wasn't the Ophiuchus's mating time. I didn't need them all going into heat on top of everything else to remind me of how alone I was.

Being here, all alone, wasn't going to help me feel any better. I had to do something to get this restless energy out, and no matter how upset I was, being under the moon always calmed me down.

I made sure that Luna had enough water, and then grabbed my purple hooded robes, draping them over me before heading outside. The night was cool around me, and I heard the sounds of wolves howling in the distance. They usually started the full moon with a pack-wide hunt in the forest, before they all split off to enjoy themselves in other ways.

I turned in the opposite direction and let my feet lift off from the ground, using my Moon Touched gift of flight to rise above the trees. Up here, where the air was clear and fresh and the moon was brighter than ever, I was safe. No one could touch me here, and no one would judge me or find me lacking. I could simply...exist.

I zoomed above the trees, feeling the wind in my hair and the moonlight upon my back, getting as far away from

Coronis as I dared. A part of me wanted to fly all night and see how far I could get before I passed out in exhaustion. Instead, I found an especially tall tree and perched upon a sturdy branch like an owl.

I gazed up at the moon, which seemed especially bright tonight. The goddess's light filled me up and magic danced inside my veins. Something about this night felt magical as if Selene herself was watching and anything could happen.

"I don't know if you're listening," I whispered, as I stared up at the moon. "But you're the only one I have to talk to."

The slight breeze rustled the trees, and no one answered me. It was rare for Selene to talk to anyone, even Moon Witches, but I kept talking anyway.

"My aunt, Celeste, I'm sure you know her. Of course you do, since she's our High Priestess. She probably talks to you all the time, doesn't she?" I gave a little laugh, feeling ridiculous. "She put me in charge of relocating the Moon Witches back to Earth, which should have been a huge honor. But none of them take me seriously because of the way I look."

I sat down on the branch and put my chin in my hand. "They all treat me like a kid. Including Ethan." I squeezed my eyes tight as the kiss replayed in my mind, along with the look of horror on his face afterward. "He's the Libra alpha. I love him, but he only sees me as a teenage girl, just like everyone else. I'm in my forties, for fuck's sake! But no matter what I do, no one ever treats me like an adult."

I picked at a spot on my robes where one of the embroidered moons was coming undone. I knew Selene wouldn't answer, but it helped just to talk to her, so I kept going. "All I want is to be an adult instead of trapped in a kid's body. If I looked even a few years older, maybe people would see the real me. Maybe then I'd have a real chance at love."

My heart twinged again as I thought about Ethan. Now that I was living on Earth I would grow older, just like everyone else—but by the time I had grown into my body, it would probably be too late. He'd be with someone else by then, and I would still be alone.

More than anything, I wanted to fall in love and have that sweeping, all-consuming romance I'd read about in my favorite books. I knew it was possible because so many of my friends had found their mates. Why couldn't I have that too?

A lone tear trickled down my cheek. "Haven't I done everything for you, Selene? For the Moon Witches? Don't I deserve love too?"

I didn't expect a response, so I was even more shocked when the moon suddenly flashed so bright it temporarily blinded me. I blinked quickly, trying to regain my night vision, and through the glowing moonlight, I saw something that resembled the outline of a woman.

"Larkin." The voice was cool and serene, like a whisper in the breeze, and I nearly fell out of the tree at the sound.

I clutched to the branch, my hands shaking. *Holy shit,* I thought. *It's really her.* I cleared my throat. "H-hello?"

"I can grant your wish," Selene said, her words like a gentle caress across my ears. "It is within my power to give you what you most desire, but there is one condition. You only have until the next full moon to fulfill your two tasks of finding love and securing a home for the Moon Witches or the spell will be broken."

Was this really happening? I started to wonder if I'd fallen out of the tree and knocked my head against the ground. Or maybe I'd fallen asleep at home with Luna on my lap. But then the vague female shape reached toward me and sent power pouring through me in a great rush, making my skin feel like it might peel off, while my teeth and eyes ached like never before. Then the moonlight faded and the night went back to normal, as if nothing had happened at all.

"I won't let you down," I whispered. "I promise."

But once Selene was gone, I immediately began to doubt everything that had just happened. I rubbed my eyes and held out my hands, but they looked the same. Selene had said she would grant my wish, but I didn't seem any different. Maybe I was losing my damn mind. After the day I'd had, who would blame me?

Coming out here hadn't cleared my head the way I'd hoped, and I just wanted to go home and crawl into my bed. I flew back the way I'd come and went into my cottage, tossing off my robes as soon as I stepped inside. Luna greeted me at the door again, and I scooped her up into my arms. She purred and cuddled against me like she could feel that I needed all the extra love I could get tonight.

I got ready for bed, and with Luna purring at my side, I fell asleep. *What a funny thing to imagine,* I thought as I drifted off. *The moon goddess, talking to me.*

IN THE MORNING, I opened my eyes and glanced around, still clinging to a small shred of hope that my encounter with Selene had been real, but my room looked the same as always. The romance novel I'd picked up a few days ago on Stella's recommendation was still bookmarked about halfway through, just like I'd left it, and the clothes I'd worn last night were perched on top of the hamper. Luna sat in her cat tree licking her fur, her tail twitching every so often. Nothing felt different, and I decided that everything really *had* been a dream. Not that I was all that surprised. There was no reason for Selene to grant me a wish, not when there were so many other Moon Witches who had begged her for help all these years.

I pulled the covers off of my body and got out of bed. As I stretched my arms above my head, I noticed that my shirt felt oddly tight against my body. I looked down and nearly had a heart attack.

I had boobs. Like, big ones. Boobs that weren't there last night.

What the fuck...

I turned to the full-length mirror on the other side of the room and stared.

And stared.

And stared.

I didn't recognize myself in the mirror. The woman before me was older, taller, and had real curves. She also had long, pure white hair. I blinked at the reflection and raised my hand. My reflection raised her hand as well. My mouth gaped, and so did the woman in front of me.

I pulled the fabric of my shirt tight. I had a waist, an actual *waist,* and my body was curvy and toned. I poked at my boob. It jiggled, and so did the boob in the mirror. I poked it again, wondering if it was a fluke. Maybe I was still asleep. I pinched myself. Ow. Okay, that had certainly felt real.

I met my gaze in the mirror. My eyes were the same, and I still had the faintest trace of freckles across my nose and cheeks. The rest of my face looked familiar, yet different. Older.

"No way," I said, but there was no denying it.

I was a woman.

CHAPTER THREE

THE FIRST THING I did with my new body was strip off all my clothes and look at myself naked. Who wouldn't?

I still couldn't believe it was real. Selene had actually granted my wish and made me older. I guessed this body was approximately in its mid-twenties, which meant I'd aged ten years or so overnight.

I grinned as I twisted around in the mirror, admiring the way my limbs moved. I'd always felt gawky and too awkward like I was stuck somewhere between the charm of a child and the grace of an adult. But now I had boobs. And a butt! And I was...pretty? I'd never felt attractive before, so this was an entirely new experience for me.

I picked up my phone and snapped a quick selfie to make sure this wasn't all some weird hallucination or an illusion. Then I debated sending the picture to all my friends in our group chat but decided that might freak them out. How was I going to explain this to people?

I sat back on the bed, staring at my feet, which were also a tiny bit bigger. "Thank you," I whispered to Selene, though I wasn't sure she could hear me in the daytime. Tears filled my eyes knowing the goddess had actually spoken to me and fulfilled my wish. With stipulations, of course. I only had until the next full moon to both find love and secure a new home for the Moon Witches. Easier said than done, especially in such a short amount of time. And if I failed, I'd be back in my younger body again.

That wasn't going to happen. I'd promised the goddess I would do this, and I'd meant it. At the very least, I would try my best.

Step one: find something to wear.

I pulled my favorite jeans out of my closet and realized this would be harder than I expected. I'd bought these jeans in Toronto when we'd stayed there with the Libra pack, but they were slender through the hips and butt. It was obvious they weren't going to fit.

I tossed them aside. Surely I had something that would fit my new body. I pulled clothes from the dresser and closet, discarding them one at a time while swearing under my breath. All of my clothes were made for a teenager's body.

Step two: ask for help.

I dialed Ayla, who picked up the phone and sounded confused. I'd quickly learned, after coming to Earth, that no one used their phones for actual calls. "Larkin? Are you okay?"

"Yes. No. I'm fine, but um, none of my clothes fit."

"Oh. Have you had a growth spurt or something?"

I laughed like a mad woman. "Something like that. Uh, could you please bring over some of your clothes? And maybe shoes too? As soon as you can?"

She was silent for a long moment, probably debating my sanity, especially since I was calling her at nine in the morning. She had a baby, after all. What was I thinking?

"I'll be right over," she said, surprising me.

"Thank you," I said, the relief obvious in my voice. I should have known my cousin would come through for me.

She arrived at the cottage thirty minutes later with baby Jack wrapped up on her chest, and in her arms, she carried both a large duffel bag and her diaper bag. When I opened the door, wearing my too-tiny pajamas once more, her jaw hit the floor, along with both bags she was carrying. It was a good thing Jack was strapped on tight.

"Wow." Her eyes roamed over me, and she seemed to be having trouble forming words.

I picked up both her bags. "It's me. Larkin."

"I figured out that much, thanks. When you called I could tell something was going on, but this was not what I expected at all. You're..." She gestured wildly with her hands in the direction of my chest. "Wow."

"I know," I said with a laugh, as I ran my hands through my hair. I was glad it was longer again—that pixie cut had been a mistake. "I'm older."

"How did this happen?"

"It's a long story. Come inside, and I'll make us some coffee."

"Good idea." She gave me another shocked look before

heading inside, and as she passed by me, I realized that I was taller than her now. Weird.

I hurried into the kitchen and busied myself making a pot of coffee, while also pulling out some blueberry muffins I'd made two days earlier. Ayla watched the entire time from the side like she wasn't one hundred percent sure it was really me. Jack, on the other hand, seemed perfectly content and entirely unphased by my new appearance. He was super cute, and though he looked a lot like Kaden, his white hair was all Moon Witch.

While the coffee brewed, I handed Ayla a plate with a muffin on it and told her everything that had happened last night. By the time I was done, the coffee was ready, and I poured it for us.

"That's incredible," Ayla said. "I've felt Selene's power before, but I've never heard her speak. She must really favor you."

"Maybe." I stared into my coffee mug. "I just hope she hasn't given me an impossible task."

"Let's start with the Moon Witch town. What's happening with that?"

"I've found the perfect place for us to live, but it's expensive. Ethan thinks we can offset some of the costs by inviting other people to live there, such as shifters who don't want to live with any of the packs. But when I brought the idea up to the other Moon Witches, they weren't excited about it. In fact, they downright refused to even consider it."

Ayla took a slow sip of her coffee, her eyes thoughtful. "I think a neutral town where different supernaturals could live in harmony is a great idea. I'm sure they'll come around to the idea eventually."

"I'm not so sure," I muttered. "Convincing them might be impossible."

"I know you can do it, especially with Ethan's help. Plus that will give you an excuse to spend more time with him, and maybe fall in love at the same time."

I groaned and covered my face in my hands. Thanks to the excitement of my new body, I'd managed to temporarily forget our awful kiss yesterday and everything else that had come with it.

"What?" Ayla asked. "I know how you feel about him."

"My feelings aren't the problem." I didn't remove my face from my hands. I could feel myself blushing, my cheeks growing uncomfortably warm. Great to know that didn't go away when my body got older. *Not.*

"He cares for you too," Ayla said. "I know it."

"As a friend, sure. But that's it." I finally removed my head from my hands. I'd have to tell her about the kiss with Ethan, something I wished I could remove from my mind forever. "When I went to visit Ethan yesterday, we accidentally kissed."

"How do you accidentally kiss?" Ayla asked, looking confused.

"We were hugging goodbye, and I tried to kiss his cheek, but he turned his head, and..." I trailed off and made a vague gesture with my hands. "He looked horrified, and it was so awkward. He said he didn't mean to do it, and that he'd never do something like that. He's clearly not interested, and never will be."

Ayla sighed. "I mean, I get it. Your body was, you know, a teenager's, and no matter how much Ethan liked you as a person, he would never cross that line. But now that you look closer to your true age, he might change his mind. You're smoking hot, Larkin!"

"Thanks." I ducked my head, still blushing.

My phone rang, startling me out of wondering how Ethan would react to my new body. I pulled it out of my pocket and looked at it.

"Oh no," I said, feeling a bit faint. "Why does he have the worst timing?"

"You have to answer it," Ayla said.

I shook my head, putting it down on the counter. The buzzing got louder, and Ethan's name continued flashing on the screen.

"If you don't answer, I will," she said.

I gaped at her. "You wouldn't."

Ayla raised her eyebrows, daring me to find out.

"Fine," I snapped, and answered the phone. "Hey, Ethan." I tried to make it casual, but I was sure I failed completely. I cleared my throat and squeezed my phone tighter.

"Hey," Ethan said, sounding a bit less confident than usual. "I just wanted to call and tell you how sorry I am once again for the awkward way things ended between us yesterday."

"You didn't have to," I said. "I mean, it's okay."

"Still," Ethan said. "I didn't mean to upset you, and I didn't want to do anything that would ruin our friendship."

"It's fine. Really. I know you're always a perfect gentleman." *Sadly,* I added in my head. From the look Ayla gave me, I might as well have said it out loud.

"Thank you for understanding." Ethan cleared his throat. "I also wanted to check if we're still good to go to Halcyon Lake tomorrow to check out the resort."

I hesitated. I wasn't sure how I'd be able to face him. Talking to him over the phone was one thing, but seeing him in person...

Ayla made a frantic motion at me, nodding her head vigorously. I rolled my eyes at her. There was no hiding my conversation from her sensitive wolf ears, and I knew she would never let me get out of this awkward situation.

"Yes," I said, squeezing my eyes shut. "I'm still good to go."

Ethan let out a breath, almost imperceptible on the other end of the line. "Good. I can't wait to see you tomorrow. What do you say about eight? I'd like to get an early start if we can. Let's meet in my office and we'll go from there."

"That works."

"Perfect," Ethan said. "I look forward to it."

"See you tomorrow," I replied, before hanging up. The longer we talked, the greater the chance I'd say something I would later regret.

Ayla stared at me. "Well?"

"Like you weren't listening to everything." I sat back in

my chair, willing my body to relax. "I'm going to look at the resort with him tomorrow."

"Good. Now you just have to woo Ethan and then you can keep this new body. But first, you'll need some new clothes."

"Did you really just say 'woo?'"

She ignored me and opened up the duffel bag. "I brought over some clothes, but you didn't exactly give me much to go on, so I did the best I could. They won't do for a day trip with Ethan though." She pulled out a couple of things and tossed them to me. "Put these on, and then we'll go shopping. You're going to need a whole new wardrobe."

I stared down at the clothes in my hands. I did love shopping, but I didn't have much money, and I was hesitant to spend it on clothes that might not fit me in a few weeks if I failed horribly. Then again, I couldn't walk around in too small clothes for the next month either. Especially not around Ethan.

"Fine, let's go shopping," I said, mustering a smile for my cousin. I just hoped this wouldn't be one big giant disaster.

CHAPTER FOUR

I TELEPORTED JUST OUTSIDE of Ethan's office at
eight AM sharp. I didn't even give myself the chance to ride
the elevator today, afraid that if I didn't go straight to his
office I'd find some way to talk myself out of it. I had no idea
how Ethan was going to react to my new appearance, and I
didn't know if we could pretend that nothing had happened
between us two days ago. Everything about today might be
awkward and terrible. In fact, I should probably turn around
and go home.

I was debating making an escape when Ethan opened
the door to his office. Shoot, he'd probably heard me with his
sensitive wolf ears.

"Hey, Larkin—" He froze the second he saw me, his
mouth still open, though the words had been cut off. His
gaze raked up and down my body, before lingering on my
face with a thousand questions in his eyes.

"Sorry, I should have sent you a heads-up or a picture or

something." I twisted a piece of my long white hair, my hands shaking a little. "But I promise it's really me."

"I know. You smell the same."

Oh my goddess. Now all I could think about was how I smelled. Was it bad? Good? Should I feel honored that Ethan knew my smell so well, or was that just a normal shifter thing? I was so out of my depth here.

Those cool gray eyes swept over me again, slower this time. Taking in every inch of me. "You look incredible."

"Oh. Um. Thank you." I was one hundred percent sure my face was fire truck red. I smoothed my hands down the front of my new jeans, which Ayla had said made my ass look smoking hot. I was also wearing a V-neck that showed off my brand-new cleavage, though now I wondered if it was too much or too obvious. I was torn between wanting Ethan to stare at me and wanting to go hide in a closet.

He cleared his throat and seemed to regain some of his composure, though it obviously took some effort. My appearance had really shaken him. "How did this happen?"

"I prayed to Selene and asked her to give me an older body. The next morning I woke up like this." Sure, that was only part of the story, but I didn't think he needed to hear all of it. Especially the finding love in less than thirty days part.

"That's amazing. Does Selene often grant the wishes of Moon Witches?"

"No, almost never." I smiled a little. "None of the other Moon Witches could believe it, even with me standing in front of them."

He met my smile with one of his own. "Maybe now

they'll listen to you a little more, knowing you have the favor of your goddess."

"That would be nice, but I doubt it."

I'd spent yesterday morning going shopping with Ayla for new clothes and shoes, and we'd run into some of the Moon Witches living in Coronis. They'd been so shocked by my appearance that I went to Celeste afterward to make sure she heard the news from me first. By the evening, it seemed like every single Moon Witch was coming by the cottage to ask me about my encounter with Selene and check out my new appearance. I couldn't blame them. Most of them had spent their entire lives praying to our goddess without receiving any indication she was listening at all. For her to not only speak to me but also grant my wish was completely unheard of, and I'm sure they were all wondering why she'd listened to me and not them. I wasn't sure either, to be honest.

Ethan tore his eyes away from me with what seemed like a lot of effort. I'd really rattled the poor man. "Are you ready to get going?"

"Yes." I was carrying Ayla's duffel bag, which I'd borrowed and filled with some of my new clothes, along with the other things I'd need for a night away, including my laptop.

Ethan grabbed his own small suitcase and then reached for the bag on my shoulder. "Here, let me."

"Oh, thanks."

As we rode down the elevator together, Ethan faced the reflective walls, and I tried to look at anything but him. He was dressed in Ethan-casual today, which meant a nice pair of dark trousers and a white button-up shirt, with the sleeves rolled back, naturally. I wondered if he ever wore jeans and a T-shirt.

"I'm sorry again about the other day," he said. "I didn't mean to make it awkward."

Shoot. I was hoping we could avoid talking about the worst kiss ever. "It's fine, I promise. How about we pretend that it never happened?"

"Is that what you want?"

"Definitely."

He gave me a kind smile. "Then that's what we'll do."

The elevator doors opened into the basement, where dozens of cars were parked. Ethan led me to a large luxury SUV that was black and shiny like it had just been washed. He opened the passenger side door for me first, then went to the trunk and began loading our luggage into it.

As we both buckled our seatbelts he said, "The resort is about a four hour drive away. I booked us rooms at a nearby hotel though, so we don't need to rush back. I want us to spend as much time as we can there so you can get a really good feel for the place."

"Is it just the two of us?" I asked, even though the answer was obvious. It was just now hitting me that I was actually going away for a night with the man I had a huge crush on.

"Yes. My beta will take care of everything while I'm gone." He motioned to the dashboard as he pulled out of the parking garage. "Do you want to pick the music?"

"Really?" I asked. Ethan was always polite, but he was also an alpha and he was always in control of every situation he was in.

"Don't sound so surprised," Ethan said, grinning over at me.

"Too late." I flipped through the satellite radio and put on some upbeat pop, the kind of thing we could sing along to, not that I was brave enough to do such a thing.

He shook his head with a smile. "This is exactly the kind of music I'd expect you to choose."

"I like all kinds of music," I said. "I can change it."

"No," Ethan said. "I meant it, you can play whatever you want. I was just teasing you."

The next four hours passed quicker than I expected. The drive was beautiful, especially since spring had fully arrived in Canada, and the scenery kept me entertained. So did the music, even though some songs had Ethan groaning, though I noticed that he hummed along to some of them too. We also talked a little bit, though we were just as content to enjoy the ride in companionable silence too.

Eventually, we turned onto a dirt road that had an old, abandoned sign that must have had the resort's name on it at some point. The elements had weathered it away until it was nothing but blank wood. As we drove down the road, the forest enveloped us like a green cloak, both protecting and sheltering us. I got the feeling that there was no one else around us for some distance, which was exactly what the Moon Witches wanted.

When the trees thinned out, I spotted the first of the

twelve cabins on the property, which was about the size of my cottage and had a hunter green roof. We continued along the road and I spotted more cabins spaced about the property, some larger and some smaller, but all in what appeared to be good condition from the outside. If they were all in good shape on the inside too they would be perfect homes for the Moon Witches.

My excitement grew as we reached the main lodge, a much larger building made of stone but with the same hunter green roof. It was only steps away from the crystal blue lake, which sparkled under the bright sun overhead. There was a small sandy beach at the edge of the lake, and multiple docks with boats already waiting there, swaying slowly in the breeze. The rest of the area was smooth green grass, with tons of space for people to gather or for us to build upon.

Ethan parked in front of the lodge and I got out of the car and breathed in the fresh, clean air. It was so beautiful and peaceful here I wasn't sure I would ever want to leave. I could already picture the Moon Witches gathering under the full moon in front of the lodge, or shifters running across the grass toward the forest that surrounded this little slice of paradise.

"It's perfect," I said.

"I knew you would think so." Ethan had his hands in his pockets, but he was watching me, not the gorgeous scene around us. "Let's start by checking out the lodge, and then I'll take you through the cabins. You'll see that most of them are in pretty good shape, although a few definitely need work."

"You've been here before?" I asked as we walked down the path to the lodge. It had tons of windows looking out onto the lake, and I bet it got amazing views at sunset and sunrise.

"Of course," Ethan said. "I wouldn't suggest any properties to you that I hadn't personally vetted myself."

As I stepped through the entrance of the lodge, the scent of aged wood and pine greeted me, instantly calming my senses. The spacious main room stretched out before me, its vaulted ceilings reaching toward the sky like outstretched arms. The large windows let in tons of sunlight, which lit up the polished wood floors and the large stone fireplace in the corner. I couldn't help but imagine myself sitting by that fireplace, sipping hot cocoa on chilly evenings while watching the flames dance. The furnishings were rustic and dusty, but they had a certain charm to them too.

We explored the entire building, and Ethan took notes on his phone of anything that might need to be repaired or replaced, before heading outside again. Together we stood on the deck that wrapped around the lodge, and I gazed out at the serene landscape spread out before me. The stillness of the lake and the forest was punctuated only by the occasional rustle of leaves or the distant call of wildlife. At that moment, I knew that this place held a special kind of magic. It reminded me a lot of Lunatera, actually.

We went to tour the cottages next, and as we made our way along the dirt road, the scent of pine needles filled my nose. The first cabin was one of the smaller ones and was nestled among the trees. It had a quaint, rustic feel that made it blend seamlessly with the natural surroundings. Inside, I found a cozy living area and a well-equipped kitchen that was a lot more modern than I'd expected. The single bedroom was small but comfortable, with a window that offered a picturesque view of the lake outside.

The next cabin we visited had three bedrooms plus two bathrooms, which would be perfect for a small family. The interior was simple yet charming, with wooden furnishings and soft, comfortable seating. Sunlight streamed in through the windows, casting a golden glow over everything. I imagined my friends spending lazy afternoons here, gathered around the kitchen sharing stories and laughter. The thought brought a smile to my face.

The more we looked around, the faster I fell in love with the place. I could already picture myself here, waking up every day and looking out at the lake. I knew that if I could only get the other Moon Witches out here, they'd love it just as much as I did. Since I knew that was unlikely, I took tons of photos on my phone, with plans to make a slideshow to show them at our next meeting. Meanwhile, Ethan made a long list of all the work that the place needed.

After we finished our initial tour, Ethan headed back to his car. "Time for a well-deserved lunch break."

He pulled a blanket and cooler out from the trunk and tilted his head toward the beach, motioning for me to follow him. I took my shoes off and sank my feet into the sand as I watched Ethan spread the blanket out.

"What's this?" I asked.

"I meant it when I said we could take our time," Ethan

said. "I packed a picnic so we could stay here for as long as you wanted. I thought lunch by the lake would be the perfect way for you to get to know the property a bit better."

I sat down on the blanket and looked at the assortment of food. He'd packed some sandwiches I recognized from a place down the road from his office. It looked delicious, and I was touched that he'd taken the time to think of this. There he went again, with his thoughtfulness and attention to detail.

"If I remember correctly, this one is your favorite," he said, handing me a banh mi sandwich.

"How do you know that?" I asked, as I eagerly unwrapped it.

He shrugged. "I remember you eating them when you stayed with our pack in Toronto."

"You remember that? That was ages ago." I was starving and the first bite was so good that I had to hold back a moan. We'd never had anything like this back in Lunatera.

"I have a very good memory." Ethan watched me eat with a smile, without touching his own food.

"What?" I asked. "Do I have something on my face?"

He shook his head and looked away, finally taking a bite of his sandwich. "No. I'm still getting used to this new look on you."

"Sorry. I know it's a big change."

He handed me a bottle of water. "In some ways, yes. In other ways, you look more like the true you now."

I was so touched by his words that I forgot all about my sandwich. Had Ethan actually seen the real me before, even when I looked so much younger than my actual age? I'd never thought it was possible, but maybe I'd been wrong all this time.

"It must have been difficult, being trapped as a child for so long while your mind continued to age," he said.

"It was, yeah." I blew out a long breath and picked up my sandwich again. "Although the true me is even older than you are. I'm pretty sure I'm in my mid-forties at this point."

"Well, you look damn good for your age," he said, raising his water bottle in a toast. I toasted him back with a laugh.

We joked around a bit more as we finished our sandwiches, and it was so easy being with him, especially in a place like this. When we were done, we watched as a few ducks chased each other around the lake, ruffling their feathers and quacking loudly.

"What do you think?" Ethan asked as we cleaned up our picnic. "Do you want to move forward with this property?"

"I love it. I know the Moon Witches will too. It reminds me of Lunatera."

"I'd hoped you would say that." He pulled out his phone again and checked something on it. "I'd like to check a few more things while we're here and take a few more notes about repairs. I'd also like to get my contractor out here to look at it sometime."

"How much do you think it'll cost to turn the place into an actual working village?"

Ethan looked up like he was doing some quick calculations in his head. "About five hundred grand."

I'd just taken another sip of water, and I nearly spit it

out. "What?" That was way more than I'd expected. The place looked pretty good to me, and I'd thought it would just take some hard work from all of us, not that huge of an investment. "That puts the total cost of everything at about four million! There's no way we can afford that. What if someone buys it before we can get that kind of money?"

"That's not going to happen."

"How do you know for sure?"

"Because I bought the resort already." He said it so casually like he was talking about buying socks and not something that cost millions of dollars.

"You did?"

"As soon as I found the place, I knew it was perfect, and I didn't want to risk losing it to someone else. If the Moon Witches didn't want it, I planned to make it into a resort for the Libra pack to escape to when we wanted to get out of the city. But this way, I can sell it to the Moon Witches whenever you're ready."

"Thank you." I felt the hot press of tears at the backs of my eyes and tried to blink them away. "You've done so much for me. For us, I mean. I don't know how we'll ever be able to repay you, and I don't just mean the money."

"It's my pleasure. You've done so much for the Zodiac Wolves, and it's only right that we help you in return."

Was he talking about the Moon Witches, or about me personally? I couldn't tell. I wanted to hug him again, but I wasn't interested in repeating that disaster. So I dabbed at my eyes and gave him a smile, while my heart nearly burst with hope and excitement.

CHAPTER FIVE

TAKING extensive notes about the resort took longer than I expected, and it was early evening by the time we packed up and headed toward the closest town to stay at the small hotel there.

As we drove there, I fantasized about what might happen if this was a romance novel. We'd get to the hotel, and they would inform Ethan that they'd made a mistake, and they only had one room, with one big bed. *And everyone knows what happens after that.*

I smiled out the car window as I thought about it, the way we'd go to sleep on two opposite sides, maybe even build a wall of pillows between us. But when we woke up, we'd be in each other's arms. Ethan would look at me and finally realize that he was madly in love with me, and we would make sweet, passionate love in the early morning light.

When the front desk girl frowned as she looked over

Ethan's reservation, I held my breath, waiting for my fantasy to come true. But then she handed us our separate room keys and I tried not to sigh audibly. Apparently, the one-bed thing only happened in romance novels. Not that Ethan would ever take advantage of a situation like that anyway. He was too much of a gentleman. He'd insist on sleeping on the floor, without a doubt.

After we each went into our separate rooms, we had about thirty minutes to rest and clean up before we'd agreed to meet up for dinner. I brushed my hair and wished I'd brought some makeup or something, not that I really knew how to use it. Besides, this wasn't a date. This was just a meal with a friend and business partner, who never needed to know that I was totally in love with him.

"I think you'll like the food at the diner across the street," Ethan said, once we'd both stepped out into the hallway. "I checked the reviews and it looks good."

"You really do think of everything, don't you?" I asked.

"I try."

The diner looked outdated but cozy, with hockey memorabilia and photos on the walls. Ethan and I squeezed into a red booth next to a window, and I breathed in the aroma of bacon and gravy.

"So, I've always been curious," Ethan said after we'd ordered our food. "What was it like during all those years in Lunatera?"

"It's incredibly beautiful and peaceful, but it's always night and nothing ever changes there. As much as I love the moon, there were times when I would have given my left arm to see the sun again. It was also a bit lonely because I was the only kid when I went to live there, and then I just...stayed that way."

"What happened to your parents?"

I stared down at my hands, feeling the ache in my chest that came with remembering them. "They were killed by Sun Witches when I was a kid."

"I'm sorry."

"It happened a long time ago." I forced a smile. "The other Moon Witches took me in and taught me everything I know about magic. It wasn't all bad. Plus I had lots of books to keep me company."

"Ah, yes. I've heard you have a book club with Ayla and Stella."

We talked a bit about books, and I wasn't surprised to find that Ethan read mostly non-fiction. Conversation flowed easily between us as we ate our food, which was delicious. I asked him about growing up in the Libra pack and learned that he wasn't the son of an alpha, like Kaden, Jordan, and Wesley, but had won the position instead. He mentioned he always wished he'd had siblings, and I learned that he liked to watch baking shows to unwind, which made me giggle.

"What?" he asked, pretending to be offended. "They're relaxing."

"Do you ever do any baking of your own?" I asked.

"Of course not," he said with a laugh. "I'm completely useless in a kitchen."

I loved the sound of his laugh and wished I could hear it

more often. "I like to bake. I'll bring you some muffins next time I see you."

His eyes dropped to my lips. "I'd like that."

Something about the way he was looking at me made me flush. I drank some water to cool myself off and convinced myself I was imagining it. Spending all this time alone with him was making my head spin.

Ethan paid the bill without letting me even see how much it was. He also opened doors for me at every opportunity and then escorted me to my hotel room.

I found myself lingering before opening my door. I didn't want this moment to end. "Thank you for dinner. And for today."

"My pleasure," Ethan said.

He didn't move to leave, and I smiled and tucked my hair behind my ear. Ethan tracked the movement and opened his mouth like he was about to say something. I waited, holding my breath, but then he gave me a rueful smile.

"Goodnight, Larkin," he said, pulling out the keycard to his room.

I let out a long, slow breath and finally opened my own door. "Goodnight."

Once in my hotel room, I leaned against the door, my heart pounding like I'd just run for a very long time. Surely that wasn't just in my head. There had been tension there, right?

Stop it. I wouldn't make something out of nothing. Getting my hopes up would only crush me further when nothing actually happened between us. Ethan was just being nice, as usual. It didn't mean he would ever see me as more than a friend.

I got ready for bed, changed into my sleep shirt and shorts, and pulled out the book I'd packed with me. I crawled into bed and settled in, ready to read a few chapters until I felt sleepy, but the book couldn't hold my attention. It wasn't a boring book, but I couldn't concentrate on it at all. I gave up after a few more pages.

I opened up my laptop instead and started working on my secret project—a spicy romance I'd been writing about a hot werewolf and a shy human girl. Naturally, the guy's name was Ethan, for now anyway. I planned to change it if I ever decided to publish my story, but at the moment I was just having fun. Eventually, I might tell Stella or Ayla about it, but I wasn't ready to share this side of me with anyone yet. It was still too new, and just for me.

I was in the middle of a very plot-heavy scene, where the werewolf was busy saving the main character—Laurel— from danger, but I wasn't interested in working on that. I started a new chapter, thinking about my daydream earlier about sharing a hotel room with Ethan. My characters would need a place to stay after they escaped from danger, where they could clean each other's wounds and have hot, sweaty sex all night.

I closed my eyes to cement the image in my mind. Ethan, all ruffled from a recent fight and a girl who looked kind of like me by his side. My characters entered the hotel and the lobby clerk frowned, just like she had tonight.

"I'm sorry," the front desk clerk said. *"We only have one room left."*

Ethan's jaw clenched as he looked between me and the woman. *"You don't have anything else?"*

"No, but it does have a king-size bed."

Something dark and feral flashed through Ethan's eyes. A hunger I'd never seen before. *"We'll take it."*

His voice came out as a low growl and the hair on my arms stood up. I shivered, though I wasn't scared at all.

I leaned forward as I continued typing, getting really into the scene. I wrote it the way I wished things had played out tonight, with a little extra danger and excitement thrown in. Heat pooled low in my belly as my characters both undressed, in order to clean their wounds, naturally.

ETHAN'S EYES *fell to my breasts and lingered, his gaze hot and heavy. Then his hand slid across my stomach, slowly passing over the bruises there.* *"I'd kill him again if I could, for what he did to you."*

I flushed, but couldn't help but lean into his touch. *"I knew you would rescue me."*

From there, it was easy to get them together. After all, there was only one bed.

"Make me feel good," I said.

I saw the war in Ethan's eyes, and I saw the moment he gave up. He slid his fingers to my slick folds like he couldn't help himself. I gasped, heat flaring in my body as he pressed two fingers inside of me.

"You're so wet for me," he growled.

His manhood was hard and hot against my thigh, and I knew how badly he wanted this too. Tension threaded the air between us, making it almost impossible to breathe.

"Take me now," I begged.

He spread my legs and

My phone rang, startling me out of the scene. I closed my laptop with a snap and quickly scrambled out of bed.

It was Ethan. Of course. He was the only person in the world who made phone calls anymore. Getting a text from him this late at night would be bad enough, but now I had to hear his voice too. What was his deal?

I could pretend that I was asleep, but what if it was important? I cleared my throat and tried to sound normal and not completely breathless from writing a sex scene with him in it. "Hey."

"Sorry to bother you, but I couldn't sleep and I was working. I wondered if you could email me a head count of the Moon Witches who might be interested in moving to the town immediately, so we have an idea of what kind of numbers we're looking at."

I relaxed. Of course he was working. "I can do that."

"It doesn't need to be tonight."

"It's fine. I couldn't sleep either."

He paused. "What are you doing?"

"Also working," I said, a bit too quickly. "I'm putting together a slideshow of the photos I took."

"I can't wait to see it." There was another pause. "I'll let you get back to work then. I'll see you tomorrow."

"Okay," I said, my heart racing. "See you tomorrow."

After I hung up, I let out a huge sigh and opened my laptop again. It was my first laptop, a Christmas gift from Ayla and Kaden, and I was still getting the hang of how everything worked, including things like backing up and saving to the cloud (whatever that was). I wasn't sure if backing up would work here in the hotel, so I copied the scene I'd been writing and put it in a blank email to send to myself just in case. Then I opened another document and quickly jotted down the names and family sizes of the Moon Witches who'd expressed some interest in moving to our new town. By the time I was done, I was rubbing my eyes. I copied and pasted the info into a new email and sent it to Ethan, then closed my laptop to get ready for bed.

I got up to turn off my lights, but as I settled into bed, my phone buzzed. Now what?

I reached over to my nightstand, frowning as I saw an email from Ethan, a response to the one I'd just sent him. I clicked on it, wondering if I'd forgotten something.

Ethan's reply was short. *What happens next?*

Huh?

I scrolled down and stopped breathing when I saw what was there. Instead of the list I'd compiled, I'd sent Ethan the spicy scene I'd just written, featuring him and a girl with a very similar name to me.

I buried my face into my pillow and screamed.

CHAPTER SIX

I DOUBLE and triple-checked the message. It kept existing, unfortunately. Yes, I'd actually sent Ethan my spicy scene instead of the list. I must have messed up the copy and pasting or something. Fuck, fuck, fuck.

I wanted to die. Out of all of the stupid mistakes I could have made, this was by far the worst. My heart pounded in my throat and I threw my phone on the nightstand like it was a snake that might bite me. Then I grabbed it again and refreshed the message, reading his reply over and over.

I couldn't believe this was actually happening to me. It was bad enough that I'd sent my unpolished writing to someone unintentionally, but it was a thousand times worse because it was Ethan. There was no way to hide my feelings for him anymore, not after sending him a scene that made it very clear I thought about having sex with him. A lot.

I gripped the sheets tightly between my hands and tried to calm down enough to think. I had no idea what to do. The only thing I *did* know was that I'd never be able to face Ethan again. Maybe I could teleport back to Lunatera and stay there forever so I would never have to see him again. Yeah, that was starting to sound very appealing.

My phone buzzed again, and I nearly threw it across the room because of how much it startled me. Ethan's name flashed on the screen and I panicked all over again. I didn't want to open his message. He was going to tell me that he didn't want to continue this, that he would sell the resort and I'd have to find someone else to help me. No, he wouldn't be that mean. He was too much of a gentleman for that. He was probably reminding me we were just friends or something along those lines. A polite rejection, like what happened after our kiss.

I sighed and opened his message, bracing for the worst.

I'd love to read the rest of the scene.

I stared at the message for a few moments, trying to make sense of the words. It was pretty clear that the characters were supposed to be us. Why would he want to read more? Was he teasing me again?

I got up and tugged at my hair, trying to figure out what to do. Would there be any chance of us being able to move past this? Could we wake up tomorrow and pretend like it didn't happen? I doubted it. This wasn't an accidental kiss. No, this was so much worse. I'd shown Ethan my deepest desire, and he wanted...more? No, that didn't make any sense.

I typed and then deleted a dozen replies, sometimes

apologizing, sometimes begging him to forget I'd ever sent that email. But I couldn't seem to hit send.

A knock came at my door. I froze, my heart beating even faster. There was only one person it could be.

I waited for a long moment. Maybe I could pretend I'd gone to sleep, and he'd leave me alone.

The knock came again, gentle but insistent, and then Ethan's voice floated through the door. "Larkin, are you okay?"

He didn't sound upset, but he was good at controlling his temper. I didn't respond, but I moved closer to the door and held my breath.

"I didn't mean anything by my comment, and I don't want you to be embarrassed or upset," he said. "Please open the door."

I chewed on my lip, shifting from foot to foot. I didn't think I could face him.

"I'm not leaving until I know that you're okay," Ethan said.

There was a hint of alpha in his voice that made me weak in the knees. I found myself opening the door before I even realized what I was doing.

"I'm so sorry," I said, but the rest of my apology got stuck in my throat as I caught sight of him. He was shirtless, with all of his muscles and tattoos on display. The only thing he wore was grey sweatpants that did little to hide his body or the outline of his cock. My gaze caught on that, and I swallowed. I quickly looked away, but there was nowhere safe for my eyes to land on. He looked like he'd just rolled out of bed, his hair mussed and imperfect for once. I could imagine him running his hands through it, and that led to thinking about *me* running my hands through it, and then along the rest of his body.

Meanwhile, Ethan's eyes were caught on my legs and my too-tight shorts. He tore his gaze off of them, but then it snagged again on my breasts, which were snug against the fabric of my shirt. I'd forgotten to buy larger sleep clothes during my shopping trip with Ayla, and my old ones were stretchy enough that they worked for now, even if they were a bit revealing. I resisted the urge to cross my arms.

Ethan cleared his throat and finally managed to look at my face. I burned hot under his gaze, and it felt like he'd put his hands on my body instead of his eyes.

"Are you okay?" he asked.

"I'm so sorry," I said again. "I didn't mean to send you the story."

"It's okay." His lips quirked up into a small smile.

I shook my head, my cheeks flaring. "I can't believe I did that. I've been playing around with writing, but it didn't mean anything. I understand if you're upset though."

"I'm not upset."

I let out a long breath. "Can we forget it ever happened?"

"No, I don't think we can."

"We can't?" I asked, the panic spiking again.

He leaned against the doorframe, so close I could feel the heat off his naked skin. Shifters always seemed to run hot. "I didn't know you were a writer."

I should have stepped back and closed the door, but I couldn't bring myself to move. "I'm not. But I'd like to be."

"Well, you could have fooled me. I thought you'd sent me a published book at first."

I blushed and looked down at my feet. Now he was just being nice. "I've never had a relationship, so books are the closest I've ever gotten." I didn't know why, but I felt the need to keep explaining myself. As if this moment wasn't embarrassing enough. "I've never even had a real kiss."

"Really?" Ethan asked, raising his eyebrows.

"That little peck we had at your office was the only kiss I've ever had," I admitted.

He leaned closer. "I can't believe that."

I motioned to my body with one hand. "No one would kiss me before."

Ethan's eyes dropped to my body once more and lingered just a bit too long before he met my gaze again. "You looked like a kid before, and that was..." He paused and tilted his head to the side. "Confusing."

"And now?" I asked, the words coming out breathless and hopeful.

"Now..." He stared down at me, and his gray eyes seemed to go dark with something like hunger. I could see him warring with himself, just like the Ethan in my story, and then he reached for me.

He swept me into his arms like something from a movie, and then his lips captured mine in a searing kiss. This was no accidental brush of lips like before. No, this kiss was slow and deliberate and everything I'd always dreamed about. I had no idea what to do, but that didn't matter because Ethan was completely in control, his tongue sweeping across my lower lip and sliding into my mouth. Every coherent thought fled my brain, and all I could do was melt against him and try not to collapse into a puddle on the floor.

I put my hands on his shoulders, needing something to hold onto, but the feel of his bare skin under my palms made me gasp. He was half-naked and pressed up against me and oh my goddess this was actually happening. Ethan was really kissing me, and it was real, not just a fantasy in my head. Somehow, it was even better.

He finally pulled back and ran his hands down my arms. "There. Now you've had a real first kiss."

I couldn't say anything. My legs felt like they were going to give out from under me, and I was having a hard time focusing on anything except Ethan's mouth. But then his words finally penetrated the haze of lust and warmth clouding my brain.

Was he just taking pity on me? Right. That was the only reason he would kiss me.

"Thanks." I stepped back quickly, avoiding eye contact. "I'm not a total loser anymore."

His brow furrowed. "Larkin—"

I grabbed the door to my room and started closing it. "I should get to bed. See you tomorrow."

Ethan hesitated for a moment before nodding. "Goodnight."

I practically closed the door in his face, my eyes watering as emotion swept over me. That kiss had meant everything to me and nothing to him. It hadn't been real, and somehow that made it even worse than our accidental kiss.

It was real for me though. I touched my lips. They felt warm and a bit swollen. I replayed every second of our kiss in my head, wondering if it had meant anything to him, but I couldn't tell. I didn't know enough about this sort of thing. Maybe he kissed tons of girls like that.

Or maybe he actually liked me too, and now I'd sent him away like an idiot. That might have been my only chance with him, and I'd blown it. I sighed as I headed back over to my bed. How was I supposed to find love if I freaked out when a man kissed me?

My phone buzzed on the nightstand, causing me to jump. I didn't want to check it, but I couldn't stop myself. I reached over and saw Ethan's name on the screen.

I expected him to apologize or say that we could pretend all of this never happened, like the other time we'd kissed.

I meant it, I really liked your story and I want to know what happens next. But don't worry, your secret is safe with me.

I set my phone down, unsure how to respond. He hadn't mentioned the kiss at all, but at least he wasn't going to tell anyone about my writing. I couldn't imagine sending him any more of it though. One scene had been enough to embarrass me for the rest of my life.

I crawled into bed and pulled the covers up to my neck, but I had a feeling I was going to be staring at the ceiling all night, replaying that kiss in my head over and over.

CHAPTER SEVEN

IN THE MORNING, neither of us said anything about the kiss or the scene I'd sent him. In fact, we barely talked at all on the way to the resort, and once we were there I told him I wanted to fly over the property so I could see it from all angles. It was true, but it was also an excuse to avoid him as much as possible. Ethan took some more notes, and at one point I spotted him as a wolf roaming through the nearby woods. I quickly flew in the opposite direction.

Eventually, I grew tired of flying and landed on the beach. I kicked off my shoes and dug my feet in the sand as I gazed out over the lake. It was still today, without any wind, and looked like a giant piece of glass, reflecting the blue sky and the pine trees.

Footsteps sounded behind me, and I turned to find Ethan with the same blanket from yesterday tucked under his arm. He smiled at me and spread it out across the sand, then took a seat.

"I hope you don't mind some company," Ethan said.

I hesitated. "Not at all."

"About last night..."

I held up a hand. "It's okay. We don't need to talk about it. Really."

Ethan looked like he wanted to protest this, but the expression on my face must have made him change his mind. He leaned back instead and stared out over the water. "I'm jealous of your ability to fly."

"I'm jealous of your ability to shift into a wolf," I said, grateful for the change in topic.

He chuckled softly and patted the blanket next to him. "Come sit down. I promise I won't bite."

Saying no to Ethan was impossible, so I found myself sitting beside him, stretching my legs out in front of me. "Happy now?"

"Very." He was looking at me now, not the lake, and having all his undivided attention on me made my breath hitch. I wanted him to kiss me again, but I knew that was unlikely.

"We should probably start heading back to Toronto," I said.

"We will soon enough." "I wanted to talk to you about your story."

I tensed, preparing for the worst. "What about it?"

"Did you decide what happens next?"

"I think you know what happens next." I wanted to cover my face with my hands.

A slow grin spread across his face. "Are you going to finish it?"

"I don't know."

"I hope you do. It was hot."

My mouth fell open. "Really?"

He reached over and took a piece of my hair and tucked it behind my ears. "I didn't know you thought about me that way."

Maniacal laughter escaped me. "Of course I do. I mean, who wouldn't? Just look at you."

His eyebrows shot up at my confession. I wanted to look away, feeling flushed again, but his hand lingered in my hair and then moved to my neck. He drew me toward him and then his mouth was on mine. The kiss started slow, a tentative exploration, but then I wrapped my arms around his neck and let go of all my hesitations. If he was kissing me again, that meant it wasn't pity that he'd felt for me last night. He actually wanted this. Wanted *me*.

He dragged me onto his lap and kissed me harder, teaching me how to use my lips and tongue without even saying a word. He tilted my head and took what he wanted while giving me so much more. I gave up all control to him, knowing he would never do anything to hurt me.

He growled a little in his throat as his lips moved across my jaw and then pressed to my neck. He breathed me in, his tongue sliding across my skin. "You smell so good. You taste even better."

No one had ever talked to me like that before. It was like

something one of my book boyfriends would say, except it was even better because it was Ethan.

He lowered me down onto the blanket and moved over me, claiming my lips again. He spent an eternity kissing me like he was in no hurry at all. I tangled my hands in his hair, growing bolder with every second that passed and began to kiss him back harder. My hips lifted up of their own accord, seeking him out, and I gasped when I felt his hard length against me, pressing through our clothes. Something electric went through me at that feeling. I'd never once been the object of anyone's desire before, but Ethan actually...wanted me. The thought turned me on more than anything else.

Then his mouth was on my neck again and his hands were cupping my breasts and this intense need filled me, like nothing I'd ever felt before. "Ethan," I moaned.

"Larkin," he said in response, and hearing him say my name with such a throaty growl made me shiver. "Maybe we should finish that scene together."

"Yes," I said, clinging to his shoulders. "I want that. Show me all the things I've read about in books but never experienced."

"I can do that, as long as I make one thing clear first." He moved to lay beside me, lightly running his hand across my belly. "This thing between us... It has to be temporary. We can have some fun together, but I can't promise you anything more than that."

My heart stuttered. "What do you mean?"

He sighed and looked away, his face pained. "It's a shifter thing. I could find my mate at any moment, maybe even at the next Convergence, and I don't want to hurt you when that happens. I've seen relationships torn apart too many times because of a new mate bond. And as the alpha of my pack, I have to find my alpha female. It's my duty. I'm sorry."

I swallowed hard. Something dark and ugly twisted in my stomach as I realized that the next Convergence was the day before the next full moon. There went any hope of getting him to fall in love with me. Of course he would want to find his true mate. He was a shifter, and he needed to be with another shifter—not a Moon Witch like me. I'd always known that.

But this would be my one chance to experience this kind of passion with the man of my dreams. I was already too far gone at this point—there was no turning back now. Even if he didn't fall in love with me, I'd rather have one month with him than nothing at all.

"I understand," I said, forcing a smile. "We can be friends with benefits."

He looked surprised. "Are you sure? Maybe we should stop now before this goes any further. I don't want to hurt you or do anything to ruin our friendship. I care about you a lot."

"I'm sure. I want this." I saw the hesitation on his face and sat up straighter. "I know I looked like a kid a few days ago, but I am an adult and I can make my own decisions. I'm tired of only reading about sex in books. I want to experience it myself, and I can't think of anyone better to do it with than you. I trust you and I feel comfortable with you. And besides, I'm not looking for anything serious anyway. Not right now."

Tension drained from his face and he smiled again. "I'm glad you trust me, and that we're on the same page."

I felt a bit guilty lying to him about that last bit, but he didn't need to know that I was already hopelessly in love with him. There was nothing that would change that, not even the threat of impending heartbreak when he inevitably found his mate.

Was I making a huge mistake? Probably. But I'd waited for too many years to be intimate with a man, and I was really tired of being a virgin.

Ethan's fingers traced along the hem of my shirt. "What do you want to learn about first?"

"I don't know." I wanted everything, but the thought of having sex at this very moment on the beach was also overwhelming. I wished I was one of those confident heroines in the books I read about, who went from virgins to sex goddesses from one page to the next, but that wasn't me. I was too shy, too awkward, too nervous. I'd never even been naked in front of a man before. "I'm not sure I'm ready for...you know."

"That's fine." Ethan stroked the smooth skin along my belly and began pressing soft kisses to my collarbone. "We'll start slow, and you can tell me if anything is too much."

"Thank you." I relaxed again into his touch. I couldn't imagine doing this with any other man. He was the only one I trusted in this way and I knew he would take good care of me.

He hummed his approval against my skin as his fingers slipped under my shirt and explored my breasts through my bra. I gasped as he circled my nipples, which were so hard it was almost painful. It felt so good, I wanted him to keep touching me forever.

He gently pushed me back down to the blanket and then kissed me again, making my head spin. As his tongue stroked mine, his hands continued their exploration under my shirt, moving down to my hips, then sliding over my jeans, stroking my thighs. My hips jerked forward, seeking more, and in response, Ethan's hands cupped the spot between my legs.

"Is this what you need?" he asked.

I nodded, moaning softly. No one had ever touched me there before. Ethan popped open the button on my jeans and then lowered the zipper while I held still, not even sure I could breathe. He carefully yanked my jeans down a little, giving him access to my panties underneath. I started to get nervous again, but then his mouth was on mine and I relaxed again. His fingers pushed aside the fabric and then he was touching me *there* and I forgot everything else.

Ethan's mouth left mine, trailing kisses along my jawline until he found my earlobe. He nipped the sensitive skin and whispered, "You're so wet for me. I can't wait to feel you. To be inside you."

One of his fingers dipped inside at this, just a tiny bit like he was coating himself in my wet heat. Then he went exploring, and everything felt so new and so sensitive as he stroked and teased me. I gripped his arms, feeling this pressure building inside me, making me want to chase it down. When he finally touched my clit, my body jerked and I sucked in a breath. He gave me a satisfied smile and then captured my lips again like he couldn't get enough.

He slowly pushed a finger inside me and I was glad his mouth was back on mine to stifle my cry. Ethan was kissing me and touching me at the same time and it was almost too much for my body to handle. His finger pumped in and out, his thumb rubbing along my clit until I couldn't hold back anymore and let out a long moan. I was breathing so hard and fast, that I had to push Ethan's mouth away from mine to catch my breath.

"That's it," he said. "Let go. Let me feel you come."

His words pushed me over the edge and my body tightened around his fingers. I clenched the blanket underneath me and tilted my head back to the sky as my body shuddered and the orgasm swept over me. Ethan's lips found my neck again and it was so good, and so much more than I expected. I'd never had an orgasm from anyone but myself before, and I was starting to see what all the fuss was about.

He removed his fingers and brought them to his lips, tasting me, and somehow that was the most erotic thing I'd ever seen. Then he lowered himself onto the blanket next to me, one arm draped over my chest. "How was that?"

"It was perfect." I leaned over and kissed him softly. "Do you want me to do anything for you?"

"Not this time. This was just for you." Ethan stroked my hair and tucked it behind my ear. "I'm going to have so much fun showing you everything you've read about in your romance novels."

"I can't wait."

Even if I couldn't have him forever, it would be worth it to have him just for this month.

CHAPTER EIGHT

A FEW DAYS LATER, I found myself back in Ethan's office for a Zoom meeting with the other alphas to discuss opening up the Moon Witch town to a few wolf shifter families. I was a bit nervous since it was my first time attending one of these meetings and I was the only non-shifter present, but Ethan ran the meeting smoothly. He was good at steering the alphas back to the topic at hand if they got sidetracked, and all of the alphas seemed interested in our proposal. It seemed there were a lot of shifters who felt out of place after the breaking of the mate bonds and the creation of new ones, who weren't sure which pack to live with.

Ethan also somehow got each of the packs to donate money to our cause, reminding them that the Moon Witches had been instrumental in freeing the wolves from the Sun Witches. He also pointed out that a neutral town would be beneficial for everyone. In the end, the Zodiac Wolves would jointly cover a quarter of the costs of our loan, which was more than I could ever have hoped for.

Things were really starting to come together for our town, and I knew if we had a solid plan in place, most of the Moon Witches would come around.

As soon as the meeting ended and everyone disconnected, Ethan said, "That went even better than I thought it would."

I leaned back in my chair, finally allowing myself to relax. "I can't believe you got them to agree to give us all that money."

"Me either," he said with a short laugh. He got up and went over to the bar area. "Would you like some green tea?"

"That would be lovely."

He prepared the tea, using an electric kettle on the bar, while he talked. "Have you made any progress with the Moon Witches?"

"A little. Over the last few days, I've been talking to some of them individually and showing them pictures of the resort. They all agree that the location is perfect, and I think some of them are coming around to the idea of letting a few wolf shifter families live there too."

"How did you convince them?" He handed me a mug and our fingers brushed. I couldn't help but blush at the contact, even though we'd done much more at the lake. It was all just so new and exciting.

"By explaining that we need people who have skills they don't have, along with the extra income." I wrapped my hands around my mug and breathed in the tea. It was still too hot, but I liked the comforting feel of it in my hands. "I think they take me more seriously now that I'm older. They're all treating me differently since Selene granted my wish."

"I'm glad they're finally giving you some respect, though I wish they'd done it all along."

I shrugged. "Whatever makes them listen, I guess."

We sipped our tea while we chatted more about the meeting, and it was so easy being with him. I'd thought that after the other day, things might be awkward between us, but if anything, we'd grown even more comfortable together. In fact, we'd been chatting every night since I got back from our trip when Ethan had texted me to make sure that I'd gotten home safely. I'd responded with a picture of me snuggled up with Luna on the couch, and then he'd called me to ask me about my cat. The next night he'd called me again to ask how my day went, and from there it became a regular thing. It was so easy to talk to him, and we chatted about everything from his business to my favorite books and our childhoods. The only problem was that it was becoming harder and harder to remember that this was just temporary. I had no idea how I would be able to let him go when this was all over.

Once we'd finished our tea, Ethan set his mug down and fixed me with an intense stare. "You're too far away. Come over here and sit on my lap."

I raised my eyebrows at his sudden commanding tone, which I had to admit, was pretty hot. "Someone is bossy today."

"It's been a few days since I've gotten to kiss you. I missed you."

A little thrill ran through me at his words. I stood up slowly and walked over to him, then leaned against his desk. "Did you?"

Ethan ran his hand along my side, then yanked me down into his lap. I let out a small noise of surprise, but it was lost in his mouth as he kissed me. I wrapped my arms around his neck and kissed him back freely, no longer nervous like I was the last time we'd done this.

"Have you had a chance to finish that scene you were writing?" he asked, as his hands cupped my ass. I could feel his cock hardening between us and shivered at the thought that I was doing this to him.

"No," I said, playing with the collar of his shirt. "I can't believe you actually want to read more of that."

"Hmm." His hands moved down to my thighs and he gripped the fabric of my dress. "Maybe you need some more inspiration."

"What do you have in mind?" I asked, my voice coming out breathlessly. If it was anything like last time, I knew I'd be almost drowning in pleasure no matter what he did.

He tilted my head up and began kissing my neck again. I wondered if he would bite me there like I'd heard some shifters did. But no, that was only something they did with mates.

"I can't stop thinking about you," he murmured against my skin. "I have to taste you again."

"Yes," I whispered. His words made my lovesick heart flutter, and I clutched him tighter.

He picked me up then and set me down on the edge of his desk, then moved between my thighs. He gripped the skirt of my dress and met my eyes. "I want to go down on you."

I inhaled sharply. I liked that he was straightforward with what he wanted and that he gave me the chance to say no if I wasn't ready. I'd read about oral sex in books, and I was excited to see if it was as good as everyone described.

"Do it," I said and then wondered where this newfound confidence had come from.

His eyes flashed with something like pride and a wicked smile crossed his lips. He yanked my dress up to my hips. "I've been thinking about how this dress would look around your waist ever since you walked into my office."

He ran his hands along my bare thighs, then spread my legs wide so he could move between them. My panties, which were already soaked in anticipation, were dragged down my legs and dropped onto the floor. Then he gazed down at me with something like reverence.

"You're so beautiful, Larkin," he said.

I almost came on the spot, and he'd barely even touched me yet. No man had ever said those words to me before. The best part of it was, I could tell he meant it.

His strong hands gripped my thighs as he lowered his head between my legs. He looked up at me, his dark eyes flashing with heat. "Eyes on me. I want you to watch me tasting you."

He held my gaze as he slid his tongue between my folds. I nearly jumped off his desk, it felt so shockingly good, and his hands gripped me tighter.

"Be a good girl and stay still," he said with a little growl. "I'm not going to rush this."

Oh fuck. I nodded, unable to speak. I was desperate for him to keep going and I would do anything he said at this point.

He began licking and sucking me, his tongue exploring me, and I gripped the edge of the desk. It was like nothing I'd ever felt before. He went slow at first, tasting me, savoring me, and I couldn't stop moaning. Every flick of his tongue against my clit made me shudder, but he was taking his time and not letting me orgasm.

"Please," I groaned. "Ethan..."

"I like it when you say my name like that."

He licked me harder, faster, his hands gripping my thighs, holding me down. My hips bucked against his mouth, and the pressure that had been building inside me was threatening to explode. My hands moved to grip his hair, pressing his face closer to where I needed him most. He let out a low groan and devoured me like he couldn't get enough.

His eyes stayed on mine the entire time, drinking in every reaction like he wanted to memorize them all. My thighs quivered and I moaned, feeling myself getting closer and closer. His fingers gripped me harder and his tongue was relentless as it sought out my pleasure.

"Ethan!" I cried as my orgasm hit and I nearly shot off his

desk. I lost all sense of time and space as the pleasure rolled through me like a storm, unstoppable and completely overwhelming. I shook and trembled in his grip, while Ethan's gaze remained locked on mine, his eyes ravenous. And he didn't stop.

I tugged at his hair, trying to push him away and pull him closer all at once, my body shaking. It was too much. I couldn't take any more of it, or surely I would die. Why wasn't he stopping? Was he actually trying to kill me?

He held me in place, making sure I couldn't escape. My back arched and my pussy ground against his mouth and somehow I was coming again, even harder than before, and all I could do was cry out his name over and over. This orgasm was like nothing I'd experienced before, and when it was over, and he was finally satisfied, I swore I'd gone on some kind of out-of-body experience.

He didn't stop until my body finally stopped convulsing. Only then did he slide his tongue from me, a smug smile on his face. He stood up and dragged me into his arms.

I fell against his chest, completely boneless. "What did you do to me?"

He slowly rubbed a hand against my back. "Sorry, I couldn't stop. You taste too fucking good. I could do that all night."

"I've never...more than once..." I could barely speak.

"No? Well, get used to it. Now that I know I can give you multiple orgasms, one is never going to be enough for me."

I searched his eyes, but it seemed like he was telling the

truth. He actually wanted to please me as much as possible —even without asking for anything in return.

His cock was hard, straining through his pants, and I pressed my hand to it. "Ethan...I want..."

He took my wrist and dragged my hand up to his lips, kissing my knuckles softly. "I know. Me too. But not here. Not tonight. I want to take it slow and make your first time special."

I nodded, because truthfully I wasn't sure I could take any more, and I appreciated his thoughtfulness.

Ethan threaded his hand with mine and pressed a kiss to my jaw. "Why don't you come to my place two nights from now?"

"I'd like that," I said, with butterflies in my stomach. I'd never been to Ethan's home before, and I couldn't wait to see it.

He pressed another kiss to my forehead. "It's a date."

CHAPTER NINE

"LARKIN, YOU LOOK AMAZING!" Stella said as she threw her arms around me. Her large pregnant belly bumped against me and I laughed.

"She's a total hottie now," Harper said with a grin, making me blush.

"How do you feel?" Mira asked me.

"I feel...great. Like I'm finally myself on the outside."

"That's so wonderful," Madison said.

"Give the girl some space," Ayla said, waving them away. We were in her house for our monthly book club meeting, but my friends had all surrounded me as soon as I'd arrived, wanting to check out my new appearance in person. I'd sent them a picture in our group chat a few days ago, explaining what had happened, but they'd been eager to see it with their own eyes.

We all settled in around Ayla's living room, where she'd already set out some snacks and drinks. The book club had started a few months ago as a way for us all to keep in touch now that Mira and Stella were so far away and everyone was so busy. Madison, the Virgo alpha, was our newest and most surprising addition. I'd only met her in passing before, but we invited her to join our group after we'd discovered that she liked romance novels as well, and she quickly became a good friend.

We spent a few minutes pouring wine (for everyone except Stella, who pouted), enjoying the charcuterie spread, and catching up on what was going on in everyone's lives. In truth, our monthly book club was mostly an excuse for us all to get together and drink, eat, and gossip. Ayla and Mira especially appreciated it because it gave them a break from mom duty while their mates watched the kids.

"So what did you think of the latest book?" Ayla asked as she poured herself more wine.

This month's pick was a reverse harem novel, and I'd read it before everything started happening with Ethan. At the time it had seemed really exciting, but now I could hardly remember what it had been about.

"It had a good balance of plot and steam," Mira said. She tended to like books with lots of action and twists and often read thrillers along with romance novels. "I liked it."

"I would love to have multiple mates," Harper said with a sigh. When we started this club, she hadn't read a book in years. Now she couldn't get enough. "Can you imagine?"

Stella snorted to her left. "I can barely handle one mate. More men just seems like more work. Besides, Jordan would never share. He wants to murder anyone who even looks at me."

"Same here," Ayla said, shaking her head. "One is enough for me."

Madison grabbed some more crackers and cheese. "I'm going to agree with Harper on this one. I think multiple mates sounds fun. You could make a schedule for everything from sex to cleaning and give everyone separate tasks. Ooh, or a spreadsheet!"

"That's very Virgo of you," Mira said, and Madison laughed.

I was smiling, but my mind was a thousand miles away. I couldn't stop thinking about Ethan and what we'd done yesterday, or what we were planning to do tomorrow.

"Larkin?" Stella asked.

I blinked and looked around. All of the girls were staring at me. I took a sip of my wine and cleared my throat. "Sorry. I spaced out for a bit. What did you ask me?"

"Do you want multiple partners?" Harper asked. "Or are you more of a one-man kind of girl?"

"Oh. Um. I don't know."

"What's going on?" Stella asked. "Is something wrong?"

I downed the rest of my wine in one big gulp. "No. Why would you think that?"

Stella narrowed her eyes at me. "You're usually so excited to talk about books, but you're being really quiet. You've barely said a word to us all evening."

Mira gave me a sympathetic smile. "Is it the new body? I'm sure it's a big change."

"No, I bet it has something to do with Ethan," Ayla said, wiggling her eyebrows at me. "The two of them went on an overnight trip together."

"What!" Stella nearly jumped out of her seat. "Why is this the first I've heard about this?"

Harper grabbed another piece of salami. "Ooh, did you share a hotel room?"

"Please tell me there was only one bed," Madison said.

"No, we had separate hotel rooms," I said. "I'm pretty sure the one-bed thing only happens in romance novels."

"Not true," Ayla said. "It happened to Kaden and me. But go on."

I tried to keep my voice casual. "We went to go check out the property that is going to be the new Moon Witch town and spent the night out there."

Harper gestured for me to go on. "And then..."

I grinned a little. "And then we kissed."

"You kissed!" Stella shrieked.

"I knew it!" Ayla said with a smug look in her eyes.

"That's great," Mira said. "We all know you've liked Ethan for a long time."

I blushed. "We um, did some other stuff too. I think we're going to have sex tomorrow night."

All the girls gasped and shrieked at this, basically losing their damn minds, while my face went totally red.

"Details!" Harper shouted. "We need details!"

"No, we don't," Madison said, throwing a pillow at Harper. "We're just happy for you."

"See? I told you this would work out," Ayla said.

My heart clenched at that and something must have passed over my face because suddenly all the girls looked worried.

"What's wrong?" Stella asked.

"Oh no, was it not good?" Harper asked.

"No, it was great," I said. "But it's just a fling. It can't last."

"Why not?" Mira asked while Madison poured me another glass of wine like she could tell I needed it.

I took a sip before I spoke again. "Because he's a shifter and I'm not. Sooner or later he will find his mate—maybe even at the next Convergence. So he told me we can have some fun for a while, but that's it."

"I'm sorry, Larkin," Ayla said, and the other girls responded with similar words.

The mood in the room took a sad turn, with everyone giving me pitying looks. This was why I shouldn't have said anything. Now I'd ruined our fun book club night.

"It's fine," I said, though I could already feel the hot pressure of tears at the backs of my eyes. "I always knew it wouldn't work out. I could never be his mate or his alpha female. After all, I'm not a shifter."

"Well, that's just dumb," Madison said.

I blinked at her. "What?"

She leaned forward. "Look at me and Ayla. We're both only half shifter and we're both alphas. Why can't you be one too? Who says his alpha female can't be a Moon Witch?"

"Would the other alphas accept that?" Mira asked.

"Who gives a flying fuck what the other alphas think," Stella said.

Ayla nodded. "Don't give up hope. Selene gave you this new body for a reason, after all. Trust in the stars and the moon."

"I'll try," I muttered.

"And if he hurts you, we'll kick his ass," Harper growled, her wolf side coming out a little.

I laughed a little and wiped my eyes. "Thanks, guys. I won't give up. But even if it doesn't work out, I'm going to enjoy myself while it lasts. And to answer your question, I think I'm a one-man kind of girl."

None of them pointed out my hasty and obvious change of subject, and we sank back into the usual book club talk with ease. The knot in my throat didn't release the entire time, but I managed to stay engaged for long enough to convince them that I really was okay.

We wrapped up the night by choosing our book for next month and then the girls all gave me a hug and told me to keep them updated. We went out onto Ayla's porch and said our goodbyes before splitting up. Harper got in her car to drive back to the house she shared with her brother, while Ayla teleported Mira and Stella back to their pack lands. I'd offered to take Madison back to the Virgo lands and we moved down to the grass so I had enough space to open a portal.

"Can I talk to you quickly before we leave?" she asked.

"Sure," I said.

"Our discussion earlier got me thinking about something..."

I raised an eyebrow. "About multiple mates?"

Madison gave a short laugh. "No, about half-human shifters. There are more of them than people realize, and most of them are packless. Many of them are birthed by human women and have no idea what shifter life is like or even which pack they should belong to. Some of them are abandoned when they shift and left to fend for themselves. Others are kicked out of their packs for being part human, or raised as outsiders like Ayla was."

"I didn't know it was such a big issue."

"It's a problem that many of the alphas don't want to acknowledge. I'm working to change that now that I'm the Virgo alpha, but I'm only one person. The Virgo pack accepts all half-human shifters who want to join us, but it would be nice if there was somewhere where the packless could live."

My eyes widened. "You want them to live in our town?"

She shifted on her feet. "I was hoping the Moon Witches might consider it. A lot of these people have useful skills and experience from living among humans for most of their lives. They'd make a great addition to your town."

She made a good point, but I was overwhelmed thinking about adding even more people to the town. "I'll talk to Ethan about it, and the Moon Witch council will have to agree. But I'll see what I can do."

"Of course," Madison said with a smile. "Thank you so much."

I opened up a portal and we entered Lunatera, then I made another portal to take her back to the Virgo pack lands, which Ayla had brought me to visit mainly for this exact purpose. Their forest was especially green when we arrived with wildflowers blooming everywhere. I hadn't visited every pack yet, but so far the Virgo lands were the most beautiful out of any I'd seen.

When I returned to my cottage, I immediately sat down in front of my laptop. Talking about books with my friends always inspired me, and I knew exactly the way to finish the spicy scene. My fingers flew across the keyboard while my fictional characters went at it all night long. By the time I was done, I was breathless and wet.

I opened up an empty email, addressed it to Ethan, and pasted the finished scene into it. Then I held my breath and tried to convince myself to press send. He'd asked for it multiple times, but what if he was just humoring me? Or what if the scene was terrible? What if he read it and was like, "Wow this girl really has no idea what sex is like, maybe we should call tomorrow off?" My mind spun with all sorts of horrible scenarios. But Ethan was also the only person who knew about my writing, and it thrilled me a little to share it with him. What if he didn't hate it?

I gathered up my courage and sent the email, then shut my laptop immediately. Otherwise, I would stare at my screen all night wondering if he'd read it yet. Instead, I busied myself by getting ready for bed. It was late, anyway. Ethan was probably asleep already.

My phone rang, startling me out of my thoughts. I quickly picked it up from my nightstand.

"Why do you always call?" I asked in a teasing voice. "Don't you know phones are for everything except phone calls these days?"

"I call because I like hearing your voice."

"Oh..." He had me blushing again.

"Thanks for sending that scene to me," he said, his voice low and husky. "It was hot... But our night together will be even hotter."

My breath caught. "Oh?"

"I'll see you tomorrow," Ethan said and hung up before I could even say anything else.

I stared at my phone, my heart racing. I had no doubt he'd make good on his promise.

CHAPTER TEN

I STOOD outside the door to Ethan's condo and tugged on the bottom of my little black dress. It had moons on the hem, and I hoped that Selene would give me some strength for tonight. All day I'd been a complete mess, flitting back and forth between nervous and excited like a hummingbird, and now the anticipation was almost more than I could handle.

My driver and bodyguard, Arvin, rang the doorbell. He was a very muscular shifter with graying black hair, and he'd picked me up from outside Ethan's office and driven me here. I'd told him I could walk up to Ethan's condo on my own, but he'd explained that the alpha had told him to make sure I arrived safely, and he wasn't leaving until he'd finished the job.

Ethan opened the door and his face lit up at the sight of me. "Larkin, welcome. Come on in." Then he turned to Arvin and shook his hand. "Thanks for escorting her here."

Arvin bowed his head. "Of course, alpha."

"Say hello to the wife and kids for me."

The man cracked his first smile. "I will."

Ethan shut the door and turned to me, but I was busy picking my jaw up off the floor. His condo was incredible, like the kind of thing you only see in movies. It was two stories and all open concept, with a sleek staircase leading upstairs. Floor-to-ceiling glass walls offered breathtaking views of the glittering Toronto skyline, and the downstairs living area was spacious and modern, with marble floors and soaring ceilings. The furniture was sleek and minimal, in neutral tones, but a few pieces of art added a splash of color here and there.

"You look stunning," Ethan said, drawing my attention back to him.

"So do you." He was wearing a black dress shirt with the sleeves rolled up, showing off the tattoos on his arms. Somehow he got even more handsome every time I saw him. How was that even possible?

He pulled me into his arms and gave me a kiss that left my head spinning. "I'm so happy you're here."

"Me too. Your place is beautiful."

"Thanks. I'd like to get a house with a yard and all of that someday, but for now, this works for me."

He took my arm and led me toward the kitchen, which was huge and just as beautiful as the rest of Ethan's place. A tall woman with short hair dyed pink was pulling something out of the oven, and she waved at me with a smile.

"This is Soleil," Ethan said. "She has the best French

restaurant in Toronto, and I hired her to make us something incredible tonight."

"You honor me, alpha." Soleil gave us a little curtsy. "Tonight I've prepared a three-course meal featuring fresh oysters in a lemon-wine sauce, lobster risotto with saffron, and Quebec duck roasted in citrus honey with heirloom carrots. Then for dessert, a fruit tart with strawberries, raspberries, and blueberries."

I'd never eaten anything so fancy in my life and I was blown away that Ethan had arranged all of this for me. "That sounds incredible."

"I do hope you enjoy it. Everything is ready, I simply need a few minutes to plate it."

"Thank you," Ethan said. "You can go when you're ready. I will serve us."

Soleil looked like she wanted to argue, but finally nodded. "Yes, of course."

Ethan led me to a dining table next to the huge windows, which was already set for two, with some candles and a bottle of wine already open. He pulled out my chair for me and then went to get our first entree. I took a moment to glance at the view of Toronto, but my eyes caught on the waning moon overhead. It was a small sliver, a reminder that I was almost halfway to my deadline. I tore my eyes away as Ethan put our first course in front of us and then sat down. Soleil slipped out the front door, giving us our privacy.

I stared down at the beautiful food in front of me. "I feel like I'm underdressed. I had no idea tonight would be so fancy."

"You're perfect." He reached across the table and took my hand. "I hired Soleil because I'm the worst cook in the world, and I didn't want to scare you away with my burnt grilled cheese sandwiches."

"So you do have flaws," I said with a laugh.

"One or two." His eyes glimmered with amusement as he poured wine for us. "Don't tell anyone."

"I doubt anyone in your pack would believe me anyway. They seem to adore you."

"I've tried to do right by them ever since I became alpha."

"How did you become alpha anyway?" I asked as we began eating. "I know you didn't inherit it, but I've never heard the full story."

"The previous alpha did a lot of things that were harmful to the pack's future. He'd inherited the position from his own father, and he didn't really care about being alpha except as a way to hold power over the other shifters. My mom was an accountant for the pack, and she would complain all the time about how he was going to bankrupt us. The alpha kept asking her to do some illegal things, but she always refused. My dad feared the alpha would come after our family, so he sent me to the US for college, and then I went to business school there too. When I came back to Toronto to start my own business, the pack was in bad shape. I challenged the alpha for his position, and I won."

"What happened to the previous alpha?" I asked.

Ethan's brow pinched. "It was a fight to the death."

"Oh. Right." I should have known that, but I still had a

lot to learn about pack life. "And your parents? Are they okay?"

"They're fine. My parents were well-respected in our pack and the previous alpha never went after our family in the end."

"That's a relief. What does your dad do?"

"He's retired now, but he used to be a lawyer. He kept the pack out of trouble." He took a sip of his wine and studied my face. "Do you want to talk about your parents or is it too hard?"

"I can talk about them, but there's not much to say. They were Moon Witches who left Lunatera because they wanted to have a kid. We spent a lot of my childhood moving all over the US, running from the Sun Witches, and my parents took whatever jobs they could find. They tried so hard to give me a good childhood and keep me safe, but the Sun Witches found us when I was ten. My parents fought them off and used their last breaths to send me to Lunatera. My aunt Celeste raised me after that."

"You must miss them a lot."

"I do. They were both so kind. But I'm trying my best to honor their memory by bringing the Moon Witches back to Earth, just like they would have wanted."

"I'm sure they're proud of you."

"I hope so."

We moved on to our next two courses, and they were both unlike anything I'd ever tasted before. Ethan explained that Soleil's father was from the Virgo pack, who lived in

Quebec, and he'd also been a chef. Then talk turned to the Moon Witch town again.

"Have you thought of a name yet?" Ethan asked.

I took a bite of the duck, which was so tender I almost moaned. "I was thinking of calling it Eventide. I originally wanted to name it something related to the moon, but now that all sorts of people might be living there, I thought Eventide fit better."

"It's perfect."

I set down my fork. "That reminds me. Madison asked me yesterday if we would allow some half-human shifters to move to our town. Specifically, the ones that didn't belong to a pack."

"I think that's a great idea. Do you think the Moon Witches will agree to it?"

"I'm not sure, but they might be more sympathetic to half-humans than full shifters. After all, they're outcasts, like we are."

Ethan frowned and looked out the window. "They shouldn't be outcasts. One of the first changes I made when I became alpha was to make sure that no half-human would ever be kicked out of my pack. I know Jordan and Wesley have made the same change, along with some of the other alphas. A few are still resistant though, but we're working on them."

We finally moved on to dessert, and although I was already so full, the fruit tart was impossible to resist. "This is so good. I think I'm having an orgasm in my mouth."

Ethan laughed and leaned over, licking a tiny bit of

cream off my lips. "Save some of those orgasms for me." He grabbed a fork and poked at his own tart. "Have you done any more writing after that scene you sent me?"

"Not yet." I finished my tart and pushed my plate away. "I hope you finish the story."

"Would it have a happy ending?" I hoped he got my double meaning.

"Of course. Isn't that a requirement for romance novels?"

I laughed, surprised. "You've done your research."

He leaned back in his seat and fixed me with a gaze that made me shiver. "I've been catching up on some of your favorites and I'm almost done. If you give me a list, I'll gladly read more."

"I'm impressed."

"I wanted to get an idea of what you liked." He stood up and crossed the distance between us, then kneeled down at my feet. He removed my heels and began massaging my feet.

Our eyes locked in a charged gaze, the tension between us crackling in the air, palpable and intoxicating. "And did it help?"

"Oh yes." He trailed his hands slowly up my legs. "Although I don't think I'm morally gray enough for you, and we probably should have been enemies first, judging by your reading preferences."

"You really did read all those books!" I took his face in my hands. "But you're better than any book boyfriend, and friends-to-lovers might be my new favorite trope."

Our lips met in a fervent kiss, a fusion of longing and hunger that had been building all night. This time I controlled the kiss, my fingers splayed across his rough jaw, showing him without words how much I cared for him. He gripped my thighs, spreading my legs so he could lean in even closer, but it wasn't enough.

He rose to his feet and dragged me up with him, his lips still locked with mine. Then he grabbed my ass and picked me up, wrapping my legs around his waist. He was so strong he made it seem easy, and I clung to his shoulders as our tongues danced in a sensual rhythm. My short dress was hiked up to my hips and I could feel his cock pressing through his trousers against the lace panties I'd worn just for him. I thrust forward, unable to help myself, and he let out a groan that vibrated at the back of my throat.

"I've never wanted anyone as much as I want you." He pressed his forehead against mine as we both caught our breath. "Have you bewitched me?"

"I sure hope so."

He adjusted his grip on my ass, getting a better hold on me, while also dragging me against his cock in a way that made me moan. "I think it's time to go upstairs."

CHAPTER ELEVEN

ETHAN CARRIED me up his staircase while I clung to him and pressed kisses to his jaw and neck. I didn't have shifter senses, but I was pretty sure he was the best thing I'd ever smelled or tasted.

The second story was like a big open loft, containing a large bed covered in red and pink rose petals. Candles on the side tables gave the space a soft, romantic glow, and I was overwhelmed by how thoughtful he was.

"You did all this for me?" I asked as he walked us toward the bed.

"I wanted tonight to be perfect."

He set me down and turned me around, then brushed my hair to the side so he could press a hot kiss to the back of my neck. While I stared out at the tiny sliver of the moon, he slowly unzipped my dress and lowered it to the floor, following it with a trail of kisses down my spine. He unhooked my bra and let it fall next, leaving me in only the lace panties.

A low growl escaped his throat at the sight of them. "Did you wear these for me?"

I nodded, not trusting myself to speak at this point. I'd never felt sexier than I did in that moment, standing before him in nothing but a tiny bit of black lace.

"Take them off," he commanded in a deep voice.

I did as I was told, slipping the panties down and stepping out of them. Ethan moved behind me and reached around to cup my breasts in his hands. His fingers were rough, yet his touch was gentle, and I arched back against him, wanting more. He teased my nipples, circling them, pinching them lightly, doing things to me I'd never known I wanted. Then his mouth was on my neck again, and I felt the slightest scrape of his teeth, which made me shiver.

"Tell me what you want," he said, his breath hot against my skin.

"Touch me," I whispered.

He reached down and cupped my pussy, and a little moan escaped my lips. "Here?"

I pressed against his hand, which was all the response he needed. He found my clit and started moving his finger in small circles. I was already soaked, and after just a few strokes, my knees felt weak. I leaned against him, reaching back to hold onto his head, which was still bent low over my neck as he sucked and nipped my skin.

"I'm going to make sure you're nice and ready for me." He slipped one finger, then two, inside me, and I cried out.

His thumb kept circling my clit while his other hand played with my breasts. He pinched and rolled each nipple, and soon I was gasping and moaning, grinding against his hand and desperate for more.

He was stroking me in exactly the right spot, and I was already close. It was almost embarrassing how fast he could get me there. When my knees began to shake, his hand slid down from my breast and wrapped around my waist, holding me up. My entire body shook, and I cried out his name. He kept touching me, dragging out the orgasm until I was spent and collapsed against him.

Ethan spun me around, and then he was kissing me again. This time his hands were on my ass, and I could feel the heat of his body through his clothes.

I tugged at his shirt. "You're wearing too many clothes."

"Then do something about it."

My hands trembled a little as I unbuttoned his shirt, but I was done being awkward, shy, nervous Larkin. Tonight I wanted to be as confident as one of the heroines in my favorite books.

I pulled off his shirt and took a moment to run my hands over his broad, muscular chest and the Libra pack mark there. I loved the feeling of his warm skin beneath my fingers as I studied his tattoos—a wolf, a moon, some branches, the Libra constellation, and more. Next, I undid his belt buckle, then the button of his slacks. I pushed them down, leaving him just in black boxer briefs, but I couldn't go on from there. It was just too much.

Ethan seemed to sense this and held my gaze as he

stripped out of the boxer briefs, leaving himself completely nude.

I swallowed hard as I took him in, from his muscles to his tattoos to his very large cock. Over the last few months, I'd seen plenty of shifters naked—they weren't exactly modest—but this was different. This was Ethan, and he was even more beautiful than I expected.

"You can touch. Anywhere you want." He took my hand and pressed it to his flat, toned stomach.

I stroked my hand over the ridges of his abs, and then moved lower. I couldn't look away from his cock, and the thought of having that inside me was terrifying, yet also strangely exciting. After a second spent hesitating, I wrapped my hand around his cock. He let out a sharp breath, almost like he was in pain. Emboldened, I gripped him tighter, stroking up and down his length, then brushed my thumb over the head of his cock. I loved the feel of him in my hand and the way his breath sped up as I continued stroking him.

"You're so big."

"Don't worry. I'll fit you just right." He gripped my wrist. "But that's enough playing for now. It's my turn again."

He pushed me back onto the bed, scattering rose petals everywhere. My entire body ached with desire for him, and I spread my legs wide, inviting him between them. For a moment he only stared at me, and then he tilted his head back and closed his eyes like he was praying.

"What is it?" I asked, nervous he was having second thoughts about this.

"You're so damn beautiful." His eyes swept over me again. "I was thanking Selene for granting your wish."

I flushed with heat at his words, and then his head was between my thighs, and he was licking me until I was writhing against the bed. He brought me almost to orgasm...and then stopped.

"Tonight I'm going to make you come on my cock."

Fuck. I had no idea Ethan had such a mouth on him, but it turned me on even more. Before I could respond, he moved to the nightstand and pulled out a package of condoms.

"Oh, um, we don't need those," I said.

He ripped open the box. "I don't want to take any chances since you're human."

"It's okay. I went and got birth control earlier today." Ayla had convinced me to do it, reminding me she was the product of a shifter and a Moon Witch.

Ethan's eyebrows shot up. "Did you? That was smart thinking. But you didn't have to do that."

"I know, but I wanted to." I took the package of condoms from his hand and tossed them aside. "I want to feel you completely."

Something feral entered his eyes, a glimpse of the wolf inside him. He pushed me back on the bed and climbed over me, his cock rubbing between my thighs. "Are you sure you want this? Last chance to tell me to stop."

"I want it. I want you." I reached up and touched his face. "Show me everything I've been missing."

Ethan gripped his cock in his hand and slowly guided it

inside of me. He kept his eyes locked on mine and I felt every single inch sliding into me. There was a small, uncomfortable stretch as my body adjusted to him, but nothing painful. I'd heard some girls say the first time hurt a lot, but that wasn't true for me.

"Damn, you're so tight." He closed his eyes, his face strained. I could tell he was holding himself back, making sure he didn't hurt me. He was fighting for control, and I loved that I could do this to him. "Are you okay?"

"I'm good." I wrapped my arms around his neck. "Don't stop."

He let go and thrust inside me, making me gasp. My eyes fluttered shut as he bottomed out. This was it. He was finally inside of me.

He moved slowly at first, testing to see how I responded. I could tell that he was still holding back, and if I could think for more than a few seconds at a time, I would have told him that he could go harder, that I wouldn't break.

The more he moved, the better it felt, and soon I was trembling and gasping as he picked up the pace. I'd already been close to orgasm thanks to his tongue, and I could feel myself getting closer and closer.

He withdrew his cock and then thrust inside me, harder this time, and my hips rocked up to meet him. I tangled my fingers in his hair, needing to grip onto something as my instincts took over. I clung to him, arching up to meet him thrust for thrust, but I still needed more.

"Please," I begged.

He responded by sliding his hands under my ass, lifting

my hips, and hitting a spot that made me gasp. I wrapped my legs around him, trying to get as close to him as possible. Our bodies moved together like we'd been doing this our whole lives, like we were meant for each other. Pleasure swept through me like a tornado, turning me inside out, and stealing all the breath from my lungs.

He slowed his thrusts and gave me some time to recover, while he stroked my hair and stared into my eyes. "Are you okay?"

"I'm great," I said. "But I want you to come too."

"I will after I give you another orgasm."

A soft laugh bubbled out of me. "I'm not sure I can have another one."

He grinned. "I do love a challenge."

"I have a question though," I said slowly.

He propped himself up on his elbows, with his hard cock still sheathed within me. "What is it?"

"I feel like you were holding back. Is that true?"

"I had to. With my shifter strength, and my wolf so close to the surface..." He brushed his nose against my neck, breathing me in like I was an intoxicating drug. "I don't want to hurt you."

I gripped his hair tighter, forcing him to look at me. "I know you would never hurt me. I want everything from you. All your strength, your animal side, everything. I can take it."

"You have no idea what you're asking for."

"I do." I clenched my pussy around his cock. "I trust you."

He shuddered a little and then pulled out of me. I worried he was going to say no, but then he turned me over.

"If this is what you want, then I need you on your hands and knees."

I did as I was told and positioned myself, spreading my legs wide. I felt completely exposed like this, but also excited. He lined up behind me and rubbed his cock against my ass, then slid into my pussy again. With his hands on my hips, he guided himself deep inside, so deep it made me cry out. It was almost painful but not quite.

After a moment, he pulled out and then drove his cock inside me with a forceful thrust. I cried out and pushed my hips back against him, showing him I wanted more. He hardly gave me time to recover before he slammed into me again, his fingers digging into my hips.

"You take my cock so well," he growled, as he pounded into me at a relentless pace like he couldn't stop.

This was what I'd wanted. The real Ethan, losing control over me.

The sounds coming out of me were loud and animalistic, and I was sure I'd have bruises on my hips later. I didn't care. I liked the thought of him marking me like this.

One of his hands reached around to find my clit. He circled his fingers around it and drove his cock into me with a primal intensity that made me moan and writhe against him.

Ethan was breathing hard and his thrusts became more erratic. "Come for me, Larkin. Do it now."

As if my body was answering his command, I came hard, screaming out his name. In return, he let out a feral growl as his own climax overtook him, his warmth spreading deep inside me.

He collapsed on the bed and dragged me with him, wrapping his arms tight around me. I curled against him, enjoying the feel of his naked body pressed against mine.

"You're incredible," he said, pressing a kiss to my forehead. "How do you feel?"

"Amazing," I said truthfully.

"Stay right here." He got up and went to the bathroom, then returned with a warm, wet washcloth. He gently spread my legs again, and cleaned me up, making me feel in a whole new way.

I love you. The words were on the tip of my tongue, but I swallowed them down. No man wanted to hear that right after sex, especially when he'd already told me this had to stay casual. But I felt it, deep in my bones, and knew Ethan was the only one for me, as long as I lived.

Now if only I could make him feel the same way.

CHAPTER TWELVE

I WOKE to the feel of something amazing happening between my thighs. I moaned and shifted as pleasure shot through me from the feel of something warm and wet sliding in and out of my pussy. Someone was going down on me, and it was the most mind-blowing way to wake up.

"Good morning," Ethan said, lifting his head to give me a wolfish grin. Then he went back at it, and I gasped as he suctioned his lips over my clit and started eating me out in earnest. I was pretty sure his tongue was magical because it sent sparks of pleasure along my entire body. He had me shaking and crying out within minutes, my thighs clenching around his head while the orgasm completely decimated me.

"What a way to wake up," I mumbled when I could finally breathe again.

He moved up the bed and pressed a kiss to my mouth. "I read about it in one of the books you said you liked. That blue alien one."

"Seriously?" I laughed at the thought of him reading that book, but it only made me love him more.

His cock pressed into my hip, and I took it in my hand. I wasn't sure I could take any more orgasms at this point, but I wanted to please him too. I stroked him a bit, but I wanted to do more.

"I want to take care of you too," I said, pressing on his shoulder to make him lie back.

"I'll take whatever you want to give me."

I slid down his body, trying not to show how nervous I was. Ethan's hot gaze followed me as I settled between his legs. I licked a stripe up his cock, surprised by how good he tasted, and then sucked on the head.

Ethan sucked in a breath. "You're doing so good."

I took as much of him in my mouth as I could, and covered the rest with my hand. Ethan draped his hands over his head, letting me be in control completely.

He let me set the pace, but couldn't stop himself from thrusting a little into my mouth. I wanted to impress him, so I sucked harder and tried to take him deeper. His hand dropped to the top of my head and he threaded his fingers through my hair. I glanced up and his eyes were shut tight, his bottom lip trapped between his teeth. I felt powerful in that moment, knowing I was the one to make him lose control.

I didn't stop until he was coming down my throat and my eyes were watering. I swallowed every drop, wanting all of him, everything he could give me.

He pulled me up, and we lay there, both breathing heavily, staring at each other.

"I don't think I'll ever get enough of you," he said as he ran his thumb across my swollen lips.

I closed my eyes and hoped that was true.

WE TOOK A SHOWER, where he gave me another orgasm with his hand, and then we managed to make it out of the condo to eat breakfast at a delicious cafe down the street. It was such a beautiful day we were even able to eat outside.

"Since it's the weekend, do you want to go on a tour of Toronto with me?" he asked, as he took a sip of coffee. "I'd love to show you around the city."

"I did live here for a while with your pack," I said, before taking a bite of my omelette.

"I know, but you didn't venture out of the hotel much. Not that I could blame you at the time, but now there's no danger of us being attacked by Sun Witches or vampires. I'd love to show you some of my favorite places in the city, along with the neighborhood where the Libra pack lives and works."

"I'd like that," I said, though a part of me wondered if this was a bad idea. I was already head over heels in love with Ethan, and spending more time with him would only make things more confusing for me. He claimed he wanted to stay friends, but then he treated me like his girlfriend and said the most amazing things to me. How could he be so romantic and sweet, yet also want to remain casual? I didn't get it, but maybe this sort of thing was normal for him, and I just wasn't wired the same way. I'd never been in a relationship before, after all. Maybe this really was just friendship with sex on the side.

Over the next few hours, Ethan took me around in his car to see some of the tourist sites. We went up CN Tower and gazed across the city, went shopping at St. Lawrence Market, and took selfies in front of the Royal Ontario Museum.

Afterward, he took me to the neighborhood where the Libra pack lived and worked. It was a cool, hip area with lots of boutiques and trendy outdoor restaurants with string lights hanging between the buildings. I spotted a few shifters walking down the street, who waved at Ethan as we passed by.

"This area used to be very rundown and mostly abandoned when I became alpha, but I saw its potential," Ethan said. "I bought up the properties and leased or sold them to members of the pack, who live in nearby homes or apartments."

We passed a house for sale that looked beautiful, and I stared at it in the side mirror for a long time after we passed it. I would have loved to live in a house like that, but I wasn't going to stay in Toronto. Soon I'd be four hours away in Eventide, and Ethan would still be here, with his pack, and whoever he found to be his mate.

By the time we returned to his condo, it was getting

dark. When we stepped inside, I was shocked to see a woman already there. She was Black, with short brown hair and a designer suit, and leaned against the kitchen island like she'd been inside Ethan's condo many times before. She looked vaguely familiar, and a spike of jealousy and panic shot through me.

"I thought I gave you today off," Ethan said as he walked toward the kitchen.

The woman snorted. "You know I don't like days off."

He chuckled and rested his hand on my lower back. "Larkin, this is my beta, Macy."

"It's nice to see you again," she said, offering her hand.

Now I remembered. We'd met briefly before while I was staying with the Libra pack, although I hadn't known she was Ethan's beta at the time. I shook her hand and gave her a warm smile, relieved that my jealousy was unfounded. "Likewise."

"Macy acts as my assistant and helps to run my life, my business, and my pack," Ethan explained. "I would be completely lost without her."

"Yes, you would," Macy said without missing a beat. "I'll get out of your hair, but I just came by to drop off these papers since I knew you wouldn't be back in the office until Monday. Make sure you sign them."

"Thank you. I totally forgot." He turned back to me, and said in a stage whisper, "This is why I need her."

"How was your dinner last night?" she asked, as she headed for the front door.

"Excellent," I said. "I've never tasted anything like it."

Her face lit up with a smile. "Soleil will be so pleased to hear that."

"Soleil is her mate," Ethan added.

"Oh, how lucky you are to have a mate who is also such an amazing chef," I said.

"Yes, very lucky." She paused in the doorway and eyed me for a moment. "You should come to the next pack meeting. I'm sure everyone would love to see you."

"I'm not sure that's a good idea." Why would I attend? I wasn't a shifter. Attending a pack meeting seemed like something a serious girlfriend would do, and Ethan had made it clear he didn't see me that way. I imagined all the Libra shifters staring at me, wondering why a Moon Witch was among them.

"I think it's a brilliant idea," Ethan said. "I would like you to be there."

I gaped at him, feeling more confused than ever. "Why?"

"I'd love to get your opinion about some of the things we'll discuss there. Also, you can meet my parents."

Meeting his parents? Wasn't that a big step in a relationship? But we weren't in a relationship, right? Or were we? I was more confused than ever, but also afraid to ask him. I wasn't sure I was ready to hear his answer.

"I'll think about it," I said, which basically meant yes. Ethan smiled like he knew this as well.

Macy grinned, her eyes gleaming with something like satisfaction, and then she said goodnight and slipped out the door.

Ethan immediately wrapped his arms around me and

nuzzled my neck. "Can you stay another night? I'm not ready to say goodbye to you yet."

"Yes," I said, already melting against his touch. How could I say no?

"Good. I'm not letting you out of my bed until morning." He picked me up and carried me upstairs to make good on his promise.

CHAPTER THIRTEEN

A KNOCK on my door startled me out of my reading. I'd been going over the loan documents Ethan had sent me, but all the confusing legal and financial terms made my head spin and I wasn't making much progress. I set down my pen, relieved to have an excuse to take a break, and got up to open the door.

Killian stood outside my cottage, wearing a dapper gray suit with a vest and a cravat, like something out of a historical romance novel. He was probably the most beautiful man I'd ever seen, which was saying something since I was always around shifters nowadays, who all seemed to be blessed with super attractive genetics. But his beauty was graceful, poised, and timeless, so different from their rugged, feral appeal. All vampires seemed to have that beauty too, although Killian was the only one I considered a friend. Most of the other vampires I'd met had been trying to kill me.

Seeing him standing under the bright afternoon sun made me smile. Ever since the Sun Curse had been broken, he spent as much time outside during the day as possible. Sometimes I'd catch a glimpse of him walking through the woods, his head tilted up to catch the sun on his face.

"Hey," I said, as I opened the door wider.

"Hello Larkin," he said in his smooth voice, which still had a bit of an English accent even after all this time. Though Killian had originally been from Ireland, he'd spent most of his long life in England before joining us in Lunatera and becoming the mayor of our town there. "I apologize for stopping by unannounced, but I wondered if we might chat about a few things over a pot of tea."

"You're always welcome here."

He swept into my house and settled himself in the armchair by the fireplace, giving Luna a rub while I went to make some tea. Killian had already seen my new body a few days ago when I'd been shopping in Coronis, so I knew he wasn't visiting to see if the rumors were true. I assumed he was here to ask me one of his never-ending questions about computers or smartphones, like when he'd come by declaring he needed to visit a place called Google to search its archives. I'd somehow managed to keep a straight face as I opened up a browser and showed him that Google was not a physical library as he'd thought. Even so, he was catching on faster than a lot of the older Moon Witches, many of whom simply refused to even try to use modern technology.

When I returned with a hot pot of tea and two mugs, he flashed me a warm smile, showing a bit of fang. "Thank you, my dear," he said, as he took a mug from me. "You do always make the best tea."

"Only because you taught me how to do it properly," I said as I settled down into the other chair. Though Celeste had raised me like her own daughter, Killian had always been there for me too. For much of my life, he'd been the only male I spent time with on a regular basis. Lunatera had men in it, of course, but they were few and far between.

"It's an important skill to have."

I took a sip of my tea. "What brings you here today?"

"I wanted to speak to you about this town you're starting. Would I be welcome there?"

"Of course. You may not be a Moon Witch, but you're still one of us. You know that."

He stroked Luna, who had curled up on his lap. "I had hoped so, but things are changing these days. I've heard talk that you're trying to convince the others to allow some shifters to live there too."

I paused with my mug halfway to my mouth. Vampires and shifters had once been mortal enemies, with a long history between them of bloodshed that wouldn't just disappear overnight, even though they were at peace now. "Is that going to be a problem?"

"Not at all. In fact, I think it's a brilliant idea." He gestured around us with an elegant hand. "We've been living for months among the shifters without any problems. They've taken us in and helped us get settled in this world. Even me, a vampire. This is proof that our kinds can all live together in harmony."

"I'm so glad you think so." I smiled at him over my mug. With Killian's backing, I had no doubt that many of the Moon Witches would agree too. A large number of them were not-so-secretly in love with him, though he'd never shown interest in anyone since his wife died.

"I do. In fact, I was wondering if some other vampires might be able to settle there too."

I nearly dropped my tea. "Other...vampires?"

"Ever since the truce, I've been working with the vampires, witches, and wolves to smooth everything over. It hasn't been easy, but I've been surprised by how many vampires want peace between us all." He poured us both some more tea. "Right now most of our kind live in Europe and in isolation. Many wish to stay over there and continue as they always have been, but there are some who would like more of a sense of community, especially now that the Sun Curse has been lifted and they would have an easier time traveling overseas."

"I'm open to the idea, but how would we know if we could trust them?"

Killian nodded as if he expected this question. "I would personally vouch for all of the vampires that would live there. We would be very careful in who we chose, keeping the numbers very small at first, and then opening it up to more only if it went well and there was enough space."

"I trust your judgment, but I'm not sure the other Moon Witches will be okay with it. You're the only vampire most of them have ever met. Convincing the shifters might be even harder." I leaned back and sighed as I stared out the window at the beautiful spring day. I didn't want to give Killian any false hope because I didn't know how the others would react to having vampires in what was originally going to be a small village for the Moon Witches. It seemed like everyone suddenly wanted to move to my little town, and I wasn't sure if I could handle trying to keep the peace between everyone. Even with the help of other Moon Witches, it might be too much. But that gave me another idea.

"I have faith that you can convince them," Killian said.

"I'll do my best, on one condition. I want you to be the mayor of Eventide, at least for the first year. You're the only one I trust to manage the town and help it grow, while also keeping the peace between everyone."

Killian's eyes widened slightly. "Are you sure? I thought you would want the job."

I shook my head. "I don't know anything about running a town, but you did it for years. We could really use your expertise in this matter, and I think it would do a lot to convince the Moon Witches to allow vampires to live there too."

"Hmm, I do see your point." He spent a moment rubbing Luna as he considered. "Very well. I will be the mayor of your town—Eventide, is it?—for one year's time. After that, the town will hold an election to select the next mayor."

"Perfect," I said, feeling like a huge weight had been lifted off my shoulder.

He put Luna on the floor, who protested with a little meow, then rose to his feet in one smooth motion. "'Thank you for your help. I'll let you get back to whatever you were doing when I interrupted."

"It's always good to see you," I said, as I opened the front door. A warm slant of sunshine shone in, and Killian smiled as it hit his face.

"I don't think I'll ever get used to it," he said, closing his eyes. "The feeling of the sun."

"You're so dramatic," I said and gave him a hug.

He embraced me in return, patting me on the back. "I'm very proud of you, Larkin. I hope you know that."

Someone cleared their throat, and I looked over Killian's shoulder to see Ethan standing a few feet away in front of my cottage. He was holding a bouquet of red and pink roses, while a Moon Witch portal was closing behind him. A scowl crossed his face, one of the first I'd ever seen him wear.

"Hey!" My heart leaped at the sight of him. I hadn't expected him to show up out of the blue. "Do you know Killian?"

"We've met." Ethan's eyes narrowed as he looked at the vampire. "What are you doing here?"

Killian smiled wide enough to show a bit of fang, his face amused. "I simply came to chat with Larkin for a moment. Don't worry, I'm already on my way out."

"Good," Ethan said. He crossed the distance between us and pulled me against him, kissing me long and hard, and definitely way too intimate with Killian being only a few steps away.

"Ethan!" I pushed back against him, horribly embarrassed. I couldn't believe how rude Ethan was being, which was so unlike him. But Killian laughed and shook his head, then wandered down the path with his hands in his pockets, muttering something about alphas.

"What is going on?" I asked. "Why are you acting like this?"

Ethan ran a hand through his hair and the tension in his shoulders disappeared completely when Killian disappeared into the trees and was out of sight. "I'm sorry. I don't know what came over me. I saw him hugging you and I lost my mind."

"You were jealous?" I asked, finding it hard to believe.

He rubbed a hand across his jaw. "Yes, though I hate to admit it. Nothing like that has ever happened to me before. I'll make sure to send him an apology."

Something warmed inside of me at the thought of Ethan getting so possessive over me. "You have nothing to be jealous of. I've known Killian my entire life. He's like an uncle to me."

"Good." It came out as almost a growl, and I couldn't help but shiver as I heard his voice drop so low.

"Come inside," I said, dragging him in and shaking my head. Ayla and Stella had told me all about how possessive their alphas got, but I'd never expected it to happen with Ethan and me. He was acting, well, like I was his mate. Which wasn't possible. "What are you doing here?"

"I wanted to surprise you." He handed me the roses. "Sorry for showing up unannounced but I missed you so much. I had to see you."

I tossed the roses on my kitchen counter and wrapped

my arms around his neck, kissing him. "I missed you too. And I'm sorry, I should have invited you to visit sooner. My cottage is just a lot more humble than what you're used to."

"I love it. It's very you. But I'd really like to see your bedroom."

I let out a shrill shriek as Ethan lunged for me. He caught me around the waist and I laughed as he lifted me up and carried me to my room.

"Cute," he said, before laying us both down on the bed. "Now take your clothes off and get over here. I want you to sit on my face."

"You're so bossy," I said, as I tore off my clothes, my pulse racing with anticipation.

"You like it." He gestured for me to come closer. "Now bring that wet little pussy over here so I can taste it."

Oh my goddess, when he said things like that I would do anything he demanded. I climbed over him, feeling a bit awkward, but he gripped my thighs and dragged me into position. I grabbed the headboard as his hot breath teased against me.

"Ride my tongue," he said. "You're not going to hurt me."

Then he buried his face in my pussy like it was the best meal he'd ever tasted. I cried out as his mouth and tongue licked and sucked until my thighs trembled. His hands remained steady, pulling me down harder onto his face, and my hips responded, moving against him.

I moaned, tossing my head back as he suctioned his lips around my clit and started working it in earnest. He set a brutal, relentless pace, and I could feel my orgasm coming upon me quickly. My legs quivered with pleasure, and I held onto the headboard for dear life as my climax swept over me. Thank goodness I wasn't a shifter, or I'm sure I would have broken it in two.

I moved back a little, slumping on his chest as I caught my breath. He looked up at me with a satisfied smile, licking his lips.

"I need you," I said, moving down his body, fumbling with his clothes with trembling fingers. Why did his shirt have so many buttons?

He gripped his shirt and tore it open, giving me access to his chest. I ran my tongue along his tattoos and his muscles, unable to get enough of him. He helped me open his trousers and push them down, freeing his beautiful cock. I took him in my hand, feeling how hard he was. Fuck, I needed him inside of me right now.

"You want my cock?" he asked, looking up at me with a feral hunger in his eyes. "Then ride me. Show me how much you want me, how much you've been thinking about this. I want you to bounce on my cock until you come on it."

I moaned again as I moved over him and slid the length of him along my folds. I was so wet from him eating me out that the head of his cock slipped right in, and it was like coming home. I sank down onto his cock slowly, dragging out the moment. I wanted to savor the feeling of this, along with the way he looked at me, his head propped up on my pillow, his eyes dark and possessive. I never wanted to forget it.

"You look so good like this," Ethan said, his voice coming

out a little hoarse. "Now be a good girl and fuck yourself on my cock."

I ground against him, slow and dirty, and so, so good. I'd never been on top before, and I loved being the one in control, taking what I needed from him. Ethan let me set the pace at first, and I rolled my hips and felt him deep inside me, enjoying the friction between our bodies. He played with my breasts and I arched my back, giving him better access, while I started riding him in earnest. My old bed squeaked and rattled as I moved faster, hitting that perfect spot over and over again.

He gripped my hips and thrust up against me. I pressed my hands against his chest, needing to touch him and steadying myself at the same time, as it all became too much for me. I lost control as I was hit with wave after wave of pleasure.

"My turn," he said, and then flipped us over in one smooth motion so he was on top, his cock still buried so deep inside of me I hardly knew where he began and I ended. He gripped my hands and yanked them over my head, while he rolled his hips in a way that kept my orgasm going and going.

"You're mine," he growled, his fingers tight around my wrist.

"I'm yours," I said, wrapping my legs around his hips. "I've always been yours. From the moment I first saw you."

He groaned as I said those words and unleashed himself upon me, fucking me hard and fast, not holding back at all. I heard my bed squeaking dangerously, the headboard slamming against the wall with every thrust, and

I was suddenly very glad that Stella didn't live here anymore.

Ethan growled and bottomed out one last time. He came just as the bed frame snapped with a loud, sharp noise, and we tilted dangerously. I grabbed onto Ethan and screamed as the mattress hit the floor.

"Did we break the bed?" I asked as I clung to his neck.

He lifted his head and looked around like he was in a daze. "I think we did."

I burst into laughter, and after a moment, he joined me. He collapsed onto the broken bed next to me, and we giggled until we were both breathless. I curled into his side, and he draped an arm over me.

"It was worth it," he said, as he tucked me against him. "I'll buy you a new one. Until then, I think you should stay with me."

"Was this all just an elaborate plot to get me back to your place?"

"I wish I was that clever." He pressed a kiss to my forehead. "No, I just don't want to let you go."

Then don't, I thought as I snuggled up against him.

CHAPTER FOURTEEN

THE NEXT FEW days were like a dream come true. I moved into Ethan's place in Toronto, while we waited for my new bed to arrive, and he decided to work from home. During the day, we spent our time getting everything ready with Eventide. There was an overwhelming amount of paperwork related to it, but Ethan helped explain it all to me so that it made sense. Every day, Macy seemed to show up with more, but somehow we got it all filled out and signed.

We met with architects and city planners, and together we mapped out a layout for what our new town would look like. Ethan also started reaching out to contractors, deciding on which ones would be the best fit for the various projects. Ethan's attention to detail was incredible and he asked all sorts of questions that I wouldn't have even thought to ask. We'd also worked out a way to get more people living in Eventide to start since there were only twelve cottages at the moment—we'd have the others live in RVs temporarily, while other housing was built. There was certainly enough land for them, and it would allow us to bring in many more people who could help get the town started.

While Ethan was working on other projects, I took the time to visit some of the Moon Witches and talk to them about my ideas, showing them the slideshow and the layout of the town. They were still hesitant about allowing outsiders to live with us, but more and more of them were beginning to come around. Celeste had scheduled a council meeting in Lunatera in a few days, and the matter would be voted upon then. I could only pray to Selene I'd done enough.

At night—and sometimes during the day too—Ethan was determined to act out all of the best scenes from my favorite books. He wanted to show me everything, and I was an eager student.

I'd never been so happy in my life, but every night I gazed out at the Toronto skyline and saw the moon over-head, getting larger and larger. My deadline was approaching and I never forgot that I could lose all of this soon. I'd done everything I could to secure a home for the Moon Witches, but finding love was proving to be more difficult. There were times when I swore Ethan looked at me like he was madly in love with me, but other times I succumbed to doubt, convincing myself he would find his true mate at the Convergence. He had to attend it as his pack's alpha, and there was nothing I could do to stop him. If his mate was there, all of this would come to an end.

And if not—what then? Would my love for him be

enough for Selene? I didn't think so. But I didn't know what to do, other than pray that he cared for me as much as I cared for him.

One sign that he cared was that he was insistent I come to the Libra pack meeting. It was held at night in the event space of the hotel I'd lived in while staying with the Ophiuchus pack. We'd had our holiday party here, and I remembered how sick to my stomach I'd felt as I'd watched Ethan dance with Stella, convinced that they were mates. I would be even more heartbroken now when he did finally get his real mate.

I rubbed my hand over my heart and tried to push it out of my mind as Ethan led me through the room, smiling and nodding at the other shifters. There was a small stage up front with a few chairs and microphones, and that was where he led me now. He directed me to sit next to him, to my surprise, and I wondered what the rest of his pack thought about this. While Macy took a seat beside me, I gazed out at the audience and found most of them were giving me curious looks, though I didn't sense any hostility.

There were a lot of shifters present, more than I expected, but Ethan was known for trying to keep the peace and making sure that all members of his pack felt heard. I looked around at both familiar and unfamiliar faces and wondered what it would be like to stay here in Toronto with him. I loved the city, especially now that I'd had time to explore it with Ethan, and could see myself making it my home.

Ethan started the meeting and most of the focus faded

from me. He talked about pack matters that I didn't really know much about, but I listened closely and tried to follow along. He invited other shifters to bring up any concerns they had and addressed them as best he could. Most of the pack members were completely civil, except for one man who had a grievance with some members of the Taurus pack. Ethan listened to him without interrupting and tried to offer some reasonable solutions, but the man remained unsatisfied and sat down in a huff when he was done speaking. Macy quickly moved on to the next person.

At the end of the meeting, Ethan introduced me and told everyone how we were working together on a new town for supernaturals to live in harmony, and that if anyone wanted to be considered for it, they should submit an application to him. I bit my lip and didn't point out that I hadn't gotten the Moon Witches to agree yet, but I was flattered by Ethan's confidence in me.

After the meeting, most of the shifters left, but a few lingered to discuss some things. Ethan took my arm and escorted me over to an older couple standing on the side of the room. The woman was on the shorter side but had her son's clear gray eyes, while the man was tall and had broad shoulders, along with Ethan's dark hair.

"Larkin, these are my parents, Renee and Bob," Ethan said.

"It's so nice to meet you," I said, shaking their hands.

"The pleasure is all ours," Renee said. "You've done so much for our people."

I flushed. "Not as much as your pack has done for me.

The Libra pack offered me sanctuary when I needed it most and I will always be grateful."

"I heard you were the one who started the service of opening portals between packs," Bob said.

"It was the idea of the Cancer alpha female, but yes, I made it happen."

"Genius," he said.

"I love it," Renee added. "My sister is a Scorpio and now we get to visit her family whenever we want. Without having to pay ridiculous airline fares or worry about making sure my passport is up to date!"

I laughed, pleased to hear it was working out. "I'm glad we could be of service."

"Ethan, my dear, a lovely pack meeting as always." Renee kissed his cheek. "Larkin, I hope we get to see you again soon."

"Keep up the good work, son," Bob said, and then he took Renee's hand and they exited the room.

"Your parents are so nice," I said to him, as we watched them leave.

"They are." He was about to say more when someone called his name. "I'll be right back."

Ethan moved away to talk to a group of people, including that man who'd had the issue with the Taurus pack. He started arguing with Ethan, who held his hands up and tried to keep everyone calm. I chewed on my lip as I watched them both, and hoped that it didn't turn into a real problem.

Macy came to stand beside me, looking both beautiful

and sophisticated in a sage green suit jacket with a cute skirt. "How did you like the meeting?"

"It was fun to watch, although I didn't understand half of what they talked about. I liked watching Ethan manage it all."

"You know, Ethan has had a lot of lovers before you, but he's never brought them to one of these meetings before, and he's never introduced them to his parents." She gave me a knowing smile. "He's showing you off to everyone like you're his alpha female."

"Oh. Um. I'm not sure that's true."

"Trust me. I've known Ethan a long time." She looked over at him with warm eyes. "Ethan has also never taken so much time off work, or been so possessive or obsessed with anyone. He's acting like you're his mate."

"That's not possible," I said. "I'm not a shifter."

"So what?" Macy put a hand on my arm. "I'm not saying this to try to get your hopes up, but he has all the signs. Trust me, I went through the same thing when I mated with Soleil. We were inseparable for a month, and I've heard with alphas it's even worse."

A tiny bit of hope bubbled up in me, but I tried to quash it down. "We're not mates. We can't be."

Macy cocked her head to the side. "How do you know for sure? Have you tested it?"

I stared at Macy for a few moments, the hopeful part of me swelling. I knew how other shifters activated the mate bond—they shifted into wolves and locked eyes. But I couldn't shift, so how would that even work? Besides, I'd seen him as a wolf before many times, although we'd always been fighting at the time, or a good distance apart. Had we ever locked eyes while he was a wolf? I wasn't sure. We'd never actually tested it. We'd both been so convinced from the beginning that it was impossible for us to be mates, that we'd never even tried.

Macy opened her mouth to say something else, but before she could, raised voices caught our attention. On the other side of the room, the angry shifter towered over Ethan, using his size and height to try and intimidate him.

"You can't play both sides," the male shouted, clenching his hands into fists.

"Let's sit down and talk about this," Ethan said, without backing down. "I'm sure we can find a solution."

"Fuck that," the man snarled. "I don't want to talk. All you do is talk and I'm tired of it." He poked Ethan in the chest. "I'm challenging you for the position of alpha."

A gasp went up around the room from the few remaining shifters. Macy immediately moved to stand at Ethan's side, crossing her arms. I remained frozen, unsure if I should get involved or not. Would they actually fight to the death right here where we had our holiday party? Surely not.

Ethan's eyes narrowed and his voice became low and deadly, though still calm. "You don't want to challenge me for the alpha position. We can resolve this another way that doesn't involve your death."

"Fuck that," the man spat.

He shoved Ethan once and I stepped forward, ready to

summon moon magic if needed, but Macy held out a hand to me to tell me to stop. This was shifter business, and they didn't want me to get involved. Only Ethan could settle this now.

Ethan stared at the other man for a long moment. "Very well. I accept your challenge."

A murmur went through the assembled Libra pack members. A lot of them looked uneasy, and a few looked outright worried. I wondered how long this had been brewing, and why today was the day that had set the male shifter off.

Ethan started stripping out of his clothes, handing them to Macy. The assembled shifters all drew back, giving both Ethan and the male shifter enough room for a fight. The other shifter stripped down as well, tossing his clothes out of the circle. The two men stared each other down for a few moments, and then Ethan shifted, becoming a huge and majestic gray wolf with piercing eyes.

He let out a low growl that sounded like a warning but didn't attack. The tension rose, and I was pretty sure we all held our breath as we waited for the other male to shift and for the fight to begin. But then the man swallowed hard and took a step back, sweat beading on his forehead.

"You're right," he said to Ethan in a quiet voice. "I don't want to fight you. I rescind my challenge and acknowledge you as the Libra alpha."

He dropped to his knees and bowed his head in submission. Ethan growled once more, low and long. It vibrated through my chest, even from this far away. Then he brushed his nose against the man's shoulder, which seemed to mean something to the shifters because the tension broke. A collective sigh went through the shifters around me, and almost everyone relaxed. Ethan stepped back, and the male shifter got up and brushed himself off, then walked out of the room.

Ethan trotted over to me in wolf form and rubbed against my legs. I reached down and rubbed his head between his ears, feeling his soft fur. Shifters were so odd. I wasn't sure I'd ever think like they did, no matter how much time I spent around them.

I bent down and wrapped my hands around Ethan's furry neck, and he licked my face. Then I pulled back enough for our eyes to meet, and I held my breath. I waited for any sign that there was a mating bond between us, hoping it would magically activate, or however that worked. But nothing happened, and my hope crumbled to dust.

Ethan had been right all along. There was no mating bond between us. He'd meet his true mate at the Convergence and I'd be left alone, wondering if I could ever get over him. I'd go back to my old body and have nothing but memories from our time together.

My heart broke as Ethan looked away, his tail drooping. Had he been hoping for something, too? Tears burned in my eyes and I blinked them back, trying not to cry in front of everyone. Ethan nudged me with his nose and I put my hands in the soft fur at the nape of his neck. He leaned against me as I stroked his fur, and together we mourned what might have been.

Eventually, Ethan pulled away, and he went back to Macy and got his clothes. While he dressed, she came back over to me.

"See?" I said, the heartbreak making my voice shake. "No mating bond. Just like I thought."

Macy put her hand on my shoulder and squeezed. "That doesn't mean anything. Mating bonds don't always happen immediately. Soleil and I have known each other our whole lives, but even after the Sun Witch spell was removed, it took us a while for our bond to activate. But it finally did when we went on a full moon hunt together a few months ago."

"You're just saying that to make me feel better."

"I'm not," Macy said. "Libras are notoriously indecisive. Sometimes we just need a little push. Don't give up on him, okay?"

I nodded, though I didn't really mean it. Any hope that I had of being mated with Ethan was now gone for good.

CHAPTER FIFTEEN

AFTER THE PACK MEETING, I told Ethan I needed to return home to plan for my own meeting with the Moon Witch council. My new bed was delivered the next morning, and though he and I talked every night and visited each other as much as we could, I worried we were nearing the end of our time together.

When I arrived in Lunatera, I stared up at the moon overhead, wondering if Selene was listening. "I did my best," I told her. "I found love. Even if it was only temporary, doesn't that count?"

She remained silent on the matter, so I put up the hood on my purple robes and continued down the beach, to where the Moon Witch council was gathered near Celeste's house. My aunt stood in the center of the other witches, wearing a black and silver robe with her moon crown resting on her brow. Ayla stood beside her in her own purple robes, and she gave me a thumbs-up as I approached. I knew I could count on her to be on my side, even if no one else was.

"We meet tonight under the watchful eye of Selene to discuss the matter of our new home on Earth," Celeste said. "Our youngest daughter Larkin has been tasked with this burden, and has asked us to gather tonight to vote on the matter of allowing other supernaturals to join us in this new town she is starting."

I gazed around at the faces I'd known my entire life. They'd raised me and taught me everything I knew about magic, but they'd also never taken me seriously in my younger-looking body. They'd seen me as a perpetual child, even after I'd been an adult for years. I hoped they'd finally listen to me tonight, and that my argument was strong enough to sway some of the more hesitant Moon Witches.

"Larkin, you may speak now," Celeste said.

I nodded and stepped forward into the center of the circle. All of the gathered witches watched me, waiting patiently. "For centuries our people have lived in Lunatera, hiding from the threat of the Sun Witches, and we were safe —but at what cost? We have allowed ourselves to become stagnant, so isolated by living in a realm with no time that we have fallen behind. Like the moon and the tides, we must change and adapt to survive, and we must do that on Earth. But we can't do it alone."

One of the other Moon Witches, a cranky old lady named Paola, snorted. She was one of the ones who always talked over me or dismissed me. I ignored her and continued speaking.

"There are so few of us left, and we have been away from Earth for too long. To truly have a town that will sustain us for generations to come, we need teachers, electricians, and plumbers. We need all sorts of people who have different skill sets to make it into a community. We need income from a wide variety of sources to help pay for it all, and we need fresh blood if we want to raise a new generation of Moon Witches. There are so few male Moon Witches left—our survival depends on us breeding with outsiders. Allowing other supernaturals to live in Eventide is the answer to all of our problems."

"How will it be decided who can live among us and who can't?" a male Moon Witch named Erik asked.

"We will collect applications from everyone who is interested and a small committee will decide on who to invite," I said. "We were thinking of starting with five individuals or families from each group to start, and then adding more as needed."

"I thought you said there were only twelve cabins," Mariel, one of my distant cousins, asked me. "How will we fit all these extra people in the town?"

"A good question," I replied. "We plan to rent a small fleet of RVs, where people will be able to live while more housing is being built."

"Shifters and vampires are dangerous creatures," Rowena said. She was the oldest witch in Lunatera, and I wasn't sure she would ever leave. "What makes you think it will be safe for our people to live among them?"

"Killian has lived among us for years, and he has never

harmed anyone. He will help us choose other vampires that will not be a threat to us. As for the shifters, we have been living among them for months. I've been with them for even longer. They have done everything they can to protect us and help us adapt to living on Earth again. The thirteen alphas have also agreed to combine their assets and pay off one million dollars of our loan, as a thank you for our help in freeing them from the Sun Witches."

A low murmur went up among the council at that and Celeste smiled and gave me a nod.

"The time for supernaturals to be divided is over," I said. "The vampires and shifters have made a truce. Our war with the Sun Witches is over. We can live in harmony together, in a town where no one is an outcast or an enemy. Eventide will be that place."

I bowed before them, signaling that I was done speaking, and then stepped back to take my place among their ranks.

"Thank you, Larkin," Celeste said, her eyes beaming with pride.

As I glanced around the circle, I noticed similar looks from many of the other witches too. I practically glowed as I realized that for the first time, they were seeing me as more than just a kid. I'd proven myself to them by securing Eventide with Ethan's help, and with the confidence I'd found over the last few weeks with him.

"I've heard enough," Celeste said. "As our High Priestess, I move that we allow other supernaturals into our town, under the guidance of Larkin and a small committee she will form to oversee it. Are there any objections?"

No one said anything. Many of the Moon Witches bowed their heads or nodded, the matter concluded. Others looked skeptical but kept their mouths shut. I couldn't believe it. Not a single one said anything against me. This had to be a new record.

"Then this matter is settled, and our meeting is adjourned," Celeste said. "May Selene watch over us all."

The others repeated her blessing and then the meeting broke up, with some of them going back to their homes here, while others opened a portal to Coronis. I finally relaxed, the last of the tension from the past few days letting up when I realized that I'd accomplished my task. I'd secured Eventide for the Moon Witches, and we were well on our way to becoming a community that would be welcome to anyone.

Celeste walked over to me and gave me a warm hug. I leaned into her embrace. She'd been like a mother to me ever since my parents had died and her approval meant a lot to me.

"You've done an amazing job," she said, as we pulled apart. "Thank you for all of your hard work. I know the town will be in good hands with you. It's no wonder you have Selene's favor."

"Thank you for trusting me with this task. I wasn't sure I could do it at first."

She touched my cheek. "I knew you could. You've always been the best and brightest of us. My little moonbeam, all grown up." She stepped back. "Now I must return home to work on some things. Would you care to join me for dinner?"

"I would, but I need to get back to Earth." Ethan was meeting with some contractors at Halcyon Lake, and I wanted to immediately tell him the good news.

"I understand." She kissed my cheek. "Come visit me soon."

"I will."

After Celeste walked back to her house, Ayla grabbed me in a hug. "That speech was incredible. You blew everyone away. Did you practice it in advance?"

"A little. I worked out all the points with Ethan over the last few days. I wanted to make sure I said everything I needed to."

She arched an eyebrow. "How are things going with him?"

"I don't know." I bit my lip. "It's almost the full moon, and I'm not sure what will happen then."

"He loves you. I know he does. Maybe you just need to tell him how you feel."

Her words stayed with me as I transported into what would soon be Eventide. A few trucks were parked outside of the lodge, and I spotted Ethan standing with a few other men, their heads bent over a map. He raised a hand and waved when he saw me, then said something to the other men and started toward me.

"How did it go?" he asked, then gave me a kiss.

I laughed at the excitement in his voice. "They said yes!"

"I knew they would." He slipped his arm in mine and we strolled toward the lake together. "Tell me everything."

"I gave them the speech I'd prepared and they actually listened to me for once. They asked me a few questions, and then Celeste said she was convinced and none of the other Moon Witches spoke out against her decision. I couldn't believe it!"

"I'm not surprised at all," Ethan said. "You're incredible. You can do anything once you put your mind to it."

"I couldn't have done it without you," I said, wrapping my arms around his neck.

We kissed as all around us the sky faded from blue to black as the last bit of sunlight vanished. The other men called out their goodbyes and got in their trucks, and we waved at them and they drove away. Then Ethan wrapped me in his arms as we gazed out at the lake. I leaned against him as we watched the moon come out from behind a cloud. It was almost full, just a tiny sliver away from being complete. I was almost out of time.

"Are you planning to live here with the Moon Witches?" Ethan asked.

"Yes, unless..."

"Unless?" He traced a nonsensical pattern across the bare skin of my upper arm.

I glanced up at the almost full moon and remembered Ayla's words. The Convergence was in two days. This might be my last chance. I had to be brave.

"Unless you want me to live in Toronto with you," I said.

Ethan went very still, his body tensing against mine. I wished that I could take the words back immediately. They hung in the air between us, and for a moment I couldn't even breathe.

"I would like that," he said. "But my fate is controlled by the stars."

"Why can't you choose your own fate?" I asked, turning around to face him.

He closed his eyes briefly like he was in pain. "I wish I could. But shifters...we don't get to choose."

"Why not?" I asked, stepping back from him.

"It doesn't work that way. I could meet my mate anytime, and I would have no choice but to be with her. It could even happen at the next Convergence." He shook his head. "I've seen too many relationships torn apart by mate bonds in the last few years. I don't want to hurt you like that."

"It's too late for that." The wind whipped at my hair, making my eyes water. "I love you, Ethan. I always have, even when you barely looked at me."

"Larkin, I care about you too, I really do. I want nothing more than to be with you. But we're not mates, no matter how much I wish that we were."

"Is there any hope for us?" I asked, with a hitch in my voice.

"No. That's why I said from the start this could never be serious." He looked out at the lake with sorrow in his eyes. "I know I did a poor job of keeping that distance between us though, which is my fault. I guess... I guess I wanted it to be real too. I'm sorry."

His words hit me like a punch to the gut. Somehow it was even worse hearing that he cared for me and wanted to be with me too, but couldn't. In his mind, it was impossible for us to be together, all because I wasn't his mate. And maybe he was right.

"We should end this now then, before it goes any further," I said, while my heart shattered in my chest. "Before the Convergence."

"Larkin, I..." He reached for me but then stopped. "I didn't want it to end this way."

"I didn't want it to end at all," I whispered, as a tear finally slipped down my cheek. I brushed it away with the back of my hand and turned around, unable to look at Ethan for another second. It hurt too much.

I launched myself into the air and flew over the water, the wind blowing back my hair. At the end of the lake I banked up and over the trees, not knowing where I was going, only that I needed to get as far away from the man I loved as possible.

CHAPTER SIXTEEN

A LOUD KNOCK came at my door, startling me out of staring at yet another page of a book I couldn't focus on. I set it face down next to my glass of red wine. I'd gone through several bottles over the last two days, and they were piling up on my kitchen counter. I knew that eventually I'd have to deal with them, just like I'd have to deal with everything, but now wasn't that time. Luna opened her eyes from where she was curled on the couch next to me and made an inquisitive noise deep in her chest. She'd kept me company these last few days, letting me cuddle her. She seemed to realize that I was heartbroken and often sat on my chest, purring. She was rarely this affectionate, so I knew it had to be pretty bad for her to be acting like this.

I stood up and went to the door, wondering who it could be. It was the night before the full moon, the same night of the Convergence. All of the shifters I knew were there, celebrating being wild and free, or whatever they did there. I wasn't interested. I wanted to sit in my cottage and never go outside again if I could help it.

I'd been trying so hard to not think about tonight or what it would entail, but it was impossible to avoid. Usually when I had problems I wanted to escape from I would read a book, but that wasn't working anymore. Every book reminded me that the characters were on their way to the happy ending I would never get.

I opened the door and tried not to groan out loud. Usually, I'd be happy to see all of my best friends, but not tonight. Ayla stood on the porch, while Madison, Harper, Stella, and Mira all stood behind her.

"Why are you here?" I asked, trying not to sound annoyed. I failed. "Shouldn't you be at the Convergence?"

"Wow," Stella said, putting a hand over her heart. "Is that any way to greet your best friends, who've come to save you from yourself?"

"I don't need any saving," I muttered, crossing my arms.

"We're here to take you to the Convergence," Ayla said.

"No way." If I had to be in the same place as Ethan trying to get a mate, I might actually have a nervous break-down. I flopped back onto the couch and picked up my glass of wine. I took a healthy gulp of it and watched as they all filed in after me.

Stella raised her eyebrows at the wine bottles. "Damn, did you drink all of those yourself?"

"This is a judgment-free zone," I said, raising my glass. "If you're going to judge, come back a different day."

Mira immediately began cleaning up my empty wine bottles. "We came because we're worried about you."

I sighed and scrubbed a hand over my face. I knew I looked like a mess. I hadn't changed my pajamas in days, and I'd thrown my hair up into a messy bun earlier without brushing it. I'd cried on and off for what felt like an eternity, and I was sure that my eyes were all red and puffy. I'd always been an ugly crier and getting this new body hadn't fixed that.

"Get off your butt and get dressed," Harper said, kicking my foot lightly. "We're going to the Convergence and you're coming with us."

"While I appreciate the sentiment, I'm not interested." I picked up my book and flipped to a random page. I couldn't focus on it, but they didn't know that.

"You're holding your book upside down," Madison said.

I let out a frustrated noise and set it back down. Luna startled and jumped off of the couch. She stretched, yawned, and then sauntered into my bedroom, giving us all a nasty glance. I wanted to follow her. "While I appreciate you all coming to check on me, I'd rather you left me alone with my heartbreak."

"What if I fight Ethan for you?" Harper asked, bouncing on the balls of her feet. "Would that at least make you feel better?"

"I already told Ethan that he's in trouble," Stella said. "I can rally all the Leos behind me if I need to."

Ayla rolled her eyes. "No one is getting into any fights or

pack wars. But I do think you should come to the Convergence. I spoke to Ethan earlier today when we were all setting up for the Convergence and he was a mess. The Libras are worried about him. No one has seen him act like this before, according to what Macy told me. He's just as miserable as you are."

I snorted. "I highly doubt that. He's the one who said there was no future for us."

Madison put a hand on my shoulder. "Everyone can see that you two are meant to be."

I closed my eyes. "I wish that was true."

"Sometimes people need a second chance to see what's been in front of them all along," Mira said.

"I know that worked for you," I said. "But it's different for me. I'm not a shifter. I'm not his mate. The stars must have someone else in mind for him."

Ayla huffed. "Sometimes you have to defy the stars and fight for what you know is right."

"Yeah," Harper said. "Fuck the stars!"

I couldn't help but laugh as I looked at all of my friends around me. They'd taken their time to come and make sure that I was okay, and to try to convince me that this was something worth fighting for. With them by my side, I felt stronger. Maybe I really could try one more time. I had one more night before the full moon, after all.

"Am I even allowed at the Convergence?" I asked. "I thought it was only for shifters."

"You'll be escorted in by four alphas," Stella said, lifting her chin. "No one will dare to challenge us."

"Fine," I said, heaving a huge sigh. "I'll go. You're right, Ethan is worth fighting for."

"You are worth fighting for," Ayla said. "Now go take a quick shower and get dressed. We don't have all night."

"Thank you," I said. "Thank you all for coming to help me."

"That's what friends are for," Madison said.

"We'll clean up while you get ready," Mira said, wrinkling her nose as she picked up some used tissues from off the floor.

Fifteen minutes later I emerged from my bedroom, wearing a shimmery silver gown that Ayla had convinced me to buy during our shopping spree. It hugged my curves and dipped low in the back, making me feel sexy and powerful. I'd added a silver tiara with a moon on it, which Celeste had given me years ago. I'd never been brave enough to wear it before, but shy, awkward Larkin was a thing of the past. Ethan had made me feel so comfortable and safe with him that I'd become someone else, someone I liked a lot more. I wasn't ashamed that I wasn't a wolf. I was a Moon Witch, and that was enough.

"You look so beautiful," Mira said, and Harper let out a low whistle.

"Let's go," Ayla said, gesturing for everyone to come closer. "We don't want to be late."

Ayla had us all grab each other's hands, forming a circle, and then my living room disappeared as she teleported us away. In an instant we were outside, standing in a patch of grass near some tents with the Ophiuchus symbol. More tents stretched out across the field in front of us, and where they ended, hundreds of shifters were gathered.

The girls instantly rushed me forward, toward the crowd of shifters. As we drew closer, I recognized the Aquarius alpha and his mate standing in front, giving a speech. Their pack was hosting the summer Convergence in their pack lands, and under other circumstances I would have liked to get a chance to look around, but I didn't have time. I had to find Ethan before the mating ritual started.

I searched the crowd for him, or for someone in the Libra pack who might know where he was, but I didn't recognize anyone. However, we did find Kaden, Jordan, and Wesley standing together on the sidelines.

"Where's Ethan?" I asked them.

"We haven't seen him," Wesley said.

Stella took me by the shoulders. "He's here somewhere, and you can find him. I know it sounds crazy, but trust your gut and follow it."

"Now we shall begin the mating ritual," the Aquarius alpha's voice boomed out, and my stomach dropped.

What if I was too late?

CHAPTER SEVENTEEN

AS THE MATING RITUAL STARTED, dozens of shifters around me all began shedding their clothes. I stepped back, shocked by all the sudden nudity, and then they all started shifting. I'd never been surrounded by so many wolves before, and frankly, it was a bit terrifying. Some instinctual part of my brain screamed at me to run, but I reminded myself that these shifters were my friends and allies. They wouldn't hurt me. Hopefully.

"Good luck," Harper said, as she tossed her clothes to the ground. Madison was stripping naked beside her too and I quickly averted my eyes, not needing to know what all my friends' boobs looked like. Not that they cared. Shifters had zero modesty.

"You too," I told them. "I hope you both find your mates."

They both became wolves and nudged their heads against me, before joining the other unmated shifters in the center of the circle. Ayla, Stella, and Mira were all standing with their mates on the sidelines, keeping their eyes peeled for a sign of Ethan. Harper met her twin, Dane, and they chased each other around a bit. Then two identical gray wolves raced toward them, and they collided in a tangle of fur and fangs that I guessed had to be their mate bond activating.

I scanned the other wolves in the circle but didn't see Ethan's large gray wolf. Somehow I knew I would be able to tell him apart from the other wolves, and I was certain he wasn't among them. All I saw were shifters tussling and nosing at each other as they found their mates. But where was he?

What if he had already found a mate and run off with her to seal the bond? The thought of him getting intimate with someone else at this very moment made me nearly sick to my stomach.

Wolves split off in pairs and started moving away into the forest or toward the tents to seal their bonds. Despair and jealousy filled me at the sight. I wanted what they had too. I turned away from the mating frenzy, feeling miserable and ridiculous. What had I expected? I'd known exactly what would go down tonight.

Something in my gut tugged me forward, and I remembered Stella's words. I gave in to my instincts, trusting them to lead me to the right place, and found myself walking through the tents. I wasn't sure where I was going and was beginning to feel quite silly when I came face-to-face with a very large tent with the Libra symbol on it. My breath caught in my chest as I looked at it, my heart pounding. That couldn't have been a coincidence.

I saw movement inside. Someone was definitely in there. I rushed toward the tent, intending to burst inside, but before I could, the flaps parted and Ethan stepped out.

He had a bag slung over his shoulder, and he was fully dressed. He looked a little tired and worse for wear, but just as handsome as always, and my heart hurt at the sight of him. I stayed still and waited for his eyes to fall on me. When they did, he stopped dead in his tracks, and I could have sworn I saw his jaw drop for a split second before he caught himself.

"What are you doing?" I asked, motioning to his pack. "Why aren't you at the mating ceremony?"

Ethan shook his head, still looking me over as if he couldn't quite believe it. "I decided to skip it."

"You did?" I asked, the tiniest bit of hope fluttering inside my chest.

"I couldn't do it." He dropped his bag on the ground. "I was going to find Ayla and ask her to teleport me to Coronis so I could talk to you."

"Why?" I needed to hear him say it, or I wouldn't believe it.

He stepped forward, gazing down into my eyes. "I want to be with you and no one else. I don't care if we're not mates. I'll avoid every mating ritual. Hell, I'll never shift again if that's what it takes."

My blood rushed in my ears. I could hardly believe that this was happening. After all the time I'd spent wishing and hoping, it didn't feel real. "What about your pack? You're the alpha, and they expect you to find your alpha female."

"You're my alpha female." He took my face in his hands. "I won't accept any other. And if my pack has a problem with that, then I'll step down as alpha too."

"I could never ask you to do that."

"None of it is worth it if I can't have you by my side."

He crushed his lips to mine, sliding his hands into my hair. He poured everything into this kiss, showing me how he felt with every brush of his lips and stroke of his tongue. I kissed him back, long and deep, not holding a single thing back. The rest of the universe faded away, leaving only the two of us, standing under the almost-full moon.

"I was going to come here to fight for you, to tell you to defy the stars," I said. "I guess you got to that part on your own, didn't you?"

He brushed his knuckles against my cheek. "I'm sorry it took so long. After you left me by the lake, I thought about spending the rest of my life without you, and I realized that would be torture. I don't want a mate. I just want you."

"I've always wanted you, Ethan. You, and only you."

"I love you, Larkin. Will you be my wife? My alpha female?"

"Yes, yes, yes," I said, kissing him between each word.

A smattering of applause sounded behind me, and I jumped, pulling back from Ethan. I turned around to see that most of my friends were gathered several yards away. My eyes widened as I realized that they'd probably just heard some of that.

"What are all of you doing here?" I asked. "Aren't you supposed to be..." I trailed off and made a vague motion to the woods.

Stella, who stood with Jordan, shook her head. She had her hand cupped around her very pregnant stomach and grinned at me. "We were all nearby, and when we heard you and Ethan talking, we wanted to make sure that it went okay."

I rolled my eyes with a smile. "You were just being nosy."

Everyone was there except Harper and Madison, who were hopefully off finding their mates. But my other friends were all here to support me, along with their mates, and I was touched that they'd come over to check on me, even if it was just to spy on us.

"Congratulations," Kaden said, looking between us. "I'm happy for both of you."

"Welcome to the family," Wesley said as he shook hands with Ethan.

Mira gave me a hug as well. "See? Everything worked out in the end, just like I thought it would. All it takes sometimes is another chance."

Jordan smiled at me and then clasped Ethan's hand. "I'm so glad you both figured everything out. Stella was threatening to start a pack war with the Libras, and I have a hard time saying no to her."

Stella snorted and hit Jordan lightly on the shoulder. "Not *all* the Libras. Just Ethan and anyone who supported him."

"I'm glad we could avoid a pack war," Ethan said dryly.

"It would only be until you came to your senses," Stella said with a shrug.

Jordan kissed Stella's head. "Isn't she the perfect Leo alpha female?"

A gray wolf that looked familiar loped over to us and then shifted back into a naked Madison. "I see you found him. Did everything work out?"

"It did," I said with a smile I couldn't contain.

"Any luck?" Ayla asked as she handed Madison her clothes.

"No." Madison shrugged as she pulled on her dress. "I'm not sure I'm meant to find a mate."

"Maybe not," I said. "But that doesn't mean you can't find love. Don't give up hope yet."

"I appreciate that," she said. "I'm sure if it's meant to happen, it will."

"It's been lovely to see you all, but I think it's time we said goodnight," Ethan said, as he took my hand and dragged me into his tent. I only had a brief moment to give my friends a wave before I was pulled inside, and I heard my friends laughing outside.

Ethan pulled me in for a scorching kiss, and I had a feeling I wouldn't be getting much sleep at all tonight.

CHAPTER EIGHTEEN

THE FULL MOON lit the forest and a slight breeze rustled through the trees. The sounds of shifters all around me filled my ears. We were in the middle of the Algonquin Provincial Park, which was just outside of Toronto, and the Libra pack liked to gather here on full moons and other nights when they needed to wolf out. I tilted my head up to look up at the moon, soaking in its power. It glowed so bright that I could see perfectly in the dark, even under the shade of the trees.

Earlier that day, I'd signed the final loan documents from Ethan, finalizing everything with Eventide and officially making it the Moon Witches' new home. We'd also decided to build our own cabin there so we could spend as much time as we needed in Eventide to get the place up and running. I knew there would be a lot of hard work ahead of us, but it would be worth it. Ethan's contractors were already getting started on fixing everything, and within a couple of weeks, it would be ready for people to start moving there. Soon more construction would begin, building houses, stores, and everything else we needed to turn the place into a real town. I was so proud that I'd managed to pull it off, and I honestly still couldn't really believe that it was real. Everything had worked out perfectly, but I couldn't have done it without Ethan.

I kept expecting to wake up and realize that this was all a dream, but no matter how many times I pinched myself, I was still here, standing next to Ethan in the forest, still in my older body.

"Ready?" he asked, his eyes shining with love.

I nodded, not trusting myself to speak. He took my hand and led me through the throng of Libra pack members, who parted around us. Most of them smiled at us as we passed by, though some eyed my purple Moon Witch robes with confusion, or looked conflicted when they noticed that Ethan held my hand. I knew that they weren't all ready to have a non-shifter as their alpha female, but I'd win them over eventually, just like I'd won over their alpha.

Ethan escorted me through the crowd until we stopped below two huge trees that created an archway. A hush went through the other shifters as he pulled a black jewelry box out of his pocket and handed it to me. I opened it and found a gorgeous necklace with a Libra symbol studded with diamonds on a thin silver chair. It glittered in the moonlight as Ethan took it out and held it in front of me.

"Larkin, with this necklace you become a member of our pack. Do you accept?"

"Yes," I said, my hands trembling slightly. I cleared my

throat and repeated it louder, so everyone could hear as well. "A hundred times, yes."

He moved closer and secured the necklace on me, then gave me a glorious smile, his eyes full of love. I touched the necklace for the briefest moment before Ethan swept me into his arms and kissed me. It was the kind of kiss that showed everyone he was claiming me, and all around us, the Libra pack exploded into cheers and whistles. I melted into him, as I did every time he touched me.

He reached down and squeezed my hand once more before stepping back and turning to address the pack. "Please welcome Larkin Aetos of the Moon Witches, the newest member of our pack, and my alpha female."

The crowd cheered again and my cheeks grew warm with so many eyes on me, but I stood confidently by Ethan's side and gave everyone a smile. I had a pack now. I was an alpha female. I had no idea what exactly went along with all of that, but I was eager to find out.

Macy was the first to come up to us, with Soleil by her side. "Welcome, Larkin," she said, bowing her head low. I stepped forward and gave her a hug, and she whispered, "Told you so."

She stepped back with a smug smile on her face and gave me a wink. Soleil greeted me next by kissing both my cheeks, and then one by one, every single pack member came up and welcomed me as a member. Some gave me hugs, some bowed their heads, and some simply gave me a terse nod. But every single one of them recognized me.

When it was done, Ethan gave me a proud smile before

turning back to face his pack. "Now it's time to hunt. The moon goddess is watching us intently tonight. Let's make her proud."

All around us, Libras started undressing and shifting, and the forest was soon filled with the sound of howls as they set off on their hunt. I couldn't help but shiver a little as I listened to them. I'm sure I would get used to it eventually, but it would always be both strange and wonderful being the only human in a wolf pack.

Ethan began shedding his own clothes. For once, he'd worn a black T-shirt and jeans. I had a hard time not staring at him as he took them off. Then I remembered, I was his alpha female. I could stare as much as I wanted.

"I'll see you soon," he said, as he folded his clothes neatly and put them under a nearby tree with his shoes.

"I'll be flying right above you." I'd never participated in a wolf hunt before, and I wasn't sure I wanted to either. Watching from overhead seemed like the perfect way to be involved without getting too close.

Ethan kissed me once more before he pulled away and shifted. Within seconds, his large gray wolf was nudging my hand with his big wet nose. I bent down to place a kiss on it.

Our eyes met under the light of the full moon and something weird happened in my chest. A massive tug, drawing me toward the wolf in front of me, tethering our souls together. Suddenly I was not one person but two, like my heart had been divided in half and split between two bodies.

The mate bond!

Was it possible? I pressed a hand to my chest, finding it

hard to breathe. Awareness of Ethan washed over me in new ways I'd never expected, and then came the overwhelming desire. I wanted, no, I *needed* him.

Ethan shifted back and caught me in his arms. "Are you okay?"

I touched the rough stubble on his jaw, staring up at him. "Is this what I think it is?"

"You're my mate," he said, his voice filled with awe. "How is it possible?"

"I don't know. Why did it happen now and not before?"

Ethan began pressing soft kisses to my face, my jaw, and my neck. "Maybe I wasn't ready before. Maybe the stars listened to me and let me write my own destiny. I don't know, and frankly, I don't really care. All I care about is that I don't have to worry about being mated to anyone else ever again."

Or maybe it was Selene, I wondered, as I glanced up at the full moon shining down on us. In the end, it didn't really matter why it had happened. All that mattered was that I was Ethan's and he was mine, and no one could ever doubt that it was meant to be.

"The mating bond isn't complete yet though," Ethan said, as he began sliding my robes off of me. He kissed my neck, his teeth scraping against my skin, and I sensed he was growing more wild by the second. Desire flooded me, an intense urge to have Ethan inside me, unlike anything I'd ever felt before.

"Are we going to consummate our bond right here in the

middle of the forest with your pack in earshot?" I asked, only half teasing as he unclasped my bra.

"You'd better get used to it." He grew claws and tore my undies off like they were paper. "You're mated to a shifter now. Sometimes we have to give into our feral instincts."

I grinned as I hooked one of my legs around Ethan's hips. He was already hard, his cock pressed against me. "I wasn't complaining," I said as I reached between us and stroked his length a few times. "It's just like that new scene in my book, the one I'm writing right now. Which I think I have an ending for, by the way."

"Oh?" He gripped my ass and hauled me up, wrapping my legs around his waist. "I can't wait to read it."

Ethan backed me up against a thick tree and rubbed his cock against me, and I moaned and dug my fingers into his skin. The bark was rough against my back, but I didn't care. All I wanted was Ethan inside of me now. Making me his, wholly and completely.

"I love you," I gasped. "Now take me. Here, like this."

He didn't hesitate to obey. He slid into me, filling me up, and making us both groan. I felt the coiled tension in his body, and I knew he wasn't going to be gentle with me tonight. Good. I loved it when he let go of his control and let me feel his power. I wanted to be sore the next day, so that whenever I moved I remembered our night together.

He began to move, fucking me against the tree, slow at first and then faster. The sounds of the forest grew louder, the trees whispering, the wind caressing my skin, and the moon above shining brighter, as if they were all there, celebrating this moment with us. Somehow I knew this was because of my new connection to Ethan—I was tapping into his enhanced shifter senses. I also felt how much he loved me, and how good it made him feel to be inside me, claiming me. I was beginning to understand why mates were so obsessed with each other. This was intense.

Ethan's eyes were dark and feral as he thrust up into me. "You look so good like this. Taking my cock with the symbol of my pack—*our* pack—around your neck."

"I'm never taking it off," I told him, before capturing his mouth in a ravenous kiss, my teeth grazing against his lips. His animal instincts were affecting me too, it seemed.

His hands dug into my ass as he moved me up and down on him. He set a fast, brutal pace, his eyes staying on me the whole time. I gripped tight onto his shoulders, letting my nails sink into his flesh as I struggled to stay quiet.

"Let them hear," Ethan growled. "I want them all to hear the moment I claim you for my own."

He adjusted his angle and hit me in exactly the right spot. My head fell back, hitting the tree, but I barely noticed the slight pain. All I could feel was the pleasure, the way Ethan's cock stretched me, filled me, claimed me. He pushed me toward an orgasm hard and fast, and pretty soon it was impossible to keep my voice down. Tonight, he wanted me screaming.

He latched his mouth on the side of my neck, where he sucked and licked at my skin. "I'm going to bite you where everyone will see. I want them all to know you're my mate."

"Yes!" I'd secretly wanted this ever since I'd heard about

mates biting each other. I knew it would hurt, but I didn't care. The thought of his teeth inside me turned me on more than anything else. "Bite me, claim me, make me yours."

His canines sank into the side of my neck and sent a wave of pain through me, making me cry out. But then the pain receded and all I felt was an intense pleasure unlike anything I'd ever felt before. It traveled throughout my entire body and mixed with the intense sensations between my thighs, pushing me over the edge. I came, my body convulsing and shaking, and I screamed so loud I was sure everyone in the forest could hear me. Ethan's climax followed mine immediately, his entire body tensing, and his cock throbbing deep inside me.

He kissed my neck in the spot where he'd bitten me, and then lowered us both to a spot of grass on the forest floor. My body pulsed with a mix of pain and pleasure, but I didn't regret a single moment.

"Are you okay?" Ethan asked. "Did I hurt you?"

"I'm fine." I reached up and used a little bit of magic to heal the bite on my neck, just enough so it wouldn't hurt anymore, along with my scratched-up back. The magic was cool and soothing against my inflamed skin, and I sighed in relief. "Don't worry. I can take it."

"You're amazing." He pressed a kiss to my neck, my jaw, my lips. "My mate. I love you so much."

We lay there together for a few, long minutes, gazing up at the night sky and catching our breath. Ethan's body was hot against mine and I closed my eyes, luxuriating in the feeling of having him so close. With the mate bond, I had an entirely new awareness of him, one that would take some time to get used to.

"You should go join the hunt," I said eventually, once we'd both recovered enough. "It's probably almost over and they'll want you to be there."

Ethan lazily slid his hand along my thigh. "Are you sure? I'm sure they wouldn't mind me staying here with you."

"I'm sure." I gave his arm a squeeze as we sat up. "I'll be right above you. Go ahead, and I'll join you in a minute."

He gave me a smile that was all alpha. "Fine, but when we're done, I'm taking you back home, and I'm sorry to say you won't be getting any sleep."

I laughed and rolled my eyes. He gave me one more long heated kiss before stepping back and turning into a wolf again. He did a quick circle around me before running off into the forest after his fellow pack members. I watched the area he'd disappeared into, the foliage swaying before settling in place. I knew I'd be able to find him easily enough. The mate bond between us would lead me right to him.

I picked clothes up off the ground, dressing quickly. My undies were shredded, thanks to Ethan's claws, but I'd make him buy me some new ones. Once my robes were back on, I flew up above the trees until I found the highest one and perched on a branch near the top. The wind was stronger up here, and I gripped on tight as I looked around. The forest stretched below me for miles, untouched and perfect, and I heard the distant sounds of howling. The hunt was still going on, and I hoped Ethan would be able to get there in time to help them bring down a deer or two.

I tilted my head up toward the moon. It was so bright tonight, almost too bright to look at directly. "Thank you," I said softly to Selene.

For a moment, nothing happened, and I wondered if Selene had heard me. Then, like a cool hug, I felt her presence around me. It enfolded me completely and I closed my eyes and smiled. Somehow I knew that I'd done it. The spell was complete, and I would get to keep this body. Every wish of mine had come true. I had secured a place for my people to live, and I had found true love.

With that knowledge bolstering me, I lifted into the air and flew off to join Ethan and the Libra pack.

My pack.

EARTH BLESSED

MADISON & KILLIAN

CHAPTER ONE

AS A VIRGO, healing was more than just my pack's power, it was a calling. As the Virgo alpha, it was also my duty.

I stepped through the shimmering portal and out onto the grass in front of Eventide's lodge.

The lake was as smooth as a mirror without any wind to stir it, and the tall trees around it reflected perfectly in the still water. The little cabins nestled around it looked picture-perfect and idyllic. It was hard to imagine that just a short time ago vampires had attacked the people living here.

Four of my pack mates came through the portal behind me. I'd chosen them because they were not only strong healers, but strong of heart and mind too. They'd be able to handle whatever horrors we faced.

The problem with being a healer was that people only needed us when they were ill or injured. Seeing so much suffering and misery could be hard on an inexperienced healer, and it was one of the things the Virgo pack trained to overcome. But some were better than others at it.

Many people called me the best healer in the Virgo pack, but that wasn't true. I was simply the best at keeping a cool, practical head when shit went down. That was how I saved Wesley during the Cancer massacre when others in my pack fled in fear. It was also how I kept shifters alive during and after the Sun Witch battle when everything was chaos. Today I would use that same skill to take care of the people of Eventide.

Larkin was the last one through the portal and she closed it behind her. "Thanks again for coming on such short notice."

"It's no trouble at all," I said. "This is what we do."

"We've put the injured people in the gathering room in the Lodge for now." She gestured for us to follow her, and my healers fell into formation behind me.

I'd been to Eventide many times over the last two years, ever since Larkin founded it with the help of her mate, Ethan. I'd been instrumental in selecting the half-human shifters who now lived in the town, and I'd visited often to make sure they settled in and were doing well. The town had grown quickly, beyond all expectations, mostly thanks to Larkin and Ethan's hard work and strong vision. But today it was in lockdown, with few people on the roads except for the shifters and vampires who were patrolling and acting as security.

Larkin had converted what was once the resort lodge into the town hall, though they still called it the Lodge. She led us inside, past a small lobby with a cozy fireplace, into a spacious room where they held events and meetings. Emergency cots had been set up around the room, and the scent of blood and rubbing alcohol was strong. About twenty people were injured, some moaning softly, others completely passed out. A few Moon Witches in purple robes were walking down the aisles, doing what they could to help. They looked relieved when they saw me enter with my fellow Virgos.

I squared my shoulders and turned to my healers. "Start with the most badly wounded first. Don't forget to drink your water, eat the snacks we packed, and take breaks every hour. We can't help them if we're not at our best."

The four women nodded at me and split up, taking sections of the room. They each had a backpack packed with medical supplies, healthy snacks, and a refillable water bottle—part of my protocol for any healer out in the field.

"I'm so sorry this happened," I said, giving Larkin a hug. "But we'll take care of everyone."

"I know you will." She looked across the room with obvious concern in her eyes. "I need to go speak to some of the Moon Witches about the town wards. I'll be back later."

After she left, I turned my attention to the room and breathed in deeply. My healers had settled in already, but I smelled something I didn't like at the far end of the room. That was another thing we trained in, using our shifter senses to detect illness, disease, and infection. I made my way over there and my heart clenched as I recognized the girl in the corner. Sarah was only sixteen, a half-human shifter I'd helped move here a year ago, along with her fully human older brother, who'd gotten custody of her when their mom ran off. The awful smell came from a wound on her stomach, which had been hastily bandaged, but was bleeding through already.

I grabbed the nearest chair and dragged it over, then began removing the bandage to check how bad the damage was. Her eyes opened and she blinked blearily at me.

"Madison?"

"Hey, Sarah. I'm going to heal your wound, okay?" I gave her a warm smile, keeping my worry for her off my face. "Don't worry. You're going to be fine."

She gritted her teeth as I removed the bandage. Underneath were long, jagged scratches that I recognized as being from a vampire's long black nails. I'd seen plenty of similar wounds back when we were fighting the Sun Witches and their loyal vampires. These nails must have been coated in something vile because the wound was seeping black pus. For a full-blooded shifter, it probably wouldn't have been a problem, but half-humans didn't have the same healing capabilities.

"What happened?" I asked, as I held my hands over her stomach and concentrated on forcing the poison out.

"I was in the forest with some of my friends. We heard some crows making a huge fuss so we went to see what was going on." She shuddered a little, her voice going high-pitched. "The vampires came out of nowhere. We ran, but they were so fast. We tried to stop them from getting to the town but there were too many. We held them off as best we could until Sloane was able to ring the warning bell, but one of them got me."

"You did an amazing job," I told her as I wiped up the nasty black stuff with a cloth. Anger welled up in me at the thought of these vampires attacking some kids, but I pushed it aside. I couldn't heal with an angry mind. "Think how much worse it would have been if you hadn't been so brave and strong. Your actions saved many lives today."

"Are my friends okay?" she asked with tears in her eyes.

"Everyone is going to be fine," I said. Larkin had already told me there were no casualties, which I found surprising. "I brought four other healers with me from the Virgo pack and we won't leave until you're all in perfect condition again."

"Thank you." She gripped my hand and her eyes fluttered shut.

Her wounds were deep, and I worked on them for some time while she rested. She was so young, I wanted to make sure she didn't have any scars or long-term problems from this injury.

When I was done, she was completely healed, with no trace at all that she'd even been wounded except for a touch of redness in the area, which would fade within a few hours. She would need to rest for another day or so to regain her strength though.

I moved to the next cot, where a male Moon Witch I didn't know had some deep cuts on his arms and legs. He gave me a weak smile while I dragged over my chair and got to work.

While I was finishing up with this second patient, I noticed the other healers all staring at someone by the door. I turned around and then understood why. Killian, the mayor of Eventide, had just entered the room and was speaking to the patient on the first cot. I wasn't sure if they were staring at him because he was a vampire, or because he was so ridiculously handsome it was impossible not to look at him. He had wavy black hair and a face so beautiful I would have believed it was Photoshopped if I wasn't viewing it in person. Every movement he made seemed like the most graceful action ever taken, and when his gray eyes locked on mine, my heart did a wild somersault.

Something in my gut urged me toward him. My legs started to get up, but then I shook my head to fight it off. What was wrong with me? I'd met Killian before a few times but had never spent much time around him. We'd had a few interactions before, but I wouldn't call him a friend. More like an acquaintance, at best.

Even though I'd always found him handsome and charming, I'd avoided dealing with vampires ever since my aunt, the former Virgo alpha, was killed by the vampires working with the Sun Witches. I knew it was unfair to lump Killian in with those vampires since he'd always been allied with the Moon Witches, but I couldn't help my wariness.

I focused on the Moon Witch again, making sure he was completely healed and resting well. Only then did I get up and cross the room to speak to Killian.

"Madison," he said in his lilting voice, touched with a bit of a British accent. He bowed slightly and took my hand, pressing a kiss to my knuckles. "You and your Virgos have my deepest gratitude for everything you've done for my people."

I wasn't usually one for blushing, but the touch of his lips to my hand made me feel warm all over, even though his skin was icy cold. He was like something out of Bridgerton or one of the historical romances I sometimes read. He even wore a suit that looked straight out of another century, though his shirt was torn in one spot and had a touch of blood on the collar. A sword hung from his waist, which only made him even more dashing.

"We're happy to help," I said.

He lightly touched my elbow and guided me outside the room, giving us a little more privacy. "It means a lot that you came here personally."

"This town and its people are very important to me."

"Yes, of course. It's thanks to you that we have so many half-human shifters here." His brow pinched together. "I'm devastated that so many of them were injured during the attack."

I leaned against the wall, feeling the fatigue from healing two people settling in. "Injured, but not killed. Are you surprised by that?"

"Not at all. Bolstering the town's security and preparing for an attack was one of the first things I did as mayor. I've personally spent many hours over the last two years training our people to fight in preparation for something like this."

My eyebrows shot up. "Were you expecting an attack?"

"Yes and no. We didn't know of any immediate threat,

but we knew that a town like this came with many risks. When you take in outsiders and rejects, and mix together people who used to be enemies, there will always be someone who has a problem with that. Focusing on preventing an outside attack also brought our people together and prevented them from fighting amongst themselves."

I had to admit, I was impressed. Larkin had once told me he'd been mayor of the Moon Witch town in Lunatera, and I could see why she'd asked him to take the position here too. "It seems to have worked."

His eyes flashed with something deadly, reminding me that no matter how civilized he looked, he was a predator. "We will defend this peaceful community with everything we have."

"Why do you think the vampires attacked?"

He let out a long sigh. "There is a small faction of vampires who don't approve of our truce with the shifters. This town, with its mix of shifters, witches, vampires, and even a few humans, is downright offensive to them. They've been harassing us for some time now, sending threats, destroying some of our supplies, things like that. But they've never attacked us directly before."

"Some of the injured had some sort of black poison in their wounds. Do you have any idea what that is?"

"Black poison?" He crossed his arms as he considered. "Hmm. There is a poison some vampires once used. It slows down healing in both vampires and shifters. But I haven't heard of anyone using it in a very long time."

"That's concerning," I said. "Do you think they'll attack again?"

"I hope they've learned their lesson. If not, we will be ready."

I'd never spent so much time alone with Killian, and I was starting to wonder if it was a bad idea. Every second made me like him a little more. Staring into his gray eyes was hypnotic, and each time he spoke, it was like a soft caress against my skin. I had the strongest urge to kiss him too. This had to be some kind of vampire magic.

His eyes studied me intently, and then he pressed the back of his cold hand to my forehead. "Madison, darling, you're looking a bit pale. Perhaps you need to eat."

I jerked back from his touch. "Yes, probably."

"Can I get you something?"

"No, thank you, I have snacks in my bag." I gestured toward the room. "I should get back to work."

"I won't keep you from it." He placed a hand on my shoulder. "Thank you again for coming, and please let me know if you need anything."

I hurried into the room and pulled out my water and a granola bar. I'd ignored my own advice about taking breaks, and now I was a mess because of it. Yes, that was definitely the problem. It had nothing to do with this ridiculous desire to kiss a vampire. Nothing at all.

CHAPTER TWO

I SPENT SEVERAL HOURS HEALING, and by the end of it, I was wiped out. The other Virgos and I had managed to heal everyone who needed it, and most of the injured were able to return to their own homes to rest. Only a few, including Sarah, needed to be watched overnight. Two of the Moon Witches volunteered to stay with them while I rested, assuring me they would get me immediately if anything changed. The other Virgos were taken home by Larkin, who thanked them profusely for coming to the town's aid.

It was late by the time I left the Lodge, and the town was quiet. Larkin had offered me her cabin to stay in for the night—she'd planned to return to her home in Toronto—but I needed some time outside first to unwind after such a long, difficult day. I walked down to the lake and stood on the shore for a few minutes, looking up at the moon. The clouds were rolling in, covering most of the sky, and it seemed as though it might rain soon.

I quickly undressed, stashed my things in a small fishing hut nearby, and shifted. Once my wolf was free I shook out my gray fur and stretched my back, then inhaled the cool night air, breathing in its scents. I dug my claws into the earth beneath my paws, allowing it to ground me. Being a wolf made me feel closer to nature, which was exactly the kind of meditation I needed after a day of healing.

I turned away from the lake to head toward the forest that surrounded it but stopped in my tracks. Killian was walking up behind me, his movements so quiet I hadn't heard him approach, even with my enhanced senses. A shot of instinctual fear hit me, but then was replaced by the strongest urge to go to him. I couldn't resist it this time. My wolf had a mind of her own, and she wanted *him*.

He took a step toward me. "Madison—"

Whatever he was about to say was lost as our eyes met. Worlds collided, stars exploded, and I died and was reborn in an instant. The new me was irrevocably tied to Killian on some primal level that I could barely understand. All I knew was that he was *mine*.

My wolf lunged at him, knocking him down, and I licked his face. Instead of freaking out or fighting me, he wrapped his arms around me and stroked his hands down my fur.

"What is happening?" he asked.

His words brought a tiny bit of sense into me and I

pulled back. *Mine, mine, mine,* my wolf growled—and then I realized what was happening.

Killian was my mate.

No. That couldn't be possible. A mate bond with a vampire?

I couldn't believe it.

I shifted back quickly, needing to both get my wolf under control and speak to Killian about what was happening and whether he felt it too. But as soon as I was human again, a wave of lust washed over me. I drew in a sharp breath and Killian's eyes flashed with hunger. His arms were still wrapped around me, only now I was naked and on top of him, and I wanted him so badly I couldn't breathe.

My mouth was on his in an instant. His hands slid down to grasp my ass, positioning me right where I needed him, and I could feel how affected he was by this too. My hips rolled against the hard bulge in his pants like they were possessed, seeking the friction only he could give me, while our tongues danced together. He was wearing too many clothes. My claws would fix that.

The press of his fangs against my bottom lip jolted me out of the haze of lust.

What the fuck was I doing? He was a *vampire*!

I scrambled off him, breathing heavily, my pussy throbbing. He rose to his feet in one swift, graceful movement and stared at my naked body with unbridled lust, his mouth open a little and his fangs on display. Then he shook his head and blinked, regaining control of himself in an instant.

"My deepest apologies," he said, smoothing his shirt and looking at anything but me. "I don't know what came over me."

I crossed my arms over my breasts, trying to hide the fact that my nipples were so hard they could cut glass. "It's not your fault. It was the mate bond."

He paused and met my eyes again. "Pardon?"

"You're my mate." A nervous laugh escaped me. "I don't know how it's possible, but it's true."

His mouth opened and closed. He ran a hand through his perfect black hair. His eyes strayed to my body again and then looked away while he swallowed hard. "Perhaps you should put some clothes on so we can discuss this."

"Yes," I said quickly. "Good idea."

I bolted into the fishing hut and got dressed, then stood there for a moment, afraid to go back out. If I stayed in here long enough maybe this feeling would fade. There was no way this could actually be a real mate bond. There had to be some other explanation.

But the feeling didn't fade. If anything, it only grew stronger with each minute. I sensed Killian outside. His arousal, his confusion. His hunger.

I pulled myself together and stepped out. I was the Virgo alpha. I couldn't lose my head over a vampire.

The sight of him standing there with his hands in his pockets hit me like an avalanche, crushing me with feelings I couldn't stop. I closed my eyes, willing them to disappear, but it didn't work. The mate bond wouldn't be denied.

"I'm sorry," I said. "I don't know how this is happening."

He gave me a smile that only made it all worse. "There's no need to apologize." He offered me his arm. "Why don't we return to my cabin? We can talk there."

I ignored his arm, worried about what might happen if I touched him again. "Lead on."

His cabin overlooked the lake and it only took us a few short minutes to walk there. It was one of the smaller, original ones that had come with the land and had a quaint, cozy feel on the outside. His front door was unlocked and he led me into a small living room with a fireplace. The furniture looked antique and had lots of rich, dark colors.

"Would you like something to eat?" He asked as he closed the front door behind me. "You must be exhausted after healing so many people."

"Thanks, but I'm okay. Larkin brought us all some food earlier."

"How about some tea then?"

"That would be great."

He stepped into a kitchen that was surprisingly modern and turned on an electric kettle while I leaned on the counter and watched him. The mate bond silently thrummed between us, but I tried my best to ignore it. While we waited for the kettle to boil, he turned to me and crossed his arms. For some time, we simply stared at each other, gathering our thoughts while fighting the urge to rip each other's clothes off.

"I guess we'd better talk about it," I finally said.

He let out a low chuckle. "I suppose so." The kettle boiled at that moment and he took it off and began preparing a pot of tea. "I didn't know it was possible for vampires to experience a mate bond."

"I didn't either," I said. "Honestly, I wasn't sure if it would ever happen for me at all."

Killian cocked his head. "Why not?"

"I'm half human, so I wasn't sure if I would get a mate. I thought it would have happened by now. I've been to a lot of Convergence mating rituals at this point." I hesitated but figured it would be best to get everything out in the open from the start. "I also can't have children. I thought that might be a factor too."

"I'm sorry to hear that."

I shrugged and tried to ignore the lump in my throat that came whenever I talked about this. "I had ovarian cancer when I was younger, and it affected my reproductive system."

"Was your pack not able to heal you?"

"Even the best healing can sometimes leave you scarred for the rest of your life."

He inclined his head in response. "If it makes you feel better, I can't have kids either."

Relief washed through me. I'd always worried that if I did find my mate, they would be upset that we couldn't have kids together.

Killian gestured for me to sit in his living room and then handed me a mug that said, "I vant to drink your coffee" with a bat on it. I held it up and raised my eyebrows at him.

"I know," he said with an overly dramatic sigh. "I don't even like coffee, but my friends seem to find great humor in buying me the most ridiculous mugs." He showed me his mug, which had a grumpy-looking Dracula cartoon on it with the words, "Mornings suck."

I laughed a little and then took a sip of my tea. "What would your friends think of you being with a shifter?"

"People in Eventide would have no problem with it. We have all sorts of relationships here and no one minds. I'm more worried about how your kind will react to the Virgo alpha being mated to a vampire."

I leaned back in the antique chair, which was more comfortable than I expected. "I'm worried about that too. Even though the shifters and vampires are allies now, there's still a lot of tension between us."

"Indeed. This attack only proves that many of my kind don't want vampires and shifters to mix."

"It's not just vampires. Many of the shifters are still wary of vampires." I wrapped my hands around my mug, soaking in the warmth. "I have to admit that I was one of them."

"Why is that?" Killian asked, and I was relieved that he didn't sound offended or upset.

"The vampires that were working with the Sun Witches killed my aunt, the former Virgo alpha." I closed my eyes briefly, willing the memories away. "I was the one who found her. I tried to heal her, but it was too late."

"I'm sorry you went through that. I heard about those attacks, but I assure you that I was not affiliated with that group of vampires."

I opened my eyes and gave him a weak smile. "I know. I

don't blame you for it. But I haven't rushed to make any vampire friends either."

"I understand that," he said. "If there is anything I can do to make you feel more comfortable, I will try."

"Thank you for offering, but it's just something I have to work through myself." Especially now that I was mated to a vampire.

"I understand needing time to work through your grief and trauma." He stared into his mug with a mournful expression. "I had a wife once, long ago. Amelia was a Moon Witch and I loved her dearly, but the Sun Witches took her from me."

The pain in his voice made my heart ache for him. "I'm so sorry."

"I spent years hiding in Lunatera, as if I could escape what happened, but the grief never left me. Time there stays frozen, and so did my pain. It was only when I returned to Earth that I was finally able to begin to move on. But even so, I never thought I would find love again." His gaze met mine. "I certainly never expected a mate bond with a shifter."

The mate bond pulled between us, stronger this time, and we both sipped our tea, looking away quickly. I wondered if he was picturing me naked, or if I was the only one having those thoughts.

"Can this even work between us?" I asked. "Even if we ignore the shifter-vampire issues, I'm the alpha of the Virgo pack, and you're the mayor of Eventide. I'm not sure I can do a long-distance relationship."

"Actually, I was planning to step down from mayor next month anyway."

"Really?" I asked, surprised.

"It was always meant to be a temporary thing," Killian said. "I was more than happy to help Larkin out with getting Eventide on its feet, but I only agreed to be mayor for a year. Somehow that's turned into two, but now the town is up and running and it doesn't need me anymore. It's time they have an election to find someone new."

"But becoming my mate would mean moving to the Virgo pack and becoming my alpha male. You would give up everything here to live with a bunch of shifters, many of whom might hate your guts."

"I've faced many challenges in my long life. I'm ready for the next one." Killian reached a hand out to me, palm up. "If you're willing to have me, I would like to at least give this thing between us a chance."

I started to reach for his hand but then paused. "Are you sure? If not, you could reject me, and this could end now. We don't have to go through with this."

"I'm sure. Maybe this will be what we both need."

I let out a breath and took his hand. I'd tried to keep myself from feeling any hope from the moment the mate bond activated down by the lake. I'd wanted a mate for so long, and even though Killian was as unconventional as you could get, I couldn't help but feel excited that he was mine.

Killian rose to his feet and cupped my chin in his hand. He stroked his thumb across my cheek, and I shivered. It had been so long since anyone had touched me like this. I'd had fun a few times at the Convergences I'd gone to, but there had always been something missing. *A mate bond.* It flared between us, stronger than ever.

I leaned into his touch and his thumb ran across my lips, while his gaze searched mine. He must have liked what he saw there because he slowly and deliberately wrapped one arm around my waist, tilted my head up, and claimed my mouth with his own.

Kissing Killian was a full-body experience. His skin was cool, a nice contrast to my shifter heat, yet somehow I still felt hot all over. I slid my hands around his neck, teasing the back of his silky hair. His fangs tugged at my lower lip, but this time it didn't shock me. I ran my tongue over their sharp points, wondering how it would feel to have them biting me.

He tilted my head to the side, kissing down my neck. His fangs brushed against my skin and I held my breath, trembling a little in anticipation. But then he groaned low in his throat and pulled away from me.

"Why did you stop?" I asked, trying not to feel rejected.

"Madison, you are more lovely than words can describe, and your blood... It sings to me. I desperately want to sink my fangs into you and taste how sweet you are. I want to do so much more with you too. But I think we should stop for tonight."

"Why?" I asked, reaching for him again. "The mate bond... It won't be complete until we make love."

"I know. That's why I want to wait." He pressed another kiss to my lips, which did nothing to quell my desire. "You must be sure this is what you want—a life with a vampire by your side." His gaze dropped to my neck. "One who won't be able to resist the taste of you."

I trembled a little at the thought, but it was from desire and not fear. "You're probably right. We should try to get to know each other first before we rush into anything."

"Exactly." He stepped back and shoved his hands in his pockets like it was the only way he could stop himself from touching me. "Do you want to stay here tonight?"

I was having my own trouble not reaching for him again. "If I stay, I don't think we'll be able to keep our hands off each other. I'll stay at Larkin's place."

He nodded and escorted me to the door. "I'll let you go then, but have no doubt that I will be thinking of you all night long. And tomorrow, we will meet again."

I started to lean forward to kiss him goodnight but then stopped myself. If I kissed him again, I wouldn't be able to leave. "Goodnight."

I stepped outside, even though my heart was begging me to turn around and go back in. Killian was right though. This had all happened too fast and was so unexpected. We both needed some time to get over the shock of it and figure out what we truly wanted. Though I had a feeling my decision wouldn't change by the morning.

CHAPTER THREE

IN THE MORNING, I went to the Lodge to check on the four remaining patients. All of them had recovered nicely and had no further issues to report. I did a small amount of final healing on each of them and then sent them on their way. Sarah gave me a big hug and I promised to visit her and her brother again soon.

Killian found me while I was packing up my supplies. My breath caught at the sight of him standing in the door-way, wearing dark gray trousers and a light blue button-up shirt.

"Care to join me for lunch?" he asked, before kissing my cheek.

How could I say no?

"What did you do this morning?" I asked as we stepped out of the Lodge and headed for the main part of town.

"I worked with some of our security team to strengthen the town's defenses in case the hostile vampires returned."

He offered me his hand. "And I thought about you quite a bit."

I hesitated for a second before taking his cool hand. "I thought about you too."

"Do you still want to do this?"

I'd barely gotten any sleep last night. My brain had been too loud, thinking about all the reasons why being mated to Killian was a terrible idea. But in the morning, I decided I didn't care. I wanted him anyway. "Yes, as long as you do."

He squeezed my hand. "I do."

We strolled together down the main road and I admired all the new stores and restaurants that had popped up. Eventide was about two years old at this point, growing faster than anyone had expected. It turned out there was a huge need for a town where all supernaturals could live freely. A few more people were out walking around today compared to yesterday, doing their grocery shopping or getting a bite to eat.

I looked down at our joined hands, wondering what people would think. But everyone we passed greeted us warmly, some stopping to ask Killian questions about the attack, and a few thanking me for healing their family members. No one seemed to care that we were together.

Killian led me inside a cute little cafe with his hand pressed to my lower back in a way that sent a trickle of lust down my spine. "This place is owned by a Moon Witch couple named Erik and Patricia. They're good friends of mine."

"Erik?" I tilted my head. "I think I healed him yesterday."

"You did," said a female Moon Witch with light blond hair who wore a long, flowing dress that showed off her baby bump. She gave us a friendly smile and handed us two menus. "Please sit wherever you would like. Lunch is on me today."

"You are too kind," Killian said as he led us to a table by the window.

"How is Erik doing?" I asked.

"He's fine, but I made him stay home today to rest, just to be safe." Patricia touched my arm lightly. "Thank you again for healing him."

She took our drink orders and then went behind the counter. Killian reached for my hand across the table and ran his thumb over my knuckles.

"Patricia and Erik were uncertain about coming to Earth, but they wanted to have a family, which was impossible in Lunatera. Like me, they had a hard time adjusting here at first, but now they are thriving."

He sounded so pleased by this that I couldn't help but smile. "The entire town seems to be thriving. Every time I come here, it seems like another store has opened and five new houses have been built."

He chuckled. "The town has been growing rapidly, it's true. I believe we're almost to two hundred people now."

"Wow. I had no idea."

"We started out with mostly Moon Witches—about twenty of them at first. Larkin and our committee then invited a few shifters, half-humans, and vampires to join them. But once the town was truly established and word got out, more

Moon Witches were excited to join our community, along with everyone else. I'd say we're about one-third Moon Witch, one-third shifter, and then the last third is a mix of vampires and half-humans. We even have three humans living here."

"The fact that you've been able to keep the town peaceful with such a wide variety of supernaturals is a true testament to your skill as mayor."

"I wish I could take all the credit, but I've had a lot of help. It also helps that the people here really want this experiment to work." He looked down at our joined hands with a smile. "It benefits all of us to not be divided anymore."

We chatted a bit more about the town before our food arrived. Killian had ordered a chicken dish, and I paused as I watched him take a bite.

"What is it?" he asked.

"I guess I never realized that vampires ate food before."

He laughed. "Of course we do. How could a body subsist on blood alone?"

I ducked my head, feeling embarrassed. "I suppose most of what I know about your kind is from superstitions and myths."

He grinned. "Most of the beliefs about vampires are wrong, just like the ones about werewolves."

"But you do need blood, don't you?"

"Yes, that part is true, though not as much as you might expect."

"How often do you need it?" I paused. "Sorry, is that too personal a question"

"Darling, you're my mate. Nothing is too personal between us." He leaned forward and lowered his voice. "If I drink only from animals, I need blood every two or three days. Human blood is stronger—I can go a week or so then. And shifter blood is the most potent of all, or so I've heard. I've never had a chance to taste it...yet."

The hunger in his eyes awakened the lust in me, which was always there ever since the mate bond had activated. I found myself crossing my legs, suddenly all too aware of how much I wanted him to bite me. I'd never felt this way before. I blamed the mate bond.

"Would you be able to survive with only one person's blood?" I asked, my voice coming out huskier than I intended. The thought of him drinking from anyone else sent a wave of possessiveness through me.

"If they were strong enough, yes." He gave me a wicked grin that showed the tips of his fangs. "I have no doubt an alpha like yourself could handle it."

I wasn't so sure. I was still half human, after all.

I spent the rest of the day with Killian, getting to know him while we explored Eventide some more and checked in on the residents there. I could tell how much they loved and respected him, and I felt guilty for taking him away soon. At the same time, I knew he would be an excellent partner for an alpha like myself.

We found ourselves back at his cabin just as the sun went down. Killian turned toward the sight of it dipping below the horizon with awe in his eyes.

"For centuries I was unable to walk in the sun," he explained. "I try not to ever take it for granted now."

"Your life has been so very different from mine. I want to know everything about you."

"You will, darling." He wrapped his arms around me and kissed me under the faint glow of the sunset. "But I've lived a very long life. It will take some time to get to it all."

I dragged his mouth to mine again, wanting more of him. His delicious scent filled my nose as I melted into his arms. The mate bond hummed its approval, and the need inside of me grew. Our kiss turned filthy, our hands roaming each other's bodies, and I wondered how I would ever get enough of him.

When his mouth moved to my neck, I moaned. He kissed and sucked there, his tongue trailing across my skin, his fangs grazing me lightly. He shuddered a little, then started to pull away.

"Don't stop," I said, clasping my hand to the back of his head.

He pressed his nose to my neck, breathing me in. "Your blood calls to me. The temptation to bite you is hard to resist."

I tangled my fingers in his hair. "Then stop resisting."

His hands tightened around my waist and then his fangs sank into my skin. I moaned at the mix of pleasure and pain and clung to him, my knees going weak.

"Killian," I breathed and closed my eyes. My body lit up with desire, and pleasure like I'd never experienced coursed through me. As he sucked on my neck, my pulse began beating out of control, my clit throbbing. I rubbed my hips against him, needing relief, needing *more.*

His arms wrapped around me tighter while his mouth kept doing wicked things to me. I pressed him harder against my neck while draping one leg around him, rubbing my needy pussy against the bulge in his pants. He groaned and thrust back at me.

The sensation was too much. I let out a wild cry as an orgasm rocked through me, so fast it took me by surprise. My knees gave out, but he caught me and pulled me against his chest. A moment later, he broke free of my neck, looking dazed and slightly shocked.

"I've never experienced anything like that before," he murmured.

"Me neither." I touched my neck. I felt two tiny bite marks there, already healing. "Does it always make people feel that way?"

"If we want it to be pleasurable, yes, though it's never been so intense for me before. We can also make it extremely painful, to the point of making the person pass out, but I haven't done that in a very long time."

I rubbed myself against him again, feeling the aftershocks of pleasure coursing through me. "I don't want you drinking from anyone but me."

"That won't be a problem. Your blood is..." He shuddered a little as he licked his lips. "Exquisite. Delicious. And so very powerful."

I nuzzled his neck. "I want to bite you too. To mark you as my mate."

"You will, my darling." He pressed a kiss to the spot on my neck where he'd bitten me and then pulled away. "But I think that was enough for one night. Anything more might kill us both."

Why did he have to be so damn sensible? I forced myself to take a step back from him. As much as I wanted to seal the mate bond, I understood his desire to wait too. "I have to go back to the Virgo pack lands tonight, but I want to see you again soon."

He nodded. "I need time to get my affairs here together before I can move there. But I would love for us to visit each other until that time."

"I'd like that too." I grinned. "I'll make a schedule."

"That's very organized of you."

"Welcome to life with a Virgo."

A MOON WITCH named Selin took me back to Haven, the Virgo village. The first thing I did upon returning home was send a text to the group chat with all my best friends— Ayla, Mira, Larkin, Stella, and Harper—asking if they could get on a video call with me ASAP. I knew they were all busy with their mates and kids, but I really needed to talk to them about this situation.

My friends came through for me though, and an hour later we were all in a Zoom call.

"What's going on?" Ayla asked. Her second baby, Maia, was asleep in her arms. "Is everything okay?"

"I'm guessing we're not here to talk about book club," Stella asked.

"I hope not." Harper pulled a face. "The book this month was boring."

Mira made an affronted noise. "I thought it was romantic."

"You just like a slow burn," Larkin said. "But seriously, are you all right Madison?"

As I looked at their faces, I felt nervous all of a sudden. Earlier it had seemed easier, but the prospect of telling all of them that my mate was a vampire was suddenly daunting. I tucked my hair behind my ear. "Um. I have some big news to tell you."

"What is it?" Larkin asked.

I drew in a long breath. "I finally found my mate yesterday."

"Congratulations!" Ayla said while the others cheered.

"I knew you'd find your mate eventually," Mira said, smiling at me. "It was just a matter of time."

Larkin held up a hand. "Wait. You were healing in Eventide yesterday."

"That's right," I said.

"So who is it?" Stella asked.

"Um..." I glanced nervously around, which was ridiculous since I was in my kitchen alone. But I couldn't even say it out loud.

"Don't keep us in suspense any longer!" Harper said.

"It's Killian," I finally said.

Every single one of them looked at me with an expression of complete shock.

"That's..." Ayla couldn't seem to find a good word. "Not what I expected."

"Wow," Larkin said. "Just... Wow."

They all started talking at once, almost yelling to be heard over one another. None of them looked upset, just stunned and excited, and I relaxed a bit.

"I can't believe it!" Stella was saying, over and over again.

"A shifter and a vampire, this has to be the first time!" Mira added.

"What was it like?" Harper asked. "Did he use his fangs?"

"We haven't sealed the mate bond yet."

"Why not?" Stella asked.

"It's all so new and unexpected. We want to get to know each other a little first. Honestly, I'm worried about how we're going to fit into each other's lives, or how my pack will react once I tell them. Or the other alphas, for that matter."

"Don't worry about what anyone else thinks," Ayla said. "If you and Killian are happy together, that's all that matters."

Mira nodded. "Everyone knows that all sorts of new and different things are happening now that the forced mate bonds have been lifted. You might be the first to mate with a vampire, but I doubt you'll be the last."

"Be brave," Stella said. "You might get some people who aren't happy with it at first, but they'll just have to get over it."

"Yeah, and if not, we'll *make* them get over it," Harper said.

I rolled my eyes at her.

Larkin put her hand to her chest. "How romantic. I'm so happy for you, and for Killian too. I couldn't think of a better match for both of you."

"You know our mate bonds have never led us astray." Ayla gave me an encouraging smile. "Remember how shocked we were to find out that Stella and Jordan were mates?"

"Or Larkin and Ethan," Stella said. "They had the first known mate bond between a Moon Witch and a shifter. People were shocked at first, but they soon accepted it."

"We'll always be by your side, and we'll support you no matter what," Larkin said.

I blinked back tears. "Thank you, everyone."

"So he really hasn't used those fangs on you yet?" Harper asked.

I let a slow smile spread across his face and the girls hooted and hollered. "He did bite me earlier tonight."

"And?" Harper asked, leaning forward.

"It was good," I said. "And that's all you're getting."

"Oh, come on!" Larkin said. "I need new material for my next book."

Everyone laughed and the tightness in my chest relaxed. Just knowing that I had my friends on my side made me feel so much better. After talking with them, I knew that I'd be able to find a way to make this work. For my mate, it would be worth it.

CHAPTER FOUR

THE NEXT FEW weeks passed in an absolute whirlwind. I traveled so much between Eventide and Haven that I felt like I was never in one place for very long. Killian and I spent as much time together as we could, going on dates, getting to know each other, and slowly introducing everyone to the idea of a shifter being mated to a vampire.

As I'd expected, not everyone had been open to hearing that my mate was a vampire. The Virgo pack was confused and skeptical, some even getting visibly angry when I'd broken the news. One woman had shouted that I shouldn't be so quick to forget that the last Virgo alpha had been killed by a vampire. I'd managed to keep my cool and had calmly pointed out that I could never forget that, since I'd been the one to find her dead. I reminded them that Killian wasn't the one who had murdered her, and we couldn't judge one person based on the actions of others. No one else said anything after that, but I could tell that many were still very skeptical and uneasy. I worried someone might challenge me as alpha, but things changed once Killian started coming to visit the village. As expected, he charmed everyone he met, even some of the grumpiest old biddies in our pack, and soon no one questioned our mate bond in my pack.

I wished the other alphas were so easy to convince. A few of them were openly accepting of our mating, like Ethan and Kaden, but some of them were wary of Killian even though he had a good reputation among the shifters. Many of the other alphas had lost family members to the vampires too. It also raised the question of what this meant for the shifters going forward. First Ethan had been mated to a Moon Witch, and now this. Would more shifters start having human or vampire mates?

In the end, there was one thing that everyone could agree on—mate bonds could not be denied, even when they couldn't be understood.

Killian spent much of his time packing his things and preparing the town to elect a new mayor. There were no more vampire attacks or sightings, and things calmed down enough that he felt safe leaving the town. After a month, Killian officially stepped down as mayor of Eventide and put someone in charge temporarily until the town could vote in a replacement. The people of Eventide threw a big party for him on his final night, and we danced together under the stars and drank too much wine. The next morning, he moved into my house. I tried not to feel overwhelmed as I watched him move all of his stuff in. It was all happening so fast and was such a huge change, but I wasn't as nervous as I thought I would be either. I'd waited so long for my mate, and being around Killian just felt right somehow. I suppose it was no different than if I'd met my mate at the Convergence anyway. Shifters were used to things moving quickly when mating bonds were involved. If it hadn't been for the vampire issue, we would have been fully mated already.

And tonight we finally would be.

I met Killian at the heart of the village, in the grand central square under a towering, ancient oak tree that served as a sacred gathering place for the Virgo shifters. Under its branches, the pack elders often convened to discuss matters of importance, guided by the wisdom of generations past. Tonight all the pack was gathered around to watch the two of us pledge ourselves to each other, even if some of them were unsure of our mating.

I wore a long green dress that hugged my curves and matched the color of my eyes, along with a flower crown on top of my head. The pack parted around me as I walked, bowing their heads to show their respect, as I took my place under the huge oak tree and waited for Killian to join me.

A whisper went through the assembled shifters and they stepped aside to let Killian through. He wore a black Regency-era suit with a white shirt and a moss green cravat that matched my dress. He was so beautiful that I temporarily forgot my name, let alone what I was supposed to say to my pack. How could he be my mate?

He flashed me one of his charming smiles and pressed a kiss to my hand. "You are exquisite."

"So are you," I whispered, before raising my voice so

everyone could hear. "Killian O'Malley, do you accept the mating bond between us, which would make you not only a member of the Virgo pack but my alpha male?"

"I do," he said without any trace of doubt or hesitation.

A murmur went through the Virgos, and they all shifted a little closer, trying to get a better look at him.

I opened my hand and offered Killian the ring inside, a simple silver band with the Virgo symbol on it. Larkin had given me the idea after showing me the Libra necklace Ethan had made for her. "This ring is a symbol of your place in our pack, as my mate and my partner."

Killian took it and slid it on his finger. Then he reached into his pocket and pulled out a silver signet ring that looked very old. It was engraved with a raven and studded with tiny diamonds.

"This is the crest of my vampire house, House Corvus. I would be honored if you would wear it."

My eyebrows shot up. I'd never heard him mention vampire houses before. Even though we'd spent lots of time together over the past month, he'd remained vague on a lot of details about his past. I'd have to ask him about it later.

I slid the ring onto my finger and held it up to let it sparkle in the moonlight. "I love it. Thank you."

We moved together and kissed in front of everyone. Heat rose in me like it did every time we touched. I'd gotten very good at ignoring the tug of the mate bond, but I was ready to give in to its pull finally.

All around us, the Virgo pack cheered or politely clapped. After we broke away, the party began in earnest.

Food and drinks were passed around, and Killian stayed close to my side, his hand on my lower back. Everyone, it seemed, wanted to speak to him. Some were excited, and some wanted to get a better feel for him, I could tell. Killian accepted all the interest courteously and smiled as he shook hands and answered questions.

Eventually, the party died down, and I took Killian's hand and led him away from the crowd. "Walk with me."

"I'll follow wherever you lead, darling."

We left the central square, passing the little shops and cafes that surrounded it. Haven was in Quebec, and much of our architecture had a French feel to it, while also being built in ways that blended seamlessly with the natural landscape.

"I do love this village," Killian said. "It reminds me of a charming little town I visited in southern France."

"When was that?" I asked.

"Sometime in the early eighteen hundreds. I can't remember the exact year."

I nodded and was reminded again of the huge age gap between us. Killian had told me once that he was three hundred years old. Meanwhile, I was turning thirty this year. I wanted to know so much about his life, but he seemed pained whenever he talked about it. I suspected it was because many of the memories reminded him of his wife.

We walked past the large herb garden where we grew aromatic plants known for their healing properties, and then I led Killian away from the square, past the houses with moss-covered roofs and wooden doors carved with celestial motifs and the Virgo symbol. Our houses blended in perfectly with the forest around them and were built in harmony with the earth.

As we moved further into the forest, the houses became further and further apart, and I led Killian down one of the many wandering trails that meandered through the woods.

"It's beautiful here," Killian said. "I hope your pack will come to accept me."

"They will. The Virgo pack is known for its hospitality and sense of community. We're the only pack ruled by a female alpha, and we do not have any warriors. We never choose sides in any pack war, and we will always heal anyone who needs it. Haven is a safe, peaceful village where everyone is welcome and accepted." I gave him a wry smile. "Though that doesn't mean we're weak or that we don't gossip."

"I believe it," he said with a laugh. "I've already met some very spirited ladies in your pack."

We continued on until I brought us to a small clearing with soft grass and pale pink wildflowers, where the canopy opened up to reveal the moon and stars overhead. I did a little twirl in the middle of the clearing, holding Killian's hand, and then he pulled me against his chest.

"I'm ready," I said, as I reached up to undo his cravat.

He touched my cheek, staring into my eyes. "Once we do this, there is no turning back. You'll be mated to a vampire for the rest of your life."

"I know. I want that. I want *you*." I kissed him, running

my tongue over his fangs, and his fingers tightened around my waist in response. "Not only because you're my mate, but because you're Killian. The man I've grown to love."

"I love you too." He nipped at my lower lip. "And I want you. More than I've wanted anyone before."

He slowly slid my dress off, pressing a kiss to every spot of skin he uncovered, until it pooled at my feet on the ground. I stepped out of it and began undressing him next, removing each piece of clothing and then running my hands along his pale, cool skin. His body was like a Greek sculpture, with smooth muscles that looked like they'd been carved from marble. As he stood before me, completely naked, I took a step back to stare at him, my mouth watering at the sight of his large cock straining toward me.

Killian let out a breath. "It's been so long since someone has looked at me like that. Especially someone as lovely as you."

I draped my arms around him. "Don't tell me that ladies haven't been throwing themselves at you for years."

"Oh, they have," he said with a wicked grin. "But I never got this far with any of them. It's been a very long time since I've done this."

He lowered us down to the grass and our bodies tangled together as we kissed and touched.

I could feel the heat burning between my thighs, and when Killian ran a hand over my nipple and then down to stroke between my legs, it was like he was lighting a fuse that had been waiting for him.

I gasped, my back arching. "I don't think I can wait anymore."

Killian rolled onto his back, pulling me on top of him so I was straddling his hips. "Then claim me as your mate, my alpha queen."

His hands grasped my thighs as I sank down onto his cock, gasping as it stretched me. I ground against him, reveling in the feel of having him inside of me, so deep that it felt like he was hitting places no one else had.

My fingers dug into his chest, and when I began to ride him, he looked at me like he wanted to devour me whole. Pleasure ran through me as he started thrusting up into me, meeting me stroke for stroke. We fell into a perfect rhythm together, his cock hitting me in all the right spots, and I threw my head back, moaning as I rode him harder and faster.

As he continued to thrust into me, the moon and stars overhead were growing brighter, like they were shining just for us. Killian's gaze met mine, his eyes glowing silver under the moonlight, and I could feel the bond between us pulsing. It hummed a tune that sounded like, *mine, mine, mine.*

"Come here." He pulled me down toward his mouth and I moaned as he started kissing me. His lips moved to my neck, the scrape of his fangs against my skin driving me wild.

I wrapped my hand around his throat. "I'm going to mark you as my mate tonight."

He gave me a sinful grin, showing his fangs. "Only if I get to bite you in return."

"I wouldn't have it any other way."

We rocked together, kissing and touching, and I felt the bond between us tighten, a glowing string tying us together. Pleasure began to build within me, my breaths quickening, and I brushed my lips against the smooth skin of his neck. I inhaled sharply, breathing in his amazing scent, and then felt my canines grow. He groaned as they nipped at him and I could tell that he was close too.

I pressed my hands to the ground on either side of his head as I sank my teeth into his neck. The taste of him exploded on my tongue, and as it rushed through me, the bond between us came to life. I could feel his emotions and sensations—all the love, desire, and pleasure coursing through him like we were sharing a body.

My claws came out, digging into the earth as pleasure rocked through me. I tilted my head back and cried out as the orgasm shook me to my core.

I was still gasping, riding the wave of pleasure, when Killian turned us over, flipped me onto my back, and sunk his fangs into my neck. The rush of ecstasy that followed was enough to send me spiraling once again. We were both coming at the same time, our bodies and minds linked as he drank my blood. My claws raked across his back and he groaned, his cock pulsing inside of me.

When the euphoria began to fade, Killian's fangs retracted from my neck, and he licked the blood from the wounds he'd made, his tongue gliding across my skin. He kissed his way up to my mouth, his tongue tangling with mine.

"You taste so good." He pulled me close and we settled down in the grass together. "Better than anyone else I've drank from before."

"I never knew it could be like that." I touched the bite on his neck and the claw marks on his back. *Mine*, my wolf growled. "Did I hurt you?"

"I'm a vampire, love. I can take it." He played with my hair. "Besides, I know a really good healer."

I laughed and kissed him again, while he held me tight. We stayed there, suspended in time in that little grove on the outskirts of Haven, with the stars spinning above us.

There was no turning back now. I was mated to a vampire.

CHAPTER FIVE

I WOKE UP SLOWLY, with Killian's arms wrapped around me. I smiled even before I opened my eyes. We'd woken up like this every morning for the last week, ever since we'd made it official.

The days had passed quickly, but we were settling into mated life together. Every morning we had breakfast together and then went for a walk, checking in on the other residents of Haven. Most of my pack had accepted him completely, and he was inundated with requests for him to join various committees or clubs. He promised he would consider all of them, and though he seemed content with getting to know the pack and spending time with me, I sensed he felt a bit aimless. He'd had such an important role in both Eventide and Lunatera, and I worried he wasn't sure what to do with himself in Haven.

"Good morning," I said, and Killian hummed in response. The sun streamed in through the curtains in my bedroom, and Killian looked ethereal in the early morning light. I didn't think I'd ever get used to how handsome he was.

"Good morning," Killian responded and brushed hair away from my eyes.

I sat up slowly and stretched. "I'll go make breakfast."

Killian stretched slowly, like a cat enjoying the sunshine. "I'll be down soon."

I headed to the kitchen and made myself coffee, while also setting the kettle on for Killian's tea. Once that was going, I went about making breakfast. I loved cooking and I was glad I'd been wrong about vampires not eating.

Killian came down a few minutes later, wearing only a pair of black pajama pants. He pressed a kiss to the side of my neck and poured himself some tea.

"Who taught you how to cook?" he asked.

"My aunt," I said.

"Not your parents?"

I shook my head. "I was mostly raised by my aunt, the former Virgo alpha. She didn't have a mate or any kids of her own. My mom was her sister, but she left the pack for a while to train in the US as a nurse."

"And your father?" Killian asked.

"He's a human doctor. She met him in Texas, where he still lives with his wife and my half-brothers. You've been to his land actually—it's where we fought the Sun Witches for the last time."

"Ah, yes, I remember." He leaned against the counter

while I whisked some eggs in the skillet. "Your parents aren't together?"

"No, they split up not long after I was born. My mom wanted to raise me in the Virgo pack and he wanted to stay in Texas. I got the sense it was never very serious between them. I'm still friendly with my dad though and we visit each other when we can."

"And your mom?" he asked softly.

I stirred the eggs for a few heartbeats before I answered. "A few years after my mom took me back to the Virgo pack, she was healing a human in a nearby town who was sick. It went badly, and she lost the human. I guess the humans blamed her for not being able to heal their family member, so they hunted her down and killed her."

"I'm sorry." Killian put a hand on my shoulder and squeezed.

I leaned into his touch and closed my eyes for a moment, missing both my mom and my aunt so much that it made my heart ache. Then I let out a breath and went back to cooking.

"After that attack, the Virgos withdrew from healing humans," I said. "But I want to change that. Shifters can heal most injuries on their own, and we're not at war anymore, but humans are always getting injured or sick. What is the point in having the power to heal if we don't use it on those who need it the most?"

"How does the rest of the pack feel about that?" he asked, sipping his tea from his "Mornings suck" mug.

"They're scared, which I understand. We would have to

be careful how we go about it to not expose what we are to humans. But I think if we could do it, we could help a lot of people."

"It's a worthy goal," he said, but he was frowning.

"What is it?" I asked.

"Do you have a plan in place to keep your pack safe from possible attacks?"

"No shifters would ever attack us because they want access to our healing and know that we always remain neutral in any conflict. As for humans, our village is hard to find, which has kept us hidden from them over the years. The only time we've been attacked in the last few years was when the vampires killed my aunt."

"I know the Virgo shifters don't fight or cause harm to others. It's one of your main beliefs and I respect that, but I'm worried about what might happen once you venture back out into the world again, completely unprotected."

"Maybe you can help me brainstorm ideas for that," I said. "You did such a good job with Eventide."

"I would be happy to help."

We sat down to eat together, and I found myself wondering about Killian's past once more. "Tell me about your family. Your childhood. Everything."

"There's not much to tell. I grew up on a sheep farm in Ireland, but it was so long ago I barely remember those days, or even my parents for that matter. I moved to London in my early twenties and became a vampire when I was twenty-nine." He paused and stared down at his omelet, and I sensed he wanted to say more, but then he shook his head.

"My mortal life is a blur, just a blink of an eye in the long centuries that followed."

"How did you become a vampire?" I asked.

"I met a woman in London who took a fancy to me. She turned me, and then when she got bored of me, she left and found another. Vampires are not like shifters—we are often solitary creatures who spend our lives in the shadows. Eventually, she was killed in France by an angry mob who found out what she was. They dragged her out into the sunshine." He said the words calmly as if her death hadn't bothered him much.

I played with the signet ring on my finger. "Did she give you this?"

"No, I had that made just for you." He closed his hands over mine. "All vampires belong to the house of the vampire who created us. By wearing that, it shows that you belong to me."

I had about a dozen more questions, but he rose to his feet and began to put away his empty plate. "I forgot to mention it yesterday, but the people of Eventide have asked me to come back today to help with the mayoral election. Is it all right if I go?"

"Of course," I said, as I began to help clean up. "You don't need to ask my permission."

"You are my alpha," he said, kissing my cheek. "But also my partner. I would turn them down if you needed me here."

"No, I'm actually busy today also." I perked up thinking about my plans. "I'm visiting a nearby town where I'm going to look at a potential property we could use as a healing center."

He paused. "Do you want me to come with you? I'll tell them I can't make it."

I shook my head. "No, don't do that. I'm just meeting with a realtor. It should be perfectly safe."

"Very well." He pulled me in for a kiss. "But I'm going to miss you."

"I'll miss you too, but I'll see you tonight." I still couldn't get enough of him. I'd heard that new mating bonds were like this, especially with alphas, but I wasn't sure if that would be true for us. We were unconventional in every way, but even so, I could hardly keep my hands to myself when we were in the same room. And if another shifter tried to touch him? I found myself growling and becoming possessive in a way I'd never felt before.

Mated life was weird...but wonderful too.

THE RAIN POURED DOWN SO thick that I could hardly see past the dim glow of my headlights. I squinted and turned my wipers on higher, but it didn't seem to matter. There was too much rain, and I was driving well under the speed limit to account for that.

I'd left a while back, after seeing Killian off to Eventide, when the rain had just been a slight sprinkle. I was shocked by how quickly it had turned into this downpour. The fog was getting worse too. I slowed down even more as I neared the next turn, and turned my blinker on even though there was no one else out on the road. I was lucky I'd been to this town several times before or I might have missed the turn and gotten lost.

This road was smaller and completely empty, and I only made it a short distance before something crashed down in front of me, nearly giving me a heart attack. I screamed and slammed on the brakes, narrowly avoiding hitting a large tree that had fallen in the road.

I pressed a hand to my chest, willing my pounding heart to calm, while adrenaline coursed through me. After the initial shock passed, I muttered a low curse. The tree was too big to drive over, blocking the entire road with its thick trunk and branches. I'd have to move it and hope that no human drove by and wondered how I was so strong.

I pulled to the side of the road and got out of my car, tugging the hood of my jacket over my head. The rain drenched me immediately, but I started toward the tree, eager to get this over with.

Sudden movement and the flutter of wings caught my eye. I paused, shielding my face from the torrential rain as a dozen or so crows appeared out of the fog, flapping their wings above me. A murder—wasn't that what they were called?

I vaguely remembered Sarah telling me she'd heard a bunch of crows before the vampire attack, and instinct made me sprint back to my car—but I was too late. The crows descended and then transformed into vampires, similar to the way we shifted from wolves. Though shifters were stronger than vampires, they had us beat in speed, and they circled me in the middle of the road.

I turned, trying to keep them all in my sight, but it was impossible. My heart thudded in my chest as I thought of the attack on Eventide and knew this had to be the same group.

"What do you want?" I asked.

Unfortunately, they didn't look like they were interested in talking. One of them snarled at me, drawing his lips back to display long fangs. Some of the others had their long nails out, which looked like talons in the dim light, and something black dripped off of them.

Another vampire stepped forward and the others looked at him as if for guidance. I wondered if he was their leader. He had long black hair that reached past his shoulders and was as inhumanly beautiful as every other vampire I'd seen. He was dressed in a long black coat and looked sort of familiar, but I couldn't remember if I'd seen him before or not.

"Come with us quietly," he said in a low, rich voice. "And no one else in your pack will get hurt."

Panic shot through me and I considered fleeing, glancing toward my car. If I could break out of the circle of vampires and make a run for it, I might make it. But how would I do that? I wasn't a fighter, and I was vastly outnumbered. Even if I could escape, his threat to my pack stopped me in my tracks. But he didn't want to kill me—he wanted me to come with him. Why?

I sighed and raised my hands. "I won't run or fight."

The vampire gave me a smile that was beautiful and terrifying all at once. "Smart girl."

He motioned to one of the vampires behind me. I turned, but the vampire moved so fast that he was just a blur, catching my arm in one hand. Before I could react, he jabbed a syringe in my neck.

I waited for something to happen, as did the vampires. Eventually, I rolled my eyes. "I'm a Virgo," I said, but they still looked confused. "Like all of the earth element packs, I'm immune to poison. That includes most sedatives."

"I guess I'll have to do this the old-fashioned way then," the leader snarled and stalked toward me. I tried to back away, but the vampire who had injected me held me tight. The leader grabbed my chin and pushed my head to the side.

I realized what he was going to do a moment before he did it. "No, please," I said, but it was too late. The vampire's fangs cut into my flesh, and I gasped, my whole body going taut with the pain.

Unlike Killian's bite, this was awful, and for one horrible moment, I thought I'd scream from the pain. Then, mercifully, my vision started blackening around the edges. The last thing I heard was the leader laughing.

CHAPTER SIX

I WOKE UP SLOWLY, feeling like my head was stuffed full of fabric. My mouth was dry and a sharp pain throbbed behind my eyes. For a few moments, I didn't remember where I was or what was happening, but as I blinked up at an unfamiliar ceiling, it all came rushing back. I reached for my phone to call for help, but then remembered it was in my purse, which I'd left back in my car. Damn.

I couldn't tell where I was, but the walls, floor, and ceiling were all a dark, damp stone. Each of the outer walls had two tiny windows, letting in a bit of light, but they were too small to crawl through. I peered outside, but saw nothing except some branches that blocked my view of anything else. It had stopped raining at least.

I stood up slowly and paced the length of the room. Room was a generous word—it was more of a cell with two dirty, bare cots. One of them I'd been put on after I'd passed out from the vampire's bite, and the other one was shoved into the opposite corner. There was a bucket in one of the corners right below the window, and nothing else.

I tried the door handle, but I wasn't surprised to find it locked. I sighed and sat on the cot again and felt my neck. The bite had healed already, and other than the pounding in my head, I seemed to be fine physically and I still wore the same damp clothes. Why had the vampires taken me captive?

I didn't have any way of telling time down here, but it couldn't have been more than an hour before I heard the sound of a key in the door. I looked up just in time to see the vampire who had bitten me walk in. I crossed my arms over myself to suppress a shiver.

He looked me over, his eyes cold and practical. "Do you know who I am?"

I shook my head. I still couldn't figure out why he looked familiar.

The vampire gave a wry smile. "I'm not surprised. My brother likes to forget that I exist at all."

"Your brother?" I asked.

The vampire gave me a mocking bow and gave me another bloodless smile. "My name is Cormac. I'm Killian's younger brother."

"I didn't know Killian had a brother." Now that he'd said it, I could see the resemblance. Why hadn't Killian told me about a brother? That seemed like the kind of thing you should tell your mate.

He sneered. "Like I said, I'm not surprised."

"Why are you holding me captive?"

"I want to make my brother suffer like I have suffered all these years. Once I learned that he had a shifter mate, I knew this would be the perfect opportunity to draw him out."

I raised my eyebrows. "Were you behind the attack on Eventide too?"

"That town is a disgrace. Leave it to my brother to become mayor of such a wretched place."

"Why do you hate him so much?"

He paused, his eyes very far away. "When I was mortal, Killian and I both loved the same woman. After a long courtship where we both tried to win her over, Bridget chose me, and I thought that would be the end of it. Killian left Ireland after that." His haughty, beautiful face showed the first traces of sadness, but when he looked back at me, they disappeared just as quickly. "A few years later, Bridget and I both grew very ill. Once I learned that Killian was a vampire, I begged him to save us. He turned me, but not my wife. He refused to help her, and I had to watch her die. He did it just to punish me."

Something awful clenched in my stomach. I remembered how Killian often changed the subject when I asked about his past, but surely this couldn't be true. Killian was kind and gentle, nothing like Cormac. "That doesn't sound like Killian."

"You poor thing," he said, his voice dripping with condescension. "Just because you're mated to him doesn't mean that you really know him."

He moved so fast that my eyes couldn't track it, and then

he was holding my wrist. I flinched, but all he did was look at the ring on my finger.

"Did Killian tell you about the vampire houses?" he asked. "What House Corvus really means?"

"Not really," I said.

Cormac let go of my hand just as fast, and I curled it back into my body. "Typical of my brother. Killian gave you that ring because he used to be the leader of our house. But after he married that Moon Witch, he stepped down and walked away. He disappeared for a century or two, and I became the leader in his absence. I hoped he'd skulked off to die somewhere by himself, but I wasn't so lucky. Now that he's back, he thinks that he can take over the house again."

"Killian doesn't have any interest in that," I said.

"You're wrong," Cormac said flatly. "Killian is a cold-blooded vampire warrior. He's nothing like your soft little Virgos who don't even know how to fight back. You have no idea what you've brought into your midst. You're going to be sorry you ever let him find out where you're hiding."

I swallowed hard. Everything he was saying seemed so wrong. I couldn't believe him. But then again, how much did I really know about my mate? It was obvious he'd been keeping a lot of secrets from me. Could I have been completely wrong about him?

The door opened, and I thought Cormac was leaving, but instead, another vampire ushered in a small boy carrying a baby in his arms. The boy looked no older than five or six and had dirty, matted brown hair. The baby in his arms was probably about six months old and I guessed it was a girl based on the pink hat on her head. Alarm went through me at the state of their clothes and how haggard they both looked.

Cormac motioned for the boy to step closer to me, and he did without questioning it. The kid kept his eyes downcast, and I could see that he was shaking a little.

"These shifters serve my House," Cormac said with a hint of disgust in his voice. "But they're sick or something. They need healing."

I wasn't sure how a baby and a ragged-looking kid could serve a vampire house. I took a deep breath in, letting their scents wash over me. Infection, as expected.

"They're half human," I said. "Their human side makes it so they can still get sick, and when they're injured, they don't heal quite as fast as full-blooded shifters, and their wounds can become infected."

"You will heal them both," Cormac demanded.

"I'll need some time alone with them."

"Heal them now and make it quick!"

There was nothing that made me more angry than people who abused or mistreated kids. I rose to my feet and met his eyes, letting a bit of my alpha wolf reveal herself. My words came out in a low growl. "If you want them healed, I need food, water, clean clothes, wipes, and diapers. And several hours alone with them. Do not test me on this."

Cormac stared back at me, but I refused to back down. Not on this matter. Sure, he was the head of a vampire house, but I was the fucking Virgo alpha.

"Fine." He snapped his fingers, and the other two

vampires left the room. "You'll get everything you need, but don't try anything. If you're hoping to find a way to escape, it won't work. This room is heavily guarded, and there's no other way out."

I'd worry about escaping later. Right now all I cared about was helping these kids and keeping them safe.

Cormac left the room, and over the next few minutes, the vampires brought in everything I'd asked for, setting them on the empty cot in the corner. Eventually, the lock turned again, and we were alone.

The boy's head jerked up and he glared at me. He set the baby down on the cot, and then shifted into a small gray wolf, shredding his clothes in the process. He snarled at me, baring his canines, and it would have been cute if he hadn't been so scared.

"It's okay. I'm not going to hurt you." I held my hands up, trying to show him that I wasn't a threat, and then carefully extended one out for him to sniff.

The kid crept forward slowly, always keeping himself between me and the girl. His hackles stood on end, and I had no doubt that if he was faced with a human, he could do some serious damage to them, even as small as he was. He sniffed me cautiously and his ears, which had been flattened to his skull, perked up and swiveled toward me. His tail wagged once, and then he shifted back. He looked much more bright-eyed now, even though I could still tell that he was tired and worn down. "You're like me!"

I nodded and smiled. "Yes. I'm part wolf too."

He sat on the cot, his legs swinging off the edge. He was

naked and dirty but didn't seem to notice. "You're a prisoner here too."

"I am, but I'm also going to help you out. Is this your sister?"

He shook his head while I gently picked up the baby and unwrapped her from her blanket. She stirred, her eyes opening sluggishly. She looked at me, but I wasn't sure if she really saw me or not. I took her temperature as best as I could with the back of my hand and listened closely to her breathing, which had a creaking sound.

"My name is Madison," I said. "What are your names?"

"I'm Louis." He came to sit beside me, watching what I was doing, but not getting in my way. "I don't know her name, but I'm calling her Edie. That was my mom's name." He looked away after saying that, and I could sense that there was a lot of deep pain there.

"What happened to your parents?" I asked.

"The vampires killed them."

I swallowed hard. I knew all about losing family members to vampire attacks, but I couldn't imagine what this kid had gone through. "How long have you both been here?"

Louis shook his head. "I've been here for a while. I don't know how long. They keep me locked up. Edie just got here not too long ago."

I nodded, and we fell into a brief silence as I changed Edie's clothes and her diaper, then used some wipes to clean her as best I could. I'd finished her diagnostic, and I could tell that she was malnourished and had croup, as evidenced by her weird breathing.

"I'm done checking her over," I said as I swaddled her back in her blanket and put that pink hat back on. She slept through it all, and that worried me. "Can I look at you next?"

Louis shook his head. "I'm fine, but she's been breathing like that for a while. It's getting worse."

My heart went out to him. He was so young, yet he had the weight of protecting this baby on his shoulders. He also didn't trust me yet, but I'd wear him down eventually.

"How about I heal her first, while you clean up as best you can and put some new clothes on?"

"Okay."

I focused on healing Edie for the next few minutes. It was harder to heal children, especially babies as young as she was, but I'd done it before. It might take a little more time since they were so small and I had to be very gentle, but I had no doubt that I could help her.

"Are you really healing her?" Louis asked, once he was a little bit cleaner and wearing fresh clothes.

"Yes, I am."

He frowned as he watched me, but there wasn't much to see in cases like this. No healing light, no wounds closing up. Edie's breathing did stop making that horrible noise though, and soon she opened her eyes and actually seemed to notice us. She reached for Louis, who took her hand.

"She's better!" he said, his eyes wide.

"She'll be even better after we get her something to eat and drink."

Louis rushed to get her some baby food in a pouch. Cormac's vampires hadn't bothered to bring us any formula or milk though. No wonder she was malnourished. These vampires had no idea what to do with a baby obviously. I dribbled a little bit of water into her mouth and she perked up a bit, enough to start sucking on the pouch.

While I fed her, Louis tore into some bread like a wild animal and devoured some yogurt. It broke my heart to see the kids treated this way. I knew that it had probably been quite some time since Louis had sat down at a table and eaten a proper meal, and I wondered if the vampires forgot to feed them sometimes. It was clear that they didn't know how often Edie would need to be fed since she was showing signs of malnutrition.

"How have things been for you here?" I asked eventually as Louis sat back on the floor, having finished all the food.

"Not good. I've been trying to figure out how to escape but it's too hard. The vampires are so strong and fast."

My heart broke a little more with everything he said. "I'm strong and fast. I bet you are too."

Louis puffed up and said, "I am." He deflated a moment later. "But I got injured too. It slows me down."

Edie had finished her pouch and promptly fallen asleep again. Her breathing sounded much better, though it would probably take a bit more healing before she was completely healed. I wanted to go slow with her and not shock her system too badly. I wrapped her up in a clean blanket and put her down on the cot, away from the edge.

"I'd like to heal you now," I said, turning to Louis. "If you'll let me try."

Louis thought about it for a few seconds. "Okay," he said, and then turned around and lifted his shirt up. I'd avoided looking at him before when he was naked, so I'd missed these horrible wounds on his back, which seeped with black pus, just like the wounds I'd seen in Eventide. These were clearly made by a vampire's claws, and worst of all, they'd gotten infected and now were red and no doubt very painful.

"They did this to you?" I asked, shaking with rage.

"When I tried to escape, the vampires hurt me," he said.

I closed my eyes and tried to keep my breathing even. I'd never been violent in my life, happy to stay a pacifist and follow my pack's ideals, but the anger that flowed through me in that moment was overwhelming. I wanted to murder every single one of the vampires, starting with Cormac. Ripping his head off would only satisfy a little bit of my sudden, violent urges. How could someone be so cruel to a child?

I inhaled through my nose and exhaled through my mouth a few times, centering myself before I opened my eyes. "I'm sorry they did this to you, but I can make the pain go away."

He nodded and I lightly touched his back. He flinched, but as soon as it became clear I wasn't going to hurt him, he relaxed. His skin was too hot, riddled with the infection.

Energy passed from my body to him, drawing out the infection and the poison first, then knitting his skin back together from the inside out. It didn't take long, and pretty soon, there weren't even scars left over. I smoothed my hands over his tiny, uninjured back as if to reassure myself that he really was better, and then helped him tug the shirt back down.

"Is that it?" he asked, twisting around as if to check his own back.

"That's it," I said. "You did a good job of holding still."

Louis opened his mouth to say something but yawned instead.

"Healing really takes it out of you," I said. "Don't worry, you can get some sleep. I won't let anyone hurt you again."

"Okay," Louis said, yawning again. He curled around Edie and was out almost instantly.

I stretched out on the other cot and watched them both sleep. A warm surge of love and protectiveness swelled in my heart, unlike anything I'd felt before.

I wouldn't leave them here. When I escaped, I'd be taking them with me.

CHAPTER SEVEN

I WOKE to the sound of Edie crying. I couldn't remember falling asleep. I'd intended to just rest my eyes for a few moments, but healing always took a toll on the healer's body too, and I'd let the kids eat all the food. My stomach growled, but I ignored it.

I quickly picked Edie up, holding her close. One whiff told me that she needed her diaper changed, and that had probably been what woke her up. I quickly unwrapped her and looked at the dwindling supply of diapers. We'd need more before long, but I didn't know when Cormac or one of the other vampires would come by next.

I peered out the window and guessed it was sometime in the early morning, by the direction of the faint sunlight. The guards outside didn't seem phased by Edie's crying, but I knew we'd only have so long before Cormac would come back and demand to know why I hadn't finished healing Edie and Louis yet.

Louis stirred on the cot opposite us and sat up, rubbing his eyes. "Is she okay?"

I nodded. "She's fine, but if the vampires come by, act weak and I'll tell them that I'm still healing both of you, okay?"

"Okay," Louis said. He watched me finish changing Edie's diaper, and I smiled over at him.

"How are you feeling?" I asked.

Louis stretched carefully at first, and then when his back didn't hurt him, more vigorously. "I feel much better! How did you do that?"

"I'm part of the Virgo pack. We have healing powers."

"What's a pack?"

"It's a group of shifters, like us. We live together and share similar traits. Sort of like one big extended family. Do you know what pack your wolf parent was from?" I hadn't seen a pack mark on him, so I was guessing he didn't know.

Louis shook his head. "My mom wasn't a wolf, and I didn't know my dad. I didn't even know there were other people like me until I met Edie, but she doesn't turn into a wolf yet."

"She will in another two or three years," I said.

"I can't wait," Louis said.

He reached out and took Edie from me, holding her gently. He smiled down at her and then started making silly faces. Edie had stopped crying after I changed her diaper but now she giggled at Louis. She reached up and touched his face as he scrunched his nose at her and wiggled his eyebrows.

I watched them both for a few moments. They clearly were very close. Louis obviously felt protective of her, but he also clearly cared for her. No matter what happened once we got out of here, I'd make sure that they could stay together.

I had to get them out of here before the vampires came back and tried to take them away from me. Somehow we'd have to escape, but I didn't have a plan. I'd told Louis that I was fast and strong, which was true, but I didn't know how to fight. I didn't even know how many vampires there were out there, or what awaited me on the other side of the door. All I knew was that I had to try.

I stood up and carefully tested the door again. It was still locked, of course, but I didn't know how thick it was. I pressed against it, debating whether my shifter strength was enough to break it down or rip it off the hinges. The other alternative was to wait for the vampires to return and use everything I had to take them out. Even if it meant killing them.

A tapping noise on one of the tiny windows caught my attention. A large crow stood on the windowsill, seemingly trying to get my attention. The vampires who had taken me had shifted into crows, but why would one of them be outside my window? I worried it might be a trick, but something told me it wasn't.

And then I felt my mate's presence.

"Killian," I breathed, as I rushed to the window. It was rusted shut after many years of being left closed, but my shifter strength was good for opening a window at least. I wrenched it open and let the crow inside. Killian hopped in and halfway to the floor, he flowed into his regular form. Unlike shifters, he somehow managed to keep his clothes on when he became a bird, which seemed very unfair.

He pulled me into his arms and I slumped in relief, knowing he would get us out of this awful place. "Madison, love, are you all right?"

"I'm fine." I pulled away and spotted Louis backed into the corner, his face pale with fear. He held Edie and growled at Killian. I quickly stepped between them. "It's okay. He's not going to hurt us. This vampire is a friend."

"He turns into a crow like the others," Louis said.

"That's true, but I'm not with the other vampires," Killian said. "I'm here to get you out."

"This is Killian," I told Louis. "He's my mate, which is like my husband. Killian, this is Louis and Edie. Your brother has been holding them captive. Speaking of, you have a lot of explaining to do." I poked a finger at his chest. "I didn't know that you had a brother, or that you could turn into a crow. Both of those seem like important things you should tell your mate."

Killian had the grace to look a bit ashamed. "You're right—I should have told you. I'll explain everything later, but this whole place is about to be attacked by our allies. I'm getting you out of here." He glanced at Edie and Louis. "All three of you."

"How did you find me?" I asked.

He shrugged. "When you didn't return last night, I

called our friends and we started searching for you. We found your car, and from there, I followed the mate bond."

There was a flurry of noise outside of the door, including a shout, a growl, and the sound of something heavy hitting the floor. I tensed, but Killian didn't look concerned, his eyes fixed on the door. Another scuffle sounded, and there was the definite sound of fighting. I took Edie from Louis and shoved him behind us. Louis shifted into a wolf and pressed against my leg. He was so brave, and my heart swelled with so much love and protection toward him.

There was a moment of silence, and then the sound of the key in the door. When it swung open, all I could see was two dead vampires, and no one else outside. Then a very naked Kaden appeared out of thin air, making me gasp.

"The way out should be clear," he said. "Follow me."

He shifted back into a huge black wolf and sprinted off. Killian unsheathed his sword and gestured for us to follow the Ophiuchus alpha.

"Stay next to me," I told Louis as we exited the room we'd been trapped inside. We seemed to be in a basement, and I quickly took the stairs up to the main floor, clutching Edie to my chest. Louis stayed glued to my legs the entire time, while Killian was right behind us.

We emerged into a huge, old house that looked to have been abandoned several years ago. Two male vampires rushed us as we entered the living room, but Kaden leaped on one and bit him in the neck, while Killian loped off the other's head with his sword. They moved so quickly and with such deadly precision, dispatching both vampires before they even got close to me or the kids. Maybe I should have been worried that Cormac was right about my mate being a cold-blooded vampire warrior, but all I felt was relief.

Killian was *my* cold-blooded vampire warrior.

We continued through the house, past dusty, old furniture, toward the exit. Through the windows, I caught brief glimpses of a huge fight happening outside. A huge white wolf—Ayla—shot moon magic out of her mouth at a vampire, blasting it back. Wesley, also in wolf form, took the vampire down, tearing off his head. Behind them, Larkin and Ethan worked together in a similar way, her moon magic lighting up the area, before Ethan's fangs and claws finished the vampire off.

We reached the back door of the house and Kaden burst through it and leaped upon a vampire who tried to get in our way. Killian sliced its head off with the flick of his sword, and then the kids and I were outside, rushing after them.

Across the lawn, a group of four wolves seemed to be moving in tandem, taking down vampires left and right. As I drew closer, I recognized Harper and her brother Dane. Their twin Gemini mates were with them, fighting as a deadly force together.

Jordan stood a little further off, a wreath of fire surrounding him. A black wolf—Stella—ran in a tight circle around four vampires, forcing them to huddle together, and then Jordan used his sun magic to light them on fire in one amazing burst of heat and light.

I felt a stab of pride watching my friends, along with a burst of love knowing they'd all come so quickly to save me. But then came the fear, because there were so many vampires, and I couldn't stand the thought of losing any of the people I loved.

Killian led us toward a group of parked cars, but I stopped when I realized Louis wasn't by my side anymore. He was still in the doorway, cowering with his tail tucked between his legs.

"Louis!" I yelled, but he bolted back into the house.

Kaden shifted back and held out his arms. "Give me the baby. I'll keep her safe while you get him."

"Thank you." I passed Edie to him, knowing there was nowhere safer. Kaden and Edie disappeared from sight a second later, while Killian turned to take out another vampire.

I ran back toward the house—and straight into Cormac. His nails had grown long and were dripping with black poison. He reached for me and I narrowly avoided the blow, stumbling back.

Louis appeared out of nowhere, growling and moving in front of me. Protecting me from Cormac. He lunged at the vampire, who sneered and slashed his long, sharp black nails at the kid. Louis was able to dodge the first blow, but not the second, and let out a loud, startled noise of pain as the claws tore through his side. He hit the ground and I screamed.

Cormac gave me an awful smile and moved so fast that I couldn't escape. He gripped me tight and pulled me against him, his poisoned nails gripping my neck. He turned me around in time to see Killian running over to help us.

He pulled up short once he saw that Cormac had me by the throat. "Cormac," he said, his voice low. "Please, let her go. We can talk this out."

"You're going to watch your beloved die now," Cormac said, stroking my skin with his nails. "Just like I did."

Killian raised his hands in surrender and took a few steps forward. "You know I did everything I could to save Bridget."

"Liar! You let Bridget die because you were jealous."

"That's not true. I tried to save her, but I was too late."

"We both know you never got over the fact that she chose me over you. That's why you let her die." He gripped me tighter, shaking me a little. "Then you married that Moon Witch bitch and walked away from our people. But I took care of her."

"What are you talking about?" Killian asked.

"I made sure the Sun Witches knew where you were living." He ran a claw down my neck to my breasts. "Now another one of your women will die today."

"Let her go and I'll do whatever you want," Killian said. "You can take me instead."

My eyes kept darting to Louis, curled around himself on the ground, whimpering softly. He was bleeding a lot and he would die if he didn't get healed soon. I needed to find a way out of this, but I was running out of time.

There was one thing I could do, something I'd never tried before. Something my mother told me to never do except as a last resort to save someone. Something the Virgo pack kept as a closely guarded secret.

I reached out with my healing energy and wrapped it around Cormac. It was easy with his nails on my throat and his body pressed against mine. Instead of healing him, I inverted the power, using it to tear him apart from the inside out.

Everything that could be healed could also be hurt. The same magic that allowed us to repair wounds also gave us the ability to cause them. I channeled all my rage and hatred for Cormac and his vampires into my power and smiled when he began screaming.

He let me go and stumbled back while his body jerked and spasmed. He leaned over and vomited up blood, which also leaked from his eyes. Oops, I might have overdone it.

I had no regrets.

"What have you done to me, you bitch?" he screamed.

Cormac lunged for me with his claws, but Killian was there in an instant. He snarled and brought the blade down. It sank into Cormac's chest, and then Killian pulled it out with a wet sucking noise. He raised it again as Cormac fell to his knees, and beheaded his brother in one powerful swipe.

As the head hit the ground, I crouched over Louis and willed every bit of my healing power to help him. He twitched underneath me and let out a soft whimper. I held my breath as I healed him, watching his eyelids flutter until they opened. He licked my hand, his ears twitching, and I rubbed his furry head. He was going to be okay.

He shifted back and crawled into my lap. "Madison?"

"It's going to be okay," I said, as I wrapped my arms around him. His bottom lip wobbled, and the first of the tears welling in his eyes spilled out. I soothed him, rubbing my hands up and down his back. "You were so brave to try and protect me. I'm never going to let anything bad happen to you again."

Killian kneeled beside us and touched my face, checking to make sure I was all right. I pressed my cheek into his hand and searched his eyes. I knew we had a lot to talk about once this was over, but for now, I was relieved to have him by my side.

All around us, the sounds of fighting died down as my friends took out the rest of the vampires. They killed every single one of them, and I felt no guilt or remorse about it. Those vampires had taken me hostage and hurt small children. None of them deserved to live.

As soon as it was safe, my friends all crowded around us, making sure we were okay. Kaden handed me Edie, and I held her in one arm, with Louis in the other, while Killian held me in return.

We were safe.

CHAPTER EIGHT

"ARE you sure you don't need us to stay a little while longer?" Ayla asked, hovering on my porch like she was hesitant to leave.

"I'm sure," I said, giving her a hug. "Go home to your kids. Poor Mira must need a break by now." Mira was watching all my friends' kids while they came here to rescue me.

"She's happy to help out, just like the rest of us," Stella said.

"I think most of us would rather fight than wrangle a ton of toddlers and babies anyway," Harper added, wrinkling her nose.

Larkin laughed. "Seriously, Mira had the hardest job."

"We really appreciate all your help," I said. "And your mates too, of course." The men were off chatting with Killian a few steps away, patting each other on the back and promising to have a tequila tasting night soon.

"Don't hesitate to call us if any vampires return," Ayla said.

"I will, but I'm sure we'll be fine," I said.

"Yes, you will," Harper said, wrapping an arm around my shoulders. "I'll be staying for the next few days with Dane and my mates to keep an eye on the village. You'll be completely safe with us here."

Stella smirked. "I doubt the vampires will be back after the serious butt-kicking we gave them."

"All the wine and cheese is on me for the next book club," I said. "Seriously, I owe you guys."

"No you don't," Larkin said, giving me a squeeze. "This is what friends are for."

We all hugged each other and said goodbye, and then Ayla teleported them away, presumably to get their kids from Mira, while Harper and Dane went off to set up patrols around Haven. Once they were all gone, I turned around to find Killian standing behind me. I gave him a tired smile as we went back into the house. We still had to talk about a lot of stuff, but I knew that we'd get there eventually.

"I'm going to put Louis to bed," I said.

Killian nodded. "Do you need help?"

"No, thank you. I think he's still a bit wary of you."

Louis was curled up on the couch, covered in a blanket, watching a cartoon with eyes that were almost closed. After we'd gotten home from the attack, I'd healed him again and fed him a hearty meal, while members of the Virgo pack gathered supplies for us. Within hours, they'd brought clothes, toys, a crib, and other baby supplies—everything we needed to take care of both kids for the next few days. They also brought us enough food to fill our fridge and our freezer so we wouldn't have to cook. I was so impressed and touched by how my pack rallied together to help us however they could.

"Let's get you to bed," I said, turning off the TV.

Louis nodded and got up to take my hand when I offered it. Together we walked upstairs, and I took him to the guest bedroom that was now set up as a temporary kid's room. Back when this had been my aunt's house, the room had been my bedroom, and it made me smile to see it full of toys again.

Louis looked totally exhausted, and I quickly had him brush his teeth before tucking him into bed. Edie was fast asleep already in a crib on the other side of the room. I knew that Louis would sleep easier having Edie in the same room as him.

"Are we really safe here?" Louis asked as I tucked the covers in around him and sat on the bed beside him.

I pressed a kiss to his forehead. "We're safe, I promise. No one will ever hurt you again."

"You're sure?" Louis asked.

I could see genuine fear in his eyes, and I knew that it would take a while for him to trust me and this place. "I'm sure. I will protect you, and so will Killian and the rest of the Virgo pack. We have some really tough warriors from the Ophiuchus and Gemini packs patrolling tonight as well."

"Okay." He gripped my hand tight as he fell asleep, and

I smiled as I watched his little furrowed brows even out. His hand slowly relaxed, but he didn't let go of me.

A fierce love ignited in my chest as I looked at him and Edie. I'd never felt anything like this before, but I knew that I'd do anything to protect these kids and make sure that nothing bad happened to them ever again. The two kids would have a long road of mental and emotional recovery ahead of them, as well as physically getting their strength back up. They were both malnourished, but I had a feeling that the emotional scars would last a lot longer than the physical ones. After the trauma they'd been through, they'd need a lot of care, but they were both strong and I would help them however I could.

I carefully extracted my hand from Louis's after his breathing evened out and I was sure he was asleep. Then I went to check on Edie, touching her cheek lightly. She had the cutest little brown curls on her head, now that she'd had a bath and was clean again. Her breathing sounded good, and I sensed she was doing much better after my healing.

I left the door halfway open for either of them to make noise if they needed anything. My own bedroom was only a few feet away, and a part of me wanted to throw myself into bed immediately. The last two days had really taken it out of me, but I wanted answers from Killian before I fell asleep. It wasn't that I didn't trust him, but he'd omitted a lot about his past. I wanted to hear the story from his point of view.

I heard Killian in the kitchen and headed back downstairs to meet him there. He was opening a bottle of red wine, and he gave me a small smile as I sat down at the island.

Killian came around the counter to wrap his arms around me. "I'm sorry about all of this. I didn't realize that when I left Eventide I would bring the vampire threat with me. I never meant to put you in any danger."

I pulled away from him. "I think it's time you tell me the truth about your past. Starting with how you can turn into a crow."

He poured us both a glass of wine. "All vampires belong to a House, which are similar in many ways to your Zodiac packs. Each house has a different animal we can turn into. House Corvus, as you've seen, can turn into crows or ravens."

"Why didn't we know this about vampires before?" I asked.

"It's one of our greatest secrets, and even though we are at peace now, it's not something we would readily share with most shifters or witches." He swirled the wine in his glass. "You have to understand that we have been hunted nearly to extinction over the last few centuries. For most of my life, both shifters and witches were our enemies. Shifters wanted to kill us on sight, and we were unable to walk in the sunlight until a few years ago, thanks to the Sun Curse. We existed only by staying hidden and keeping our secrets close to our chests. Most of the old vampire Houses are gone now, or decimated to almost nothing over the course of the last few centuries. Some of them, like House Strigidae, who can turn into owls, only have a few members left in Europe. It's rare to see any of them, as most of them are in hiding."

"Wow," I said, taking a moment to process all this new information. "What about the vampires who were allied with the Sun Witches before?"

"Those were members of House Desmodus, who can turn into bats. They are the largest House and have members all over the world, but even their numbers are much smaller compared to what they used to be."

"Bats?" I asked, my lips quirking up. "Like in Dracula?"

"Indeed," Killian said. "They've inspired many of the folklore and superstitions about vampires." He paused. "And then, of course, there was House Lupus."

"Lupus, as in wolf?" I asked, nearly spitting out my wine. Surely there weren't vampires that could turn into wolves. We would have known about that.

"Yes. House Lupus could turn into wolves, but they're long gone now."

"What happened to them?"

He took my wine glass from me and set it down on the counter. "Many centuries ago, the witches used the vampires from House Lupus to create shifters. Then the witches wiped them out so their secrets would be buried with them."

"What?" I asked, nearly knocking over my glass of wine. Wolf shifters came from *vampires*? It seemed like a joke, but when I looked at Killian's face, he wasn't laughing. He looked deadly serious. "How is that possible?"

"I don't know how they did it," Killian said. "It was long

before my time or my sire's. But the story is passed down from vampire to vampire as a warning to never trust the witches again. It's one of the reasons I stepped down as leader of my House when I fell in love with a Moon Witch. The other vampires would never accept our union." He gave a bitter laugh. "Ironically, during my time in Lunatera living with the Moon Witches, House Desmodus decided to partner with the Sun Witches in return for walking in the sun again. Of course, we saw how poorly that ended for most of them."

"I can't believe it," I said. "Does anyone else know this?"

"Some of the witches do, I'm sure," Killian said. "I've told Kaden, Ayla, Larkin, and Ethan, but we've collectively decided to keep that information secret until relations between wolves and vampires improve."

I picked up my wine again with trembling hands and took a long sip. "I can't believe that the information was kept secret all this time."

"It's another thing the witches kept secret, like the fake mate bonds. Someday we'll make it common knowledge again when our people are ready. My hope is it will bring vampires and shifters closer together, but I suspect we will need a few more years of peace before that time."

"What happens to House Corvus now?" I asked, playing with the ring on my finger.

"I'm not sure how many of us are left, or what they will do now without a leader." He sighed. "My brother seems to have destroyed our once great and noble House."

"I still can't believe you didn't tell me you had a brother."

"I'm sorry. I would have told you about him eventually, and about everything else too." He refilled both of our wine glasses. "As you might have noticed, I have a hard time talking about my past."

"No kidding," I said dryly.

"Memories of my past usually bring me nothing but pain, and I try to think of them as little as possible. They say time heals all wounds, but when you live an immortal life, I find they often fester instead."

"Sounds like you need a healer to help you out with that problem."

He arched an eyebrow. "Perhaps that's why I was mated to one."

"It might help you to talk about these memories instead of burying them," I said. "Tell me what happened with your brother."

He stared off into the distance, growing very still as he spoke. "We grew up in Ireland together on a sheep farm. I was meant to inherit the farm, but my brother wanted it. He wanted everything I had, and we had an intense rivalry our whole lives. Naturally, we both wanted the same woman too. Bridget."

"Cormac said she chose him over you."

"She did, and my brother and I nearly killed each other over it. After we'd pummeled each other into the dirt, I realized I'd had enough. He could have her, and the farm, and everything else. I left for London and never looked back."

His voice became low and mournful. "We didn't speak again for years. I became a vampire and was something of a rake in those days. I barely thought of home at all. But then he wrote to me and told me they were ill, and I rushed home. Even after everything, I couldn't let my brother die. I tried to turn them both, but Bridget was too weak by that point, and she died instead of becoming a vampire. Cormac has blamed me for her death ever since, and I believe he also resented me for making him a vampire."

"I'm sorry," I said, taking his hand.

"I hoped we could move past it someday, and I tried to repair our relationship a few times. I even brought my wife to visit Cormac many years later, but now I know he sent the Sun Witches after us in retaliation." He stared down at our joined hands. "I should have seen how much evil was in his heart then, but I didn't want to believe it. He was my brother, after all. So I hid away in Lunatera, turning my back on my vampire nature and my past as much as I could. When I came to Earth, I hoped I could start fresh, without the burden of my previous mistakes weighing on me. But I should have known they would come back to haunt me." He pressed a kiss to my knuckles. "I'm so very sorry you were put in danger because of my mistakes, but I'm relieved that Cormac will never hurt anyone I love again."

"I'm still sorry that it ended that way between you," I said.

"We stopped being brothers a long time ago, but I didn't want to admit it. I'm just glad that you are all right, and that we were able to rescue the kids too."

"Me too."

"What did you do to Cormac at the end there?" he asked. "I've never seen anything like that before."

"The easiest way to explain is that I used my healing powers to do the opposite." I gave him a wry smile. "The Virgo pack has secrets too."

"So it seems."

We finished our wine and I got up to put our glasses in the dishwasher. "Thank you for rallying my friends to help so quickly."

Killian came up behind me and pressed a kiss to my neck. "I would have done anything to save you. *Anything.* But I'm worried about the Virgo pack and how defenseless it is. What if I hadn't been able to get our friends to come to our aid so quickly?"

"I'm worried about that too, but I'm not sure what we can do about it. The Virgo pack will never become warriors." I'd often worried about this same problem ever since becoming alpha but had never come up with a good solution. "So far, remaining hidden has worked for us."

"Yes, but that might not work any longer, especially if you plan to venture out among humans again." He turned me around and took my face in his hands. "Let me become your pack's protector. I'll devise a defensive plan, just like I did for Eventide, and I'll make sure you don't have to betray your ideals, while still keeping your people safe. I could get a few others to help me, maybe some loyal vampires I trust with my life. Perhaps someday House Corvus and the Virgo pack can stand side by side, but only if I can get my House in line first."

I leaned into his touch. "I think that's a great idea."

Killian smiled and opened his mouth to say something else, but before he could, a cry echoed from upstairs. Edie.

"She's probably hungry," I said.

"I'll get her, while you get a bottle ready," Killian said.

"Deal."

He walked upstairs while I prepared Edie's formula, sending a silent thanks once more to the Virgos who had brought us everything we needed to take care of a baby. I faintly heard Killian talking to Edie, and then her crying got louder. He reappeared a few minutes later, gently rocking Edie in his arms. She'd finally settled down a bit, and once I handed him the bottle, he gave it to her like he'd done this before.

"How do you know how to do this?" I asked.

"I've been alive for a long time," Killian said with a grin. "Even though I never had any kids of my own, I have some idea of what they need."

Edie relaxed against Killian, seeming content to eat. I loved seeing him be so gentle with her. She finished the bottle and promptly fell asleep again, while Killian continued rocking her.

"What are you planning to do with the kids?" he asked.

I hesitated. "I should probably send them to Eventide to live with the other half-human shifters there."

"But...?"

I leaned back against the counter and sighed. "But I

don't want to. I know I just met them, but I feel something for them. A connection."

"I know." He stroked Edie's hair and smiled. "She's a lovely baby. And Louis is so strong. He has a real fighting spirit."

My heart squeezed thinking about how he'd thrown himself in front of me earlier. "He's so brave, but he's going to need a lot of therapy after what he's been through."

"Maybe he needs to grow up in a place of peace and healing." Killian met my eyes with a smile. "Like the Virgo pack."

I inhaled sharply. "What are you saying?"

"I think we should adopt the kids."

"You do?" Tears welled up in my eyes and spilled over my cheeks.

"Only if you think it's a good idea, of course. You clearly care for them, and I do too. I also feel some responsibility for them. They were taken by my House, after all. I want to make things right with them." He wrapped his free arm around me, the other one still holding Edie. "But mostly, I'd love to add them to our family."

I hugged Killian, pressing Edie between us. "That's exactly what I want, but I was scared to admit it out loud. I wasn't sure if you'd want it too."

"Don't ever be afraid to ask me something." Killian rubbed a hand over my back and pressed a kiss to the top of my head.

I wiped at my tears and nodded. "In the morning, let's talk to Louis and ask him what he wants to do. I think he'll want to stay with us, but I don't want to force him into anything."

"No, he's had enough of that. He might need a little time to settle into the pack, but I think he'll want to stay."

"Me too."

CHAPTER NINE

I OPENED the window in my kitchen and breathed in deeply. It had rained recently, and dew sparkled on the leaves of the nearby trees and on the petals of the recently opened flowers. I could smell their sweet floral perfume, along with the other scents of the forest around us.

A loud bang to my left startled me, and I glanced down. Edie giggled as she opened the cabinet again. She peered inside, before letting it close again with another bang. Then she stood up and toddled around me to the other side of the sink, reaching for another cabinet. This one was baby-proofed, and she tugged and tugged on it to no avail.

"Sorry, flower, that one's not for you," I said, as I moved to pull some ingredients out of the fridge. Edie always liked to stay in the kitchen with me while I made breakfast. She'd started showing more interest in helping me cook, and I was excited for when she was older and could start helping.

She walked over to me and grabbed my pants, looking up at me. "Mama?"

I quickly picked her up, elation running through me. I kissed her forehead and hugged her close. "That's right," I said, and it came out a little choked. "I'm Mama."

"Mama," Edie said again, tugging on my hair, which she loved to play with.

"I love you, my sweet girl." I kissed her again and set her down, my heart nearly bursting with happiness.

A small gray wolf suddenly bolted into the kitchen from the back door with a few leaves in his fur. Louis and Killian went for an early morning run every day, mostly to burn off some of the kid's boundless energy. He panted and wagged his tail as he looked up at me with a wolfish grin.

"Yes, breakfast is almost ready," I told him. I knew what that grin meant. "Go put some clothes on and then you can eat."

He cocked his head at me and let out a little whine.

I shook my spatula at him with a smile. "You know the rules. No wolves or naked kids at the table."

He huffed but then shot out of the room in a gray blur. Claws clicked against the hardwood as Louis scampered up the stairs. He had so much energy, but I was glad to see him thriving. I'd rather he be energetic than closed off and sluggish like he'd been when he started living with us. Watching Louis come out of his shell was a treat.

Killian stepped inside, wiping his boots on the mat, and grinned as he leaned against the counter to give me a kiss. "Can I help?"

I shook my head. "It's almost ready. You can put Edie in her chair though."

Killian kissed me once more, before leaning down to pick up Edie. "And how's my favorite girl this morning?" He lifted her up high and she squealed happily. Killian had surprised us all by becoming an excellent dad, helping me out way more than I would have initially thought he would. There were plenty of long nights—Louis often had nightmares, and getting Edie to stay in her crib all night was an issue—but he took it all in stride.

Louis came pounding back down the stairs, on two feet this time instead of four, wearing shorts and a T-shirt with dinosaurs on it. He sat down at the dining room table. "I'm starving, is breakfast ready yet?"

"Nearly." I knew for a fact that Killian had fed him before they went for their run, but he was always starving. He was tall for his age too, even for a shifter. I couldn't even imagine how big his appetite would be the more he grew.

Killian pulled Edie's highchair out from the corner and set her down in it as I put the plates down on the table. Louis politely waited for all of us to sit down before he dug in, even though he was eyeing the food like he hadn't had anything to eat for a week. He'd had seconds and thirds at dinner last night, but if anyone had asked him, he would have said it had been *forever* since he'd had anything to eat.

Killian pulled my chair out for me and then sat down opposite me. I'd made us all a hearty but simple breakfast of eggs, bacon, and toast. The kids drank milk, while I had coffee and Killian had tea. For the first minute or two, none of us talked as we dug into our food. I glanced around at my family, finding it hard to believe it had been a year since we'd all found each other. Somehow it seemed both longer and shorter, all at once.

"What are you doing today?" Killian asked, before taking a sip of his tea. He still used that same ridiculous Dracula mug, naturally.

I straightened, excitement going through me. "I'm going to look at potential locations in nearby towns for our new healing center."

I'd decided to ask Ethan for help since he'd done such a good job finding a location for Eventide. Quebec was a bit out of his normal range, but he'd found me some nearby buildings that had potential, and today I was going to check them out. We were going to open the healing center an as "alternative medicine" practice, calling what we did "energy healing" or something similar that the humans might understand and accept. I'd done a lot of research into reiki, acupuncture, and similar things, and I thought we could use those as a mask for what we were really doing. Doing this would protect our identity as shifters while also allowing us to heal people who needed it.

While I was still busy with Edie and Louis, as well as my duties as Virgo alpha, I knew that it was time to start doing this as well. I couldn't wait to get the center up and running. It would be a lot of work, but it would be worth it in the end. The Virgos were ready to come out of hiding and start helping more people.

"Let me know how it goes," Killian said.

"I'll send you pictures." I dabbed Edie's mouth with a napkin. She laughed and took the napkin from me. I let her keep it. Maybe she'd clean her hands too. "What about you?"

"I will be training the wardens again today," Killian said. "We're going to be ready when you open this center."

Killian had been just as busy as me over the past year. Besides being an excellent dad, he'd also worked to overhaul the Virgo pack's security, putting new measures in place that would help us if we were attacked. He'd also reached out to many vampires of House Corvus and declared himself as their leader again. Bringing the tatters of House Corvus together hadn't been easy though. He'd been right that there were very few of them left, and many had been wary of the sudden change in leadership. But to his surprise—and mine—there were quite a few who were willing to follow him.

Killian had spent the last few months recruiting and training a small group of loyal House Corvus vampires who had sworn themselves to defend the Virgo pack. My shifters were initially wary of them coming to live with us, but over time they'd come to appreciate the added security and patrols. I'd been hesitant at first too, but after talking to several of the vampires and hearing that they were unhappy with how Cormac ran things, I felt a little bit better. As the months passed and they praised Killian for how he handled things, I knew that their loyalty wasn't just for show. They really believed in Killian and what he was doing here.

I also learned that many of the vampires had been longing for a community and a sense of purpose, and being among the Virgos gave them both. Best of all, there'd even been another vampire-shifter mate bond in our pack a few weeks ago. A true sign that times really were changing.

"I want to learn to fight with you too," Louis piped up. He'd been talking about this for a while, and Killian and I had debated what to do about it. On one hand, he was a Virgo now, and we didn't fight. On the other hand, things really were changing. A few other Virgos had expressed interest in learning how to defend themselves too. Killian had argued with me that everyone had the right to learn self-defense, and eventually, I'd agreed, partly because there was no stopping Louis. He was a fighter, deep in his core, and we had to love and accept him for who he was.

"You can come by after school and we'll start getting you trained," Killian said.

"Really?" Louis's eyes went huge. "Thanks, Dad!"

Killian grinned at me, looking immensely pleased. Louis had recently started calling us Mom and Dad, and every time it happened, it made my heart grow. I still couldn't believe we'd gotten so lucky.

Both kids had come so far in the last year. At first, Louis had been scared and distrustful of my mate, but eventually, he'd grown to love him, and now he wanted to be just like Killian when he grew up. He'd even asked Killian to teach him how to use his sword. And once he'd gotten over his fear and hatred of vampires, he'd started hanging around them more. He still had some issues to work through, but he had a strong heart and he was surrounded by love.

Edie, on the other hand, had already started showing an affinity for healing, like me. Just the other day, we'd been outside taking a walk in the forest and she'd found an injured bird beside the trail. I'd tried to pull her away, but Edie had already leaned down and touched its broken wing. I'd watched in awe as the bird's wing had knitted itself together right then and there before I even really knew it was happening. The bird had perked right up and flown off, while Edie clapped and giggled.

Most kids didn't come into their healing power until they were closer to ten, and it often took years to master. The fact that Edie could already heal so easily and quickly made me wonder if she would surpass me one day. She might even become the next alpha.

We finished breakfast, and I got up to clear the plates. Killian helped me load the dishwasher, while Louis made airplane noises and flew a block above Edie's head while she laughed and reached for it.

Killian wrapped his arms around me from behind. He put his chin on my shoulder and we watched our children play for a few minutes. "Have a good day," Killian eventually said. "I'll see you tonight."

He leaned forward and kissed my neck, and then let his fangs brush against my skin. I shivered as I thought about how good it felt to let him drink my blood. His words felt more like a promise than anything else, and I leaned my head back against his.

"Tonight," I echoed. As he pulled away, I touched my neck where Killian's fangs had brushed against me. One day, the issue of his immortality might become a problem. Maybe I could find a way to heal him, and make him mortal again.

He had also joked that he could try to turn me into a vampire. It might work since I was half human. Neither of us was really sure, but there would be plenty of time to find out. For now, we were happy.

Killian called for Louis to find his shoes. He would take Louis to school and then continue to the large house the vampires were staying in to start training them. We all said our goodbyes, with lots of hugs and kisses, and then the two males were out the door. As they headed out, I watched them go and picked up Edie, bouncing her on my hip as I told her to wave goodbye.

It was still hard to believe sometimes that I had a mate and a family, two things I thought I would never find. But against all odds, our misfit group had found each other. Now I had everything I could ever have wanted.

For the first time in my life, I truly felt blessed.

FATES ENTWINED

AYLA & KADEN

CHAPTER ONE

EVERYTHING HAD TO BE PERFECT.

This mantra repeated in my head all morning while I ran around like a headless chicken, and I was pretty sure Kaden was tired of me saying it too. But what did he expect? It was the summer solstice and the Ophiuchus pack was hosting the Convergence for the first time ever. As alpha female, it was part of my duty to make sure it ran smoothly. Was it any wonder I was a total mess?

I strode past dozens of tents toward the area where tonight's feast was being set up. We'd decided to use a spot just outside of the Ophiuchus pack lands in a field large enough to house all thirteen packs, with mountains surrounding it on the east and west, and a river running north and south through it. More shifters poured in by the minute, and it seemed like there were more here than there had ever been at any Convergence before.

I checked in on the people setting up the long tables for

the feast, but they seemed to have everything under control. Food was already cooking nearby, and some of my shifters were putting out drinks.

"Should we put up a tent?" a shifter named Andrea asked. "It looks like it might rain!"

I glanced up at the sky and shivered. The temperature had dropped drastically a few minutes ago and some clouds were rolling in. They looked dark and heavy with rain, which hadn't been in today's forecast. It was unusual for us to get heavy rain in the middle of June, even in this part of Canada.

"Maybe the clouds will pass," I said. *They better fucking pass.* I didn't want our Convergence to be remembered as the one where we got rained out and had to spend most of the time in our tents.

"I can hear you fretting from the other side of the field," Kaden said behind me. "Everything is going to be fine."

"Everything is not fine." I gestured wildly at the air. "Look at this weather!"

He laughed and wrapped his arms around me. "Shifters can handle a little rain."

I sighed and leaned into him. "I know. I just can't help but worry that something will go wrong."

"You've done an amazing job organizing everything. I can't imagine what could go wrong at this point."

"I just want everything to be perfect."

Kaden groaned. "Not that word again."

"I'm sorry. It's just that all the other packs have hosted the Convergence, and now it's finally our turn. It's like the final step in the Ophiuchus pack becoming part of the Zodiac Wolves."

"I understand." He played with my hair. "I still can't believe it's been six years since we officially joined the Zodiac Wolves."

"We've all come a long way since then."

Things had changed a lot in the past six years since the Sagittarius pack hosted the first of the new Convergences, free of Sun Witch control. The thirteen packs all lived in harmony now, for the most part. Sure, there had been some issues, like during the Aquarius-Taurus rivalry two years ago, but the alphas all worked through them to prevent any more pack wars.

There hadn't been any more conflicts with the vampires or Sun Witches either. The Moon Witches had returned to Earth for the most part, and Eventide continued to grow, welcoming more and more members of the supernatural community who would otherwise feel like they had no place where they belonged. In fact, it had grown so much that there was talk of setting up a similar town somewhere in the US soon.

Kaden nuzzled my neck, bringing me back to the present. "Remember when we first met at that waterfall by the Convergence?"

"Of course I remember. You were butt naked."

He gestured out at the rows of tents before us. "Look at where we are now. Hosting our own Convergence."

I couldn't help but smile at his words. "You're right. I'll try to relax and enjoy the moment."

"Why don't you take a break?" Kaden asked, leading me away from the feast tables. "You'll have plenty of time to fret later. We should spend some time with our friends and family before the Convergence officially starts."

"Fine." I glared up at the sky again, which was getting darker by the minute. "Where are the kids, anyway?"

"I think they're playing with their cousins back by the Cancer-Leo tents. Louis is with them, making sure they don't get into any trouble."

"Good," I said, relaxing a little as we began weaving our way through the sea of tents. Seeing my friends and family would definitely put my mind at ease.

Then a huge white snowflake landed on my nose.

I stopped in my tracks as white powder descended from the clouds above us, the air growing colder with every second that passed. Was that... S*now?*

Kaden held his hand out and caught a snowflake. "What the fuck?"

"How is it snowing?" I asked. "It's the middle of June!"

His brow furrowed. "I don't know."

The snow picked up quickly and people started shouting and freaking out. Everyone began covering things up or running to their tents. I couldn't blame them for panicking. No one had expected anything like this or packed gear or clothes for cold weather. It hadn't even been forecasted to rain, for fuck's sake.

My stomach dropped. I'd known something would go wrong today, but I'd never expected this. "Everything is falling apart," I said. "What do we do?"

"It will be fine," Kaden said, rubbing my arms. "The storm will pass in a few minutes. This is odd, but it's not impossible to overcome."

"We need to find the kids." I glanced around, looking to catch sight of them. "They're wearing T-shirts and shorts!"

"Ayla," Kaden said, his voice way too calm for my taste. "They can shift if they get too cold."

"Yes, of course. You're right." A little bit of the worry eased from my mind, but it wasn't enough. They were my babies and I needed to make sure that they were okay. "But I'm still going to check on them."

He nodded. "I'll come with you."

We headed for the area where the Cancer and Leo packs had set up their tents. These days, the two packs were the best of allies, and they always set up next to each other at Convergences, with the Ophiuchus, Libra, and Virgo tents surrounding them.

I didn't see the kids, but I spotted Mira and Stella chatting together, looking up at the sky. Mira was shaking her head as if she couldn't believe it, while Stella was rubbing her arms.

"Can you believe this weather?" Mira asked us as we approached.

"I've grown soft living in Arizona," Stella said. "I can't handle this shit anymore."

"Have you seen the kids?" I asked. "We thought they were around here, but we can't find them."

"No, we thought they were with you," Mira said. "We haven't seen them in a while."

"I'm sure they're around here somewhere," I said, trying not to freak out anymore than I already was. "They do love to go off exploring."

"Let's split up and look for them around the tents and meet back here," Stella suggested.

We agreed on that plan, and Kaden and I went to the Virgo tents next. Madison and Killian were both in the middle of their cluster of tents, directing people where to move things so they wouldn't get covered with snow. Madison looked up at me with a small frown on her face.

"Have you seen Louis or the other kids?" I asked.

"No. They were playing by the Libra tent when I last saw all of them." She bit her lip. "That was a while ago though, come to think of it."

"Let's check the Libra tents," Kaden said, putting a hand on my arm. "Maybe Ethan or Larkin have seen them."

This was getting worse and worse by the moment. We rushed over to the Libra tents, where we found Ethan and Larkin inside their large tent.

"What's going on?" Ethan asked. He had one hand curled protectively over his daughter, Aster, who was strapped to his chest in a baby carrier. She looked just like Larkin, even down to the little freckles on her nose and the white hair.

"We're looking for our kids," I said, and this time some of the panic slipped out into my voice. I couldn't believe no one had seen them recently. "Are they around here by any chance?"

Larkin shook her head. "We haven't seen them, sorry."

We searched around a bit more and then gathered back at the Cancer-Leo tents with the rest of our friends and family, who were all worried now. The kids were missing, and it was still snowing so hard that visibility was getting bad. Harper had joined us too at this point, also looking for her twins.

"Let's shift and try to contact them," Kaden said.

"Good idea," Wesley said.

All of the alphas undressed quickly, handed their clothes to their mates, and then shifted. They ran around the area a bit, their ears perked up as they reached out telepathically to their pack mates, while the rest of us stood around and waited.

Kaden was the first to shift back. He shook his head. "They must be out of range."

"I'll fly above and see if I can spot them anywhere," Larkin said, already lifting off the ground.

"I'll come with you," Killian said and transformed into a raven.

"Be careful!" Madison called out to both of them as they flew into the air. "The snow is getting worse."

We waited in tense silence as they flew above the camp. They both returned a few moments later, looking a little worse for wear and dusted with snow.

"I didn't see them anywhere in the field," Larkin said.

Killian landed on Madison's shoulder with a mournful *caw*, which seemed to mean he couldn't find them either.

"They must be somewhere in the forest," Stella said.

"Do you think they got lost?" Mira asked.

I gripped Kaden's hand tight as fear washed through me. "What if they were attacked?"

Kaden's lips were pressed into a thin line. I knew he was trying to stay brave for me, but he was just as worried as I was now.

"Could it be vampires?" Jordan asked.

Wesley crossed his arms. "What about Sun Witches?"

I shook my head. "I don't think it's either of them."

"And it can't be any of the packs," Ethan added. "We've all been working so hard to keep the peace."

"What if it's human hunters?" Harper asked."Like what happened to my parents?"

"Don't worry." Ethan held his hand over his daughter's head, covering her from the snow. "We'll find them."

"Nothing bad will happen to them," Stella added.

"This is what we're going to do," Kaden said. "We're going to split into four teams. Two of the teams will and search the forest on foot. Stella and Harper, you'll come with me, and we'll take the river south and try to pick up their scent along there."

"The original Ophiuchus gang, back in action," Harper said, while Stella nodded. They were both good at tracking, although Stella was the best. If they'd wandered off that way, I knew they'd be found quickly.

"Ayla, Jordan, and Wesley, you'll follow the river north," Kaden continued.

I glanced at my brothers. It had been a long time since it had been just the three of us, but I knew we would have no problem working together to get this done.

Kaden continued handing out orders. "Mira, Madison, and Ethan, you three will stay behind to search the tents and ask around. You're all good at keeping people calm, and we need someone here in case the kids come back on their own. Larkin and Killian, you'll continue searching in the air, as well as you're able to with this snow."

"Sounds good," Larkin said.

"What do we do if we find them?" Harper asked.

"One of us will send up some magic to alert the others," I said. "Larkin and Killian will see it even if no one else does."

Everyone agreed to this plan, and we quickly split up into our groups and left the others to their tasks. Wesley, Jordan, and I headed north through the camp, toward the river.

I'm coming to get you, I thought as I squinted against the snow and rubbed my arms. *Please be okay.*

CHAPTER TWO

WE MADE quick progress through the dense forest despite the snow, which was coming down in a steady fall. It mostly melted when it touched down, though it was starting to accumulate along the riverbank. Jordan used his sun magic to keep us warm. It was good to be among my brothers again, even if they spent the entire time teasing each other and making me roll my eyes at them.

"Come on, old man," Jordan told Wesley when he paused to look at something in the snow. "Keep up."

"I thought I saw a footprint," Wesley said. "Hey, who are you calling 'old man'? I'm only a year older than you. Besides, I might be old but at least I don't have pink nail polish."

Jordan held his hands up and wiggled his nails at both of us. "This is what happens when you have two little princesses at home. It's too bad you're not man enough to rock the pink."

I never would have guessed that someone like Jordan would become a full-on girl dad, but he loved it. He went to tea parties with his daughters and let them put makeup all over his face. Of course, they also kept setting their curtains and blankets on fire, but he and Stella were used to that by now.

"I'm man enough to rock any color, but all my kids want is blue, blue, and more blue." Wesley paused. "Do you think you'll have another?"

"I don't know." Jordan shrugged. "My mother wants us to try for a boy to continue the Sun Witch line and all that, but we have our hands full with those two already."

Wesley smirked. "With you as their dad, what do you expect?"

"Good point," Jordan said. "What about you?"

"Mira wants two more kids," Wesley said with a laugh. "I'm not sure I can handle any more though. My house smells like wet dog enough as it is."

Wesley was a great dad too. He'd fully adopted Adriana, who was accepted as both a Pisces and Cancer, and now he had a son with Mira too. The only problem he had was that his kids never wanted to get out of the water.

Both men had turned the Cancer and Leo packs around over the years and were truly the opposites of their own fathers in every way. Our three packs had once been at war, but now we were the closest of allies. That wouldn't have been possible with the previous generation of alphas, but we'd fought hard for peace so that our children would grow up in a better world.

"What about you, Ayla?" Jordan asked.

"Hmm?" I paused to check the snow for tracks. "Oh, we're done having kids. Two is enough."

"Are you okay?" Wesley asked. "You're being very quiet."

"Yeah, you seemed a bit frazzled today, even before the kids went missing and the snow started," Jordan said.

I blew out a long breath. "It's silly, but I've been worried a lot about the Convergence. I feel like we have to prove something since it's the Ophiuchus pack's first time hosting. But now with the snow and the kids missing, everything is a disaster."

Jordan wrapped an arm around me. "You don't need to prove yourselves to anyone at this point. No one questions whether or not the Ophiuchus belong in the Zodiac Wolves anymore."

"You've been doing a great job," Wesley said. "This is the most organized Convergence I've seen in a long time."

"Everything was going great until the snow," Jordan added, and I shot him a look.

Wesley elbowed him in the side. "Everything is going to be okay. Once we find the kids and it stops snowing, you'll see."

I was about to reply when something purple in the snow caught my gaze. I hurried forward.

"What is it?" Jordan asked.

I picked up a toy dinosaur. "Does this look familiar to either of you?"

"I think that's Henry's," Wesley said, referring to his son, who was turning four next week. "We must be on the right path."

"Let's go," I said, picking up my pace, the excitement temporarily pushing past the doubt and fear.

We sped up, encouraged that we might be getting closer, and a few minutes later we all heard something that sounded like voices in the distance.

"What was that?" I asked, stopping in my tracks.

"It sounded like—" Jordan stopped talking as we all heard it again, louder and clearer this time. It was the sound of a child shouting.

Panic sparked through me, and all three of us quickly raced forward. I dashed into a copse of trees, following the distinct sounds of children yelling. I couldn't tell if it was playful or scared, and I wasn't about to waste time trying to figure it out.

All three of us burst into a clearing and relaxed at the sight of all our kids playing together. Some of the kids were rolling around in the snow in wolf form, while others were climbing some big boulders next to a gorgeous waterfall. Some were splashing in the water, while others were throwing snowballs at each other. I watched as Maia, my three-year-old daughter, blocked a snowball with a shield of moonlight. The snow burst into a thousand little pieces and she giggled.

Relief washed through me as I looked over everyone and realized that they weren't hurt. I rushed over to Jack and Maia, who were in the middle of the snowball fight. I crouched down between them and pulled them both into my arms. A snowball smacked into my back, but I didn't even care.

"Sorry!" one of the kids said, but I didn't turn around to see who it was.

"I was so worried," I told my kids. "Don't ever run off like that without telling someone where you're going."

"Sorry Mama," Maia said in her little voice.

Jack, who was five now, dipped his head and muttered a short, "Okay." I could tell he felt bad. He probably hadn't even realized that he would worry me by running off.

"What's going on?" I asked, gesturing at the snow. "Did you do this?"

"I made snow for Sofia because she'd never seen it before." Jack motioned to Jordan's younger daughter, who was sitting by the fire and kept running her hands through the snow like she couldn't quite believe it was there.

I raised my eyebrows. He'd made an *entire* snowstorm? That was pretty impressive. I wasn't even sure I could do that. But Jack had used his sun and moon magic in combination since he was a baby, sometimes with disastrous results. We had a lot of burned curtains and frozen blankets in our house too.

"Thea made a fire to keep everyone warm because we didn't realize it would get so cold," Jack said, motioning to Jordan's older daughter, who was almost five. Jordan was crouched in front of her, talking quietly enough that I couldn't hear what he was saying.

"Can you make the snow stop?" I asked. "It's causing a lot of problems back at the Convergence."

Jack sighed. "I guess."

I watched in amazement as the clouds rolled back out as quickly as they'd come in. The sun came out again and the temperature began to warm up. Everything was still dusted in a couple of inches of snow, and it glittered like a winter wonderland in the light.

I quickly reached up and shot a big set of sparks up into the air so the others could find us. With the air clear, they'd be able to see it for a couple of miles around. I let go of Jack and Maia and stood to survey the rest of the kids.

Wesley was pulling Adriana and Henry out of the river, where they'd been splashing in the waterfall. No surprise there. Jordan's two blond daughters were sitting on the rocks closest to the fire. As I watched, Jordan waved his hand and put the fire out. A second later, Sofia waved her own hand and made the fire ignite again, while Thea giggled. Jordan raised his head to the sky and sighed.

It didn't take long for everyone else to find us. Larkin and Killian were first, soaring through the trees to find us. As soon as Killian transformed, he went over to hug Edie, who was playing in wolf form with Harper's wild twins, Kate and Nate. Louis immediately walked over to Killian and apologized, explaining that they'd never been in any danger. He got the same speech about not running off without telling anyone.

The others showed up a few minutes later, embracing their kids with relieved smiles. Snow still covered the area, but the air was warming quickly under the sun, and I knew it would melt soon.

"Since we're here anyway, we might as well play for a bit," I said, grinning at the kids. I picked up a snowball and tossed it at Kaden, who pretended to look outraged when it hit his chest.

"How dare you," he said, then grabbed his own snowball. I dodged out of the way just in time, but Jordan's snowball hit my back a second later.

After that, it turned into chaos as adults and grownups alike threw snowballs. The air filled with laughter, playful screams, and delighted squeals. Soon Jordan was cowering while being pelted with snowballs from Thea and Sofia, with some help from Wesley. Stella crossed her arms and shook her head at them.

"Aren't you going to help me?" Jordan asked.

"Not a chance," she replied. "You're on your own."

"Fine." Jordan snapped his fingers and the next snowballs all melted thanks to a wave of his hand, which caused his daughters to yell that he'd cheated. That only made Wesley laugh harder, while Jordan groaned and let them hit him with more snowballs. Some of the other kids joined in too, while I thought about how perfect Jordan and Stella were for each other.

Everyone else had been shocked by their pairing, but not me. I'd seen it from the beginning. Together they'd made the Leo pack something they could both be proud of. Jordan had mastered fire magic, as had our other brother Griffin. Meanwhile, Stella had convinced the other alphas that females shouldn't automatically join their mates' packs and that everyone should be allowed to decide where they would live.

Eventually, the snowball fight calmed down. Kaden and Jack started building a snowman while I sat with Maia on a fallen log, hugging her close to me. Mira came to sit with us with Henry in tow, who was playing with his purple dinosaur.

"It's nice to see them all playing together," Mira said. "Even if they shouldn't have wandered off by themselves like that."

"At least they were together," I said, smiling at my oldest friend. She'd settled in nicely as the Cancer alpha female and had helped the pack recover over the last few years, while also forming a close alliance with the Pisces pack. Together we watched Wesley and Adriana splash in the waterfall, and I thought about how proud I was of my brother. I'd always known he would be a better alpha than our father, and he hadn't let me down.

Across the clearing, Edie picked flowers covered in snow and offered them to Madison, who wove them into a flower crown. She placed it on Edie's head.

"I wear for the octopus party," Edie said, touching her crown.

Louis, who was climbing a boulder nearby, called out, "It's Ophiuchus, not octopus."

"Octopus," Edie said with a nod.

"Oh-fee-oo-cus," Louis pronounced.

"Oh, leave her be," Killian said, from where he leaned

against the boulder. "None of us know how to pronounce it either."

Madison and Killian had turned the shifter world upside down when they'd announced they were mates, and they'd done a lot to improve shifter-vampire relations in the last few years. They'd also done a lot for half-humans, who were no longer allowed to be outcasts of the pack they'd been born into like I'd been as a child. All the alphas agreed they would recognize half-human shifters as full pack members going forward. But Madison and Killian didn't stop there, but were also working to help humans at one of the three healing centers they'd started around Quebec.

On the other side of the waterfall, Ethan stood with Aster strapped to his chest. She grabbed hold of a branch and dumped snow onto the ground, much to her delight. Her laugh echoed around the clearing, and Larkin leaned her head against Ethan's shoulder with a content smile.

Aster was the youngest of the kids here—Larkin had wanted to wait so she could enjoy some time in her adult body first. She and Ethan had spent the last few years traveling all over the world, while Larkin also somehow published eight romance novels at the same time. Ethan continued to be the most level-headed of the alphas, while Larkin had done so much for the Moon Witches that Celeste was threatening to make her High Priestess someday.

Loud barking drew my attention as Harper's twins, Nate and Kate, raced through the snow, followed by Harper and Dane. All four of them were in wolf form and soon they were all rolling together in the snow. Jack shifted into a white wolf and joined in, and then Maia and Henry followed. Soon the middle of the clearing was full of playful snarling, snapping, and wrestling. Wesley dragged Mira over to join in too, both of them laughing.

Kaden sat beside me and took my hand. I threaded my fingers through his, and together we admired the beautiful waterfall. It reminded me of the place where I'd first met Kaden.

"So, Jack was the one behind the snow," Kaden said.

I leaned against him. "Yep. We're in big trouble."

He nudged me in the side. "He got his wandering off streak from you."

"And he got his authority problems from you," I shot back, laughing. "At least Maia is an easy kid."

Kaden scoffed. "For now. She's only three. Wait until she's a teenager."

"Now that's a terrifying thought."

Kaden grinned. "We'll get through it together like we always do."

I smiled at him. "Yeah, we will."

He wrapped an arm around me and we watched parents and kids from all different packs playing together in the rapidly melting snow. Just a decade ago, this sort of thing would have been unheard of, but now everyone here had become family to me.

We did this, I thought, squeezing Kaden's hand. We'd brought these people all together, formed new bonds between the various packs, and brought peace to everyone.

We'd changed the Zodiac Wolves forever, and I hoped that this peace would last for many more generations.

Kaden and I had been through so much together in the many years since we'd first met at that waterfall. We'd faced witches, vampires, and even death itself to be together. We'd broken spells, overcome our trauma, and had two wonderful children. We'd also worked hard to make sure the Ophiuchus was a respected pack, equal to any other. Sometimes it was hard to believe we'd come so far, but I knew the stars had brought us together to change the world.

Kaden caught the smile on my face and leaned over to kiss me. I closed my eyes as we kissed and held each other under the sunlight, knowing that our fates had always been entwined, and nothing would ever separate us. Not just us, but everyone here with us today.

I realized then that no matter what happened at the Convergence tonight, everything would be fine. We were all together, and that was what counted.

"Are you ready to head back?" Kaden asked.

I smiled at him and squeezed his hand tighter. "I think I am."

"No more nerves?"

I shook my head. "I know everything will be perfect."

And in the end, it was.

AUTHOR'S NOTE

Thank you for reading the Zodiac Wolves series and going on this adventure with me. This series has been my comfort and my escape during a very hard time in my life, and it's bittersweet to see it come to an end. You may be wondering why I did a book of four novellas to close out the series. The answer is a bit long and complicated.

In case you haven't heard, I was diagnosed with colon cancer right after Star Cursed, the second book in the series, came out. I wrote the third book, Sun Crossed, while recovering from surgery and going through chemo. By the time Zodiac Aligned came out, I thought I was done with cancer and ready to move on with my life. I planned to write four more novels in the series about my favorite side characters next.

Unfortunately, while I was in the middle of Jordan and Stella's story, my cancer returned and spread to my ovaries. At that point, I decided I needed to get these stories written immediately or I feared they might not get written at all. I changed them to novellas, though I kept all the important beats in each story. I wrote them all while going through another surgery and even more chemo, and I'm so happy to be able to give these characters their happy endings, along with a special bonus epilogue about Ayla and Kaden.

I have no idea what will happen next. Stage IV cancer is a terrifying thing to live with, but I have so many stories that I still want to write. Like Ayla and my other heroines, I refuse to give up. I hope to write many more books in the future. For now, I simply want to thank all my readers, friends, and family for your support during this time. I love you all.

--Elizabeth Briggs

P.S. If you love the Zodiac Wolves series, make sure you sign up to receive my newsletter and get access to a special bonus scene from Kaden's point of view, plus NSFW art!

https://www.subscribepage.com/moontouched

ABOUT THE AUTHOR

Elizabeth Briggs is a New York Times and Top 5 Amazon bestselling author of paranormal and fantasy romance featuring twisty plots, plenty of spice, and a guaranteed happy ending. She's a Stage IV cancer warrior who has worked with teens in foster care and volunteered with animal rescue organizations. She lives in Los Angeles with her husband, their daughter, and a pack of fluffy dogs.

Visit Elizabeth's website: www.elizabethbriggs.com

Join Elizabeth's Facebook group for fun book chat and early sneak peeks!